At three klicks, Wedge said, "Break by pairs—"

And the enemy fired. Wedge saw eight flares, two from each oncoming fighter, as the enemy launched missiles.

Wedge whipped to starboard and then instantly began to bring himself back in line with his enemies again. The maneuver yanked him out of his approach vector . . . but missiles accelerated so fast, and the enemy was firing so close, that his sideslip stood an even chance of forcing an overshoot by the missiles. He saw twin burn trails flash back along his port side and knew he was right.

A split second later, his targeting brackets crossed over one of the oncoming aircraft and flickered from yellow to green. Wedge squeezed his yoke trigger and saw his lasers, red pulses, leap out toward the oncoming aircraft—

He had a glimpse of the enemy, black fighter-craft, and then he was past them. Sensors registered an explosion behind him and three targets beyond that, headed away but beginning tight turns back in his direction.

X-WING

BOOK NINE

STARFIGHTERS OF ADUMAR

Aaron Allston

BANTAM BOOKS
New York Toronto London Sydney Auckland

STAR WARS: STARFIGHTERS OF ADUMAR
A Bantam Spectra Book/August 1999

ISBN-0-553-57418-3

Published simultaneously in the United States and Canada

Bantam Books are published by Bantam Books, a division of
Random House, Inc. Its trademark, consisting of the words "Bantam
Books" and the portrayal of a rooster, is Registered in U.S. Patent
and Trademark Office and in other countries. Marca Registrada.
Bantam Books, 1540 Broadway, New York, New York 10036.

PRINTED IN THE UNITED STATES OF AMERICA

OPM   10   9   8   7   6   5   4   3   2   1

Acknowledgments

Thanks go to:

My Eagle-Eyes (Kali Hale, Beth Loubet, Bob Quinlan, Roxanne Quinlan, Luray Richmond, and Sean Summers), who protect me from the worst of my mistakes;

The many *Star Wars* fiction authors who have added depth and detail to the galaxy far far away, most especially Michael A. Stackpole and Timothy Zahn;

Drew Campbell, Troy Denning, Shane Johnson, Paul Murphy, Stephen J. Sansweet, Peter Schweighofer, Jen Seiden, Bill Slavicsek, Bill Smith, Curtis Smith, Eric S. Trautmann, and Dan Wallace, for the resources they have contributed;

Pat LoBrutto and Evelyn Cainto of Bantam Spectra, for all their help;

Sue Rostoni and Lucy Autrey Wilson of Lucas Licensing, for the invaluable coordination they provide; and

Denis Loubet, Mark and Luray Richmond, my roommates, for keeping my head on straight even when it insists on unscrewing itself.

Dramatis Personae

Red Flight

General Wedge Antilles (Red One) (human male from Corellia)

Colonel Tycho Celchu (Red Two) (human male from Alderaan)

Major Wes Janson (Red Three) (human male from Taanab)

Major Derek "Hobbie" Klivian (Red Four) (human male from Ralltiir)

New Republic Armed Forces, Intelligence, and Diplomatic Corps

Iella Wessiri (human female from Corellia)

Tomer Darpen (human male from Commenor)

General Airen Cracken (human male from Contruum)

Captain Geng Salaban (human male from Bestine)

New Republic Civilians

Hallis Saper (human female from Bonadan)

1

She was beautiful and fragile and he could not count the number of times he had told her he loved her. But he had come here knowing he had to hurt her very badly.

Her name was Qwi Xux. She was not human; her blue skin, a shade lighter than her eyes, and her glistening brown hair, downy in its softness, were those of the humanoids of the planet Omwat. She was dressed for the occasion in a white evening gown whose flowing lines complemented her willowy form.

They sat at a table in a balcony café three kilometers above the surface of the planet Coruscant, the world that was a city without end. Just beyond the balcony rail was a vista made up of skyscrapers extending to the horizon, an orange sky threatening rain, and the sun setting beyond one of the more distant thunderheads. Breezes drifting across the two of them smelled of rain to come. At this early-evening hour, he and Qwi were the only diners on the balcony, and he was grateful for the privacy.

Qwi looked up from her entree of factory-bred

Coruscant game fowl, her soft smile fading from her lips. "Wedge, there is something I must say."

Wedge Antilles, general of the New Republic, perhaps still the most famous pilot of the old Rebel Alliance, breathed a sigh of silent thanks. Qwi's conversational distraction would give him at least a few more moments before he had to arm his bad news and fire it off at her. "What is it?"

Her gaze fixed on him, she took a deep breath and held it until he was sure she would begin to turn even more blue. He recognized her expression: a reluctance to injure. He gestured, not impatiently, for her to go ahead.

"Wedge," she said, her words all in a rush, "I think our time together is done."

"What?"

"I don't know how to say it so that it doesn't seem cruel." She gave him a helpless shrug. "I think we must go our separate ways."

He remained silent, trying to restructure what she'd said into something he understood.

It wasn't that her words were confusing. But they were the words *he* was supposed to be saying. How they'd defected from his mind to hers was a complete mystery to him.

He tried to remember what he'd thought she would say when he spoke those words to her. All he could manage was "Why?" At least his tone was neutral, no accusation in it.

"Because I think we have no future together." Her gaze scanned his face as if looking for new cuts or bruises. "Wedge, we are good together. You bring me happiness. I think I do the same for you. But whenever I try to turn my mind from where we are to where we will be someday, I see no home, no family, no celebration days special to us. Just two careers whose bearers keep intersecting out of need. I think of what we feel for one another and every time it seems 'affection' is the proper word, not 'love.' "

Wedge sat transfixed. Yes, those were his thoughts, much as he had been marshaling them all day long. "If not love, Qwi, what do you think this relationship meant to us?"

"For me, it was need. When I left the Maw facility where I designed weapons for the Empire, when I was made to understand what sort of work I had been doing, I was left with nothing. I looked for something to tractor me toward safety, toward comfort, and that tractor beam was you." She dropped her gaze from his. "When Kyp Durron used his Force powers to destroy my memory, to ensure I could never engineer another Death Star or Sun-crusher, I *became* nothing, and was more in need of my tractor beam than ever."

She met his gaze again. "For you, it was a simulator run."

"*What?*"

"Please, hear me out." Distressed, she turned away from him to stare at the cloud-mottled sky and the distant sunset. "When we met, I think your heart told you that it was time for you to love. And you did, you loved me." Her voice became a whisper. "I understand now that humans, in their adolescent years, fall in love long before they understand what it means. These loves do not usually endure. They are learning experiences. I think perhaps that you, shoved from your childhood home straight into a world of starfighters and lasers and death, missed having those learning loves. But the need for them stayed with you.

"Wedge, I was the wrong one for you. Whatever your intent, whatever your seriousness, I think that all you have felt for me has been a simulator run for some later time, for some other woman. One with whom you can share a future." Her words became raspy. She turned

her attention back to Wedge, and he could see tears forming in her eyes. "I wish I could have been her."

Wedge sagged back against his chair. At last her
words had become her own again.

"And I am at fault," she continued. "I have—oh, this
is hard to say."

"Go ahead, Qwi. I'm not angry. I'm not going to
make this harder for you."

She flashed a brief smile. "No, you wouldn't. Wedge,
when we came together I was a different woman. Then,
when I lost my memory, I became someone else, the
woman I am now, and you were there—brave and mod-
est and admired, my protector in a universe that was unfamiliar to me—and after I realized this, I could not bring
myself to make you understand . . ."

"Tell me." Unconsciously, he leaned over to take her
hand.

"Wedge, I feel as though I *inherited* you. From a
friend who passed away. You were her choice. I do not
know if you would have been mine. I never had the
chance to find out."

He stared at her for a long moment. Then a laugh escaped him. "Let me get this straight. I look on you as a
comfortable old simulator, and you look on me as an in-
heritance that doesn't match the rest of your furniture."

She started to look stricken, then she laughed in return. She clapped her free hand over her mouth and
nodded.

"Qwi, one of the things I truly admire is courage. It
took courage for you to say what you've said to me. And
it would be irresponsible, even cruel, of me if I didn't admit that I came here tonight to break up with *you*."

She put her hand down. Her expression was not surprised. Instead, it was a little wondering, a little amused.
"Why?"

"Well, I don't think I have your eloquence on this
matter. I don't think I've thought it through the way you

have. But one reason is the same. The future. I keep looking toward it and I don't see you there. Sometimes I don't see *me* there."

She nodded. "Until just now I had a little fear that I was wrong. That I might be making a mistake. Now I can be sure I was not. Thank you for telling me. It would have been so easy for you not to have."

"No, it wouldn't."

"Well . . . maybe it wouldn't for Wedge Antilles. For many men, it would have been." She turned a smile upon him, a smile made up, he thought, of pride in him. "What will you do now?"

"I've been thinking a lot about that. I've been looking at the two sides of my life. My career and my personal life. Except for the fact that I'm not flying nearly as much as I want to, I have no complaints about my career." That wasn't entirely true, and hadn't been ever since he'd been convinced to accept the rank of general, but he tried not to burden her with frustrations he was convinced arose from his own selfishness. "I'm doing important work and being recognized for it. But my personal life . . ." He shook his head as though reacting to the death of a friend. "Qwi, you were the last part of my personal life. Now there's nothing there. A vacuum purer than anything in space. So I think, in a few weeks, I'm going to take a leave of absence. Travel a bit, try to sneak a visit into Corellia, not think about my work. I'll just try to find out if there is anything to me *except* career."

"There is."

"I'll believe it when I see it."

"Keep your visual sensors turned up, then."

He laughed. "What about you?"

"I have friends. I have work. I am acquiring hobbies. Remember, the new Qwi is less than two years old. In that way, I'm still a little girl experiencing the universe for the first time." She looked apologetic. "So I will learn, and work, and see who it is I am becoming."

"I hope you'll still consider me a friend," he said.

"Always."

"Meaning you can still call on me. Send me messages. Send me lifeday presents."

She laughed. "Greedy."

"Thank you, Qwi."

"Thank you, Wedge."

He packed as though he were still an active pilot. Everything went into one shapeless bag, a bag chosen for its ideal fit within the cargo compartment of an X-wing fighter. Nothing his life would depend upon went into the bag—just clothes, toiletries, a holoplayer. More crucial items—identicards, credcards, hard currency, comlink, a holdout blaster pistol—he kept on him, so that a sudden separation from his bag would be an inconvenience rather than a crisis.

He sealed the bag and looked around his quarters. They were spacious, as befitted a general of the New Republic, and well situated high in a Coruscant skyscraper. He had only to speak a word and the quarters' computer would change the polarity of the wall-to-wall viewports to give him a commanding view of sky, endless cityscape, ceaseless streams of vessels large and small.

These quarters were clean and spare as a military man kept them. They were—

They weren't home. Neither were the smaller but equally lavish quarters he enjoyed on the Super Star Destroyer *Lusankya*, the seat of his military operations—though he was still assigned to Starfighter Command, the special task force he commanded kept him in circumstances and settings more suited to a Fleet Command officer.

Here, as there, the presence of a few mementos, of a framed holo showing his parents in a happy embrace, of friends captured at celebrations or launch zones, didn't conceal the impersonal nature of the furniture. If he received a new posting while he was away on leave, he wouldn't even have to come back here. He'd send a short message to the right department and an aide or droid would pack everything up and ship it off, and an identical one would receive it all and unpack it into a new set of quarters on some other world or station, and that would become the place where he lived.

But not home. Home was a family-owned refueling station, destroyed half his life ago with his parents still aboard, and nothing had ever come along to replace it.

He slung his bag over his shoulder. While on leave, maybe he'd be able to see in the faces and hear in the words of those he visited what it was that had turned their housing into their homes. Maybe—

His door chimed. He set the bag down again. "Come."

The door slid up. Beyond was a man, muscular, graying, a bright and often cheerless intelligence in his eyes. He wore the uniform of a New Republic general.

Wedge approached, hand extended. "General Cracken! Come in. Have you come to see me off? I wasn't expecting a military escort."

Airen Cracken, head of New Republic Intelligence, entered and took Wedge's hand. His expression did not brighten; he looked, if anything, regretful. "General Antilles. Yes, I'm here to see you off."

Something in his tone sounded a quiet alarm in Wedge's mind. "Should I be going evasive?"

That brought a faint smile to Cracken's face. "Probably. I have an assignment for you."

"I'm on leave. It's already begun."

Cracken shook his head.

"General Cracken, you're not in a position to issue assignments to me. So what you're saying is you have something you'd like me to volunteer for."

"I have something you're going to volunteer for."

"I don't think so."

"The following information is for your ears only. You're not to discuss it outside these quarters until you reach your rendezvous point."

"That explains it."

Cracken frowned. "Explains what?"

"When I was packing this morning. Why things seemed a little different. As if a cleaning detail had been through and picked up everything, putting it back *almost* exactly where it was before. Your people were through here when I was out, weren't they? Making sure there were no listening or recording devices present."

Cracken didn't reply to that. He just looked a little surly. He continued, "The world of Adumar is on the near edge of Wild Space. It was colonized as long as ten thousand years ago by a coalition of peoples who had staged a rebellion against the Old Republic, been defeated, and been spared . . . so long as they went far away and never caused any more trouble."

Wedge just stared. Perhaps if he demonstrated continued indifference Cracken would go away. That wasn't usually the way it worked, of course.

Cracken said, "According to what we've been able to gather, their spirit of rebellion and divisiveness didn't end when they found a world worthy of settling. Their history suggests they fought among themselves a number of times, eventually reducing themselves to poverty and barbarism—not once, but twice at least. Though apparently their ancient teaching-recordings survived for thousands of years; their language is recognizably a dialect of Basic." He paused as if anticipating questions from Wedge.

"I'm not curious."

"Anyway, they were completely forgotten by the Old Republic. There is no mention of them in Imperial archives, either. We were fortunate that one of our deep-space scouts stumbled across them when returning from a mapping mission into the Unknown Regions."

"If you continue to map the Unknown Regions, you'll have to call them something else."

Cracken blinked, his expression suggesting that he didn't know whether to interpret that comment as humor or not. "Adumar is heavily industrialized, and a large portion of its industrial development is military. Their weapons are oriented around high-powered explosives. Our analysts suggest that it would be a simple matter to convert a portion of their industry over to the production of proton torpedoes. General, how would you like it if the New Republic's X-wings never had to face a shortage of proton torpedoes again?"

Wedge suppressed a whistle. Lasers were the most often-used weapons of starfighters, the means by which they shot one another down . . . but it was proton torpedoes that gave some starfighters the punch necessary to damage or even destroy capital ships. "That would . . . be helpful."

"You've pushed for years for increased production of proton torpedoes. Since you made the rank of general, people have even been listening. But the New Republic has so many demands on its resources that efforts to boost production of the secondary or tertiary weapon of choice among all starfighters tends to get lost in the shuffle. It wouldn't keep getting lost if we could bring Adumar into the New Republic; then, it would just be some industrial retooling."

"So send a diplomatic mission and work things out with them."

"Ah, that's the trouble." Cracken rubbed his hands together. "The people of Adumar have no respect for career politicians. A very sensible attitude, in my opinion— though if you tell anyone I said that, I'll merely have to deny it. Do you know what sort of individual they hold in highest regard?"

"No."

"Fighter pilots. The Old Republic had its Jedi; Adumar has its fighter pilots. They love them, a case of hero worship that spans their whole culture. Their entertainments revolve around them. Social promotion, properties, titles, all accompany military promotion in their pilot corps."

"That sounds like a reasonable arrangement. Let's implement it in the New Republic."

"And so they'll talk with a diplomat. But only if he's also a pilot. Our best."

Wedge sighed. "I'm no diplomat."

"We'll assign you an advisor. A career diplomat, already on station at Adumar, named Darpen. By the terms by which the Adumari are allowing our diplomatic mission, you'll be accompanied by three other pilots, your choice, a crew of aides, including that advisor, and one ship—you'll be in command of the *Allegiance*, an *Imperial*-class Star Destroyer—"

"I remember her. From the Battle of Selaggis."

"Well, then." Cracken took a datacard from a pocket and held it out. "Your orders. You and the pilots you choose will rendezvous with *Allegiance* at the coordinates provided here. Tell your pilots nothing about the mission until the rendezvous."

Wedge offered him nothing but a steady stare. "I need this leave, General. This is no joke. Find someone else."

"*You* need. Antilles, the New Republic needs. You've never turned your back on the New Republic in its times of need."

Wedge felt his last hope slipping away, to be replaced by anger. "What's it like, General?"

Cracken's expression turned to one of confusion. "What's what like? Adumar?"

"No. What's it like to have so many resources? So that you can simply turn to your staff and say, 'I need so-

and-so for this task. Find me the button I can push so he'll do whatever I say, regardless of what it costs him.' What's that like?"

Cracken's face flushed. "You're coming dangerously close to insubordination, General."

"No, General." Wedge took the datacard from Cracken's hand. "I'm not your subordinate. And what I'm coming dangerously close to is violence. Perhaps you'd better leave."

Cracken stood there a moment, and Wedge could see him struggling against saying something further. Then the man turned away. The door opened before him.

As he passed through it, Cracken said, "Pack your dress uniform, General." Then he was gone.

Wedge's X-wing and the three snubfighters accompanying him dropped out of hyperspace at the same instant.

Unfamiliar stars surrounded them. But within visual range was something he recognized—the white triangular form of an *Imperial*-class Star Destroyer, a 1.6-kilometer-long package of destructive force.

His sensor unit tagged it immediately as *Allegiance*, his expected rendezvous. But his heart rate still quickened a bit as he oriented his X-wing toward the vessel.

For many years, Star Destroyers had been objects of dread among Rebel pilots. Wedge had fought against so many of them, participating in the destruction of some, losing friends to several. Over the years, the New Republic had captured a number of them, turning their awesome firepower against the Empire. Now they were almost a common sight in New Republic Fleet Command, but Wedge could never rid himself of the presentiment of evil he felt whenever he saw one.

His comm unit beeped and words appeared on the text screen—acknowledgment by *Allegiance* that they had recognized him, authorization for landing, and a small schematic indicating the small landing bay, suited for dignitaries, where they were supposed to put down.

"Red Flight," he said, "we are cleared to land. Main starfighter bay. Follow me in."

He heard acknowledgments from his three pilots, then began a long, slow loop around toward the Star Destroyer's underside.

Almost immediately his comm unit crackled. "X-wing group, this is *Allegiance*. You, uh, seem to be off your approach vector for Bay Alpha Two."

"*Allegiance*, this is Red Leader," Wedge said. "We're inbound for the main bay. By orders of the expedition commander." He let the comm officer stew over that one for a moment. He, Wedge, *was* the expedition commander.

There was a moment of delay—just long enough, Wedge estimated, for the comm officer to make one short broadcast to the ship commander and get one short reply. "Acknowledged, Red Leader. *Allegiance* out."

Wedge and his companions took up position beneath the gigantic vessel and rose within the spacious confines of the ship's main bay. Wedge hovered, ignoring the flight line worker beckoning to him with glowing batons, and took a look around.

Starfighters stood ready to launch into battle— A-wings, B-wings, X-wings, Y-wings, and even TIE fighters that had once fought the New Republic. Retrofitted with shields, the TIEs were now a common sight in friendly hangars. Mechanics worked briskly on fighters in need of repair or maintenance. The metal floors and bulkheads wore a dull sheen, showing age and wear but also cleanliness, rather than a shine suggesting that the captain was too concerned with appearance. These were good signs.

The smaller bay they'd originally been directed to could have been put in tiptop shape for their arrival with comparative ease, but the state of affairs in the main bay was a better indicator of how the ship was being run, and things here looked good.

Wedge finally allowed the worker to direct Red Flight to a landing spot, near the vessel's single squadron of X-wings. The unit patch on those snubfighters, showing a single X-wing soaring high above a mountain peak, identified them as High Flight Squadron. Wedge nodded. They weren't the best X-wing unit in the fleet, but they were a veteran squadron with plenty of battle experience.

As he and his fellows set down, Wedge saw the main doorway into the bay open upward and a crowd of people enter at a run. Some of them skidded as they spotted Red Flight and turned in the direction of the recently arrived snubfighters. Among them were a man in a Fleet Command captain's uniform, the usual complement of junior officers and guards, and, most odd of all, what looked like a woman with two heads, one of them shining silver.

Wedge descended his access ladder and turned to face the delegation. He felt and heard his own pilots fall into line behind him. He extended his hand toward the highest-ranking officer. "Captain Salaban. I was glad to hear you'd been promoted off *Battle Dog*."

The captain, a lean, bearded man with skin the color of tanned leather, still breathing hard, hesitated. Obviously confused for a moment as to whether he should salute properly or follow Wedge's informal fashion of greeting, he chose the latter and shook Wedge's hand. "Thank you, sir. And welcome aboard. Allow me to introduce you to my senior officers . . ."

It was a ritual Wedge knew from countless repetitions in the past. He committed each officer's name and face to memory, hoping his retention would last until the end of the mission; it usually did.

Then the captain gestured to the two-headed woman. "And the mission documentarian, Hallis Saper."

Wedge could finally give her his full attention. She was a tall woman, taller than he by two or three centimeters, with long brown hair worn in a braid and wide-open features; she looked as though she'd recently arrived from a one-shuttle agrarian world. He could not read her eyes, as they were concealed behind goggles darkened almost to opacity. She wore a brown jumpsuit festooned with belts, pouches, and pockets.

And on her right shoulder, held on a bracket affixed to her clothing, was the silver head of a 3PO protocol droid. Its eyes were lit.

"I'm so happy to meet the most famous pilot of Starfighter Command," she said; her voice was pleasant but loud, unrestrained.

"Thank you," he said. "Um, I couldn't help noticing that you have two heads."

She smiled. "This is Whitecap, my holo-recording unit. I put him together from a ruined protocol droid and a standard holocam. I added memory and some basic conversational circuitry and programming. He looks wherever I look—the goggles have sensors that track my eye movement—and records whatever I see."

"I see," Wedge said. He didn't, but the words served as building tones useful for plugging up holes where conversation should be. "Why?"

"I record a lot of interviews with children. Studies suggest that they find 3PO units nonthreatening."

"Ah. And have you had much luck with this approach?" He was pretty sure he knew the answer to this one.

"Well, not yet. I'm still working out the kinks in the system."

It would help if you started with the fact that you're a two-headed lady with eyes that children can't see, Wedge thought, but kept it to himself. "And now you're taking a temporary break from children to record starfighter pilots."

She nodded. The 3PO head remained stationary on her shoulder, unaffected by her motion. "It's a wonderful opportunity. Thank you."

"Well, you're welcome. But I'm afraid that Whitecap is going to have to suffer some additional coding. I need to be able to issue a verbal command and shut him off. Circumstances sometimes demand privacy."

Hallis fidgeted. "That was never part of the arrangement. I'll have to refuse."

"Very well. You'll be getting some very good footage of the inside of your cabin."

"Oh. Well, in that case, I accept. I'll do the coding myself."

"And then hand Whitecap over to the *Allegiance*'s code-slicers briefly for, oh, code optimization."

Hallis's smile flickered for a moment and Wedge knew he'd guessed correctly. Hallis must have intended to arrange things so that a second code issued by her would secretly override Wedge's shutoff command. "Of course," she said, but there was now just a trace of brittleness to her voice.

Wedge returned his attention to Captain Salaban. "Allow me in turn to introduce you to my pilots. I present Colonel Tycho Celchu, leader of Rogue Squadron."

Tycho offered the ship captain a salute. "Sir." He was a lean man, blond, graying in dignified fashion at the temples, with handsome features and an aristocrat's bearing. The perfection of his looks might have made him appear severe, even cruel, in earlier years, but the beatings life had handed him—the loss of his family on Alderaan at the hands of Grand Moff Tarkin and the first Death Star, capture and attempted brainwashing by Imperial Intelligence head Ysanne Isard, and suspicion on the part of New Republic Military Intelligence forces that despite his escape he had succumbed to that brainwashing and was an enemy in their midst—all had weathered him in spirit if not in form. Now, he still

looked in every way the cold aristocrat . . . until one
looked in his eyes and saw the humanity and the signs of
distant pain there.

"This is Major Wes Janson, and if you're not aware
of his exploits, I'm sure he'll be delighted to give you the
whole story."

Janson shot Wedge a cool look as he shook the ship
captain's hand. "Good to be here." He turned to the documentarian. "Oh, and, Hallis, I'm better known for my
breathtaking looks than my fighting skills, so don't forget that this is my good side." He turned his head so Hallis's recorder would get a straight-on look at his left
profile.

Wedge suppressed a snort. Janson's self-promotion
came out of a desire to entertain rather than from any serious case of narcissism, but he was as good-looking as
he suggested. Like Wedge and a majority of other successful fighter pilots, he was a few centimeters short of
average height, but Janson was unusually broad in the
shoulders, and endowed with a body that showed muscle
definition after only light exercise and was not inclined to
fat. His hair was a rich brown, and his merry features
were not just handsome but preternaturally youthful; he
was now in his thirties but could pass for ten years
younger. A most unfair combination, Wedge thought.

"And Major Derek Klivian," Wedge concluded.

The fourth pilot leaned in for a handshake. He was
lean, with dark hair and a face best suited to wearing
mournful expressions. "Captain," he said. Then he, too,
turned to the documentarian. "Everyone calls me Hobbie," he said. "And I'll get back with you on my last
name. Lots of people misspell it."

Wedge resisted the urge to look into the eyes of the
recording unit. He knew that second head would attract
his attention during upcoming events; it was best to train
himself now to ignore it. But he couldn't help but wonder
what sort of scene would emerge from this recording,

what part it would play in the documentary Hallis would be assembling. Or how he'd look beside his more colorful subordinate pilots. Wedge was, like Janson, below average height, and he thought of himself as one of the most ordinary-looking men alive. But admirers had told him that his features bespoke intelligence and determination. Qwi had said there was a mesmerizing depth to his brown eyes. Other ladies had been charmed by his hair—it was worn short, but as long as military regulations allowed, and was the sort of fine hair that stirred in any breeze and invited ladies' hands to run through it.

He gave an internal shrug. Perhaps he didn't suffer as much as he feared in comparison with extroverts like Janson. He just wished that when he was shaving he could see some of these traits his admirers noted.

"I'd appreciate it," he said, "if we could get a temporary paint job on the X-wings. Red Flight One, Two, Three, Four." He pointed to himself, Tycho, Janson, and Hobbie in turn. "A white base, but Rogue Squadron reds for the striping, no unit patch."

Salaban nodded. "Easily done."

"So," Wedge said, "what's first on our agenda— settling in to quarters or a mission briefing?"

Salaban's expression suggested that the question was not a welcome one. "Settling in, I'm afraid, sir. There won't be a briefing until you land on-planet. Intelligence decided not to provide a liaison at this time."

Wedge bit back a response that would not have sounded appropriate in the mission documentary. "We're going in cold?"

Captain Salaban nodded.

Wedge forced a smile for the holocam. "Well, just another challenge, then. Let's see those quarters."

2

Wedge was still occasionally fuming, days later, when *Allegiance* dropped out of hyperspace at the edges of the Adumar solar system. There was such a thing, of course, as overplanning. With too much time and too much desire to put every mission detail into a mission profile, it was possible to lose perspective on which objectives were most important, on which tactics were most effective.

But this was the polar opposite of that situation. He didn't know any more now about the people of Adumar than when he received the datacard from Cracken. As he sat in his X-wing, running through his preflight checklist, he had available to him only a set of coordinates on the planet's surface. Once *Allegiance* made its approach to the world—an odd, inconvenient path like an obstacle course, with direction changes at one of the system's uninhabited worlds and one of Adumar's two moons—Wedge and his three pilots would launch and make the final approach to their destination . . . whatever it was that the mathematical coordinates represented. One of *Allegiance*'s shuttles, filled with support personnel, including Hallis Saper, had already descended to make preparations for their arrival.

"Red Flight, this is *Allegiance*. Our final leg terminates in one minute."

Wedge glanced at his comm board. The minute was already counting down—his R5 unit, Gate, had also received the transmission and, on his own initiative, begun a count down. Wedge said, "This is Red Leader. Understood. We launch at arrival plus five seconds. Red Flight, are you good to go?"

"Red Two, ready." That was Tycho, as economical of words as he was of motion.

"Red Three, four lit and ready to burn." Janson's inimitable voice and enthusiasm were evident even across the standard X-wing comm distortion.

"Red Four, nothing's gone wrong yet." There was almost a hopeful note to Hobbie's dour tone.

Wedge felt *Allegiance* heel to starboard, a maneuver lasting ten seconds, and it ended just as his countdown dropped to zero. "Red Flight, launch." He suited action to words, bringing his X-wing up on repulsorlifts until it was three meters above the hangar floor, then drifting forward over the main hangar access. Below was a great dark mass featuring occasional sprinkles of light—Adumar's night side. He angled until his nose was straight down, then smoothly brought up his thrusters and shot toward the planet's surface. His sensor board and a visual check to either side showed his three companions tucked in close beside and behind him in diamond formation. He oriented toward the planet's direction of spin; *Allegiance*'s orbit was above the planet's equator.

"Leader, Two. We have company."

Wedge checked his sensor board again. It showed two red blips paralleling their course, about ten klicks from one another and ten klicks above Red Flight's course. As he watched, another two blips began rising from below on an identical course. The sensors designated them

"Unknown Type." He took a look at them with visual sensors, but could just barely make out a black fuselage and an unusual split to the rear fuselage; the distance, and vibration from the X-wing's speed, made a better look impossible.

"Presumably an escort," Wedge said. "Stay loose, Red Flight. Diplomacy first."

"Leader, Three. Diplomacy means saying something soothing as you squeeze the trigger, right?"

"Quiet, Three."

In moments, as they held their altitude above Adumar's surface, he saw the system's sun rise above the planetary curve ahead of them. Wedge's viewport automatically polarized, cutting down a bit on its brightness, but his eyes were still dazzled. He brought down his helmet goggles and kept his attention on his instruments.

Seconds later, Red Flight crossed the day/night boundary. Visual sensors showed a tremendous archipelago of islands below them, graduating to a series of larger mountainous islands, and then suddenly they were above an enormous continent, one that had to occupy at least a quarter of the world's planetary surface. Their course led them northward, over what looked like the continent's temperate zone. Through breaks in the world's cloud cover, Wedge saw sprawling cities, deep belts of greenery, and large cultivated fields. The sensor board indicated the continued presence of their escorts, who maintained a ten-kilometer distance.

As their motion carried them around the curve of Adumar, the sun rose over them and then was behind them. When they approached the far day/night boundary, Gate transmitted the next set of course corrections: reduction of speed and descent into the planetary atmosphere.

"Leader, Red Three. Why are we taking the long way around?"

"Three, it's their course, not ours. I suspect they're giving us a chance to look at the world."

"Next time they can send holos."

Wedge grinned and began the descent into the atmosphere. He brought his shields up and kept his speed fairly high. This would give the population below something to see: The friction of the atmosphere on the shields would make the X-wings look briefly like meteors shooting out of the skies. It would also give him a chance to learn more about their escorts.

The escorts ten klicks below him entered the atmosphere first—and slowed their forward speed to do so. Wedge nodded. That suggested, though it did not prove, that the escorts weren't able to handle atmospheric reentry as well as an X-wing with shielding. Above him, the high-guard escorts also slowed as they reached the barrier of the atmosphere. Soon Red Flight was far out ahead of the chase vehicles.

They descended toward Adumar's surface, soon recognizing cities with skyscrapers, cultivated fields, untouched forests, broad lakes and rivers. It was, unlike Coruscant, a pretty world.

Sensors showed more vehicles rising in their path at intervals of fifty and a hundred kilometers, but these vehicles stayed to either side of Red Flight's course, not pursuing as the X-wings passed. "A gauntlet," said Red Four.

"Maybe if they were firing," Wedge said. "Here, they're more like distance markers."

"They could keep track of us on sensors," said Red Three, "and scramble a flight if we veered off our assigned course. I'd like to know what they're doing. Show of force?"

Wedge shook his head. If this had been a show of force, they would have had a much larger unit of vehicles in the air, and would have been making much closer passes. But Wedge didn't have the answer, either. "Less chatter, Red Flight."

One blip rising into their path did so at a halfway

point between the "distance marker" vehicles, and its range to Red Flight closed much faster than the rest. It had to be heading toward the X-wings rather than attempting to pace them. As Wedge watched, the sensor board identified the blip as a group of four fighters flying in tight formation. Their course showed them heading straight toward the X-wings. "Heads up, Red Flight," Wedge said. "This may be trouble."

His comm unit came alive with transmissions, disjointed phrases crowding one another out. "Rad Flat, tha flightknife approaching your position . . . Buan ke Shia challenges Waj Antilles! Answer! . . . Rad Flat autorized to defend . . . Dyans ke Vasan challenges Was Jansan! Answer!"

"Scramble Red Flight frequency," Wedge said, and suited actions to words by activating his comm unit scrambler. Now people other than Red Flight listening in on the flight frequency would hear nothing but computer-mangled transmissions. "S-foils to attack position," he continued. "Two, you're with me. Three and Four, you're wingmen." On the sensor board, four more of the distance-marker aircraft were now breaking from their original courses and looping back toward Red Flight.

"Leader, Three. We can outrun them."

"No, Three. If this culture really is as pilot-happy as we were told, taking the most sensible course out of here might cost me credibility I need. This could just be a test of nerve."

"Leader, Four. My nerves are already tested. Can I go home?"

"Quiet down, Four." Wedge watched the range meter's numbers roll down. At two kilometers, the approaching fighters would be barely within accurate targeting range . . . but they were closing so fast that by the time the Red Flight pilots could squeeze the triggers, the computer targeting might have good locks on them. The sensor board was already uttering faint musical tones to indicate that the enemy was attempting targeting locks on them.

At three klicks, Wedge said, "Break by pairs—"

And the enemy fired. Wedge saw eight flares, two from each oncoming fighter, as the enemy launched missiles.

Wedge whipped to starboard and then instantly began to bring himself back in line with his enemies again. The maneuver yanked him out of his approach vector . . . but missiles accelerated so fast, and the enemy was firing so close, that his sideslip stood an even chance of forcing an overshoot by the missiles. He saw twin burn trails flash back along his port side and knew he was right.

A split second later, his targeting brackets crossed over one of the oncoming aircraft and flickered from yellow to green. Wedge squeezed his yoke trigger and saw his lasers, red pulses, leap out toward the oncoming aircraft—

He had a glimpse of the enemy, black fighter-craft, and then he was past them. Sensors registered an explosion behind him and three targets beyond that, headed away but beginning tight turns back in his direction.

He looped around to port, noted that Tycho was still on his rear starboard quarter. "Leader to Flight. Status?"

"Leader, Two. One vaped, two laser-damaged but apparently still flyable. I have no damage."

"Three, unhurt."

"Four, no damage yet."

Wedge didn't bother to issue further orders. His pilots knew what they were about. He and Tycho tightened their loop, an effort to come up behind the surviving pair of enemy fighters, while Hobbie and Janson split wide— if the solo enemy turned against one of them for a head-to-head run, the other would have a good shot at a side or rear quarter.

As he came in toward the rear of the enemy wing pair, Wedge got a good look at them. They were large for single-pilot fighters. They were longer than an X-wing by almost half, their bows ending in sharp points. Behind the cockpit, their fuselages split into odd dual-tail assemblies joined by horizontal bars at the rear. The wings, which crossed the fuselage just behind the cockpit, were broad where they joined the fighter-craft but narrowed like a vibroblade to a sharp point at the tips. The craft surfaces were a glossy black.

Wedge switched to the general comm frequency. "Red Flight to enemy fighters. Indicate your surrender now by descending to the planet's surface."

"No!" The enemy pilot's voice was strained, a little high in pitch. "I will have Waj Antilles or die!"

Both enemy craft attempted a hard roll to starboard and down. Wedge and Tycho stayed with them, closing to optimum firing range—two hundred fifty meters. "You're within our sights and not going anywhere," Wedge said. "This is your last chance—"

The two craft rapidly decelerated, an attempt to force the X-wings to overshoot. Wedge fired and saw his quad-linked lasers shred the black craft ahead of him, punching through the fuselage directly behind the cockpit; the craft rolled in the air, its structural integrity compromised, and disintegrated into a dozen different pieces.

Tycho's shot was more surgical. It blew through the cockpit just where the canopy met the fuselage at the rear. The fighter-craft, still intact, rolled lazily to port and began an uncontrolled plummet.

Wedge checked his sensor board. Hobbie and Janson were headed back to rejoin them.

And the other, more distant fighters, those that had turned back toward the altercation, were once again resuming their original courses, setting up the kilometers-wide corridor for Red Flight's travel.

Wedge brought his group slowly back around on course and watched Tycho's target until that fighter crashed onto a forested hilltop far below. A fireball bloomed out of the wreckage and began consuming it and the foliage around. "Red Flight to Adumar Central Control, what was that all about?"

"Rad Flat, Rad Flat, this is Cartann Bladedrome. Congratulations on four stops. Ar apologies far the inconvenience. Please resume the original course."

He switched to Red Flight's scrambled frequency. "Any of you getting any of that?"

"Leader, Three. It's Basic, but I don't want to imagine how they have to twist their faces to pronounce it. They don't sound as though this was part of the planned celebrations."

"That's my read also, Three. Let's resume our planned course. But keep your eyes open and your sensors optimal."

Moments later it was before them, the biggest city they'd seen so far, a broad stretch of skyscrapers; even the smallest of buildings, at the city's periphery, seemed to be six or seven stories in height. The sky above it was alive with small craft. Wedge's navigation computer indicated that their destination was within the city borders.

As they got closer, they could see that the city was a riot of colors, each building painted differently from the ones next to it, most of them bearing one color for walls and another for roofs and trim such as ledges and window frames. Rust, brown, red, black, and tan seemed to be preeminent.

And then there were the balconies. Every building seemed to have a broad balcony. On most of the worlds Wedge visited, a balcony might extend as far as the edge of the sidewalk, but some of these stretched out over the street, almost meeting balconies from the buildings across the way.

Cables also stretched between buildings, masses of them, but whether they carried power or communications signals, or did nothing more than add structural support or please some aesthetic sense, Wedge couldn't guess.

Red Flight's course dictated an altitude and direction that sent the four X-wings straight down the middle of one of the city's broader avenues, just above the rooftops. Wedge reduced speed for better maneuvering close to structures. As they entered the city Wedge could see people on the streets and especially on the balconies: fair-skinned humans dressed in flowing garments he could only glimpse as they flashed past. The people all seemed to be waving, pointing up at the X-wings. There were vehicles on and above the streets, long, broad transports without seats. Wedge also saw living transportation—reptilian beasts, seven to ten meters long, in colors ranging through browns and greens; the beasts possessed natural armor on flanks and necks, a sort of hard-shell banding, and they carried saddles, some of them built for multiple riders and cargo.

As the pilots got farther into the city, the buildings grew taller, but Wedge's orders mandated the same height aboveground. Suddenly they could see balconies and residents beside them, then above them, and they had to vary their altitude occasionally to miss banks of the cables stretched between buildings; yet the city builders seemed to have planned to accommodate low-level flying, because the cables were clustered at various altitudes, with gaps between them wide enough to permit easy passage of starfighters.

Sensor signals showed some of those pursuit aircraft catching up from the rear, and then Wedge spotted them visually: They were negotiating one cable-bounded passage below Red Flight, in tight formation, moving like the escorts they were probably intended to be, a score or more of the same craft Red Flight had shot down moments before.

"Not bad-looking." That was Janson's voice. "Chiefly atmospheric from the look of them."

Their path took them abruptly out from between the balconied buildings and over a plaza. It was broad, wide enough for an X-wing to do some maneuvering at reduced speed, and packed with people.

And at the boundaries of the plaza were erected display screens, each showing a different moving two-dimensional image.

They were images of Wedge Antilles and the X-wings under his command, images of battles from throughout his career.

Wedge almost jerked in surprise. On one screen were in-the-trench shots from the original Death Star, from the viewpoint of an X-wing camera mount. On another, the huge naval engagement in space above the sanctuary moon of Endor. On another, a clash between X-wings and the Ssi-ruuk in the Bakura system. All engagements he'd been involved with . . . all recordings from participating fighters, recordings that had to have been provided to the Adumari by the New Republic. Two sets of panels showed data that did not come from the New Republic, though: They were recordings of Red Flight's clash moments ago with the Adumari fighters, doubtless recorded by the fighters that had been shadowing them; the poor focus and jerking of the images suggested the recorders had been far away.

"Leader, Three. You set this up yourself, didn't you?"

"Three, Two. Less chatter." Wedge thought he detected a trace of amusement in Tycho's admonition.

The navicomputer indicated that the plaza was the terminus of their trip. He could see one area that had to be their landing zone. At the center of the plaza was a circular fountain, the centerpiece of which seemed to be a statue representing one of those split-tailed fighters aiming straight into the sky; near it was a stage with rails around the edge and a mass of people upon it, and near that was a railed-off area clear of people. Already parked on the landing zone was the shuttle from the *Allegiance*.

Wedge continued forward until he was not far short of one set of screens—the one before him showed him and Rogue Squadron, in dress uniform, in a celebration of the fall of Coruscant to the New Republic—and arced hard to starboard. He led Red Flight in a full circle around the plaza, then descended to touch down on the landing zone.

When his canopy opened, admitting a wash of heavy, humid air that made him guess this part of Adumar was in its late summer season, he was deafened by the roar from the crowd. He took off his helmet and was rewarded by another roar as his features were revealed. "Gate," he said, "close it up and run the power-down checklist. Notify me by comm if anyone approaches."

His R5 unit chirped a confirmation. Wedge suppressed a noise of dissatisfaction. He'd have preferred to have a few minutes to do his routine post-flight check on his vehicle, but the demands of this social situation obviously wouldn't permit him the luxury.

No flight crew approached with ladders, so he swung expertly over the side of his cockpit, hung off the side of his X-wing for a moment by his hands, and then dropped to the plaza surface below, landing in a crouch. The plaza surface, for all that it looked like well-fitted square stones, gave slightly under the impact of his landing; it seemed to be a prettily decorated sheet of some flexible material.

Tycho, Janson, and Hobbie joined him in moments, and Wedge spotted another individual headed their way from the direction of the stage. This man was about Wedge's height, with intelligent eyes and features framed by dark hair and a close-cut black beard. He was dressed in New Republic clothing cut similar to a military uniform but without rank or unit designations. He held out a hand to Wedge. "Sir. Delighted to meet you. I'm—"

"Ejector Darpen!" That was Janson, his voice and

expression betraying surprise—and the good cheer that meant he now had some new trouble to cause.

The newcomer glanced at Janson and shook his head regretfully. "I should have known. Wes Janson. Now my life can take on the aspect of a personal hell." He returned his attention to Wedge. "Tomer Darpen. New Republic Diplomatic Corps. I'm your liaison to the people of Adumar."

"Good to have one," Wedge said. "This is Colonel Tycho Celchu, Major Hobbie Klivian. Janson you've obviously experienced already. Mind telling us what that assault during our arrival was all about? I assume an assassination attempt."

Tomer winced. "Not precisely. They were probably young, undisciplined pilots trying to achieve some personal honor by killing you in a fair dogfight. I doubt it was anything personal."

"You do." Wedge gave him a dark look. "I take it very personally. We just had to vape four pilots in what is theoretically a friendly zone. Is this likely to happen again?"

Tomer shrugged. "Probably not. We'll adjust security measures to reduce the likelihood."

Wedge hesitated, not satisfied by Tomer's explanations; there was obviously a lot more he wasn't saying. "All right, for now. What's expected of us here?"

"Not much." Tomer gestured at the crowd. "A short speech for the assembly. Speaking of which . . ." He pulled a round silver object, three centimeters across, from a pocket. It had a clip on the back. By use of the clip, without prelude or request for permission, Tomer fixed it to Wedge's collar. "This is an Adumari comlink. This one is keyed to the speakers on the poles where the flatcams are."

Wedge raised an eyebrow. "Flatcams? They don't record in holo?"

"No, but we have some holocams up there, too, for our own records and to keep our documentarian from going mad. Anyway, please don't do anything too elaborate with the speech until you're used to the Adumari dialect of Basic; pronunciation is a bit tricky, and the crowd may not understand you. After the speech, we settle you into quarters, give you some orientation, and you can dress for the ball. That's where all the politicking and introducing really take place."

Wedge fingered the Adumari comlink. He didn't care for the familiar way Tomer had placed it on him, but he decided not to pursue the matter at this time. "We don't meet the planetary president or representative here?"

Tomer shook his head. "No, the, ah, *perator* of Cartann offers you considerable honor by not showing up here."

Wedge said, "*Perator* is what—planetary president?"

"Well, here it's an inherited rather than elected title," Tomer said. "But he has the support of the people through demonstrations of his piloting leadership during his youth. And his absence here means, basically, that he doesn't steal any of the attention the crowd would otherwise pay you." He gestured toward the edge of the landing area, where steps led up to the stage. "After you. After all of you, actually. Mere civilians, even former pilots, don't presume to walk beside active pilots unless invited."

Janson smiled. "I like this place. I'm going to go shopping for land and build myself a retreat." He fell in step behind Wedge. "Hey, boss, do you have a speech ready?"

"No."

"So you're going to sound like a complete idiot, right?"

Wedge turned to offer him a smile that was more malice than cheerfulness. "Once, maybe. But since I made general and have to do this all the time, I've developed the Antilles Four-Step Instant Speech."

Janson gave him a dubious look. "This I have to hear."

Once on the stage, Wedge headed to its center and raised his hand with a theatricality that wasn't really part of his nature—just a by-product of the numerous public-relations tours he'd taken after the death of Emperor Palpatine. The crowd roar increased, but he waved it down and the noise dropped again. He thumbed the switch on the Adumari comlink.

Step one: Remind them who everyone is in case they've forgotten. "People of Adumar, I am Wedge Antilles, and it's my pleasure to meet you at last." His words blasted out from speakers set up on four strategically positioned metal poles around the plaza.

The audience roared again, but the noise quickly modulated into a chant: "Car-tann . . . Car-tann . . . Cartann . . ." Wedge wondered what that was all about, but dismissed it from his mind. That answer would wait.

Step two: Remind them what you're here for. "And as a representative of the New Republic, I'm pleased to be present at this historic meeting of our great peoples."

The cheering became more generalized, with the "Car-tann" chants slowly dying out.

Step three: Something personal, so they'll know you're paying attention. Wedge gestured out at the flat display panels. "I must admit, I find this display very heartwarming. It's possibly the best greeting I've ever received. I'll have to find out if I can replicate it on the walls of my quarters back home." Some laughter mixed in with the shouting and cheering.

Step four: Wrap it up before you make a fool of yourself. "I expect to have more to say once I've settled in, but for now, thank you for this warm welcome." He waved again and took a step back, as if abandoning a lectern, then switched off the comlink. The crowd's cheers continued.

His pilots advanced to flank him and joined in waving at the crowd. He heard Tomer's voice from immediately behind him: "This is good. If you can just stand here and wave for a while, that'll satisfy diplomatic obligations, and then we can get you to your quarters."

"All right." Wedge took some time to look at the crowd.

They were men, women, and children, all ages, consistently light-complected, though their hair color ranged throughout the color spectrum—Wedge suspected that many of the colors were artificial in origin. Facial hair was common among the men, especially elaborate mustaches.

There was a wide variance in the color and cut of their clothing, but some consistencies as well. Males and many females wore tights and close-fitting boots in black, with long shirts with flowing sleeves. Other women wore long dresses, tight from the torso down but again with the broad, rippling sleeves. About half of the people wore headgear, some sort of tight-fitting cloth or leather skullcap matching one color from the rest of their attire; many of the skullcaps featured a sort of visor, a curved band of what looked like heavily polarized transparisteel, that fell before the wearer's eyes or could be raised up to their foreheads.

Belts were common, usually narrow single-color loops with no buckle or attachment showing. Some people wore three or four in different colors; others wore them looping from one hip to the opposite shoulder; others still wore both waist and shoulder belt rigs.

And weapons were everywhere. From most of these belts hung sheathed long blades, short blades, pistols of some variety. Wedge could see few in the audience who were not armed in some way; even the children had knives at their belts.

It occurred to Wedge, belatedly, that he could see no security detail on duty around this stage. He glanced at

Tycho; the colonel's return glance indicated that he, too, noticed the lack.

Wedge said, "Tomer, I suppose I'm not concerned if you're not, but what are you using for security here?"

Tomer's answer was tinged with amusement. "Why, the crowd."

"Ah. And what if they wanted to cause a problem?"

"Others would stop them," Tomer said. "For instance, let's say someone jumped on the stage with the intent of killing you. He'd give you fair warning, of course, and choice of weapons."

"Of course," Wedge repeated.

"Then you could choose to kill him yourself or refuse him. If you refused, he should withdraw, but might theoretically press the issue, if he was stupid."

"That's where security issues become a trifle more important," Wedge said.

"If he pressed the issue, which is a grave breach of etiquette—"

Wedge heard Janson snort in amusement.

"—then someone in the crowd would probably shoot him dead, just to please you."

Wedge glanced back at the diplomat. "Just like that."

"Just like that."

"Oh, stop worrying, Wedge." Janson's grin was infectious. "It's obvious they adore you. You could throw up all over yourself and they'd love it. By nightfall they'd all be doing it. They'd call it the 'Wedge Purge.' They'd be eating different-colored foods just to add variety."

Wedge felt his stomach lurch. He half turned to glare accusingly at Tycho. "I thought maybe you'd be able to do what I never could. Get Wes up to an emotional age of fourteen, maybe fifteen."

Tycho gave him a tight little shake of the head. "No power in the universe could do that. Not Darth Vader and the dark side of the Force, not the nuclear devastation of an exploding sun."

Janson waved at the audience. "They'd be competing for distance and volume."

"Wes, just shut up. Tomer, how is it that you know this reprobate?"

The diplomat offered a rueful shake of his head. "I was once a pilot. Briefly. Tierfon Yellow Aces. My talents lay elsewhere, though, so I ended up in a less violent service."

Janson nodded amiably. "His talents certainly did lie elsewhere. They weren't in landing. Tomer here made the Aces' list for a landing almost horrible enough to kill him two different ways."

Tomer sighed and ignored him.

"His Y-wing was shot to pieces and his repulsorlifts were dead," Janson continued. "Had to land, though, or he'd never get dinner. Luckily we were based on a low-grav moon at the time, big long stretch of duracrete serving as a landing zone. All the other Y-wings clear off the landing zone and he lines up on it, descends toward it like he was landing an atmospheric fighter without repulsorlifts. Drops his skids as he gets close. The skids take the initial impact but he bounces, so he's like some sort of hop-and-grab insect all down the duracrete. But he's lucky enough that he stays top side up. Finally he's bled off a lot of momentum, but he loses control and his Y-wing rolls. Comes to a stop on its belly and he's safe. Then"— Janson's face became more merry as he relived the incident—"his ejector seat malfunctions and shoots him off toward space. With grav that low, he achieves escape velocity. We had to send a rescue shuttle up after him or he'd still be sailing through the void, one cold cadaver."

"I saved the astromech," Tomer said. "And the Y-wing was repairable."

"Sure," Janson said. "But seeing you as that wishbone skidded to a stop, seeing you sag in relief—and then, poof! you're headed toward the stars—"

Tomer caught Wedge's eye. "As you can see, I've provided amusement for years."

"Efficient use of effort," Hobbie said. "When do we eat?"

3

One of those processional vehicles—a giant flatbed that rode the ground on wheels, with a raised front control panel where the driver stood, and with braces for the passengers to lean back against as they rode—conveyed Red Flight, Tomer, and Hallis from the plaza. It wasn't fast going; the crowd did not want to part to admit them, but preferred to shout and jump and wave to attract the pilots' attention. Wedge solved that problem by moving to the vehicle's side and reaching out to shake hands as they passed; suddenly the members of the crowd wanted to be beside the vehicle rather than before it, and the vehicle's speed increased. The other pilots moved to the sides as well, and within minutes the vehicle was beyond the edges of the crowd and heading out into the city's avenues.

Wedge saw that the city's love affair with balconies was not limited to the avenues they'd flown above. Every building on every street facing was thick with balconies. Some had rope bridges hung between adjacent balconies, and a few had such strung across streets. Wherever they drove, people thronged their balcony rails and waved down at them. The building exteriors were also decorated, on the ground floor at eye level, with panels about a meter wide by half a meter high that showed two-dimensional images. Tomer called them flatscreens, and some buildings had continuous banks of them all around their exteriors.

"I am so glad the people of this planet like to wave and shake hands," Janson said.

Wedge gave him a curious glance. "Why is that?"

"Well, what if their usual greeting for visiting dignitaries was to throw paint?"

"Point taken."

Their conveyance pulled up before one of the taller and more richly appointed buildings they'd seen, and minutes later Tomer led the four pilots into a suite of rooms on an upper floor; their support crew had already been separated off, installed in rooms lower down in the building. "These are the quarters of a bachelor half squad recently reduced in combat," Tomer said. "The survivor gladly abandoned it for the duration of your stay, for your comfort."

Wedge took a look around. The floor, again, looked like stone, this time a green marble thickly decorated with silvery veins, but like the plaza flooring it gave slightly when stepped upon. There was one main room, mostly open, with a few padded chairs around the edges. Several arched exits led to round-topped doors of a silver hue. The walls were hung with light blue draperies; just behind the top of the drapes, banks of lights shone up on the off-white ceiling, offering indirect lighting for the chamber.

Tomer pointed to four of the doorways. "Bedchambers there, there, there, and there." Two of the building porters, adolescent boys who could not stop grinning, obligingly carried the pilots' bags to those chambers.

Tomer gestured to the bank of drapes opposite the entry into the main chamber: "Your balcony there. It's a pilot's balcony, by the way."

Wedge said, "Which means what?"

"Extra-broad and reinforced, and with nothing, including cables, for a level or two above—so you can land your starfighters on it," Tomer said. "You can move your X-wings here at your leisure, or I can get a member of the support crew to do it—"

"We'll move them," Wedge said. "Speaking of those cables—what are they for?"

Tomer grinned. "Private communications from building to building, informal communications. Say you're a young lady in one building, and your young man lives in the next—"

"You run a comm cable." Wedge shook his head wonderingly. "There are hundreds of thousands, maybe millions, of them out there."

"None to your quarters, though; we've had them removed. You can put some in if you choose." Tomer gestured again. "Kitchen through there, though I doubt you'll have the opportunity to feed yourself much while you're here. If you choose to dine here and you prefer not to cook, the building comlink is behind that drape." He pointed to one of the main chamber's long walls, near the center. "Servants are standing by for any of your needs."

"Any of them?" Janson asked.

"No," Hobbie said. "Some of your needs stray too far outside human norms."

"Meaning," Tomer continued, just a trace of testiness creeping into his voice, "that a cook, a courier, a dresser, and a few others are always standing by. If you want a late-night meal or something, press the button and ask for a cook. That's all it takes." He gestured to another door. "The refresher. You'll be dealing with unfamiliar plumbing, which you'll probably think of as backworld stuff, so I'll need to show you how the devices work."

Hobbie nodded. "A refresher course."

Janson made a face. "You beat me to it."

Wedge gestured at the two doors not already identified. "And those?"

"Extra bedchambers. This was essentially a dormitory for six unmarried pilots."

"Good." Wedge nodded. "We'll set up one for workouts, and the other will be our operations center. These quarters have been swept for listening devices?"

"Oh, yes." Tomer smiled. "And they were, of course, thick with such gadgets. We've removed them."

"It sounds as though we're set up, then," Wedge said. "What's next on our agenda?"

"Get cleaned up and get into your dress uniforms; your court dinner with the *perator* at his palace is in about two hours."

"Ugh," Janson said. Hobbie made an unhappy face.

"They're not reacting to the idea of meeting the *perator*," Tycho was quick to explain. "It's the dress uniform."

"I understand." Tomer nodded, sympathy evident on his face. "I got out of Starfighter Command before the dress uniform was even designed. Umm, if you're looking for alternatives, I'm certain that the court would consider it a sign of honor if you wore local dress instead of your dress uniforms."

"Yes," Hobbie said.

"Yes yes yes," Janson said.

Wedge repressed a smile. The New Republic pilots' dress uniform wasn't too bad, but it had been designed in the depths of some government public relations department, without the input of those who would have to wear it, and many pilots just did not care for it. He cleared his throat. "That's a possibility. If you'd be so kind as to send up some examples of local dress. . . ?"

Tomer smiled. "One snap of my fingers and you'll

have your very own fashion show. I'll see right to it." He gestured for the porter, who had been hovering at the exit, to proceed him, and he left.

Wedge turned to Janson. "How well did you know him? Do you trust him?"

Janson considered. "Let's just say that he's cleaned up better than I expected."

"No, let's not just say that. Let's be a little more informative."

Janson's gaze wandered back in time. "Well, in the Tierfon Yellow Aces, he always had something going. Floating sabacc games, trade in the newest holodramas and comedies, a locker that always seemed to have some liquor in it no matter how much he sold. I never had the impression that he was a black marketeer, but he was only one notch above that. When he mustered out and no one ever heard from him again, we figured he'd gone smuggler." He shrugged. "But the diplomatic corps seems ideal for him. He can persuade and convince and scam and manipulate, and yet remain a patriot."

Hobbie offered up a rare smile. "Not a bad metaphor for the early days of the Rebel Alliance."

Tycho offered him a mock glower. "Cynic."

They were four very different men as they walked toward the Outer Court of the Royal Residence, or palace, of Cartann.

Wedge had chosen green for most of his outfit—boots, hose, belt—and had chosen a tunic in a creamy off-white. He chose to remain bareheaded. His service blaster was holstered at his hip; Tomer seemed to think that wearing weapons was more than appropriate in a social situation, though he had said Wedge would have to surrender it when in a chamber occupied by the *perator*.

Beside it hung a device Tomer had said was commonplace in Cartann, the comfan. It was a small hemisphere with a handle. On the flat side of the hemisphere were numerous little vents; at the bottom of the handle were an on-off switch and an intake vent. When switched on, the device would draw air in through the intake vent, cool it, and expel it through the other vents, making it a handy personal comfort device. Tomer had said that handling the comfan was itself an art form, with every possible gesture assigned a meaning by the Cartann court . . . but outsiders such as Wedge would be known not to understand the language of comfan manipulation. The warmth of Wedge's tunic suggested to him that he'd be better off carrying such a thing.

Tycho's tunic was a material that shimmered and changed color as it moved; depending on the angle at which one viewed it, portions ranged in hue from sky blue to a pearlescent royal blue. Most of his other garments, including a rakish-looking hip cloak, were black, but he also wore a skullcap in the same material as his tunic. The skullcap came forward in a peak over his brow, an extension that looked like the sharp beak of a bird of prey, a comparison Wedge decided was apt, and the semitransparent visor over his eyes lent him a distant, mysterious look.

Hobbie was a riot of lines and angles. His boots, tights, and belt were a basic blue, his tunic a glorious red; but every hem of every garment was decorated with trim of eye-hurting yellow, making it almost a dizzying experience to look at him walk. "There are three types of dress clothing," Hobbie had said. "The kind that offends the wearer, the kind that offends the viewers, and the kind that offends everybody. I'm going for the third type. Fair is fair."

Janson had chosen what Wedge had first misunderstood as a minimalist approach. His tights, his tunic, all his accoutrements were black—most of them a matte black, though the tunic offered a little shine. He wore no headgear. But then he capped it off with a hooded cloak that made up for the rest of his outfit's lack of drama. Nearly floor-length, it was a curtain of nebular red-purple shot through with crystalline stars that blinked on and off with internal light.

He carried his service blaster on his right hip, but also carried a new weapon. On his belt at his left hip was a sheath carrying the Adumari blastsword, "preferred weapon for settling personal disputes in Cartann," as Tomer had explained. It looked much like a vibroblade the length of a man's arm, but the hilt was protected by a curved metal guard. The blade was sharp starting a few centimeters above the guard, but the tip of the weapon was not a sharp point; rather, it was a small flared nozzle. When the device was powered up—by turning on a switch at the pommel, the knob at the very base of the hilt—the tip would fire off something like a blaster bolt whenever it contacted a solid object.

"So it's like a blaster you have to hit someone with," Janson had said. "I have to have one."

Tycho had shaken his head, looking as mournful as Hobbie for a moment. "Don't give him a new kind of weapon," he had told Wedge. "It would be like giving a lightsaber to a two-year-old."

But Wedge had allowed it, and now Janson's customary swagger swung the blastsword's sheathed blade around behind him, making it precarious to walk close to him.

Accompanied by Tomer, they paused at the arched entryway to a large ballroom designated the Royal Outer Court. Tomer stepped forward to speak to the guards on duty. There were two of them, large men armed with what looked like polearm equivalents of the blastswords. Between them, across the entryway, was stretched a sort of silver mesh material; Wedge could see well-dressed people dancing and socializing, but it was as if viewing them through a warped and mottled piece of unusually reflective transparisteel. He spotted two-headed Hallis in the crowd, her attention turned toward a large knot of men and women.

Tomer returned. "Odd," he said. "We're to be admitted, of course—this is your night! But we're not to be announced."

"You mean," Hobbie said, "nobody is going to bellow our names across the crowd, so that everybody turns and stares at us and we have nothing to say, so we stand there like idiots while they wait. That sort of announced?"

"Yes," Tomer said. "It's customary. Why the custom was suspended for tonight I don't know. You'll have to surrender your sidearms to the guards, of course."

Tomer stopped Janson's action of unsheathing his blastsword. "No, you can take that in. Blastswords are fit for polite society. It's only blasters they object to."

The semitransparent curtain flicked to one side instantly. Conversation washed out over them, as did a swell of music played on stringed instruments at a fast pace, and a wash of air that assailed Wedge's nose and informed him that perfuming was another Adumari habit.

Tomer led the pilots into the outer hall. They attracted no immediate notice. The hall itself was a tall two-story chamber, with a balcony all around the second story, thick with onlookers; its walls were draped with tapestries in a shimmering silver hue, and the lights behind the tapestries offered not quite enough illumination. Two tapestries were drawn aside, revealing enormous flatscreens on stony walls; the screens showed, in magnification, whatever stood before them.

Tomer led the pilots straight to the knot of people that held Hallis's attention. As they approached, Wedge could see that at its center was one man, unusually tall, with a close-trimmed white beard and alert, active eyes. His garments were all a shimmering red-gold; with every motion he looked as though part of his clothing were on fire. As the pilots neared, he looked at Tomer and asked, in a raspy but well-controlled voice, "What have you brought me, O speaker for distant rulers?" He spoke with the same accent Wedge had heard on the pilots who had attacked Red Flight, in which many vowels sounded like short flat "a"s, but Wedge was becoming more accustomed to it, having less difficulty comprehending it.

Tomer offered a smile that, to Wedge, looked a little artificially tolerant. "Pekaelic ke Teldan, *perator* of Cartann, smiter of the Tetano, hero of Lameril Ridge, master of the Golden Yoke, I beg you allow me to present to you these four pilots: Major Derek Klivian, Major Wes Janson, Colonel Tycho Celchu, and General Wedge Antilles, all of the New Republic Starfighter Command."

With each recitation of a name, the crowd around the *perator* offered an "ooh," especially for Wedge. The *perator* nodded in slow and stately fashion to each and extended a hand to Wedge. Wedge shook it in standard New Republic fashion, hoping that was the reaction called for, and that he wasn't precipitating a war by failing to kneel and put the hand on his forehead or some such thing. But the *perator* merely smiled.

"You are well come to Cartann," the *perator* said to Wedge. "I look forward to hearing your words and seeing your displays of skill. But first, I have a present for the four of you." He waved behind him, beckoning someone forward.

Into the open space surrounding the *perator* stepped a young woman. Her garments were all white, though festooned with what looked like ribbons and military service decorations, and she carried blastsword, knife, comfan, and pistol at her belt. She was not tall, being a double handspan shorter than Wedge, but walked with the confident gait of someone a head taller than anyone in the crowd, despite the fact that she was a year or two from what Wedge would consider full adulthood. Her freckled features were pretty, open, bearing the expression of a youth rushing recklessly into life. Her black hair was in a long braid drawn over her shoulder, and her eyes were a dark blue that seemed almost purple in the dim light of the chamber.

"This young lady," the *perator* said, "is the most recent winner of the Cartann Ground Championship. With that victory comes certain obligations and prerogatives. Pilots, I present you Cheriss ke Hanadi; I know that you have the most informed Tomer Darpen to give you outlook upon Cartann, but Cheriss will serve you as native guide throughout your stay."

Wedge gave the *perator* a slight bow. "Thank you, sir." He spared a glance for Tomer, but the career diplomat did not seem in the least curious or disconcerted; this was obviously not an unusual sort of occurrence.

"I am honored to serve," Cheriss said. She stared at Wedge with disconcerting intensity, but Wedge could detect no animosity in her expression—just curiosity. "If General Antilles wishes diversion during the evening, I have a show to put on—a non-title from some runny-nosed lordling."

The *perator* returned his attention to Wedge. "Tonight," he said, "is an informal night. Meet the heroes and nobles and celebrities we have assembled. Tomorrow is soon enough to begin the tedious affairs of discussion and negotiations, no?" He offered another smile, then turned his back on the pilots and moved away. His knot of courtiers moved with him like a set of shields moving with a starfighter. Hallis turned between *perator* and Wedge, indecisive, then stayed behind, her attention and her recording unit's gaze on the New Republic pilots.

Tomer stood openmouthed, his expression uncomprehending. "After all his curiosity about our pilots, all his arrangements—and he has not even one question for you tonight. I'm baffled." He gave Cheriss a sharp look. "Cheriss, do you know why he has chosen to conduct tonight the way he has?"

She tore her attention from Wedge to answer. "Oh, certainly."

"Why?"

She smiled in return. "I can't answer that. Not yet. I'm forbidden."

Tomer's expression turned glum. "I hate secrets," he said.

Wedge said, "Whitecap, sleep-time."

The 3PO head on Hallis's shoulder responded, in the distinctively fussy 3PO voice, "Certainly, sir," and the lights in its eyes went out.

Hallis made a noise of exasperation.

Wedge ignored her. "Tomer, a couple of questions. If he's the ruling representative of all of Adumar, why is he simply introduced as the *perator* of Cartann?"

"He is the heir to the throne of Cartann." Tomer shrugged. "Cartann is his nation. The concept of a single world government is somewhat new here. It does not invoke the sense of pride that the traditional throne of a nation does."

"Oh." Wedge leaned in close and whispered so that only Tomer could hear. "And now he has offered us the services of a guide. Is that some sort of present? Should we have brought a gift to offer him?"

Tomer smiled and whispered back, "Oh, no. Your very presence and what it means to him is present enough."

Wedge leaned back, not entirely reassured. "Whitecap, wake-time." He saw the lights reappear in Whitecap's eyes.

He turned once again into the high-beam intensity of Cheriss's stare. "Well, what's the best way to conduct ourselves at this gathering?"

Cheriss smiled and gestured. "There are long tables along those walls where there is food. You can just walk by and take what you choose. The pilots and nobles here would be most happy if you would wander, meet them, tell them of your exploits. There are so many, though, that greeting them and saying you look forward to longer discussions later will be enough. When the *perator* leaves the hall or drops his visor, this means constraints are off; you can loosen your belt, act with less restraint, issue challenges, even leave if you choose."

Tomer frowned. "When he lowers his visor? That's the same as him leaving?"

Cheriss nodded energetically. "Both are signals of distance. When he lowers his visor, he does not see with the king's eyes—you understand? He wants to stay and enjoy but not affect the behavior of the court."

Tomer looked distinctly unhappy. "How could I have missed that little detail? Are there parallels in lesser courts—"

Janson interposed his head, glaring at Tomer. "Discuss nuance later. Feed the pilots now."

Tomer relented with a smile. "Sorry. Of course. I've forgotten the role of the stomach in interplanetary relations."

It took them nearly thirty minutes to cross the thirty meters to the food. In that time, they ran across group after group of admirers, most of them pilots—male pilots, female pilots, pilots still in their teen years, pilots as old as Wedge's parents would have been if they had survived. Wedge shook hand after hand, smiled at face after face and name after name he knew he would never recall despite his best efforts. By the time they reached the buffet-style tables, all four pilots had an appetite and eagerly went after the foods ready there, despite their unfamiliar appearance. Most of the dishes consisted of bowls of some sort of meat or vegetable simmered in heavy, spicy marinades; Wedge found one he liked, what seemed to be some sort of fowl in a stinging marinade with ground spices clearly visible, and stayed with it even after Cheriss informed him that it was *farumme*, the same sort of riding reptile Wedge had spotted during his arrival flight.

"So, Cheriss," Wedge said, "what can you tell us about the Adumari fighters we encountered on our arrival?"

"The pilots or the machines?"

"I meant the machines."

Her expression became blank. "The Blade-Thirty-two," she said. "Preeminent atmospheric superiority fighter, though the Thirty-two-alpha is equipped for spaceflight and the Thirty-two-beta also has what you call a hyperdrive." She sounded as though she were reciting from a specifications chart. "It's a single-pilot craft in most configurations, with three main weapons systems—"

Someone bumped into Wedge from behind. He glanced over his shoulder; another diner had taken a step backward straight into Wedge. The diner half turned toward him, saying, "My apologies."

"No offense taken," Wedge said, and turned back to Cheriss . . . then froze. The other diner's accent was clipped, precise . . . Imperial.

He spun around. The other diner turned to face him, surprise evident on his features as well.

Despite the man's garments—he was dressed in Cartann splendor, much as Wedge was—Wedge knew he was no Adumari. He was of below average height, with short fair hair that seemed naturally unruly. His lean features were handsome but marred by a livid scar curving across the hollow of his left cheek; his dark eyes suggested cutting intelligence. His face was burned into Wedge's memory from numerous Rogue Squadron mission briefings. "General Turr Phennir," Wedge said.

The most famous surviving pilot of the Empire, the man who had inherited command of the 181st Imperial Fighter Group from Baron Fel upon that pilot's defection to the New Republic, stared at him in disbelief. "Wedge Antilles," he said, and put his hand on the holster at his belt. But there was nothing in the holster; doubtless Phennir's blaster pistol was with Wedge's at the door guard station.

Wedge heard a noise from behind, the quiet rasp of metal on leather, and knew that Janson had drawn his vibroblade. But Phennir's expression didn't change. Either he was in extraordinary control of his emotions, or he wasn't aware of Janson arming himself. Probably the latter; Wedge was directly between the two men. If Phennir attacked, all Wedge had to do was twist aside to expose the enemy pilot to Janson's counterattack. Wedge nonchalantly kept his grip on his bowl and spoon, affecting unconcern.

Wedge could see calculations going on behind Phennir's eyes. They probably matched what Wedge himself was thinking. *Best-known New Republic pilot; best-known Imperial pilot. We're here at the same time so Adumar can compare us. Can choose which of two options suits them better.*

Phennir appeared to arrive at the same conclusion. He lifted his hand from his belt and extended it to Wedge. "It seems we're here for the same reason."

Wedge set his spoon down and shook the man's hand. "I suspect so."

"You'll understand if I don't wish you luck."

"Likewise."

Phennir turned away and raised his hand in a come-along gesture. Three other men in his vicinity followed as he departed.

Wedge turned back to his pilots, saw the last motions of Janson surreptitiously returning his vibroblade to his forearm sheath; the action was concealed from the sides by Janson's ridiculous cloak, and few, if any, of the celebrants in the chamber could have observed it. Janson's face, for once, was not merry in the least.

Wedge said, "Hallis, did you get that?"

The documentarian nodded.

"Give us a few moments of peace. Take that time to broadcast what you just recorded to the *Allegiance*."

"Yes, General." She turned and moved into the crowd, for once offering no protest to one of Wedge's commands.

Wedge turned his attention to his native guide. "Cheriss, did you know that man was here? And who he was?"

She nodded, sober. "I did. My *perator* instructed me to say nothing until you two encountered one another. They had an arrival ceremony much like yours, at the same time as yours, on the far side of Cartann."

"Please withdraw a few steps."

She did, looking more distressed.

Tomer said, "Have you met him before? You acted as though you had."

Wedge shook his head. "Not in person. We flew against him at Brentaal, years ago. Tycho went one-on-one with him. Which makes you, Tycho, the expert on what we're facing."

Tycho shrugged. "He was good. Nearly my equal at the time. But he was no Baron Fel, no Darth Vader."

"He's had years to improve."

Tycho smiled. "So have we."

"True." Wedge thought back to his first debriefing of Baron Fel, shortly after the great Imperial ace's capture by Rogue Squadron. "Fel said Phennir was ambitious, with little loyalty to Sate Pestage, who held the reins of the Empire after the Emperor fell. Phennir wanted Fel to strike out to achieve power on his own, and Phennir would be tucked in right there as his wingman."

"Which doesn't mean much to us," Tycho said, "unless Phennir sees an opportunity for personal gain in this mission—enough gain to make him betray the Empire." Then he lost his smile. "The Adumari have set us up."

Wedge nodded. "That's my guess. They're going to

play us against the Empire to see who can offer the best arrangement."

Tomer's face was nearly white with shock. "They're far sneakier than I imagined. They pulled this off without our Intelligence people even knowing."

Janson snorted. "How can you be sure? Maybe Intelligence just didn't tell you."

Tomer shrugged, unhappy. "Perhaps so. I'll transmit them a request for further instructions."

"You do that," Wedge said. "But until we get further orders, we do just as we intended to—socialize, play the visiting dignitaries, make good impressions."

"And keep eyes open in all directions," Janson said.

Hobbie sighed. "Until now, I thought this was a really sweet deal."

"The Cartann Minister of Notification, Uliaff ke Unthos."

For the fortieth or eightieth time that night, Wedge offered the minimal bow and handshake required by the situation, and went to the special effort it took to keep from his face the dismay he'd felt ever since he'd recognized Turr Phennir. He also struggled to keep his nose from wrinkling; the minister's perfume seemed as sweet and strong as an orchard full of rotting fruit. "And what is the role of the Minister of Notification?"

The white-bearded man before him smiled, evidently delighted. "My role is notification of the families. When a pilot falls in combat, in training, in a duel, my office notifies all appropriate parties. I do not create the letters of notification myself, of course. I set policy. Will this week's notifications bear a tone more of regret or pride? When siblings fall on the same day, does the family receive a joint notification or separate ones? These sorts of matters are very important . . ."

Wedge kept his smile fixed on his face, but he could

tell he was hearing a speech, one that had often been re-
played. He did what he could to tune the man's voice out
while still seeming to appear interested, but all the while
kept some of his attention on the crowd, making sure
he knew where Turr Phennir and entourage were at all
times.

Then, over the minister's shoulder, at a table at the
outskirts of the crowd, he saw her.

She was seated alone and dressed in the height of
Cartann finery. Her dark blue dress, a sheath from neck
to ankle, was fitted to her slender form, except where its
sleeves flared out in Adumari fashion, and was sprinkled
with gems that glinted white like stars against a backdrop of space. Her hair, a dark blond, was piled high on
her head, though some strands had worked loose—or,
Wedge suspected, had been left loose and artfully arrayed
to look like escapees—to frame her face. She did not
wear the decorative skullcap so common in this court; instead, into her hair was worked a headdress that looked
like blue contrails rising from above her forehead and
curving back around behind her head. She held one of the
ubiquitous comfans and was gesturing with it as she
spoke to someone at a nearby table; her gestures, Wedge
saw, included the subtle motions he was beginning to recognize as Cartann hand-codes.

She was beautiful, but it was not her beauty that
jolted Wedge—not her beauty that made him feel as
though he'd taken a punch in the gut.

He knew her. He knew her name. He knew the planetary system where she'd been born—the same as his,
Corellia.

Yet when she glanced at him, when her gaze stopped
upon him and then kept moving, there was no hint of
recognition in her eyes.

Wedge forced himself to return his attention to the
minister. "Would that we had someone with your skills

and dedication in our armed forces," Wedge said. "I'm sure we have much to learn from your techniques of notification. Could you excuse me a moment? I must speak to my pilots about this."

The minister nodded, his smile fixed, and turned away, immediately speaking to his own entourage, something about the courtesy and attentiveness of New Republic pilots. Once he was a couple of meters away and still moving, Wedge gestured for his pilots.

They stepped in. So did Cheriss and Tomer.

Wedge looked at the two of them. "Shoo," he said.

"I thought perhaps you needed some advice," Tomer said.

"I am here if you need interpretation of some word or action you do not yet understand," Cheriss said.

"Tell you what," Wedge said. "From now on, when I gesture with two hands for people to move in, it means everybody. When I gesture with one hand, it means just the pilots. Will that work?"

They nodded.

Wedge gestured with one hand. Reluctance evident on their faces, the two of them backed off and hovered a few meters away at the edges of the crowd.

"What's up?" Tycho asked.

"I'm going to allow Cheriss to put on whatever show it was she was talking about. I'm going to pay a lot of attention to it."

Tycho offered a confused frown. "Why?"

"Because the hangers-on seem mostly to be concentrating on me right now. If I do this, it'll give you some freedom to act." Wedge turned to Janson. "Wes, at exactly ninety degrees to your right, about twelve meters, there's a table with a woman at it."

"Oh, good."

"I want you to wait until the crowd is on me and Cheriss's demonstration. Then break free and approach her. Tycho, Hobbie, make sure his actions aren't being noticed. If they are, give him a double-click on the comlink to warn him off."

Janson smiled. "Thanks, Wedge, for looking after me. You know, you're one of the most considerate commanders, not like Tycho here—"

"Wes, she's Iella Wessiri."

Janson's eyes widened. "What?"

Iella Wessiri was a New Republic Intelligence agent, a former partner and long-time friend of Rogue Squadron member Corran Horn. She had been very helpful to the Rogues during the taking of the world Coruscant from the Empire. Her husband Diric, an unwilling traitor brainwashed by Imperial Intelligence head Ysanne Isard, had died during those events. Corran and Wedge had both helped her through the trying times to follow, and Wedge had eventually grown interested in her himself, until things had conspired to separate them for good. His career. Hers. Ultimately, his relationship with Qwi Xux. After that began, he'd almost never run into Iella.

"If it's really her," Wedge continued, "she's probably here on an Intelligence assignment. Don't do anything to blow her cover—just be your usual obnoxious self and let her shoot you down."

"I resent the implication that she would. That any woman would."

"But suggest to her that your commander finds her interesting and would like to see her at some time. I'd like to know what she's up to. Whether she's here to support us. Whether we can help her. That sort of thing."

Janson nodded. "Understood. And if it's not actually Iella?"

"You're on your own."

Janson's grin returned.

.   .   .

Wedge spoke to Cheriss, and she spoke to some sort of functionary, and moments later that man drew a blast-sword. He thumbed it on and waved it in a circle over his head. Wherever the tip moved through the air, it traced a glowing yellow line, so his motion created a shining circle above him. As soon as he ceased his motion, it began to fade.

This attracted the attention of the crowd and conversation quelled. "We have a non-title ground challenge," he said. "Lord Pilot Depird ke Fanax challenges Cartann Ground Champion Cheriss ke Hanadi, vengeance for her defeat of Jeapird ke Fanax at the last championship."

There was applause from the crowd, which withdrew from the speaker, forming an open circle in the middle of the chamber.

Wedge turned to Tomer. "Wait, wait. I thought she was going to put on some sort of show or demonstration."

Tomer's expression was serious. "She is. To entertain you, she offered to accept a combat challenge. As the ground champion, she receives a lot of them. And you told her to go ahead."

"I didn't know that's what she meant. I'm putting a stop to this." Wedge took a step forward, but Tomer's hand fell on his shoulder and restrained him.

"Don't," Tomer said. His voice was a plea. "It's too late. The challenge was accepted. You're out of the loop. All you can do now is embarrass Cheriss and look like an idiot—you'll be demonstrating weakness."

Wedge glared, then fell back. "You could have told me."

"You spoke with such confidence. I thought you understood."

Cheriss took off her belt, handing it to the man who'd made the announcement, and drew her blastsword and knife. She held the latter in a reverse grip, the blade laid back along her forearm, and took an experimental thrust or two with the blastsword. It was not powered up and left no glowing lines behind. Her smile was no longer cheerful; hers was the delight of a predator that had run its prey to ground.

Into the circle stepped a young man. He was perhaps a year or two older than Cheriss, lean and graceful, his clothing all in blacks and yellows, his mustache stylishly trim. He whipped his hip cloak from his shoulders and threw it into the crowd, then reached to the belt held by someone at the edge of the crowd and drew a blastsword and knife. He held his knife in a more conventional grip than Cheriss did. "I am here to correct the results of an accident," he said, his voice light and unconcerned, "and to demonstrate what we all know—that wherever a ground-pounder can merely achieve, a flier can excel."

There was applause at his words. He thumbed on the power of the blastsword and twirled it before him, leaving a figure-eight pattern that glowed redly in the air.

Wedge saw Hallis trying to move through the crowd to get to the leading edge. Farther around the rim of the crowd, he saw the *perator* standing, his retinue giving him a little pocket of space.

"To the *perator*," the announcer said. Both Cheriss and the challenger, Depird, bowed to the *perator* and flourished their blades in an identical pattern, a circle bisected by a cross; Cheriss's blade was now powered up and the symbol of her flourish glowed blue for a moment before fading.

"Honor or death," the announcer said, and took a step back, putting him at the edge of the open space.

Depird wasted no time. He moved forward, not a rush but a fast stalk, until he was almost within range of a thrust from Cheriss's long blade, and raised his blastsword to a high guard, well above his head, its point unerringly aimed at Cheriss's head; as he advanced, Cheriss took a pose with her knife hand forward, her blastsword hand back, her predatory smile still in place.

Depird took a step in and thrust with his dagger, inviting a counterblow from Cheriss's blastsword, but she swept the attack away, striking the back of his hand with her own dagger hand. Depird followed through with a thrust of the blastsword, which she took on the curved guard of her sword. When his point hit her guard, there was a crack like a blaster rifle firing, and smoke rose from a darkened patch on her guard.

With a flick of arm and wrist, Cheriss disengaged her blastsword from Depird's, then swung her guard up in a punch that caught Depird full in the jaw. He staggered back, his expression outraged, and Wedge could see that a patch on his jaw was blistered—doubtless from the heat the guard had absorbed from his attack.

The crowd reacted, some members applauding, some murmuring in a disapproving tone. Tomer said, "Cheriss is considered a gutter-fighter, vulgar by the standards of the blastsword art. With this court, the fact that she wins most of the time is her primary saving grace."

Depird shook his head as though to clear it, then began to circle Cheriss. She waited for only a quarter circuit before attacking, a step forward followed by a thrust from her blastsword—and then it was on in full, Depird catching her assault on his blade and attempting a riposte, Cheriss blocking that move with the guard on her dagger and returning a full-extension thrust that caused Depird to leap back nearly into the leading edge of the crowd. Every motion of the swords was accompanied by an arc of light from their tips; every impact of a sword tip hitting a weapon guard or blade was accompanied by the sharp crack of energy emission.

"It's a very pretty sort of competition," Tomer said.

Wedge didn't bother to glare; Tomer's attention was fully on the fight. "You mean, it's a very decorative way to get killed. You're awfully unconcerned."

Tomer shrugged. "This is their planet, Wedge. Their

way of life. It's for me to understand it . . . not to try to change it."

Cheriss, backing away from an especially aggressive advance, caught Depird's blastsword blade centimeters below the tip with her dagger. She swung it out of line and brought her own blastsword point to bear in a single, beautifully fluid motion. Depird tried to check his forward motion but couldn't—his body arched away from her blade but he ran upon it anyway. There was a sharp crack, a shriek of pain from him, and he was thrown to the floor on his back. He lay there writhing, a blackened patch on his tunic at the center of his chest, smoke rising from it.

Cheriss, barely winded, set her dagger on the floor. She turned to smile at Wedge, then extended her hand toward him, palm up; a moment later, she turned it palm down.

"You get to choose," Tomer whispered. "Palm up means she spares him. Palm down means she kills him. Palm up will suggest excessive sentimentality on your part—not something the Adumari hope to see in a fighter pilot."

Wedge stared at him. "You think I should let him die?" he whispered.

Tomer shrugged. "I'm not expressing an opinion. Just analyzing actions and consequences."

Wedge put on his sternest face, his offended officer face, and stepped out into the open ring. He moved to stand over Depird, who writhed in obvious agony. The duelist was unable entirely to keep quiet; each of his breaths emerged as a moan.

Wedge studied him critically for several seconds, then raised his gaze to Cheriss's. He spoke loudly enough for all to hear. "This boy needs to learn to handle pain, so that when he does die, he does not embarrass his family." He held out his hand, palm up.

Cheriss shrugged and nodded, not apparently bothered. Some applause broke out from the audience, and some murmuring; but Wedge could see the *perator* nod agreeably, and suddenly all the courtiers around the ruler were applauding, and the applause spread from there to the rest of the crowd.

Wedge returned to his place in the audience. As he approached, Tomer, too, applauded. "A good solution," Tomer said, his voice barely audible over the crowd. "Credible."

"We're going to talk about this later," Wedge said. "And you're not going to enjoy it." He looked around for his pilots and spotted them, all three together, standing toward the back of the audience ring.

The crowd broke up, its members drifting away, and Wedge saw the *perator*'s personal retinue move toward a side exit. Two men dressed in the featureless brown livery worn by the door guards collected Depird, hauling him unceremoniously to his feet and helping him toward the main exit. Janson caught his eye and grinned uninformatively.

"Did you like it?"

Wedge turned. Cheriss, her weapons once again sheathed, stood before him. Her smile was, oddly, just a little uncertain.

"He certainly did," Tomer said.

"I thought it was a very impressive, skillful display," Wedge said truthfully. "With an interesting aesthetic component. Do I understand right that his objection to you was that you'd beaten his brother in a tournament?"

She nodded. "In the finals of the last Cartann Ground Championship. Depird's brother, unlike Depird, was one of the few pilots who really knew how to handle a blastsword. Almost a pity that he died of his injuries."

"Pity. Um, Cheriss, what purpose did the ground championship serve, other than to establish you as the new ground champion?"

She smiled. "Well, none, I suppose."

"Entertainment," Tomer said. "And continuation of a tradition dear to the hearts of the people of Cartann."

"That, too," Cheriss said.

Janson appeared beside Wedge. "News," he said.

4

They were on foot in the streets of the city of Cartann, but nearly anonymous—the people on the street accorded them not a second glance. Wedge supposed it was because they were in native dress; had they been in their New Republic flight suits or dress uniforms, he was certain they'd be mobbed. Cheriss moved on ahead of them, politely banished from the current conversation as she led them back to their building.

"You don't speak for me," Wedge said. "Ever."

The words originated in a cold spot deep in Wedge's gut, but Tomer seemed oblivious to Wedge's emotion. The diplomat merely shrugged. "I understand. But you have to understand that sometimes I can't let you say the first thing to pop out of your head. Until you know a lot more about the way things work in Cartann, you're likely to precipitate an interplanetary crisis with an ill-thought-out remark."

"Tomer, I direct your attention to the word 'let.' You've misused it. You don't 'let' me, or 'not let' me, *anything*. Understand?"

"I understand completely. You're the one who doesn't understand. You shot your mouth off tonight and precipitated a duel you immediately wanted to stop. Should I step aside, keep quiet, and let you do that again? Or something worse?"

"No." Wedge fumed for a few moments. "We have to work out a way to do this. To work together. But I'm not going to blindly follow your lead."

"It would be better for everyone if you did." Tomer caught sight of Wedge's expression. "Well, on another matter, what's this news Janson brings us?"

"Pilot news," Wedge said. "Results of some Red Flight betting. And rather than compromise myself with the diplomatic corps by letting you know just how badly I lost, I'm going to ask you to go on ahead. We'll be along to our quarters after a while."

Tomer frowned, obviously trying to figure out how to phrase a refusal, then shrugged. "Contact me by comlink if you need me." He increased his pace, said a word or two to Cheriss as he passed her, then disappeared into pedestrian traffic ahead.

"It's Iella, all right," Janson said. "She wants to see you. I mean, it didn't seem to be an urgent thing. I think she was happier to see *me*, of course. She even asked about Hobbie."

Hobbie brightened. "She did?"

"Oh, yes. 'How's old Bugbite?' she asked."

Hobbie's shoulders slumped. When first he'd met Iella, years ago, on a covert mission to Corellia, he'd been stung in the face by a local insect. Iella's partner Corran Horn, both of them then investigators with Corellian Security, had shot him down with that nickname. "She did not."

Janson's grin deepened, but he returned his attention to Wedge. "And she did want to talk to you. Underneath the shortest of the flat displays around the plaza where we landed, at midnight tomorrow. You have to make sure that you're not being shadowed. You can't compromise her cover identity."

"What is her cover identity?"

"She's some sort of computer slicer. Hired a while back to develop programs to translate and interface between Cartann computers and New Republic and Imperial computers."

"Define 'a while back,' " Wedge said.

Janson shrugged. "I'm not sure. At least several weeks, possibly several months."

Wedge looked between his pilots. "There's something very odd going on here. I had the impression from General Cracken that a mapping ship accidentally discovered this planet—which had been cut off from the rest of galactic civilization for thousands of years—a short time ago. Immediately afterward, the New Republic was supposed to have dispatched a diplomatic delegation, which immediately discovered that they preferred dealing with pilots, which immediately resulted in our being sent here. Quick, quick, quick.

"But now I find that the Adumari people have hyperdrives; they even have some hyperdrive-equipped fighters. They've brought in specialists to link up their computer systems with ours. They've contrived to bring in pilots from the Empire at the same time we're here, and even set things up so that the two opposing groups of pilots wouldn't know about one another until we bumped into one another tonight. What do you want to bet that we haven't been brought here chiefly because they love pilots? We've been brought here to duel with our opposite numbers."

"It's worse than that," Hobbie said.

The others looked at him. "You know," Janson said, "whenever the name of Derek 'Hobbie' Klivian comes up, the words 'It's worse than that' ring in my ears. Sometimes I hear them when I'm dreaming."

Hobbie ignored him. "Wedge, while Janson was politely asking Iella about her love life—"

"I wasn't!"

"—I was talking to people about things. Asking questions instead of answering them. And I found out that Adumar doesn't even *have* a world government. The *perator* of Cartann doesn't represent the whole world."

"That would certainly explain why they all seem to identify more with this nation than with their world," Wedge said. "What do they have?"

"Well, remember that all the answers I got were from Cartann loyalists." Hobbie shrugged, apologetic. "But if you read past the text stream to the data stream, it looks as though Cartann is the biggest of a large number of nations, and it controls several other nations besides. Through tradition and military. It controls something like more than half the planet. So they could set up trade treaties, that sort of thing, for Cartann, but they couldn't negotiate to bring all of Adumar into the New Republic."

"You're right," Wedge said. "It was worse than I thought."

Janson grinned. "Oh, it's even worse than that."

Wedge sighed. "Look, this is your last one. The next person after Wes who has bad news, we all just shoot him. Go ahead, Wes."

"Cheriss is sweet on you."

Wedge felt his shoulders sag. "Tell me you're kidding."

"Sorry, chief. Do you see the way she looks at you? And she gave you the decision on her challenge duel, to kill or not to kill. They say that's a really big thing here. As subtle as flowers and sweets."

"Wes, she's half my age."

"True." Janson looked resigned. "I'll help you, Wedge. I'll go break the news to her, console her in her time of grief. I'll—"

Wedge held up a hand. "Never mind what I just said. Let's just shoot Wes."

"I'm for that," Hobbie said.

"What's our strategy?" Tycho asked.

Hobbie gave him a curious look. "I thought we'd just all draw and fire. But I could count down to zero, and *then* we could draw and fire."

Tycho gave him a mock-scowl. "Quiet, you. Wedge, what's our strategy in dealing with all these serpentine politics?"

"Play dumb for now. Let everyone—Tomer, the rulers of Cartann, our own Intelligence network—think we believe everything they've told us so far. Follow Tomer's plans for use of our time with just enough belligerence to remind them we're fighter pilots. And find out what we can on our own. I'll talk to Iella tomorrow. Hobbie, Tomer said that Intelligence certified our quarters as free from Cartann listening devices—but nobody certified them free of *New Republic Intelligence* listening devices; I want you to screen our quarters and see if our own people are eavesdropping on us. Tycho, Wes, I want you to visit *Allegiance* tonight; I'll wager every credit I'm carrying that there's an Imperial capital ship orbiting Adumar opposite our ship, and I don't want *Allegiance* taken off-guard if there's trouble."

Janson spoke up, sounding hurt: "Can it be later tonight? I, uh, sort of made an appointment for this evening . . ."

Wedge just looked at him.

"I suppose not," Janson said. "Tycho, didn't anyone ever tell you that when you ask Wedge for strategy, he gives you work to do?"

The next morning, Wedge led Red Flight in a dive toward the trees, keeping a careful eye on the unfamiliar range meter. The cockpit of the Tarrvin-on-Kallik Blade-32 was unfamiliar to him; it wouldn't do to get himself and his pilots killed because he wasn't completely at home with the controls.

Or with the speed measurements, for that matter. Adumar didn't measure things by the old Imperial standards; instead of klicks per Coruscant hour, flight speed was measured in *keps*, or thousand paces (measured by the stride of some long-dead Cartann *perator*) per Adumar hour. The Adumari measurement was about eighty percent of the Imperial standard, so Wedge had to do constant conversions in his head.

When the forest below began to turn into individual trees, streams, and riders on those banded-armor *farumme* reptiles, the control console began to chime insistently at Wedge. He knew that it was the collision alarm of the system's computer, but it seemed to be set on fairly conservative numbers and distances. Only after several more moments, in which the chime became more loud and insistent, did Wedge haul back on the control yoke, bringing his Blade-32 out of its dive.

As he began to level off above the forest floor, he felt his maneuver pushing him back in the pilot's seat, felt a slight dizziness as blood began to rush from his head. A moment later, the pressure eased and the dizziness diminished. He shook his head. The Blade-32 had inertial compensators like the New Republic and Imperial fighters he was used to, but their computers weren't quite up to the task of calculating precise adjustments to keep the pilots from suffering all the ill effects of high-gravity maneuvers.

Still, he was flying again, testing a new fighter, tearing up the sky with gravity and engineering limitations his only enemies.

When he was chained to his desk and his general's duties for days, weeks at a time, he could pretend that flying was something he had largely set aside, something he returned to occasionally for enjoyment. But at times like this, it was impossible to deny his pure love of flying, his need of it. It was impossible to deny the ache it caused him when he was unable to find cockpit time. Flying was a part of him, had been since his childhood, and he felt a flash of anger at the bureaucrats and deskbound organizers who, since his promotion to the rank of general, had given him assignment after assignment that kept him far from a cockpit most of the time.

Regular fighter missions were a thing of his past, and he missed them terribly. But perhaps they were a thing of his future as well. Perhaps someday he could find himself a post, as General Salm and General Crespin had before him, that would allow him regular command of a fighter wing. That prospect gave him some hope for his military future.

He checked his sensor board, or lightboard—the screen with the green wire-frame grid the Adumari called a "lightbounce system"—and saw that Tycho, Janson, and Hobbie were still tucked in tight. Off in the distance, their escort of four Cartann fighters was still in formation.

But Wedge's visual check showed that Janson was upside down. "Janson, orient yourself," he said. "You're belly to sky."

"Negative, boss. I'm right side up. You three inverted coming out of that headache maneuver."

Wedge glanced up, saw only sky and sun above him.

Janson's voice came again, a taunt this time: "Made you look." He righted his Blade-32.

The lightboard beeped at him. It showed an incoming flight of a half-dozen Blades, four advanced, two in the rear. Wedge's communications system buzzed. "Hail General Antilles! The Lords of Dismay Flightknife issues a challenge."

Wedge sighed. He was already well familiar with some of the Adumari pilot terminology, such as the use of "flightknife" for "squadron." For the sixth time since Red Flight had commenced this familiarization run, he switched over to general frequency and said, "Antilles here. Denied."

"Another time, then. Confusion to your enemies! Farewell!" The incoming fighters began a slow loop around to head back the way they'd come.

"They love you, Wedge." That was Janson's voice.

"This is the only planet where everyone who loves me also wants to kill me," Wedge said. "All right. Opinions, people? On the fighters, I mean."

"A bit like flying wishbones," Janson said. "These Blades have the kind of mass and solidity I like in the Y-wings. But sluggish."

"I like the weapons arrangement," Hobbie said. "Two lasers forward, two lasers back. Two missile ports like the X-wings . . . but we're carrying sixteen missiles, not six. More punch against capital ships. If we could swap proton torpedoes for the lower-powered explosives these are carrying, that'd be a lot of bang."

"I've been reviewing engineering records and damage statistics," Tycho said.

Janson laughed. "While we've been maneuvering?"

"Restraining myself so you could keep up with me left me plenty of time for intellectual pursuits," Tycho said. "I also composed a symphony and drafted a plan to bring peace to the galaxy. Anyway, without shields, these things come apart under any missile hit. But they're structurally tough, more so than X-wings, so they hang together after taking more collateral damage or laser hits. I'd like to see how much maneuverability they lose with a set of shields, hyperdrive, maybe a gunner's seat installed. If it's not too great a loss, we may have a viable fighter-bomber here, something useful in fleet actions against capital ships."

"Good point," Wedge said. He rolled his fighter over and up again, decided he didn't much like the way the atmosphere bit at his flight surfaces. "All right, let's take them back to the hangar. Wedge Antilles out."

That was a code signal, the use of his full name. After

bringing his fighter around so that it was headed back toward Giltella Air Base, one of two bases close to the city of Cartann, he switched the microphone off his fighter's comm system, then pulled an elaborate comlink headset out of a flight-suit pocket. Tycho had brought these back from the *Allegiance* last night, comlinks with scrambler attachments. Wedge set its registers to a previously agreed-upon scramble code.

Hobbie had determined that their clothes were free of listening devices, but he'd found two such objects in their quarters, obviously of New Republic make. Not being Intelligence-trained, he'd said that he wasn't confident that he could find them all. That meant their quarters were not a safe place to discuss things in confidence. With Cheriss or Tomer with them most of the rest of the time, this left few occasions for private conversation between them.

Wedge dialed the power down on his headset so its signal was unlikely to be intercepted at ranges of more than a few hundred meters. He pulled off his pilot's helmet, setting it in the little cargo space behind his seat, and put on the headset. "One to Flight. Are you reading? Answer by number."

"Two, ready."

"Three, ready to run off at the mouth."

"Four, I'm a go."

"All right, gentlemen, what's news?"

"One, Four. On the lightboard, I keep seeing fighter maneuvers about one hundred fifty Adumar klicks southwest—"

"That's *keps*."

"Thank you, Three. Southwest, and with what I've been able to tell from these broken-up signals, they've been doing pretty much what we have. My bet is that Turr Phennir and his pilots are also out familiarizing themselves with the Blades."

"Good to know, Four."

"One, Three. There's something I just don't get."

"This is news?"

Wedge smiled. "Quiet, Four. Go ahead, Three."

"Why does the *perator* of Cartann assume that the Empire just won't move in here and take over? Why does he think they'll cooperate in this competition to win their favor and then just go home if they lose?"

Wedge thought about that. "Three, here's a guess. You're thinking in terms of the Empire we knew when we joined the Rebellion. Today's Empire is a fraction of that size, with a heightened sense of economy. To conquer this world, they'd have to commit and probably spend a lot of resources. To do so, they might even have to smash flat the very industry they want to obtain. The Empire would win, no doubt. But they'd lose more than they'd gain. It would probably never be a cost-effective decision."

"Good point, One. I just can never think of the Empire as anything but this gigantic thing with limitless resources."

"Back to normal communications," Wedge said. "The air base is coming up." Ahead were the familiar colors and shapes of the Cartann air base from which they had taken off—several concentric rings, hangar buildings surrounding central control buildings, all of them with elaborate balconies.

Minutes later, they had landed and returned the Blade-32s back to the flightknife that had loaned them, declined yet another challenge from that flightknife, and been rejoined by Cheriss just outside the hangar. "Did you enjoy them?" she asked, her eyes shining.

"Yes, we did," Wedge said, and led the way toward the wheeled contrivance that would carry them back into the city. "Very hardy fighter-craft." The girl's expression suggested that she awaited further praise for the Blades, so he added, "Obviously a vehicle of conquest."

She nodded, happy. "There is none better. And it is obvious that you've learned to master it very swiftly."

"Well . . . we managed not to crash," Wedge amended. "I wouldn't say we've mastered it."

"Oh, you were putting them through their paces as though you'd been flying them for years," she said. "And the Imperial fighters accepted a challenge today and shot down four members of Blood on the Flowers Flightknife."

"Shot down?" Wedge frowned. "How many survived?"

"One," she said. "Ejected, badly wounded. He'll have some scars to brag about." Her voice became a little more soft, more shy. "Will you be accepting challenges, too? Maybe tomorrow?"

Wedge, out of the corner of his eye, saw Janson grinning at him. Wedge slowed his pace and managed to step on Janson's foot before the other pilot could adjust. Over Janson's yelp, he said, "Tell me, are all your challenges live-fire exercises, or do you ever use simulators?"

Her smile faded, replaced by an expression of confusion. "What's a simulator?"

"A device that simulates what you see and feel when you're in a fighter's cockpit. It uses computers, holograms, and inertial compensators to mimic almost exactly the experience of flying, so you can get in a lot of training without risking valuable machinery or even more valuable pilots. You don't have anything like that?"

"Well . . . in other countries, pilots sometimes duel with weakened lasers matched with laser receptors, and with missiles that have weakened charges that create a large pigment cloud, so they don't have to kill one another."

"In other countries . . . but in Cartann, all your pilot duels are live-fire?"

Cheriss nodded. "Yes. Oh, not all are fatal. A pilot might eject and the winner might decide not to shoot him on the way to the ground. That's what happened today with the Imperials. When that happens, both will live. Assuming the crowd on the ground doesn't beat the loser to death for his defeat."

"How do you keep from losing pilots at an astounding rate?"

She considered. "Well, that's why the government instituted the Protocols. Pilots who wish to duel must demonstrate that both will benefit from a duel."

"For example?"

"If a new pilot wants to duel an older, experienced pilot, that situation probably fails to meet the Protocols. You see, the new pilot would benefit if he won—he would have received training at the hands of a better, and would gain fame for having killed him. But the old pilot would not really benefit. He could mark one more kill on his board, but it would be of no consequence, so he would not benefit. Therefore his commander would not approve the duel.

"But if a new pilot had invented a new maneuver or fighting technique, the older pilot could benefit from facing it. If his commander was impressed enough with the younger pilot's inventiveness, he might permit the duel."

"You say other countries perform simulated-weapons duels. Is there a loss of honor in using them?"

"In Cartann, yes. There, I suppose not—they lose enough honor just for belonging to a lesser nation."

"What would it mean if I agreed to a duel, but insisted on using simulated weapons?"

Her face went slack, the expression Wedge had come to recognize as meaning she was thinking hard. Finally she said, "I'm not sure. Either you would lose honor, or the use of simulated weapons would gain in honor."

"If I did it again and again, and won every time?"

"I think, I *have* to think, that simulations would gain in honor."

"Interesting. Perhaps, tomorrow, when we come out

here I'll ask for Red Flight to be equipped with weakened lasers and paint missiles."

Tomer had no news for them when they returned to their quarters late that afternoon. No appointment with the *perator* or his ministers to discuss the possibility of Adumar's entry into the New Republic. No revised orders from Intelligence.

They accepted a dinner invitation Wedge had received at the previous night's celebration, at the lavish home of Cartann's Minister of Trade. Yet the politician, a lean man who hobbled on an artificial leg, the result of ejecting from a disintegrating Blade-28 and being hit by shrapnel from his own fighter, had no interest in discussing trade; he wanted to hear nothing but tales of Wedge's exploits.

They dined at a long table on the minister's broad balcony—in order, Wedge suspected, that the owners of the balconies all around might see them and be envious of the minister's guests. Wedge and his pilots quickly learned to spell one another, each taking up the thread of a story in turn so that the others might eat. Cheriss kept quiet throughout, listening wide-eyed to tales of Endor and Borleias and Coruscant.

Afterward, they took the ascender—the slow-moving, rattling, open-sided Adumari version of the turbolift—down to the third floor aboveground. The building's first three stories were mostly taken up with a massive lobby, a showcase to impress visitors, and the ascender did not go all the way to the ground; visitors had to descend those three stories by a sweeping staircase, and at the outside door they would reclaim their blasters.

Janson led the way down the stairs at a half trot. "I hope we get to your diplomatic duties soon, Wedge. I really look forward to them."

Wedge grinned. "As opposed to night after night of dinners with star-struck functionaries?"

"You said it," Janson said. "I really hate all the adulation." Then, as he rounded the main curve in the staircase, six Adumari men, climbing the stairs, drew blastswords, the foremost two of them lunging at him.

Time seemed to dilate for Wedge. He saw Janson whip off his preposterous cloak and entangle the two blastswords; the weapons' points fired off, pumping blaster energy into the garment, setting it afire in two places. The other four men charged around Janson and his two opponents, passing them on the wall side of the stairs.

Wedge leaped forward onto the curved banister— polished hardwood, it did not budge under his weight and offered little friction. He slid down it as if mounted sidesaddle on a riding beast. As he passed Janson, he brought his left leg up and unloaded a kick against one of Janson's opponents, the maneuver almost pitching Wedge over the side to the floor two stories down. The blow caught the man full in the face, throwing him back and down the stairs, rolling almost as fast as Wedge slid.

Wedge regained his balance and dropped off the banister to land beside the man, who lay faceup sprawled across half a dozen carpeted steps. Wedge snatched up the man's blastsword and turned back up the stairs.

The last of the men who'd been rushing past Janson had turned again to descend toward Wedge. Janson had his own enemy wrapped up in a wampa-hug and was bending the man back across the banister; the enemy's face contorted in pain as his spine curved too far in a direction it was not meant to go. Janson's blastsword was still in its sheath; his burning cloak lay on the step beside his foot, its flames licking higher.

Cheriss had her blastsword out; she nimbly deflected the blades of two of the oncoming men. That left one to edge past her and go after Hobbie and Tycho, but as Wedge watched, the two moved in concert. Hobbie lunged toward the swordsman and jerked back just as suddenly, drawing an ineffectual lunge from the man's blade, and Tycho took the opportunity to leap full on the man, slamming him down onto the steps. In a moment Tycho was straddling the man, raining punishing blows on his face, as Hobbie retrieved the blastsword.

Wedge backed away from the man descending after him. He cursed the unfamiliar weapon in his grip. Hand to hand, or blaster to blaster, he was confident that he could at least hold his own against an attacker, but not with a weapon as esoteric as the blastsword.

Then Wedge set the point of the blastsword to the carpet at the base of one of the steps. It unloaded its energy into the carpet, emitting a sharp "bang" and a small cloud of red-brown smoke. Wedge dragged the point all the way across the bottom of the stair, sustaining the sword's blaster emission, sending up a curtain of smoke before him.

He could still see his opponent, and the man—tall, mustached, smiling in anticipation of victory—shook his head as if correcting the actions of a pupil. "You waste all your charge to put smoke between us?" he asked. "That will be your last mistake, Wedge Antilles."

"Oh, I have plenty more to make." Wedge grabbed at the flap of carpet he'd cut free and, with all his strength, yanked. The carpet resisted, the adhesive that made it conform to the shape of the stairs holding; then it gave way. The descending assassin's feet went out from under him; he flailed wildly as he lost his balance, thumped down onto the stairs, and slid down toward Wedge.

Wedge stood his ground and brought the point of his blastsword up into contact with the armpit of his attacker's sword arm. He heard and felt the impact of blaster tip against skin, smelled the familiar odor of burning flesh. His opponent shrieked and dropped his sword.

Wedge glanced back up at the others. One of Cheriss's foes was down, a mass of char where his throat should be, and as he watched she disarmed the other with an expert twirl of their locked blades. Hobbie stepped in and hit the man, a punch that seemed to start a kilometer or two behind him, taking the man in the gut and folding him over. Janson gave his own enemy a little shove and that man, already broken like a toy, toppled to crash down onto the tile floor below. Nor did Tycho's opponent look anxious to continue the fight; his face was a mass of contusions, his eyes closed.

Janson began stomping on his cloak to put out the fire. Wedge heard a smattering of applause and whistling from the ground floor. He spared the floor a glance; men and women, bright in the lavender-and-gold livery of this building's workers, were merely cheering their efforts.

"Cheriss," Wedge said. "Who's the leader?"

"You are, General Antilles."

"I mean, *their* leader."

She gestured with her sword point at the one Wedge had kicked in the face; he lay halfway between Wedge and Hobbie. He did not move, but his eyes were fluttering.

"Hobbie, get building security and see if you can get our blasters back. Wes, Tycho, pick up blastswords and poke the first one of them who offers trouble. Cheriss, help me with this one." He moved up the stairs, somewhat tentative because the damage he'd done to the carpeting made walking tricky, and stood over the man he'd kicked.

Wedge moved his sword point back and forth over the man's throat. "What was all this about?"

It took a moment for the man's eyes to track on the blastsword tip. "What else?" the man said. "Honor. The chance to kill the famous general from the stars. Tomorrow I would kill the Imperial pilot."

Cheriss gave him a less than respectful smile. "You couldn't kill a feed-reptile if it spotted you two legs and an eye. He's lying, General. He's a paid assassin."

The man scowled at her and shook his head, a mute protest of innocence.

"Cheriss, how do you know that?"

She gestured at the man, her expression one of contempt. "First, look at his clothes."

The man, like most of the attackers, was dressed in what Wedge was beginning to recognize as barely acceptable clothing for a building as prosperous as this. His clothes were stylishly black, but on closer examination, the tunic was threadbare in places, the leather of his boots shined but much worn. The blastsword lying beside him had a guard that was much scarred, seldom polished.

"So?" Wedge asked.

"Second," she said, "this." She hauled back and kicked the man hard in the side.

He arched his back and groaned. He opened his mouth, doubtless to offer a curse or threat, and then remember Wedge's sword point hovering centimeters above his face. He remained silent.

Wedge frowned at the girl. "We don't torture for information, Cheriss. That's not our way."

She turned innocent eyes to him. "Torture? Never. This time, General, *listen*." She hauled back and kicked the man again, possibly harder than before.

Over the man's groan, Wedge distinctly heard a clinking noise from beneath the man's tunic.

Cautious, Wedge pulled the tail of the tunic up through the man's belt. Beneath, attached to a second, slimmer belt, was a transparent pouch filled with shining golden disks.

"Adumari credcoins?" Wedge asked.

"Perats," Cheriss said. "Do you see Pekaelic's face on the obverse? I see at least twenty of them. Not a fortune, but definitely an improvement in his estate."

Wedge nodded to Tycho, who searched the others. He found pouches of coins, most of them about half as full as this man's, on each.

"You're saying that someone with this kind of spending money should have better garments," Wedge said.

Cheriss nodded.

Wedge returned his attention to his prisoner. "Who paid you?"

"This money is from the last man I killed," the man said.

"Then you've killed a minister or a wealthy merchant," Cheriss said. "And his family will be wealthy enough to prosecute you all the way to the grave. I'll tell the Cartann Guard what you've just admitted to. Whoever the last important man to be killed was, you'll take the blame for it."

The man opened his mouth as if to offer a denial, then shut it stubbornly.

Cheriss caught Wedge's eye and gave him a tight shake of her head. Her meaning was clear; the man wouldn't talk.

Hobbie came bounding up the stairs, leading a handful of men and women in the eye-hurting livery of the building. All wore sheathed blastswords but carried some sort of sidearms in their hands. "It's a no on our blasters," Hobbie said. "Until we leave the building."

"Rules," said the foremost of the liveried men, "are rules, I fear. But you will suffer no more inconveniences while in our building. Are we here to be witnesses to your kill, or do you wish them given over to the Cartann Guard?"

Wedge frowned at the man, who appeared to be about twenty, very fair, very exuberant. "Do you mean it's legal for me to just kill them?"

"Of course. You beat them fairly. Unconventionally, but fairly. And until you kill them, release them, or hand them over, the duel is not done."

"It wasn't a duel. It was an assassination attempt." Wedge finally remembered to turn the power off on his blastsword. "I turn them over to you for the Cartann Guard. These men were paid to kill us; perhaps the Guard will want to find out by whom."

"Of course," the young man said. "We will hold them if you wish to depart."

"Yes, thank you."

"Do you wish to take trophies?"

Wedge glanced at Cheriss. She said, "What's theirs is yours; you have won. What they carry, I mean. You cannot claim what is in their homes, at their moneykeepers'."

"I see." Wedge glanced among his pilots. "Red Flight, arm yourselves. Blastswords and sheaths. If we're going to have this happen again, I don't want us to have to rely only on fists and vibroblades."

Cheriss smiled at him. "You did very well with fists and vibroblades. You are brawlers. I like that. Cartann swordsmen are too effete."

"Thank you, Cheriss." Once he, Tycho, and Hobbie had their new blades buckled on, Wedge led the way past the helpful building guards and down to the street.

It had grown dark and cool outside in the hours of their dinner appointment, and now the streets were filled with shadowy figures and the occasionally wheeled transport. Even more rarely, a repulsorlift-equipped transport would cruise by a few meters overhead, its complement of five or ten passengers idly watching the pedestrian traffic below. Wedge kept his face down, the better to keep passersby from giving him a closer look and recognizing him.

"Cheriss, you heard his coins clinking over all the noise of the fight?"

She nodded.

"And you took out two of the enemy. That's very good work."

"Thank you, General."

"With all your talents, and your obvious respect for pilots, why aren't you a pilot yourself?" Wedge asked. He saw a little hesitation in her expression and added, "If it's personal, just tell me it's none of my business. I won't be offended."

"No," she said. "It's just—it's not something I feel shame over." Her miserable expression suggested she was lying. "But I can't learn to fly. Ever. When I go up in aircraft, even when I'm on a high balcony, I become dizzy. I panic. I can't think."

"Vertigo," Wedge said. "So you concentrated on the blastsword instead?"

She nodded. "It is a dying art. Oh, most nobles carry blastswords in public, and many commoners like myself. But the art as they practice it in their schools is stylized. They train with blaster power set to shock instead of burn, and they have rules that make some sorts of blows illegal. I, on the other hand, researched the blastsword art of centuries ago, when it was still very prestigious. I learned about alternative secondary weapons and using the environment against my enemies." She brightened again. "I can tell that you haven't trained with the blastsword . . . but it's obvious you know how to fight. The maneuver with the banister, Major Janson's use of the cloak, Colonel Celchu's skill with his fists—I would love to learn what you know."

"We'll trade, then. Teach us what you can, in the time we're here, of the use of the blastsword, and I'll let my merry band of reprobates teach you about the back-alley maneuvers they've learned."

He turned to catch the eyes of the other pilots, to make sure none of them had an objection, and saw that Janson was glum. "What's wrong, Wes?"

Janson sighed. "My cloak is all burned up," he said. "I liked that cloak."

"We'll find you one even more garish," Wedge promised. "Now, Cheriss, I hope you'll understand, but I have to be very rude to you for a minute."

"You want me to walk on ahead again," she said.

He nodded. She offered him what he took to be an understanding smile, then increased her pace.

"I'm going to leave you now," Wedge told his pilots. He checked the chrono from his pocket. As with most people who did a lot of travel from planet to planet, his chrono showed both ship's time and local time, and the local time indicated it was less than a half hour of midnight.

"You can't see her now," Hobbie said, his face grave.

"Why not?"

"You're all sweaty from the fight."

"He's right," Janson said. "You stink of sweat, and smoke, and the wine the minister spilled on you—"

"He missed me."

"I don't think so. Anyway, you're not fit for a liaison tonight." Janson put on a long-suffering face. "I'll go in your place. I'm ready for this assignment, sir." He saluted.

"This isn't a liai—" Wedge shut up and turned to Tycho. "If he keeps this up, Hobbie gets to choose his clothes for the next three days."

"Oh, good," Hobbie said.

Tycho nodded. "Keep your eyes open tonight, Wedge. We can be pretty sure the Imps put those assassins on us . . . but we can't be sure there aren't duelists out there who want to kill you honorably."

Wedge waited until Cheriss turned a corner ahead. He whipped off his cloak and reversed it so its dark interior color was now on the outside, and turned to join the pedestrian traffic heading the other way.

At this time of night, with no events taking place, the plaza where he'd made first landfall on Adumar was nearly empty. Though not illuminated by artificial lights, it was still bright enough under the shine of two moons, one of them full and quite large in the sky.

The temporary stand where Wedge had made his speech was gone, though the four poles with their speakers were still there. The spot where the X-wings had landed was empty, Wedge and his pilots having transferred their snubfighters to their balcony early that day.

But despite its echoing emptiness compared to the previous day, the plaza was not lifeless. Near where the X-wings had landed, a circle of men and women watched a blastsword duel; even at this distance Wedge could see the lines of green and violet color twirling through the air, hear the snap as a blastsword tip hit a surface. The fight continued for several more seconds, so it must not have found flesh, but moments later he heard a second blast followed by a quick shriek. Then a third blast, and applause.

Another life lost to no good purpose. Wedge shook his head.

Ahead, there was a slender silhouette waiting beneath the shortest of the dark display panels. When he was a dozen meters away, he slowed, sure that he should not call Iella's true name, but not certain as to what sort of greeting was appropriate. Finally he said, "May I approach?"

"You may." It was Iella's voice. She lowered the hood of her cloak as he reached her, and moonlight fell full on her face. She extended her hands.

He took them, then stood at a loss for words.

She laughed. "You were more eloquent yesterday."

"I do that sort of thing more often." He caught sight of another silhouette, big, probably male, deep within the shadow cast by the nearest building. "Friend of yours?"

"My bodyguard," she said. "Here, anyone with a

marginally profitable job can afford bodyguards for situations like these. Do you have one?"

"Not with me, no. She's already killed a man for me tonight." Wedge shook his head, willing away the distraction of the night's events.

"Killed—were you attacked?"

"All of us. Tycho, Wes, and Hobbie, too. We came out of it unhurt." He gestured as if thrusting with a blastsword. "Four visiting blades, cutting down assassins. Something more for the court to talk about." Iella seemed to have caught her breath and grown paler. Wedge leaned in closer. "Are you all right?"

"I'm fine. I'm not the one in danger, Wedge. You need to be careful. These peoples' affection for duels, for picking up honor coupons by killing each other, could get you murdered."

Wedge waved her objections away. "How have you been?"

Her expression remained cheerless. "Well enough. I've been working hard. Mixing fieldwork with analysis. It never gets boring."

"That doesn't sound as though you've found any one thing that you want to devote yourself to."

She shrugged, and he could sense even more distance between them. "I guess I'm not like you, that way. Listen, Wedge, I can be here, but not forever. What do you need?"

He sighed. "Duty first. I need to know what's really going on here on Adumar. I'm effectively ambassador here for the time being, and I'm in completely over my head. How long has the New Republic really been aware of Adumar?"

"You don't know?"

"No. I thought it had been a matter of days or weeks. Your presence, your cover, suggests it's been longer than that."

"Five or six months," she said. "Intelligence discovered that someone was recruiting computer slicers for hire to do interfaces between a new set of computer protocols and New Republic and Imperial standards. Intelligence got interested, put together an identity for me as a Corellian slicer, and dropped me on one of the worlds where they were hiring. It's the sort of mission we call a blind jump. When I got here, I set things up for the arrival of a team."

"What's your name here, by the way?"

She managed a faint smile. "Fiana Novarr."

"I'm sort of surprised that a hired code-slicer would be invited to an affair like last night's dinner, with the *perator* and all."

"I went in on the arm of a minister. That's not important, Wedge."

"I suppose not. So what's all this about a mapping ship finding Adumar, and suddenly they want our pilots as diplomats?"

"That's all true, but it's only part of the story. I was here for a few weeks—a temporary prisoner in theory, since I couldn't communicate offworld until actual relations were opened with outside worlds, though I did anyway—and figured out that Adumari scout ships had gotten far enough out to discover human-occupied worlds. They'd figured out that there were two big power hubs, the New Republic and the Empire. And they wanted to learn everything they could before getting in contact with either one. They wanted to have the leisure to decide which one, if any, to side with. But the mapping ship incident did happen, and it sort of accelerated their plans."

"Thus the invitation to me and Turr Phennir."

She nodded.

"How did they keep you from knowing about the Imperial pilots coming?"

"They're pretty sneaky people," she said. "Convoluted politics and secrecy are a way of life for them."

"Well, here's an important one. What sort of arrangements am I going to be able to make with them if they're not a united world? I can't do much more than open up diplomatic relations and persuade them that the Imps are bad."

"That's exactly what you're supposed to do. Other forces are working on the *perator* of Cartann to persuade him to enter into a world government."

"So all the hard mental work is taken care of. I just need to stand around, pose, look pretty for the holocams . . ."

She managed a brief smile. "That's it."

"Ie—Fiana, I'm not sure I like this place. They don't put a very high value on human life. What do you think?"

"You're right." She shrugged, a clear sign that this was something out of her hands. "It's different in other Adumari nations. Their mania for pilots is not quite as high. Dueling is not the fad it is here. Another reason for Cartann to join in a world government. It might acquire some more civilized characteristics."

"Who's your superior?"

"I can't tell you that. That's on a need-to-know basis."

"Well, I'm talking about a need-to-punch basis. Your immediate superior and General Cracken didn't give me a full briefing before I got here, and consequently I've been floundering around like an idiot. I need to know which of them to punch."

She smiled, got it under control. "Wedge, is that it? I need to get back to my quarters. It would probably do Fiana's reputation some good for her to be seen with Wedge Antilles . . . but it would also put me under scrutiny I don't want."

"I suppose so." Then a wave of something like doubt

hit him. "No, that's not it. Listen, I haven't seen you in months. And now that we've talked, I still feel as though I haven't seen you. What's going on?"

"Nothing." She presented him with a serene expression. For all he could read in it, she could have been all the way across the plaza.

"I don't believe you."

"I can't help you with that, Wedge."

"Iella, have we stopped being friends?"

She was silent a long moment. "I suppose we have."

Wedge felt his breath catch. It took him a moment to recover it. "When did that happen? *How* did it happen?"

"It's not you, Wedge. It's me." Her mask of serenity slipped, leaving her expression tired, even dismayed. "I just had another direction to go. You're not there."

"That's not an answer. That's Intelligence gibberish covering up an answer." It surprised Wedge, how hurt his tone sounded.

"I have to go."

"Every time we've ever spoken, I've been straight with you. I want an answer from you."

She put her hood up. Suddenly he could no longer see her features. "I have to *go*," she said, and turned away.

As she moved off into the darkness, her bodyguard detached himself from the building's shadow and followed.

Wedge stood there and watched her fade into the darkness of the plaza's shadowy edges. It occurred to him that this departure was just the image, the reflection of something that must have happened long ago. He just didn't remember when, and the mystery of it was like a little, stony knot of pain next to his heart.

5

That pain hadn't subsided by morning. He thought about the situation with Iella, could come to no hypothesis that covered all the facts, and set it aside for the time being. He set aside thinking about it, anyway; the ache stubbornly refused to be set aside.

By the time breakfast was done, his datapad had still received no word from Tomer about appointments with the *perator* for the purposes of diplomacy. Nor was there news on the men who had attacked them last night. Once again the day was his.

He asked Cheriss to call ahead to the air base and order Red Flight's Blade-32 aircraft to be loaded with weakened lasers and pigment-cloud missiles . . . and to spread the word that Wedge Antilles might be accepting challenges this day, but only from fighters similarly equipped.

They were already on the wheeled transport and heading toward the air base when she concluded that call. Out of the corner of his eye, Wedge saw her pocket her comlink, look at him, look toward the transport's controls, and look at him a second time.

"Is there a problem?" he asked.

"Not a problem, no. Well, maybe."

He turned toward her, but she looked forward along their travel route, avoiding his eyes. "Last night, when you slipped away . . . that was dangerous, you know."

"The Adumari have no respect for someone who can't confront danger."

"True. But if you were to die when I was supposed to be acting as guide for you, I would lose considerable honor."

"If I elude your attention, you have nothing to be ashamed of even if I get myself killed."

Her expression tightened. "Still. When you left . . . was it to see a woman?"

The answer "It's none of your business" rose to the top of his mind, he even heard it in his most snappish tone, but he restrained himself from saying it. He didn't know how badly such a response might cut her. "Yes, it was."

"If you slipped away just to avoid exposing me to something—"

"No, it was nothing like that."

"I'm not as young as I look, you needn't worry about shocking me—"

"Cheriss." He sighed and closed his eyes. "Listen. When I was your age, I borrowed a Headhunter, that's a type of starfighter, from a friend, and used it to kill the men who were responsible for my parents' deaths. A deliberate act of revenge. The whole universe changed. All the things that had surprised or shocked or offended me just the day before became nothing, instantly." He opened his eyes, sought out her gaze, and finally was able to hold it. "Like me, you've had blood on your hands from an early age. So I know you're not going to be shocked. I'm not trying to protect you."

"Was she . . . a pilot? The woman last night?"

He considered that question, wondered just how far he was willing to answer her curiosity, and said, "No."

Her face brightened. "No? No. *No.* I hope you fly well today. I mean, I know you will fly well today, but I hope others see. Remember to specify match numbers when you accept a challenge."

Wedge nodded. He'd already learned about that protocol. If he didn't "specify match numbers" when accepting a challenge, such as by saying "we accept four," the attackers could bring as many pilots as they wanted against him. The usual protocol was to accept as many challengers as he had pilots in his own flight or squadron.

He watched as Cheriss, suddenly, mysteriously transformed into a happy young woman again, trotted up to the front of the transport and leaned over the rail into the wind.

He moved back to his pilots. "Any of you understand that? Her mood swing?"

Tycho said, "I think I'd shoot myself before getting involved in this conversation."

Hobbie shrugged. "Not one of my languages, Wedge."

Janson threw up his arms, tossing his cloak back over his shoulders. It was a practice move; he'd already done it forty times this morning. He drew the cloak back around him, where Wedge could see its flexible flatscreen panels in front, the moving images they showed of Janson on the receiving stand the other night, and he nodded. "I understood her, boss. But you don't want to know. Trust me on this."

"Anytime Janson says 'you don't want to know,' " Wedge said, "it's like juggling thermal detonators. Each time you grab and throw, you know your thumb might hit the trigger . . ." He sighed and turned to Janson. "I want to know."

"You asked for it . . . You told her your lady friend wasn't a pilot, right? Cheriss also isn't a pilot. Here, she can't compete with pilots in prestige. But you saw a lady who wasn't a pilot. You just told Cheriss, 'Yes, you too have a chance with me.' "

Wedge stood there, contemplating, unconsciously rocking in place to compensate for the transport's swaying motion across the ground. "Wes, you were right," he said.

"You didn't want to know."

"I didn't want to know."

Janson grinned. "Boom."

Wedge and Tycho flew a head-to-head pass against Janson and Hobbie. As the numbers on their range meters rolled toward zero, he watched the brackets on the lightboard as they surrounded the two "enemy" Blade-32s. At first, the brackets were fuzzy and indistinct; then they grew in solidity as the lightboard sensor technology gradually improved its lock on them. At the same time, his sensor board began emitting a deep, ominous, throbbing noise, warning of the enemy's improving chance to target him.

The lightboard brackets went to full opacity at the same instant the throbbing warning hit its maximum volume. Wedge immediately rolled to port and dove, losing hundreds of meters of altitude in a matter of seconds, then came nose-up again, seeking Janson and Hobbie, who were similarly energetic in their attempt to elude a laser lock.

Wedge got the Blade-32 oriented toward his two targets, pleased with the way the starfighter increasingly felt natural to him. Visuals and his lightboard showed Janson breaking to starboard, Hobbie to port; he looped after the former and trusted Tycho to complement his action by going after the latter target.

He barely had Janson lined up in his weapon brackets when his target opened fire on him, stitching him with several blue pulses from his vehicle's rear-firing lasers.

Wedge growled at himself; unused to dueling with vehicles with rear weapons, he'd forgotten about them momentarily, while Janson, an experienced rear gunner, had utilized them from the start. But Wedge's sensor board indicated that the simulated laser damage he'd sustained was not critical. Wedge began bobbing and sideslipping, attempts to keep Janson from achieving another targeting lock, and waited for his opportunity.

It came a moment later. Janson's Blade began a quick drift to port. Wedge hit the trigger for his vehicle's missiles, launched one into and slightly left of Janson's drift, then traversed right and fired again. Janson, quick on the reflex, shied right out of the first missile's path . . . and the second missile detonated two meters ahead of his Blade, blanketing the starfighter in a thick cloud of obnoxious orange paint. Janson emerged from the explosion with streaks of orange along his flanks and a large spot of it on his forward viewport.

"I am slain," Janson said, his tone lofty. "What mischance ever brought me to this dismal world, where bags of paint would spell my doom?"

"You've been listening to the Adumari too much," Wedge said. He checked his lightboard. It showed Tycho and Hobbie, a few kilometers out, heading toward them in formation. "How'd you do, Tycho?"

"A rare one for Hobbie," Tycho said. "Brought me to one hundred percent damage with laser fire."

"Tycho's too used to really maneuverable fighters," Hobbie said. "TIE fighters, A-wings . . . the X-wing is the most sluggish thing he's ever spent a lot of time with. The Blade is just too much like flying a boulder for him."

The four formed up again, began a long loop around the broad tract of forest that Giltella Air Base had assigned for their training exercises.

"Still no challenges," Wedge said. "By this time yesterday, we'd had three or four of them at least."

"I don't think they're going to go for simulated

weapons," Tycho said. "They're so keen to see blood, Wedge. The last group of people I saw with that sort of enthusiasm for killing was Imperial stormtroopers fresh from boot camp. It's kind of unnerving."

"I still have to figure out what sort of reason to give them for simulated duels," Wedge said. "Something they'll accept within the parameters of their honor code."

"Oh, that's simple," Hobbie said. "Do to them what you do to us at times like that."

Wedge frowned. "What do you mean?"

"Tell them *what* you're doing but not *why*. Then let them speculate. Listen to them as they speculate. When they come up with an idea you really, really like, tell them 'You finally guessed right. That was my reasoning all along.' "

"I don't do that," Wedge said. "Much."

"All the time, boss."

Wedge caught a new pattern of motion on his light-board, six blips incoming. "Heads up. We have something."

A moment later, a new voice came across the comm board, a brassy one that rang in their ears: "Strike the Moons Flightknife issues greetings to New Republic Red Flight, and a challenge!"

Wedge kept his comm unit tuned to broadcast at low strength and only on Red Flight's frequency. "Tycho, call Giltella Air Base and make sure these guys are really equipped with sim weapons." He switched to the general frequency and upped his broadcast power. "Red Flight to Strike the Moons Flightknife, greetings. I will consider your challenge. Please give me the particulars about your pilots."

"I am Liak ke Mattino, captain, fourteen years' experience, eighteen war kills, thirty-three duel kills, one ground kill. I bring five pilots before you. In order of precedence, they are . . ."

Wedge listened to the litany of accomplishments with half his attention. He could have obtained the same information by tapping on the blip representing ke Mattino and the other Blades on the lightboard; the board's text screen would have then shown the appropriate data from the transponders on their fighters. But demanding an oral recitation was a good way to stall.

Tycho's reply came a minute later, toward the end of Captain ke Mattino's inventory: "Giltella confirms Strike the Moons is equipped with sims, General."

"Thanks, Tycho." Wedge switched back to general frequency. "Captain, we accept your challenge. We accept four, your choice. Standing by."

They waited while the Strike the Moons pilots chose among themselves. Two Blade-32's peeled away from the Cartann half squad and circled out to a much greater distance. Then the other four fighters banked in the direction of Red Flight.

"Break by wings," Wedge said. "Fire at will." He banked hard to starboard, Tycho tucked in behind him and to his left, and waited to see how the enemy would react.

All four enemy Blades turned to follow Wedge and Tycho.

Wedge shook his head. That was an odd tactical choice. He heard the first throbbing of targeting locks being brought against him and began evasive maneuvering. For practice's sake, he opened fire on his pursuers with his lasers, though he had no better laser locks than they did. On his lightboard, he could see Hobbie and Janson pulling into position in pursuit of the four Blades.

The laser locks grew stronger. Wedge said, "Let's give Wes and Hobbie something to shoot at," and shoved his control yoke forward, sending his Blade into a steep dive, and rotating so they still only had a side angle on him.

The four pursuers followed but did not rotate. Wedge kept up his laser fire against one of them and grinned. If he understood the simple Adumari light-bounce system correctly, the bigger the metal cross section it saw, the farther away it could get a good laser lock. In exposing their bellies to Janson and Hobbie, the four Blades had substantially increased their cross sections, which the two New Republic pilots should be seeing just about—

He saw missile streaks appear like magic lines between Hobbie's and Janson's Blades and two of the enemy craft. Paint clouds erupted, one an appalling pink, one a lavender, and one enemy Blade emerged from each. Both the "kills" broke off from the fight, moving out to meet the two pilots sitting out the conflict.

That left two. No, one. One of the remaining Blades broke away to join the other kills. As it departed, it broadcast, "Ke Mattino congratulates Antilles on a good stop."

Wedge checked his sensor board. He must have racked up enough hits to put the enemy captain in the kill column. His own Blade showed twenty percent damage; he'd picked up a couple of grazes himself.

The surviving enemy Blade came doggedly on after Wedge and Tycho. Wedge leveled off smoothly and switched his comm system back to Red Flight frequency. "Let's try a simple one," he said. "Break to starboard and rejoin Wes and Hobbie. I'll lead him back for a head-to-head against you."

"Done, boss." Tycho broke away sharply. As Wedge expected, the pursuing Blade paid him no heed, continuing on after Wedge.

Wedge juked and jinked, making himself a hard a target to hit, though he saw his simulated laser damage climb to thirty percent, then to thirty five percent. This pilot was a good shot. But his maneuvering pointed him back toward the other three members of Red Flight. As soon as his sensor board indicated that he could get a good shot at his own pilots, the blip that was the last enemy Blade changed to a kill marker and circled off to rejoin its fellows.

"A good exercise, Strike the Moons," Wedge said. "Care to go again?"

There was a noticeable delay before the enemy captain replied. "Again? The duel is done."

"Yes, but nobody's a smoking crater, and we have fuel enough for two or three more at least. Do you want to go again, maybe let the two pilots who didn't go last time come against us now?"

There was still confusion in the captain's voice, but he said, "We could do that." And moments later, four Blades, two that had taken part in the previous exercise and two that had not, broke away from the circling formation and came again against Red Flight.

Captain ke Mattino was a tiny man, lean of form and rising barely to Wedge's nose, but his long and elaborately curled mustache doubtless helped increase his personal majesty to acceptable levels. He sat opposite Wedge in the Giltella Air Base pilots' bar and nodded as Wedge spoke, every bob of his head setting his mustache to swaying.

"The problem is not in your skills," Wedge said. "It's in your tactics. In every exchange, you kept your whole group together and went with all ferocity after the highest-profile enemy . . . me. You know what that makes you?"

Ke Mattino looked suspicious. "Dead?"

"Well, I was going to say *predictable*. But predictability, in this case, meant dead, so you're right." Wedge glanced down the table, where his three pilots and ke Mattino's listened intently.

"But circumstance dictates tactics," ke Mattino said,

his voice a protest. "The greatest honor comes from killing the most prestigious enemy."

"No," Tycho said. "That's the second greatest honor. The greatest honor comes from protecting those who are depending on you. Which you can't do if you get yourself killed."

Wedge nodded. "The question is, are you earning honor so that your loved ones can be proud of you as they stand over your grave, or so they can be proud of you when you come home at night?" He raised his brewglass to drain it, but was hit by a hollow feeling as his words came back on him: The question was merely an academic one to him. He had no one to come home to. He even had fewer friends than he'd thought, having somehow lost Iella while he wasn't looking.

To disguise his sudden feeling of disquiet, he went to the bar to get his brewglass refilled, leaving Tycho to continue in charge of the conversation. Two words were still haunting the back of his mind, intruding when he wasn't absolutely focused on some other subject: *Lost Iella.*

By the time he got back to the table, the pilots there were on their feet, shaking hands. "Unfortunately," ke Mattino was saying, "other duties do demand some small portion of our time. Is there a chance you will be accepting challenges again tomorrow?"

"Until our own duties demand all our time, there's a high likelihood of it," Wedge said. "In fact, tomorrow, we may bring the X-wings over and show you how we fight at home."

"That is something I would wish most fervently to see," ke Mattino said. He saluted, waving his tight fist a few centimeters before his sternum in an odd pattern. It took Wedge a moment to recognize the motion: It was the same as Cheriss's salute the night of her duel, but without the blastsword in hand. "I hope to see you on the morrow," the captain said, then turned away, pulling his hip cloak around him in a dramatic flourish.

• • •

Today, the people of Cartann had apparently discovered that Wedge and his pilots were flying at the air base. When they and Cheriss departed the base on their rolling transport, the street was thick with admirers. They clustered up against the rails, offering things to Wedge and the pilots—flowers, Adumari daggers, folded notes scented with a variety of exotic perfumes, necklaces, metal miniatures of the Blade-32 fighter-craft, objects too numerous to catalogue. Wedge accepted none of them, preferring instead to shake hands with as many of his admirers as could reach him, and his pilots followed suit.

Their procession slowed to a halt at a major cross avenue, however, blocked by a similar parade—people thronging around an identical wheeled transport returning from Cartann Bladedrome. Aboard, Turr Phennir and his Imperial pilots accepted the gifts and accolades from the crowd. Phennir gave Wedge a mocking smile as his transport rolled serenely past the stalled New Republic entourage.

"What's his record for today?" Wedge asked.

"He accepted two challenges, and he and his pilots shot down two half flightknives," Cheriss said. "Experienced pilots, good ones. He gained considerable honor today."

"Yes, he's just rolling in the honor coupons," Wedge said. He didn't bother to refrain from glaring at Phennir's retreating parade. "They stick to the blood all over him." He caught sight of Cheriss's confused expression and waved the thought away.

Tycho, at Wedge's ear, murmured, "Phennir has known for a day or two what we just found out today. That Adumari pilots just aren't very good."

"A few of them have decent technical skills," Wedge said. "But not many. The attrition they experience has to be keeping their level of proficiency pretty low. Add that to their lousy tactical choices . . ."

"Small wonder they treat us like supermen," Tycho

said. "Us, and that happy band of Imperial murderers over there."

In the days to come, Wedge's routine requests for an audience with the *perator* to discuss diplomatic relations were met with routine refusals and apologies. But Tomer reported that rumor had it that the *perator* and his ministers were drawing up a proposal for the formation of a world government—a move, Tomer gleefully announced, that benefited the New Republic more than the Empire and therefore had to be interpreted as a slight gain for their side. Wedge, unconvinced, didn't bother to point out that the Empire would find it easier to rule this world through an existing planetary government.

Each day, Wedge and Red Flight would return to the air base and conduct training exercises with Adumari pilots. Usually Red Flight used Blades, but sometimes they flew their own X-wings, to the astonishment of the Adumari, who were impressed with and appalled by the smaller crafts' greater speed, maneuverability, and killpower.

In the first couple of days, the challenger pilots were all from Cartann, but soon afterward flightknives began visiting from distant nations with exotic names like Halbegardia, Yedagon, and Thozzelling. In spite of the contempt with which Cartann pilots treated these newcomers, Wedge made sure that Red Flight's attention was divided equally among all pilots who showed an interest.

Each day, the kill numbers of General Turr Phennir and his 181st Fighter Group pilots climbed. According to Cheriss, Phennir's popularity also rose above that of Wedge and the New Republic flyers. "The Imperial pilots," she said, "show more affection for Cartann by doing things the Cartann way; how can the people of Cartann not respond with more affection?"

"By remembering the sons and daughters they've lost?" Wedge suggested.

The pilots' nightly activities usually involved accepting dinner invitations made by prominent politicians and pilots of Cartann. Sometimes these affairs were simple dinners, sometimes lavish spectacles of entertainment, sometimes storytelling competitions among the survivors of aerial campaigns.

Wedge almost never saw Turr Phennir and the Imperial pilots at these dinners. Most were small affairs, orchestrated so that the host could showcase the pilots for a choice number of guests, and even at the larger affairs there seemed to be a growing division among Cartann nobles—on one side, those who preferred the New Republic; on the other, those who preferred the Imperials. Increasingly, the more prestigious nobles seemed to extend their invitations to Turr Phennir rather than Wedge Antilles.

Red Flight and Cheriss spent one afternoon visiting a facility Wedge hoped would one day serve the New Republic. Buried hundreds of feet below the city of Cartann, it was a missile manufacturing plant.

The Challabae Admits-No-Equal Aerial Eruptive Manufacturing Concern was a succession of enormous rectangular chambers separated by tunnels. Portions of the ceiling above each chamber were open to an upper tunnel series, and it was from catwalks along these upper tunnels that the pilots observed the details of the manufacturing process.

Chambers early in the sequence took in raw materials, including metals, man-made materials, and raw chemicals, and began processing them into components such as missile bodies, circuit board frames, wiring, explosives, and fuels. Chambers farther along would test missile body integrity, define and test the functions of circuitry, and test explosives and fuels for purity and reliability. Toward the end of the kilometers-long facility, chambers were used for final assembly and quality checking of finished missiles.

But though each chamber would have a different function from the ones nearest it, all chambers shared characteristics in common. There was a grimness to them all that lowered Wedge's spirits.

Each chamber was filled with assembly lines, conveyor belts, and other machinery, all painted in the same lifeless tan-brown. Each chamber was occupied by hundreds, sometimes thousands, of workers, men and women, all of whom wore featureless garments in a darker brown. Walls were an eye-deadening off-white; floors were a dirt-colored brown. In chambers where manufacturing processes released smoke or soot, even the air was brown. Regardless of the air color, it was always sweltering.

Wedge saw workers moving and laboring. He saw none smiling. None looked up to see him or his companions on the catwalk far above.

"Where do they all live?" he asked. "I can't remember seeing masses of people wearing workers' garments like those. Not anywhere."

Berandis, the plant's assistant manager in charge of public concerns, a lean man whose mustache was topped by a series of ridiculous curls held in place by some sort of wax, gave him an easy smile. "Well, they live wherever they want and can afford, of course. Most are in *turumme*-warrens, above."

"I'm not sure I understand."

Cheriss said, "*Turummes* are reptiles, distant relatives of the *farummes* you've seen. They dig elaborate nests in the ground. So large banks of apartment quarters built below the surface are often called *turumme*-warrens. The warrens above a plant like this are always owned by the plant."

"Some workers live aboveground, of course," Berandis said. "There are no laws to keep them in the warrens. But few can afford aboveground housing. Mostly you see it with managers, stewards—"

"Informants," Cheriss said. "The occasional parasite."

Berandis's smile did not waver, but he lowered the tone of his voice. "Manufacturing plants are the same all over Cartann," he said. "But we do offer a difference. Our missiles are the best, which is why we are the recipient of the government contract for all missiles for Cartann's Blade-Thirties and Blade-Thirty-twos. A pilot like you can stake your life on a Challabae missile and know that it will serve your purpose faithfully and reliably. This gives our workers something to be proud of."

Hobbie nodded. "I can tell. You can see the pride on their faces."

Berandis beamed, oblivious to sarcasm.

On the long walk back to their start point, Cheriss dropped back behind Berandis to march with the pilots. Her voice artificially cheery, she said, "There is another advantage to having worker quarters above plant facilities, of course."

"Which is what?" Wedge asked.

"Well, if some enemy were to fill the skies above Cartann City and drop Broadcap bombs on the plant, the bombs would only penetrate as far as the warrens before exploding. The plant would take little or no damage." Her tone was light, but Wedge detected something in it—bitterness or sarcasm, or perhaps both. He couldn't tell.

Tycho said, "You've either worked at a plant like this or lived in the *turumme*-warrens, haven't you?"

"Both," she said. "My mother worked at a food-processing plant until brownlung killed her. I worked there for a season before I was well established enough to make my living with my blastsword."

"How, precisely, *do* you make your living?" Wedge asked. "By taking trophies from the enemies you defeat?"

"No . . . though I did that at first. Now I use only blastswords manufactured by Ghephaenne Deeper-Craters Weaponmakers, and they pay me regularly so that they can mention that fact in their flatscreen boasting."

"Endorsements," Hobbie said. "I could do that instead of flying. I've had offers from bacta makers. Bacta's a sort of medicine," he added for Cheriss's benefit.

She offered a little frown. "You are not a well man?"

"I'm well enough. But the ground and I get along so well we sometimes get together a little too vigorously."

"So let me be sure I understand this," Wedge said. "Under Cartann City, there are lots of underground manufacturing concerns, huge ones, where they make missiles and preserved food and Blades and everything Cartann needs, with worker quarters—where most workers have to live because they can't afford anything else—above them but still underground."

Cheriss nodded.

"And we don't see these workers aboveground because?"

"Because they're too tired at the end of a long day of working to do much but eat and watch the day's flatscreen broadcasts," Cheriss said.

"How much of the population lives belowground, compared to what we've seen aboveground?"

"I don't know." She shrugged. "Forty percent, perhaps. But don't feel that they are trapped, General Antilles. They can always break free of the worker's existence. They can volunteer for the armed forces. They can take up the life of the free blade, as I've done."

"So the only sure way for them to get out is to risk their lives."

She nodded.

Wedge exchanged looks with the other pilots, and his appreciation for the world of Adumar dropped another notch.

. . .

Later the same day, Tomer Darpen visited the pilots' quarters with some bad news. After two days of incarceration, the surviving four men of the six who'd tried to assassinate them had escaped. "Definitely with the aid of someone in the Cartann Ministry of Justice," Tomer said. "Whoever paid them in the first place had enough money or pull to enlist the aid of a whole chain of conspirators."

"They'll be coming after us again," Hobbie said, a mournful note in his voice.

Cheriss shook her head. "They were not just defeated but embarrassed last time. They'll be instructed to come after you again to regain their honor. But instead they'll probably run. And so they'll either vanish from the face of Adumar . . . or be found dead in an alley, a warning to others who might contemplate failure."

Still, Wedge was not entirely displeased with the way things were shaping up. His informal flying school at Giltella Air Base was actually proving to be a satisfying experience. Increasingly, pilots both from Cartann and foreign nations were discussing Wedge's philosophies as much as his tactics and skills, and doing so without contempt. One Cartann pilot, barely out of his teen years, a black-haired youth named Balass ke Rassa, finally summed it up in a way that pleased Wedge: "If I understand, General, you are saying that a pilot's honor is internal. Between him and his conscience. Not external, for his peers to see."

"That's right," Wedge said. "That's it exactly."

"But if you do not externalize it, you cut yourself off from your nation," Balass said. "When you do wrong, your peers cannot bring you back in line by stripping away your honor, allowing you to regain it when you resume proper behavior."

"True," Wedge said. "But by the same token, a group of people you respect, even though they don't deserve it, can't redefine honor for their own benefit, or to achieve some private agenda, and then use it to control your actions."

Troubled, the youth withdrew from the post-duel conversation and sat alone, considering Wedge's words, and Wedge felt that he had at last achieved a dueling victory.

6

The night of the discussion with Balass ke Rassa was one of the few in which the pilots had declined all dinner invitations, giving them a chance to dine in their quarters and get away from the pressure of being on display before the people of Cartann.

As the ascender brought them up to their floor, Janson said, "They're calling me 'the darling one.'"

"Who is?" Wedge asked.

"The court, the crowds. They have tags for us all now, and I'm the darling one. Tycho is 'the doleful one.'"

Tycho frowned. "I'm not sad."

"No, but you look sad. Makes the ladies of Cartann's court want to comfort you. They're so sad about wanting to comfort you that you could comfort them."

Hobbie snorted. "And Tycho the only one of us with a successful relationship with a woman. Missed opportunities, Tycho."

They paused before the door to give its security flatcams—primitive devices by New Republic standards, but still capable of facial recognition—time to analyze their features. Janson continued, "Hobbie is 'the dour one.' Not too much romance in that, Hobbie. And Wedge is 'the diligent one.' That may not sound too romantic, Wedge, but 'diligent' has a couple of colloquial meanings here that add to your luster—"

"I don't want to know," Wedge said. The doors opened. "Say, look who's here."

Hallis sat on the monstrously overinflated chair situated in one corner, her legs up over one of the chair arms. She waved. Her recording unit, Whitecap, said, "Say, look who's here" in inimitable 3PO unit tones.

Wedge led his pilots in. "What's with Whitecap?" he asked.

"What's with Whitecap?" Whitecap asked.

Hallis made a cross face. "Oh, something's gone wrong in his hardware."

"Oh, something's gone . . ."

"I was recording some of General Phennir's challenge matches out at the Cartann Bladedrome. When the pilots were leaving, the crowd got a bit unruly and I was knocked down. Since then, Whitecap repeats back everything anyone says within earshot. I can't get him to stop."

". . . get him to stop."

Janson grinned at her. "Some days make you just want to beat your heads against a wall, don't they?"

Hobbie said, "Maybe not. The young lady might not have her heads on straight, after all."

Tycho said, "Still, I think she ought to get her heads examined."

Wedge looked at them, appalled.

"Pilots," Hallis said. "How did I ever get this assignment? Who did I offend?"

". . . did I offend?"

"Still," she said, "you'd better be nice to me. I know

you don't take me seriously, but you ought to." Her expression was unusually earnest.

". . . you ought to."

Wedge sprawled on a sofalike piece of furniture large enough to accommodate three full-sized people comfortably. "Hallis, it would be easier if you didn't look like something out of a tale to frighten children."

". . . to frighten children."

"All right," she said.

"All right."

She pulled her goggles off and set them aside. Then she reached up to press a control on Whitecap's clamp; with a hissing noise, it relaxed and the recording unit began tilting from her shoulder. She caught it as it pitched forward, then moved across the room to set it within a cabinet. She closed the cabinet door with an irritated thump; from inside, Whitecap did a credible job of imitating the noise. "Better?"

Wedge tried to make his tone neutral, nonjudgmental. "What is it, Hallis?"

She straightened from the cabinet and gave him a serious look. "Someone rappelled down to your balcony today from an upper story. I think he was doing something to your X-wings. Just scrawling something on them, I think."

In moments, they were out on the balcony, looking over their snubfighters. Hallis followed and slid the main door to the balcony shut behind her. People on balconies all around and across the street called out to them, waving.

Wedge waved back distractedly. He saw nothing changed on his X-wing's exterior, and there was certainly nothing new written on it. He addressed his astromech, which was still set up behind the cockpit. "Gate, report on any interference with this snubfighter." He brought out his datapad so the R5 unit could transmit its response to him.

Its screen came up with the words NO INTERFERENCE NOTED.

"There wasn't any that I know of," Hallis said. "I lied about that."

Wedge gave her a curious look. "Maybe you'd better explain that."

"I wanted to get you out on the balcony. There aren't any listening devices out here."

"We know there are listening devices inside," Wedge said. "We don't say anything there we can't afford to have overheard."

"That's good," Hallis said. "I came by here this morning to let you know I'd be recording the Imperial pilots, to ask if you wanted me to look out for anything in particular. But when I got here, you'd already gone. As I was leaving, I saw someone headed toward your door. And your door admitted him."

"Saves wear and tear," Janson said. "When the thieves can just walk in instead of having to break the door down."

"Did you get a good look at him?" Wedge asked.

"Better than that, I got some recordings of him. I followed him in, got in just before the door closed. Hid behind tapestries and furniture while he went from room to room. The one time I got a good look at what he was doing in the rooms, he seemed to be checking up on emplaced items—almost certainly transmitters. Then, when I left, I followed him to where he was going."

Wedge exchanged glances with the other pilots. Suddenly Hallis didn't seem so ridiculous a figure after all. Wedge had underestimated her ability, mistaking eccentricity for a basic lack of competence. He wouldn't do that a second time.

Janson frowned. "I hope you'll excuse a silly question—but how does a lady with two heads follow anyone?"

Hallis gave him an indulgent smile. "I took Whitecap off while I was tailing him, Major. I'm fully aware of the sort of commotion he causes when I wear him. But what I know—and what you *don't* know—is that people, when they look at me, only see the two-headed lady. They don't give me a close look, they don't register my features. Meaning that I can tuck Whitecap under my cloak and take off my goggles, and nobody recognizes me. I doubt even *you* would."

Janson opened his mouth as if to protest and then shut it again, his expression thoughtful.

"Hallis, are you Intelligence-trained?" Wedge asked.

She shook her head. "Sludgenews-trained. Are you familiar with sludgenews?"

Tycho made a face. "A minor evil found in many heavily populated worlds, especially in the Corporate Sector. News on which celebrities are in love this week, complete with holos recorded by someone who sneaked onto their private estates and then escaped again. Revelations on how the shapes of nebulae determine your fate. Stories about women who claim to have borne a son to Emperor Palpatine. Stores that there never was a New Republic/Imperial war, that it was all cooked up to foster wartime productivity and profit the starfighter manufacturers. Stories claiming that Darth Vader is still alive, about to lead a revolt to reinstitute the Empire. That sort of thing."

Hallis nodded. "It's a very competitive field. You learn to hustle, to bribe, to sneak, to plant transmitters, to read past the text stream to the data stream . . . or you fail and get out. I learned it all, and then I got out anyway. It's a brand of newsmaking that doesn't exactly make the galaxy a better place."

"So you followed our intruder out of here," Wedge said.

"Yes. He didn't even leave the building. He went into a room on the third floor. Third Alabaster it's called. I don't know whether it was his room or not; its door admitted him, but then so did yours. I waited around for a while to see who else might go in or come out, but its corridor is just a little too public, so I left."

"That's good work," Wedge said. "I assume that he's probably New Republic Intelligence, keeping up on us . . . but it's not safe to assume anything for too long. We'll have to find out whose quarters those are and start tracing some connections. Thank you, Hallis."

She offered him a nod.

From the corner of his eye, Wedge saw Cheriss appear at the transparent door into the pilots' quarters. She waved but didn't come through the door—sensitive, doubtless, to the fact that she might not yet be welcome. But a second later, Tomer Darpen brushed past her, slid the door open, and emerged onto the balcony, his expression dark. "I need to speak with General Antilles," he said. "Everyone else please leave."

No one budged. Wedge could feel their eyes upon him, but he gave them no signal. Wedge spoke, his tone artificially mild: "People I haven't invited over don't get to tell my guests to leave. Try again."

Tomer said nothing for a few seconds, during which time Wedge supposed he was trying to compose himself, and then said, "This is an official exchange between the diplomatic delegation to Adumar, that's me, and the point diplomat, that's you. It's not going to be entirely friendly. It may include things you don't want your pilots to hear, but obviously you can insist they stay if you must. But I'm going to have to ask this young lady to leave, if only to the next room—"

"My pilots have heard lots of grown-up words," Wedge said. "Even Janson. And this young lady is Hallis."

Tomer looked at her, confused. "Where's your other head?"

She gave him a sorrowful look. "When I was walking around today, I met a young man who had no head. Just a stump that suggested he had a long, sad story to tell. But of course he couldn't, because he had no head.

So I gave Whitecap to him. The man now has the voice and mannerisms of a 3PO unit, but they're better than nothing."

Tomer's mouth worked for a moment or two. Then he turned his glare back on Wedge. "There. Now you've corrupted her, too. That's what I came over to talk to you about. This has to stop."

"What has to stop?"

"All this business with your duels. What is this nonsense with simulated weapons?"

"A simple way to give the Adumari the encounters they obviously want so very much, without getting them killed. Or me, or my pilots."

Tomer rolled exasperated eyes toward the floor of the balcony above. "General Antilles, you're changing things. There are now Adumari pilots, famous pilots, talking about doing more sim-weapon exercises."

"Good."

"You're not here to change things! You're here to gain their respect, according to their culture, and to demonstrate that they should throw in with the New Republic."

"Meaning what? Meaning that I should stop doing duels—"

"No, that would cost you the respect you've earned in their eyes."

"—or start doing live-weapon duels?"

Tomer was silent.

"That's it, isn't it? You think I should go up in the skies day after day and shoot down eager Adumari pilots."

"That's what Turr Phennir and his men are doing."

Wedge felt cold anger creep through his guts. When he spoke again, his voice was very quiet. "So you're saying that I should win playing by the Empire's rules."

Tomer hesitated. "In this case, yes."

"Never."

"If you don't, we lose Adumar to the Empire. And

there go the proton torpedo supplies you were hoping for. And more of your pilots die, and the Empire gains new ground. All because you're too squeamish to do what common sense demands of you."

Wedge took an involuntary step toward Tomer. The diplomat jolted backward. "Listen," Wedge said, "and try to understand. This isn't some civil trial where all positions, all propositions, are equally valid until the judge decides which one is right. If we act like the Empire, we *become* the Empire. And then, even if we defeat the Empire, we've still lost—because the Empire is once again in control. Just with a new name and with new faces printed on the crednotes."

Tomer shook his head. "No. Chief of State Leia Organa Solo is in charge. It doesn't matter what we do here. Her opinions, her ethics, still define what the New Republic is."

"You're deluded."

"And you're a naive fool, and you're going to lose Adumar for us with your naivete."

Wedge offered him a tight, unfriendly smile. "Would you like this diplomatic mission to use a different approach? Turr Phennir's approach?"

"I hate to say it, but yes."

"Then get a different diplomat."

Tomer hesitated again. "Not feasible. You're just going to have to fall in line." He heaved a regretful sigh. "General Antilles, that constitutes an order."

"You don't give me orders, Darpen."

"No, of course not." Tomer shrugged, apology on his face. "These are orders from the regional director of Intelligence, and since Intelligence was actually the first division to institute activity in this system, all New Republic activities currently ongoing, including diplomatic, fall under its authority. The director has issued orders that you cease these simulated training missions."

"Who is the regional director of Intelligence?"

Tomer shook his head. "I can't tell you that. He or she likes to maintain anonymity."

Wedge offered him a frosty smile. "Well, I can tell you who the local director *isn't*."

"Who's that?"

"General Cracken. I received my initial orders from Cracken, and they didn't say anything about being answerable to one of his subordinates. When I get a message from Cracken telling me to do what you've just said, I will, of course, comply. Until then—not a chance."

"But—"

"And now it's time for you to go."

"No, we need to talk this through."

"You can leave through the door or go flying over the rail, Tomer."

Tomer read his eyes, then shook his head angrily and turned away.

Only when the door had slid in place behind Tomer did Wedge relax again. He took a long breath. "Hallis, are you recording? In any way?"

She shook her head. "General, I'm an ethical documentarian. One reason why I'm no longer in sludge."

"Good." Wedge wrestled a moment with the words he was about to say. "Are any of you wondering whether Adumar is *worth* bringing into the New Republic?"

Hobbie, his expression regretful, nodded. Janson followed suit. Tycho didn't respond, and Hallis merely looked between them, her body completely still, only her eyes moving.

Janson said, "All that stuff about them being pilot-happy . . . it's wrong. The only things they seem to want are honor and death. I would not want to fly with an Adumari pilot in my squadron."

"I can't entirely agree," said Tycho. "We've already had luck in bringing some of them around. Our training exercises have been successes. If they hadn't been, Tomer wouldn't have blasted in here, spitting smoke and aiming lasers. And I think Cheriss, in the other room, is another good indicator. She's as devoted to this whole death-and-honor thing as any Adumari I've met, but I don't think it would take too much to turn her around to a more civilized way of thinking. I think a better question is this: What effect will it have on the New Republic if we bring Adumar in the way it is now?"

"There's no telling," Wedge said. "But it's something I need to think about. I think I need a drink."

"Oh, good," Janson said.

"Alone."

Inside, Cheriss had advice to offer—rather too much of it, until it became clear to her that Wedge really meant that he wanted some time alone. Then she settled down and merely asked, "Do you want a brewtap where you will be recognized and mobbed, one where you will be unrecognized, or one where you will be recognized but ignored? And do you want one with entertainments or shadowy corners?"

"Unrecognized," he told her. "Shadows."

"Garham's-on-the-Downstream," she said. "Hold on."

She went to the closet off the main room, the one where enormous quantities of clothing had been delivered their first day in Cartann. Clothes remained there until selected by one of the pilots, at which time they would end up in that pilot's armoire. But this closet was still mostly full, Tomer's people keeping it well stocked from day to day. Cheriss reached in and brought something over to Wedge: a face mask, made to cover its wearer from upper lip to forehead, in a lavender material with the appearance of suede but the weight of foamed plastic.

Wedge looked at it. "Lavender. I have bad memories of lavender clothing. I don't think it's me," he said.

"Precisely my point."

"Ah. A good point, too." He put it on, put up the hood of his cloak, and turned to his pilots. "Well?"

Janson affected surprise. "Who are you? What have you done with Wedge?"

Wedge sighed. "Always good to have a pal in the audience."

Garham's-on-the-Downstream was not quite what Wedge expected. It was no dive. Less than two city blocks from his quarters, it boasted expensive columns of stone, curtained booths, excellent service, and decent drinks—though most of them were variations on two types of drink, an ale ("brew") and a liquor ("hard") derived from Adumar's most common grain, *chartash*.

It was, however, set up for privacy. It had an entrance off a darkened side street, the low-yield lighting cast shadows in every corner, and the booths all offered privacy. Unfortunately, the booths were all full at this hour, so Wedge took a chair at the bar, in the most shadowy corner.

He nursed a brew and watched the people of Cartann. He pondered their fates and his own.

It was a simple question, really. If Adumar were magically to pull a world government from its sleeve, and all Wedge had to do to entice that government to join the New Republic was fight a few pilots who were anxious to duel him to the death, could he refuse?

No, there was a second question. If Adumar joined the New Republic, who would be the better for it?

First things first. On the occasions he bothered to think about it, Wedge considered himself a soldier. He had joined a cause, the Rebel Alliance, that was aligned with his particular set of ethics and beliefs. He obeyed orders and risked his life in order to achieve a set of ends he believed in. He issued orders and risked the lives of others likewise.

But the pilots who wanted to come against him here

were not enemies. They were potential allies . . . ones who wanted to kill him, or die at his hands, in order to profit from the so-called honor to be had from such a fate.

The others in the brewtap were men, mostly, though one in ten or so was a woman. Wedge assumed from the posture and conversation of these women that they were like the men here—pilots or minor nobles out for a night of drinks and anonymous trouble. The fact that none had sidled up to him with a glib offer told him that there were no professional companions here.

The people at the bar exchanged smiles and bitter comments, wove their hands around in the air to illustrate some piloting maneuver, argued at first quietly and then with increasing heat and volume about some common acquaintance or romantic rivalry. It was just the same as almost any bar Wedge had visited. With one difference: One of the arguers extended a fist, the knuckle of his middle finger protruding, and lightly rapped the chin of the other. The second man stiffened and nodded. The two of them tossed coins on the bar top and rapidly departed, their hands already on the hilts of their blastswords.

Wedge shook his head. There it was again, the dueling, the almost maniacal disregard for the value of life. Would it harm the New Republic to have such a vital culture—one so inexplicably devoted to the futile snuffing out of lives—join it?

If he was to be honest with himself, Wedge had to admit that it would probably do the New Republic no harm. Visitors from other worlds to Adumar would probably not get caught up in the dueling mania, while Adumari pilots joining the New Republic military were very likely to have their perspectives broadened by what they experienced out in the galaxy. Wedge could already see this happening with the pilots he flew simulated duels against.

So that answered the second question. Bringing Adumar into the New Republic would do no harm, and would offer the potential for increased proton torpedo production.

Which left the first question. If the way to bring Adumar in involved some of these duels—live-fire, not simulated—could Wedge do it?

Wedge wrestled with that one. He decided that other questions remained unanswered, questions critical to this whole mission: What were the conditions of victory? What exactly needed to be done to convince the *perator* of Cartann to side with the New Republic?

Tomer had hinted that it was a popularity contest. Wedge and Turr Phennir were struggling to achieve as much popularity with the people of Adumar as they could. Whenever the *perator* got around to making his decision, whichever pilot was most popular would give his side an edge—perhaps the decisive edge.

But agreeing to those terms, implicitly or explicitly, made all eight pilots, New Republic and Empire, toys of these death-loving Adumari. They had to keep killing—and, perhaps, dying—until the Adumari tired of the game and got around to their decision.

If Wedge could bring it down to a specific duel or event, for example a one-on-one with Turr Phennir, whose outcome unquestionably determined Adumar's choice, then he'd participate. That would be a military action against a clear enemy, with a clear result. It was this preposterous notion of building public acclaim until someone arbitrarily decided that the contest was done that galled him.

Final question: If General Cracken supported the local Intelligence head's orders, mandating that Wedge begin the slaughter of Adumari pilot-duelists, what would he do?

No matter how he thought his way around the

problem, the answer always came back: *To do this would be to dishonor myself and my uniform. I would refuse those orders.*

With that finally came another thought: *Which means I would have to face court-martial or resign my commission.*

Wedge suddenly found himself short of breath.

It wasn't the thought of losing his rank that hit him; it was the realization that leaving the military would be the same as abandoning what little remained of his life.

His home system, Corellia, was closed to him; joining the Rebel Alliance had put him on the enemies list of the Corellian Diktat, the ruler. His family was gone, parents dead and sister missing for long years. Almost everyone he knew was associated with the New Republic military, and the few long-time friends who weren't, such as Mirax Terrik, had busy lives that intersected his only infrequently. If he resigned, most of these people would disappear completely from his life, leaving him as alone as a pilot who ejected into space with no hope of rescue.

The bleakness of that vision settled as a chill upon him. It was all the more frightening because he knew that even in the face of what it would cost him, he would have to refuse orders insisting that he do things Tomer's way. If he didn't, he might as well be Turr Phennir, flying for the Empire.

Had a decision like that cost him the friendship of Iella Wessiri? Had the moment come and gone without him noticing? He didn't know. But on the eve of perhaps losing what was left of his life, he resolved to see her and find out.

"Yes, another. And this time, a bit stronger."

It wasn't the words that attracted Wedge's attention, but the accent: the clipped, precise tones of Coruscant, or of a dozen worlds that emulated the former Imperial throne world.

Within a nearby booth, its flap held open for the mo-

ment by a bartender, was a man in dark, somber Adumari dress. His body could not be seen within the folds of
his voluminous black cloak, but he was of only average
height, and his face suggested that he was lean. His hair
was gray, his features sharp and suggesting intelligence.

Wedge knew that face. When the bartender hurried
off to fetch the man's drink and let the flap fall back into
place, Wedge rose and set a few coins on the bar top. He
parted the flap covering the booth and slid into the seat
opposite the man.

The gray-headed man offered him a cool smile. "I
have a blaster trained on you," he said. "Perhaps you'd
better leave."

"You'd do the Empire a big favor by pulling the trigger," Wedge said. "Admiral Rogriss."

The man frowned. The gesture was a bit exaggerated, as though he were more drunk than he looked. "I
know that voice, don't I? I certainly know the accent. Is it
you, Antilles?"

Wedge raised his mask.

Rogriss brought his pistol up and then set it on the
tabletop. "I'd never shoot you," he said, "not even for
the bounty on your head. I want to see how you get out of
this mess you're in. Or, more likely, how you fail."

At close range, Wedge could offer the man a closer
inspection.

They'd never met in person, but Wedge had seen his
face on recorded transmissions. Five years ago, Admiral
Teren Rogriss had surreptitiously aided the Han Solo
task force pursuing the Warlord Zsinj. As Han Solo's opposite number, chief of the Imperial task force hunting
Zsinj, Rogriss had risked charges of treason by cooperat-
ing with the New Republic, commanding an *Interdictor*-
class cruiser in collaboration with Solo's task force.
Later, he'd led the Imperial effort to to win back territo-
ries left disorganized by Zsinj's death.

Today, Rogriss seemed little changed, though a bit of

the fire and animation Wedge remembered from the recordings seemed to be gone. Perhaps it was the effect of alcohol. "What's a much-decorated fleet commander doing on a backwater mission like this?" Wedge asked.

Rogriss offered him a half smile. "Fleet commander no more, General. Battling with Warlord Teradoc and your Admiral Ackbar for Zsinj's leavings, I fared rather poorly. I'm sure you heard."

"I did. But that happens a lot to Ackbar's opponents."

Rogriss shrugged. "I cost your New Republic a lot in that struggle. I've nothing to be ashamed of. And I remain an admiral, but with just one ship under my command, the *Agonizer*."

"An Imperial Star Destroyer," Wedge said. So Rogriss's ship had to be the counterpart of the *Allegiance*, orbiting Adumar opposite the New Republic ship. "That's still prestigious."

"Says the man who normally conducts business from the bridge of a Super Star Destroyer."

"Admiral, have you ever wondered why the Emperor gave such nasty names to his Star Destroyers? *Executor, Agonizer, Iron Fist, Venom*?"

"I've heard every schoolboy theory ever proposed on that matter."

"This one comes from Luke Skywalker—"

"Having exhausted the schoolboys, we now turn to the farmboys? How charming."

"—who has a certain perspective on the matter the rest of us don't. He thinks it all has to do with corruption, with the seduction of the not-too-unwilling."

Rogriss gestured for him to keep speaking, but his expression suggested that he'd heard it all before. The bartender brought Rogriss his drink, and Wedge waited until the man departed before continuing.

"Put a man or woman in a situation where the actions he's obliged to take, such as serving Emperor Palpatine, are a certain path to personal corruption. Fill his ears with words saying that his actions are honorable ones. But surround him with constant reminders of the wrongness of what he's doing. Our victim will cling to the words but will, at some level, always be aware of the wrongness—he can't escape it. The symbols, such as the names of ships he commands, won't let him forget. He's always aware of his descent, of his slow transference to the dark side. Skywalker thinks the Emperor found this knowing acceptance of corruption, this half-accepting, half-struggling process, particularly delicious."

Rogriss pointed his finger at Wedge as though it were a loaded blaster. "You Rebels remain so very self-righteous," he said. "Always speaking of honor, as though you invented the concept. I've spent my whole life in honorable conflict. I've conquered worlds to bring civilization to them—literacy and medicine and sanitation and discipline. I've fought the forces of chaos to keep galactic civilization from flying apart. I've had only a few weeks of each year to spend with my own children. I've made all these sacrifices . . . only to be lectured about honor by someone a generation younger than I am. That's reward for you."

"You're not drinking here, alone, anonymous, because you like the company. Or because you like the local brew, I'll bet. You're here wrestling with a question of honor, aren't you?" Wedge was speculating madly, but the fact that honor seemed to be such a sore point with Rogriss made his wild shot more likely to strike home.

"What about you?"

"I was," Wedge admitted. "I solved it. And you?"

Rogriss drew himself up stiffly. The action, made a little unsteady by the amount of alcohol he'd had to drink, was perhaps not as dignified as he'd hoped. "Where duty is clear, there is no question about honor."

Wedge laughed. "I wish that were so. Well, I'll leave you to keep wrestling. Best of luck, Admiral." he rose and departed.

Out on the street, he went to considerable effort to make sure that no one followed him—that no aide of Rogriss's meant to do him harm. But he saw no shadows pacing his and could finally relax on his way to his quarters.

7

An hour later, Wedge and Janson were in their flight suits, sitting in a small conference office on the *Allegiance*, with steaming cups of caf on the table beside them, datapads open, and scrolling data before them. "So my question is," Janson said, "why me? Why didn't you bring Tycho up with you? He's your wingman. And he's better with records."

"I need someone to be in charge on the ground when I'm up here. For example, if there's a diplomatic emergency."

"I can be in charge on the ground."

"Oh, that'd be good. You and Hobbie running through the streets of Cartann, leaving destruction in your wake, taking charge when a delicate political disaster strikes. Here's an example. A noble of Cartann comes to you and says, 'I know we have no diplomatic relations yet, but I'm here to request asylum in the New Republic.' What do you say?"

"Is she good-looking?"

"Thanks for making my point." Wedge gestured at Janson's datapad. "What have you got on Rogriss?"

Janson sighed and returned his attention to the screen. "Wife dead. Two children surviving. Daughter Asori, twenty-eight, status unknown, which could mean anything. Son Terek, twenty-four, in the Imperial Navy." He shrugged. "Nothing helpful. You?"

"Maybe." Wedge shook his head over Admiral Rogriss's career record—what of it was known to the New Republic, anyway. "His postings—after he was of sufficient rank to have an influence on them—seem to be awfully unambiguous."

"Meaning?"

"Meaning most of them have been duties where he fights the New Republic. What's interesting is where his name *doesn't* show up. There's no known association with any operations like the Death Star, or governorship of nonhuman-populated worlds, or projects we later found out are associated with Imperial Intelligence, anything like that."

"You're talking about Rogriss?" That was Captain Salaban, entering the conference room with a tray of pastries. He set it down in the center of the table and took the third chair, then put his booted feet up on the tabletop.

"That's right," Wedge said. "What's the opinion of him in Fleet?"

"Wily old so-and-so," Salaban said. "Loves strategy and tactics for their own sake. An intellectual. Doesn't much like to stick around for a slugging match."

"We noticed that in the Zsinj hunt," Wedge said. "We're trying to figure out what his commanders might have recently called on him to do that it would send him to some shadowy bar to get seriously drunk. To get belligerent on the subject of honor."

Salaban, chewing on a pastry, shrugged. "Coo bee anyfing," he said, then swallowed. " 'Scuse me. Pound the surface of Adumar flat if they don't side with the Empire? If the *Allegiance* weren't here to keep him in check, he could do that. Eventually and with tremendous losses."

Janson shook his head. "That'd be a fair fight. He'd enjoy preparing for that, coming up with tactics to swing the battle his way. That wouldn't offend his sense of honor."

Salaban nodded. "Well, he *is* coming up with some sort of tactics, just as I am. There's going to be a fight here. *Allegiance* against *Agonizer*."

Wedge gave him a curious look. "How do you figure?"

"Well, it's like this. The Empire can't afford for Adumar to fall into New Republic hands. They know as well as we do what it means to us to have that explosives production. So if we, I mean you, win over the Adumari and they decide to sign on with us, it's a certainty that the Imps will break their word. They'll call in additional ships and attack both the Adumari and the *Allegiance*, and we are in for one serious furball."

Wedge and Janson exchanged a glance. Wedge said, "Wait, scan backward a little bit. What 'word' will the Imps break?"

"That was—oh, that's right, you were already on the ground for that little ceremony, weren't you?"

"I suppose so."

Salaban put on an expression of annoyance. "Shortly after our arrival in-system—after you notified us that the Imps were here and we confirmed *Agonizer*'s presence— a representative of the Cartann government visited. He said that in order to ensure the honorable continuance of these negotiations, the government would have to offer its words of honor that if Adumar decided for the Empire, we'd leave system within the hour and not return except under 'formal banners of truce or war.' "

"And did they get these assurances?"

Salaban nodded and speculatively eyed another pastry. "Took a day or so, but they got a formal transmission from the Chief of State's office. Not from Organa

Solo herself; scuttlebutt has it she's on a diplomatic mission too, to the Meridian sector. Anyway, the Adumari were supposed to notify us if they failed to get the equivalent word from the Empire, and they haven't notified us, so I assume it's two-way. I just expect the Empire not to honor their agreement."

"That's it," Wedge said. "Probably. Like you, Rogriss is at the center of that word of honor. And he expects the Empire not to stand by it. But his personal impulse is to do what he's sworn to do, or at least what he's had to maintain to Adumar that the Empire has sworn to do."

"Well, it begs a question." Salaban stared at a second pastry, sighed to indicate his surrender, and picked it up. "Which is this: So what? We have one more promise about to be broken. If my opposite number is honorable enough to feel some shreds of guilt as he breaks it, so what?" He bit into the pastry as fiercely as if taking a chunk out of his Imperial counterpart.

"It's a fluctuation gap in their shields," Wedge said. "A weakness the Imps may not be aware of in their plan to take Adumar. It's not even relevant if the Adumari side with the Empire in the first place. But if they don't, it's something I might be able to use. I also ought to forward these little notions to General Cracken, and some questions I have about how much the Chief of State knows about policy on this operation. Set me up for a holo-comm transmission, would you?"

Salaban shook his head. "Caw bappoug. Awm assageg—"

"Chew your food, Captain."

Janson grinned. "These kids."

Salaban swallow his mouthful. "We're in a comm blackout. All messages have to be cleared through the local Intelligence head before being sent on. Record what you want and I'll put it through his office for review."

Wedge kept his smile on his face, though his mood had just gone dark again. "Never mind. Some other time." He rose. "Come on, Wes, back to Cartann. Thanks, Captain."

"Anytime."

Janson snagged a handful of pastries. "Can't let Salaban have all these. They'll kill him."

In the corridor, Wedge said, "When you found out Iella's Cartann identity, did you get her address?"

Janson nodded. "Her name, address, everything."

"I need to see her. Tonight. As soon as we get back to our quarters and change into native dress."

Janson winced. "Am I going to get any sleep tonight?"

"Sleep when you usually do. During pilot briefings. During missions."

"Oh, that's right."

The quarters of Iella Wessiri—or Fiana Novarr—were some distance from Wedge's quarters, in a part of Cartann where buildings seldom rose over six stories, where balconies sometimes sagged in the middle, where the glow bulbs illuminating the streets and flatscreens mounted on building exteriors were often burned out or flickering their way to uselessness. Still, the clothing on pedestrians—showy and colorful, if often a trifle worn—indicated that the residents of this area were far better off, financially, than the drones and drudges Wedge had seen in the missile manufacturing facility.

Iella's building was a shadowy five-story rectangle situated between two taller constructions, with a single entrance leading to the ground-floor foyer. There was no security station, no building guards, not even an ascender. They took four flights of steps up to Iella's floor, Janson switching off power to the flatscreen panels on his cloak in order that he not glow at an inopportune moment.

There was no answer to their knock at her door. Wedge waited half a minute, knocked again, waited a while more, and shrugged. "We wait," he said. He surveyed the hallway they were in. Iella's door was near to the stairwell; on the far side of the railings that guarded the stairwell was a corridor leading into blackness. "There," Wedge said.

They were in luck. The corridor led to no more rooms, but to a curtained-off window overlooking the street. They could wait just around the corner, keeping an eye on Iella's door, exposing themselves to very little danger of being seen while they watched.

"I know a game to help us while away the time," Janson said.

"Sure."

"First, let's go back out and meet a couple of women."

"Wes."

"Well, it was a thought."

Minutes later, a silhouette, a cloaked figure, approached Iella's doorway . . . and then bypassed it, moving on to the next door. It knocked quietly, waited, determined that the door was locked, and then looked around. Finally, it came creeping in the direction of Wedge and Janson.

When it was a few meters away, the figure apparently realized that two men already waited in that shadowy nook; it stopped and put its hand on its belt. Even in the dimness Wedge could see the handle of an Adumari pistol. Wedge drew, but heard the rasp of metal on leather from beside him and was not surprised to see Janson's blaster leveled first.

The newcomer, his pistol in hand but not aimed, leaned forward. Wedge saw glints of his eyes beneath the hood of his cloak. "You are not here for me, Irasal ke Voltin?"

Wedge shook his head, slowly, not taking his attention from the man's pistol.

With his blaster, the newcomer pointed toward the doorway whose knob he had tried. "You wait for him?"

Wedge again shook his head. Wedge pointed to Iella's door, the only other doorway visible from their position. He dared not speak; his accent would give him away as a non-Adumari.

"Ah. She of the glorious hair. Are you here from rage—" he touched his fingers, still wrapped around the pistol butt, to his heart—"or from love?" He touched them to his lips.

Wedge touched his own fist to his lips.

"Ah. Then we do not conflict. Frothing disease to your foes, then." He turned his back on the two pilots and stalked away. Wedge and Janson watched him ascend to the floor above, and occasional creakings from that floor suggested that the man had taken up position at the stairs' edge, where he could look down upon the doorway of his target.

"You know," Janson said, "how I really sort of liked this place when we got here?"

Wedge nodded.

"Well, it's worn off."

Wedge grinned. "I thought you liked high romance and skulking and impossibly shallow love affairs and everything they have here in such abundance."

"I do. I just don't like all the competition. Really, Wedge, when you can't even do a stakeout without bumping into six or eight other guys in the same corridor, on the same mission—"

"Hold it."

Another figure climbed the dimly lit stairwell, emerging onto their floor, heading unerringly toward Iella's door. It was another silhouette, but Wedge estimated that it could correspond to someone of Iella's build wrapped in a bulky hooded cloak. Again he cursed the Adumari fashion sense.

Signaling for Janson to remain where he was, Wedge moved quietly forward along the railing. The person had paused at Iella's door, and Wedge could now hear a series of low musical notes emanate from the door or nearby—possibly a sonic cue for a lock, he concluded.

He was only a couple of meters away when the person at the door shoved it open and triggered a switch within, blinding Wedge with unaccustomed light. He blinked against the glare, raising one hand to shield his eyes from it—and discovered that the person at the door was now facing him, blaster pistol in hand, held in a very professional-looking grip.

"State your business," Iella said. "Or keep quiet and I'll just shoot you."

Wedge pulled the preposterous lavender mask away from his face.

He still couldn't see Iella's face, but her voice certainly didn't soften. "Oh. You. Once and for all, I'm not going to tell you any more offworld stories. Go home." She put away her blaster and beckoned him forward. Once he was close enough, she whispered, "Don't say a word." Then she grabbed him by his tunic's ornate collar and dragged him into her quarters.

Inside, he had an impression of a small outer room lined with shelves loaded with electronic equipment; beyond was a larger, darkened chamber, the air within it warm and musty.

After closing the door and resetting her lock, Iella reached up to the top of one of the shelves, reaching over a decorative rim well above eye level, and drew down a device that looked like a datapad but with a series of sensor inputs at one end. She waved this slowly along all four sides of the door, and various digital notations appeared on the screen. Then she pointed it into the darkened portion of her quarters and hit a button; the screen filled with data. She nodded, cleared the screen, and set the device back up where she found it.

"All clear," she said. "No new listening devices. Wedge, you can't be here. You'll compromise my identity." Her tone was pleading, not angry.

"I need your help," Wedge said. "Help I can't get from channels. Help I can get only from you."

She led him into the next chamber and triggered the light switch. This was some sort of receiving room. The floor, ceiling, and walls were all brown wood, perhaps comforting and warm at some time in the past, now slightly warped and occasionally stained. A woven circle lay on the floor as a rug; the room's other furniture consisted of a flatscreen on the wall, a sofalike object that seemed to have been fashioned like the wing of an old model of Blade aircraft, and what Wedge recognized as an inexpensive computer terminal desk of Corellian make.

Iella slid out of her cloak. Today, she was not dressed in garments suited to social affairs; she wore trousers and boots in brown and the standard Adumari flare-sleeved tunic in a subdued rust-red. She sat at one end of the sofa. "All right, Wedge."

He remained standing. "You told me earlier that when you got here, you weren't supposed to send messages offworld—your employers wouldn't let you—but that you did anyway. I inferred from your words that you were able to smuggle in or get access to a holocomm unit for your reports to your superiors."

She nodded.

"I need access to it."

"I can't give it to you. Orders."

"Yes, I know. You're under direct orders from your superior not to permit any communications with the New Republic without his review. I'm asking you to break those orders."

A touch of distress worked through the armor she wore instead of expression. She quickly got herself back under control. "Maybe you'd better explain that."

"All right. First, I know that your boss, the regional head of New Republic Intelligence, is Tomer Darpen."

This time her expression didn't change. "I can't confirm or deny that."

"I don't want you to. I'm not trying to wring some sort of admission out of you, Iella. This is just something I figured out . . . eventually. Darpen kept speaking on behalf of the local Intelligence head, as if he were privy to his thoughts. He kept issuing me orders and expecting me to follow them, meaning that he's either very stupid or very used to having his orders obeyed, both out of keeping with the sort of role he was playing. So I conclude that Darpen is not just a diplomat, but also a major player with Intelligence.

"Anyway, he came to me today and ordered me to stop doing my sim-weapons training with Adumari pilots. Some of them are picking up the habit, which means we aren't playing this diplomatic game by their rules, and he thinks that's a very bad thing."

Iella managed a soft smile. "He ordered you."

"I'm usually pretty good about taking orders—"

"If occasionally reinterpreting them rather thoroughly—"

"But only when there's a clear chain of command. Tomer Darpen isn't in it. My fear is that he's going to get in touch with General Cracken and get the confirmation of his orders that he needs . . . but in such a way that Cracken is still not aware of what it means. The live-weapons dueling, me and my pilots having to kill a lot of eager flyers who just want to achieve a little personal honor . . ."

Iella nodded. "So you want to give Cracken the whole story, so he can issue orders, or refuse them, based on the complete picture."

"Yes."

She sighed. "Wedge, I can't help you. My chain of command is *very* clear, and so are my orders. What you're doing now, provoking the regional Intelligence head, is a sort of contrariness that Admiral Ackbar or the Chief of State will excuse you for. What you're asking me to do is deliberate disobedience of direct orders. I can't."

"Oh." Suddenly deflated, Wedge sat on the opposite end of the couch. "Well, then. I'll find a new plan. Perhaps I'll send Janson and Hobbie back in their X-wings to deliver my message. It will just take longer. Maybe too long."

"I'm sorry," she said.

"Me, too."

"Is there anything else I can help you with?"

"Yes." Stirring from his momentary depression, Wedge faced her. "Admiral Rogriss is in command of the *Agonizer*. I need a way to get in touch with him without alerting his subordinates . . . or our people."

Her eyebrows went up. "Better not let my superior hear about that. He'll think you're conspiring with the enemy."

"I hope very much to conspire with the enemy. Can you do it?"

"I think so. It may take some time. Anything else?"

"No." He sighed. "Wait. Yes, there is."

She waited.

"Iella, if General Cracken orders me to play Turr Phennir's game with the aerial duels, I'll refuse. I'll resign my commission." He saw her jaw drop. "When I do that, that's my whole life, packaged up and fired out a missile port. I have to start over from the ground up: new career, new friends, new world, maybe even a new name.

"Since I'm on the verge of losing everything I have left, I need, I *really* need, to find out how I lost something earlier. So I don't do it again with anyone else. I need to know how I lost your regard."

She stared at him as if stupefied for long moments. Finally she shook her head and said, "Wedge, you *never* lost my regard. You never lost my respect."

"Then how did I lose your friendship? Where did it go, how did I chase it off?" He felt a hard knot forming in his throat, and it made his voice raspy.

"It's not like that. It's nothing you did. It's something I did." Her expression lost all self-assurance. "Wedge, let's not do this now."

"When? Iella, we can't do it when I'm a civilian, being shipped back to Coruscant in disgrace for a mission I never wanted in the first place. Now's the time." He slid toward her, the knot in his throat threatening to cut off his speech altogether. "Please, because we were friends. Tell me how we stopped. Was it my relationship with Qwi?"

A flicker of pain crossed her face. "No. Yes. It's related to that."

"Well, that certainly clarifies matters."

She lashed out, striking his shoulder with her open palm. The blow nearly shoved him off the sofa. "Don't make light of it. This is very hard for me."

"I'm sorry." Wedge rubbed the stinging from his shoulder and resumed his seat. "I'll just listen."

Her words were a long time in coming. He saw her struggle with them, as if trying to find the perfect angle of approach on a target that had none. Then tears came, just two of them. She brushed them away and finally spoke. "When Diric died . . . the *way* he died, still struggling with his brainwashing, still a tool of the Empire, and I had not just his loss to deal with but all that shame, you and Corran were there for me. Making things better. Whenever I flailed out, looking for support, my hand would fall into one of yours. That made all the difference. And when I gradually got better, when I eventually figured out that the galaxy was just going to keep spinning and I could keep functioning within it, you didn't wander away. It wasn't a 'You're all better now, so it's back to work for me.' I can't tell you what that meant to me.

"And gradually, I began to wonder . . ." She was silent for long moments. "To wonder if maybe there was a chance for you and me."

He gave her a nod. "I had those same thoughts."

"But I told myself, 'It's too soon to be thinking about that.' I told myself that for a long time. I just accepted the time we had together, like after the whole *Lusankya* affair. I coasted."

"I didn't want to put pressure on you," Wedge said. "Any pressure. That would have been . . ."

"Morbid?"

"Opportunistic? Crude? Janson-like?"

She managed a little smile. "Looking back on it, after a while, I don't suppose you *could* have thought I was still interested in you. We became just pals, like Corran and I are, while I waited for, I don't know, that final signal from somewhere deep in my mind that I was all ready to start my life up again. That signal never came, or I missed it, and we were apart so much of the time . . . and one day there she was, Qwi Xux, the neediest little thing in the galaxy, hanging off your arm . . ."

Wedge cleared his throat. "Um, I'm not sure—"

"And I realized I'd waited too long. It was *my mistake*. I hadn't told you the truth about the way I felt, I'd waited for you to make a first move you were too ethical to make, and all these expectations I'd made in my mind blew apart like the Death Star. One second, solid and permanent, the next second, countless millions of little white specks of nothingness."

"So, ultimately, I lost your friendship by getting involved with another woman."

Iella shook her head. "Not exactly, Wedge. It wasn't what you did. It was because, after you did it, I couldn't stand seeing you. It hurt every time I saw you, knowing that I'd thrown away my own opportunity. And you can't be friends with someone who cuts out your heart, even unintentionally, every time you run into him."

"You know we're not together anymore. Qwi and I."

She nodded, but her expression did not lighten. "Wes Janson told me the first night he ran into me, at the *perator*'s court."

"And?"

"And what? And she's gone, and so maybe we can start all over again?"

Surprised by the heat and anger in her voice, Wedge drew back. "Something like that."

"Wedge Antilles, I don't care how much it hurts. I will not be number two to some feather-brained—"

A small explosion next door vibrated the wall and burned a hole, the diameter of a finger, in it. Wedge grabbed Iella's sleeve and pulled her down to the rug with him. He drew his own blaster.

Iella grabbed the barrel, kept him from swinging it into line. "Don't," she said. "It's—"

Another shot penetrated the wall at about eye level. From the other quarters Wedge could hear shouting, the sound of pottery shattering.

"—just my neighbor, Garatty ke Kith—"

There was the familiar crack of a blastsword going off, and a yelp of pain.

"—and his feud with—"

"Irasal ke Voltin," Wedge said.

"You *know* him?"

"You meet a lot of people when you're an ambassador."

There was one final crash, something like a hundred kilos of meat being violently slammed the floor, and quiet fell again.

"That will probably end the feud," Iella said.

Wedge rose and offered her a hand up. He holstered his sidearm. He was surprised at how much energy the motion took. Suddenly his endurance seemed to have abandoned him. "Back to the subject. So what you're saying is that I hurt you so badly that we can never be anything to one another again."

Iella looked as though she were reviewing something—the last several things she'd said, perhaps the last several years of her life. Finally she said, "I suppose that is what I'm saying." She looked on the verge of tears again. "I'm sorry, Wedge. I am. But I think you'd better leave."

"It's not leaving that's hard anymore," he said, scarcely recognizing his own voice. "It's finding somewhere to go." He turned toward the door.

Adrenaline jolted through him. The shock that hit him was that of a man realizing that he was about to step into a trap or a firefight, something that could end his life in a second.

It couldn't be a precognitive warning. Outside of a cockpit, his pattern recognition skills didn't afford him warnings like that . . . and besides, had there been danger beyond the door, Janson would have communicated with him.

No, the danger was more personal. It was indeed a matter of *Step through that door and your life is over,* but in a very different way. "Just how stupid do you think I am?" he asked.

"What?"

He turned to face her again. His energy was back. He felt it burning within him. And he now knew the nature of the one last barrier standing between the two of them: Her injured pride, shielding her from further harm . . . but also shielding her from *him.* "How big an idiot would I have to be to walk out that door?"

"I don't understand, Wedge. I just wish you'd go."

"Yes, it would be easier that way. Less risk of humiliation." He moved to stand before her again. "Now, listen. For years, even when we didn't see one another for ages, I knew that you were a part of my life. Until a few nights ago, when you said we weren't friends anymore. Since then, I've been in mourning. Not just missing a friend, but grieving for a lost part of my life.

"It took me a while to figure that out, and to understand just how much I need you to be in my life. As my friend, and *more* than my friend, for good. Now you tell me it can't happen. Because of mistakes. I made some, you made some, and now our chances are all behind us?" He shook his head vehemently. "No, Iella. That would be another mistake, and the older we get, the less time we have to bounce back from them. I'm tired of making mistakes."

He put one hand behind her neck, the other around her waist, and drew her to him. She looked at him, surprise in her eyes.

"You're a grown woman and in training," he said. "If you want me out of your room, it'll take you just one knee and a little leverage to put me out. But you can't just tell me to go, not this time. I love you. I'm not going to meekly walk away." He pulled her face to his and kissed her.

He had a glimpse of her widening eyes. Then he was lost in the sweetness of her lips.

He could have tensed against the impact he was sure would follow, but did not. If this was to be the last kiss he was ever to have from her, he wanted to enjoy every millisecond of it.

And the milliseconds stretched into full seconds, and her arms snaked around his neck and held him tight. Finally, it was a need for oxygen that forced him to break their kiss. He held her tight, looking into eyes that were wide but not alarmed, lips that were curved ever so slightly into an enigmatic smile. "If I'm lying in a ball in the corridor," he said, "I'm doing a tremendous job of hallucinating that I'm not."

"Now's not the time to joke," she said.

"Very well."

She put her fingers up in his hair, turned his head this way and that, and looked at him as though seeing him for the first time. "So this is the cockpit Wedge," she said. "The one the enemy has boxed in, and suddenly he snaps and goes off in an unanticipated direction, changing all the rules."

"That's me."

"It's very becoming. I wish you'd shown him to me before. Why aren't you like this on the ground?"

He shrugged. "I've never been all that comfortable on the ground. But I'm learning."

"I'd say you were." She kissed him.

When they broke for air a second time, Wedge noted, without surprise, that they were seated on her sofa again. He hadn't remembered getting there, but supposed that the sofa legs were not as close to buckling as his were.

"What you said before," Iella said, a whisper against his mouth, "about being in your life for good, sounded a lot like a proposal."

"Let me make it formal." Wedge pulled back, to stand, to adopt a traditional pose, but Iella didn't release him.

"Later," she said. "After Adumar. Let's just say for now that I'm willing to stop making mistakes if you are."

"It's a deal." He supposed she wanted to hear the words in surroundings less alien, in times less stressful.

"But you need to understand something. No matter what a great leader you may be, Intelligence doesn't take orders from Starfighter Command."

"Or the other way around."

"Right. Or the other way around."

"I can live with that."

Her expression became worried. "Can you live with this? Wedge, I'm an Intelligence officer. If my superior tells me to, I may end up on the opposite side from you."

"Just until this Adumar mess is over," he reminded her.

She nodded. "But will you be able to forgive me? If I

have to throw a net over you and ship you offworld because of your damned fool cockpit-jockey antics?"

"I'd forgive you. Though I won't have to." He gave her a confident grin. "You wouldn't be able to catch me."

Her return smile was that of a well-fed predator. "I have the feeling I can catch you anytime I want." She kissed him again.

When Wedge finally left Iella's quarters, Janson moved out from his hiding position to join him. Janson was not graceful going down the stairs; one of his knees tended to pop, and his posture was stiff.

"You're getting old, Wes."

"I am *not* old. I'm stiff from waiting for hours in that stupid corner. With just three pastries off the *Allegiance* to sustain me. Hiding out from all the other skulker traffic. Did you get what you wanted from Iella?"

Wedge turned a surprised face toward Janson. "*What?*"

"The holocomm access to General Cracken? Did she say you could?"

"Oh, that. No." He felt his smile return. Wes was merely baiting him, as usual. "Say, what happened next door, anyway?"

They reached the bottom of the stairs and marched, Janson hobbling, through the foyer toward the street. "The guy we met hit the guy who lived there just as he was going in. They fought for few seconds, and then there was a lot of quiet, and then the guy we talked to came staggering out of there with the other guy across his shoulders. Dead, I think. And me without anyone to bet with."

They reached the street. Wedge was struck sideways by a blast of intense light; he stumbled, threw up his sleeve to block the glare. "Sithspit! What's that?"

"That's the sun, Wedge. It's after dawn."

"Well, it offends me. Turn it off."

"It's a hundred thirty, hundred forty million klicks from here."

"Go up in your X-wing and shoot it down for me."

"You're acting very strangely, chief. Come on, this way." Janson tugged Wedge in the direction of their quarters. "Something else odd happened during the night."

"What?"

"In the darkest, quietest hours—you hardly ever even heard someone swinging on a cable from balcony to balcony, and there were barely two knife fights out there to keep me awake—I thought I heard breathing."

Wedge afforded him an amused glance. "You breathe, don't you? In between fits of bragging, that is."

Janson shook his head, for once completely serious. "When I was just sitting there with my back to the wall, I thought I heard the creak of someone on the stairs. Coming up, I think. I turned to look around the corner and there was no one to be seen . . . though the entire stairwell wasn't lit, of course. Someone could have been standing in the deepest shadows, the way I was in that hallway. I waited and didn't hear anything more, and then I held my breath and listened. I thought I heard someone breathing over there, but eventually there was a roaring in my ears—"

"That old lack of oxygen thing will get you every time. How much brain damage did you suffer?"

"Wedge . . ."

"And, more importantly, was it to any of the parts of your brain that you use, or was it in the majority portion?"

"Wedge . . . I really think someone was spying."

"Well, you should have introduced yourself." Wedge moved over to the street curb and walked along its very edge, balancing like a high-wire walker.

"Wedge, stop acting like a kid. You're embarrassing me."

·   ·   ·

Wedge had been asleep in his quarters for five minutes when he became aware of a noise from the main room: shouting, crashing of furniture. Sleepily, he pulled on a robe and stumbled over to open his door.

Tomer Darpen was in the main room, walking in circles around the main table. Tycho stood slumped, yawning, in the doorway to his room. Hobbie was sprawled on the main room floor, immediately behind him a tipped-over chair showing how he'd come to end up prone, and was carefully aiming a comlink at Tomer and thumbing its on-off switch as though firing a blaster at the diplomat; his expression was groggy enough to suggest that's exactly what he thought he was doing. Janson emerged in his own doorway, his robe askew, and if glares were lasers Tomer would have been the victim of a dual-linked direct strike.

Tomer was speaking in a voice loud enough to awaken sleepers on the floors immediately above and below: "—very promising indeed, but we need to be there with our best faces on . . ." Making the turn at the end of the table, he caught sight of Wedge. "General! Excellent news."

"Excellent enough to persuade Hobbie to spare your life, I hope," Wedge said.

Tomer glanced at the semiconscious pilot. "Maybe even that good. As you know, the *perator* of Cartann, two days ago, flew in representatives of all of Adumar's nations for purposes of discussing the foundation of a world government."

"I didn't know," Wedge said. "Did you include that in a briefing you sent us?"

"I—uh, oh." Tomer looked abashed, gave Wedge an apologetic look. "My mistake. I thought we'd done so. At any rate, we've received word from the *perator*'s palace that they'll be making an announcement on that subject this morning."

". . . ths mrnng," said the cabinet beside him, its words muffled.

Tomer glanced at it. "What's this?"

"Wt's ths?" said the cabinet.

"Cabinet," Wedge said.

"I know it's a cabinet, but it's talking."

". . .ts tlkng," said the cabinet.

"Oh, that," said Janson. "It's the Cartann Minister of Crawling Into Very Small Spaces."

Tycho nodded. "He bet Wedge that he could fold himself into that cabinet, around the shelves and all."

Hobbie finally found his voice, though it was gravelly from lost sleep. "Never bet against Wedge," he said. "The minister gets to stay there until he admits that it was a stupid bet and Wedge doesn't owe him anything."

Tomer looked among them, his expression making it clear that he knew they were kidding . . . and yet there was still a trace of uncertainty to it. "Anyway," he said, "be ready and at the *perator*'s palace in an hour, please."

". . . hr, pls," said the cabinet.

"We'll be ready," Wedge said.

When Tomer was gone, Wedge opened the cabinet. Whitecap was still there, but less of him; the back of his head was open, and it was evident that hardware once mounted within him was missing.

"Looks like Hallis did some scavenging," Tycho said.

"Looks like Hallis—"

Wedge shut the cabinet against further words. "Where is she, anyway? Haven't seen her recently."

Tycho shrugged. "Haven't seen Cheriss either, not since some time last night. I think we're being abandoned by our retinue."

Janson moved to the closet of not-yet-claimed Adumari garments. "What to wear, what to wear . . ."

"Dress uniforms, please," Wedge said.

The others groaned.

"No, this is an official diplomatic function. From now on, at all such functions, it's dress uniforms. Issue blasters and vibroblades, but no blastswords. We're not Adumari, and it's time to stop legitimizing their bad behavior; we won't emulate them in any way." Wedge clapped his hands together. "Let's go, people."

"Great," Hobbie said. "Who brought the old Wedge out of retirement?"

8

The New Republic officers' dress uniform—designed in committee long ago, implemented months or years before Wedge was even aware of its existence—was not the fashion disaster its wearers made it out to be.

It started with a black sleeveless turtleneck body stocking and boots. Over it went a white jacket, a V-necked garment that fastened at about navel level and below. A broad red band ran along the left hem of the garment, up over the shoulder and at an angle down the back, with a rank designation in gold on the red band above the wearer's left breast. A gray belt over the jacket completed the outfit.

There were variations to the uniform, with Starfighter Command utilizing black body stockings and Fleet Command preferring gray, for instance. Higher-ranking officers often preferred instead, and were allowed, to wear somewhat costlier and better-kept versions of their day uniforms in formal circumstances.

It was, Wedge thought, the body stocking that most wearers objected to. Flight suits and pilot day uniforms were baggy things festooned with pockets. They were comfortable. The wearer could carry his datapad, plus amusements and weapons for a half squad, in those pockets. The dress uniform body stocking had no pockets, and the jacket had only a couple of small ones—barely large enough for datacards. Too, the body stocking revealed any extra weight its wearer might be carrying, a fact not at all appreciated by image-conscious officers . . . and pilots were often the most image-conscious of all.

But the uniforms tended to have an effect on their audience. When Wedge and his pilots strode into the Outer Court of the Royal Residence, where they'd had their reception the first night, the crowd assembled there voiced an appreciative "ooh" that was music to Wedge's ears. He raised a hand to wave jauntily to the crowd, his smile projecting confidence, not betraying the slight queasiness he felt as the court's miasma of perfumes began to assault him.

"I feel fat," Hobbie said.

'You're not fat," Janson said. "Except—never mind."

"What?" Hobbie said.

"Nothing."

"No, tell me. I've been working out. I've been good. You just can't work on everything."

"That's right," Janson said. "It's scarcely noticeable."

"Where?"

A woman—already tall, her height amplified by the way her brown hair was piled atop her head—moved up beside Wedge. "I found out who that other room belongs to," she said.

Wedge looked at her, then peered closer. "Hallis?"

She looked exasperated. "Yes, Hallis."

"Sorry, you still look different with only one head."

"Men always tell me that . . ."

"What other room?"

"The one where the man went after he'd been through your quarters."

"Ah, that one." Wedge nodded. "It belongs to Tomer Darpen."

She looked crestfallen. "You already knew."

"No, I guessed, based on some other evidence I've picked up. It's very valuable to me to have your confirmation. Your work wasn't wasted. Where is your recording unit?"

She pointed to her hair. The elaborate combs holding her hairstyle in place each featured several crystals, plus smaller stones, some of which seemed to be glowing. "The lenses and microphones are up here, and I have cables down to the processor and storage memory, which are on the small of my back. I can even zoom with sight and sound."

"Less menacing that way. I think you'll get further with children with a rig like this."

"I suspect you're right." Clusters of Adumari began to converge on the pilots. "Time for me to leave. I'll talk to you later." She moved off into the crowd, drawing her cloak around her, effortlessly becoming an anonymous Adumari woman.

Wedge steeled himself for another endless round of handshaking and introductions. But the diplomatic ritual was to have an unexpected benefit: The fifth introduction he received was from the Cartann Minister of Cognitive Machinery, and on his arm was Iella Wessiri. Today she was in another sheath dress, this one ranging from red to yellow-gold depending on the angle from which one viewed the material, and how it hung upon her; when she was in motion, it was like watching fire walk. "This young lady," the wispy-bearded minister said, "is, like yourself, an otherworlder, and has expressed an interest in meeting the famous pilot. I plucked her from work today so that she might do so."

"I'm delighted to oblige," Wedge said. When he took her hand, he felt something crinkle in his palm. Iella withdrew her hand and departed with her minister, leaving Wedge with a scrap of flimsi in his hand and a happy memory of her dazzling smile.

As inconspicuously as he could, he glanced at the flimsi. On it was written a note—the name "Rogriss," followed by a series of numbers, recognizable as a specific communications frequency.

Wedge nodded. That would be the frequency the admiral kept one personal comm unit tuned to—something only his executive officer and one or two others aboard *Agonizer* should have known. Wedge couldn't begin to guess how Iella had come by the knowledge; he was just glad she had. He pocketed the scrap.

As the introductions and handshakes continued, he scanned the assembly. He caught sight of Turr Phennir and pilots, standing in a tight little quartet, all in Adumari dress. Phennir was scowling, definitely unhappy, and Wedge grinned at him. It was possibly the most minor of victories—Wedge and pilots had upstaged the Imperial flyers with their distinctive uniforms and entrance—but Wedge was happy to accept any victory he could get.

More invitees crowded into the hall and began to segregate themselves into large groups. Wedge tried to puzzle out what the divisions meant.

The *perator*, once again in gold, was surrounded chiefly by ministers and other courtiers; that group was easy to define. Tomer Darpen hovered at its edges, prevented by his alien status from moving closer to the center and hearing what the *perator* was saying, prevented by his own nature from moving farther away.

Wedge saw in two other groups pilots he'd flown against in simulations training. Most seemed to be on the periphery of one group of thirty or so well-dressed nobles, while a couple were with a different group of similar size. Wedge noted that the garments of these groups tended to be slightly different in cut and style than those he was used to, and realized that the pilots he recognized were all from nations other than Cartann. That was it, then; these were delegations from other nations.

Another group was of Cartann nobles—Wedge saw Iella and her minister among them. Iella noticed his attention, gave him a smile; then she was back in character and responding to something said by one of the men in her vicinity. Most of that crowd constituted men and women dressed in similar stuffy fashion, which suggested that this was a crowd of ministers, but the fact that they were well away from the *perator* said that they were a group the ruler had no particular need to consult—minor functionaries.

Turr Phennir and his pilots were at the center of their own knot of people. One of Phennir's pilots, a tall redheaded man, had his hand out before him as if grasping a TIE fighter's yoke; his hand shook as though he were firing on a target, and his eyes were wide, animated. The group around him made noises of admiration. Phennir was not paying attention; his gaze was on Wedge.

"Before the day's events begin," called a courtier, "a diversion. Ground Champion Cheriss ke Hanadi accepts a title challenge from Lord Pilot Eneboros ke Shalapan."

"That explains where Cheriss is," Tycho said, and craned his head for a better look.

The crowd in the vicinity of the *perator* moved back to make an open circle; Wedge headed that way.

Cheriss was already in the center of the circle, stretching, going through a few practice thrusts and lunges with her blastsword's power off. Her appearance was different from the way it had been in the previous blastsword match; her intensity was there, but she wore no predatory smile. She also looked tired, a little disheveled, not her meticulously neat self.

Into Wedge's ear, Hobbie said, "She's wearing the same clothes from yesterday."

Beside him, Janson nodded. "Not like her. Such a clean girl. Even when she's stabbing people."

"Quiet," Wedge said. "There's something wrong here."

Her opponent, at the edge of the crowd, was very tall and lean, with an elaborately curled brown mustache and a goatee that tended more toward blond. Friends or assistants to either side of him were binding up his flowing sleeves so they would not interfere with his motions. When he was ready, he nodded to the speaker, who in turn caught Cheriss's eye. She thumbed on the power of her blastsword and its tip began leaving blue trails through the air. Her challenger also flourished with his blade, its tip leaving traces of a more purple-blue behind.

The announcer called for salutes to the *perator*, then signaled for the fight to begin.

It didn't take long. The challenger moved in with a thrust that was little more than an initial probe. Cheriss swept it aside and, in the same motion, threw herself forward, a daring counterstrike that left her exposed . . . but caught her enemy in the rib cage. There was a crack and a flash of blue light, and with a cry her challenger went down.

Cheriss looked to the *perator*.

The ruler of Cartann shrugged and put his hand out, palm down—the signal that the defeated man should die.

Cheriss slowly shook her head and turned her back on the defeated man and the *perator*. She moved into the crowd, leaving the fight behind. The audience parted for her, many of its members offering a low noise of surprise.

"Did she just do what I thought she did?" Wedge asked. "Give the *perator* the choice on what happened to her opponent, and then defy him?"

"That's what I got out of it, boss," Hobbie said.

The *perator* was scowling now, but lost the expression when a minister stepped up to him and began talking. In moments, the ruler had apparently forgotten the fight, and friends of the challenger picked the injured man up to carry him from the hall.

Wedge moved through the crowd in pursuit of Cheriss. When he caught up to her, she was speaking to the man who had announced her fight. ". . . standard acceptance for ke Seiufere," she said. The man nodded.

"Cheriss, a moment of your time?"

She glanced at Wedge, and he was taken aback by what he saw in her expression. Before she had always been so animated, so full of energy and cheer; now her eyes seemed dull, lacking passion or interest. "A moment, yes," she said.

"What are you doing?"

She offered an indifferent shrug. "While I have been acting as your guide, I have let other duties pile up. Such as attending to the many challenges I receive. I am merely clearing some of those away now." She suppressed a yawn.

"You haven't changed since yesterday. Have you slept?"

She shook her head. "I don't need sleep to deal with these pretenders." She looked over Wedge's shoulder and her expression became even more mournful. "You'd best go. Someone might grow suspicious . . . for no good reason at all." She turned her back on him and moved into the crowd.

Wedge turned to look. Immediately behind him was Tycho, alert and intent as ever. That didn't make sense; why would Tycho "grow suspicious"?

But over his shoulder, a few meters back, doing a very good job of looking innocuous, stood Iella.

Wedge froze and continued to scan the crowd in that direction. Who else could have provoked such a response from Cheriss? He noted and dismissed a double dozen faces. No, she had to have been referring to Iella.

But she shouldn't have known Iella's face. To know it, she had to have . . . Wedge calculated the times any of the New Republic pilots had been in contact with Iella. No, Cheriss had to have seen it last night. She had to have been the quiet stalker Janson had heard. She must have been outside Wedge's quarters when he and Janson returned from the *Allegiance* last night, must have followed them to their meeting with Iella, must have later gotten a look at Iella's face by some means.

And now she was—

"We are doubly blessed," called the announcer. "Ground Champion Cheriss ke Hanadi, not content with a single victory this day, accepts a title challenge from Lord Pilot Phalle ke Seiufere."

The crowd moved out to open another circle, and there stood Cheriss, this time opposite a squat plug of a man who looked as though he had tremendous upper body strength. Blond, with shoulder-length yellow hair and a mustache that trailed and swayed limply, the new challenger stared at Cheriss with real anger in his sea-green eyes.

Wedge swore to himself. The fight was already under way by the time he was able to maneuver himself to the front of the crowd. Nor was this a quick and easy battle like the last one; Wedge saw Cheriss and her opponent exchange assault after assault, each time deflecting blast-sword blows with deft parries or by the more punishing method of catching the explosive blows on the guards of their swords. Within moments the air was thick with the delicate, colorful traceries of the movements of blast-sword tips and with the acrid smell of blaster impacts, which became almost strong enough to overpower the perfumes.

Cheriss's opponent, strong and fast, seemed to have no problem swatting aside Cheriss's assaults before her blade point endangered him. Some of her thrusts, breath-taking in their speed and intricacy, snaked around the guard on his left-hand dagger, but these he took with equal skill on his blastsword guard, always disengaging immediately and moving forward in aggressive attack, driving Cheriss into retreat. Soon both Cheriss and her opponent were breathing heavily, sweat running from beneath their heavy and elaborate clothing.

Cheriss, slowing, swept her opponent's point aside with the knife she still held in her distinctive reverse grip and leaped forward into a lunge. Her opponent riposted, his blastsword moving her tip out of line while his remained in line—but her lunge took her body lower than it customarily did, and suddenly she was skidding past him on her knees. Cheriss struck backward without looking and her blastsword point took her opponent behind the left knee. He yelped loud enough to drown out the blaster sound of impact, and collapsed onto one leg; before he could begin to recover, before he could force his body to work through the pain and shock of blast impact, Cheriss rose, spun, and tapped him once on each arm. He shrieked once more and slammed to the floor. Smoke rose from his wounds and the air filled with the smell of burned flesh.

The audience applauded. Cheriss, looking far more tired and shaky than Wedge had ever seen her, bowed her head to the crowd, then looked to the *perator*.

This time the ruler did not bother to give her a cue. He turned his back on Cheriss and her downed opponent. The crowd uttered a rippling noise of surprise. Cheriss turned her back on her opponent and moved into the crowd.

Wedge headed for her. But before he could take half a dozen steps through the milling crowd, the announcer called out, "Attend! Before this day is given over entirely to demonstrations of the blastsword art, the *perator* wishes to address us, and all the world, on the matter of today's gathering."

The crowd went into motion again, its elements dividing by what looked like random motion into its earlier groupings. Wedge lost track of Cheriss and sighed. He returned to his pilots. Tomer and Hallis joined them a moment later.

"Nice timing with the New Republic uniforms," Tomer said. "It turns out the *perator*'s going to broadcast worldwide. And the Imp pilots, in local dress, don't even stand out in the crowd. You couldn't have done better."

"Nice to know I've accomplished *something* on a diplomatic level," Wedge said.

Tapestries high up on two of the walls drew aside, revealing the flatscreens Wedge had seen on the night of his arrival on-planet. The screens showed confused, wavering visions of a crowd—this crowd—and then settled in on the face of the *perator*, who was smiling, golden, looking as perfect and imperishable as a statue. The *perator* was looking off to the side, talking to someone; he received some sort of cue, for he turned directly into the flatcam view and his smile broadened, became dazzling.

"On this historic day," the *perator* said, "I address all of Adumar—something I find I will be doing often.

"We have now had time to see that Adumar does not exist in a void. Rather, we share the universe with other worlds, and collectives of worlds. Hidden for centuries by distance and forgetfulness, we find ourselves now within easy reach of new friends who would embrace us as equals—except for one important manner in which we are *not* their equals."

A murmur rose in the ranks of the audience, and many of its members looked at Wedge and his pilots, at Turr Phennir and the Imperial flyers. The expressions of some were curious; those of others graduated toward resentment or suspicion.

"I find," the *perator* said, "that we lag behind these united worlds in only one characteristic—one which is easily corrected. We are a world divided by ancient borders, national identities that serve only to keep us apart and to fragment our ability to make wise decisions affecting all Adumar. I am grateful to our visitors from other worlds and their gentle manner of demonstrating this to us."

"We haven't demonstrated anything," Wedge whispered. "We haven't been able to talk to him."

"True," Tomer said, also in hushed tones. "But he's been absorbing information we've passed on to him. Records, histories, encyclopedias."

"In consultation with the rulers and representatives of other nations," the *perator* said, "we have come to an agreement that the establishment of a unified world government for Adumar will allow us to interact with outside worlds more effectively, permitting the establishment of trade and exchange of knowledge."

"This is good," Tomer whispered. "This is excellent."

The *perator* drew himself more upright, and his expression turned from cheerful benevolence to a leader's awareness of history and import. "So," he said, "on this memorable day, I hereby establish the government of the world of Adumar. With both humility and trepidation I take the reins of command of a united world." There was a stirring, a growing murmur, from one portion of the audience, but he continued, "This new government will be structured as an outgrowth of the government of Cartann, and will be centered in the city of Cartann to allow for an instantaneous and effective implementation of rule." He bowed his head in humility.

Portions of the audience applauded. But a riot of noise erupted from one large cluster of the audience—the one, Wedge saw, that was dominated by foreign dignitaries. "Wait!" cried one dignitary. He surged ahead, out of his cluster of crowd and toward the *perator*'s, waving his hands, his flared sleeves rippling with all the colors of the rainbow. "There has been no vote—"

"Liar!" That was a shout from a deep-voiced representative wearing muted greens; even his hair and beard were green. "You cannot unilaterally—" The rest of his shout was drowned out by the rising volume of applause and shouts from elsewhere in the audience.

Not one of these angry declamations was broadcast over the flatscreens on the walls. Wedge supposed that a directional voice pickup was being used so that the *perator*'s words, and only his words, would be broadcast.

Wedge glanced at Tomer. "Is what I think is happening actually taking place here?"

Tomer, confusion on his face, kept his attention on the *perator* and shrugged.

"You know what they call it when one ruler declares a world government and the rest don't agree?" Wedge asked. He could recognize the anger, the taunting quality, in his own voice. "We get a war of conquest. Lasers and missiles fired on civilian populations."

"Shut up," Tomer said.

The *perator* finally raised his eyes to look out over his worldwide audience again, and a gentle smile returned to his lips. "Today is the last day of the old Adumar," he said. "Prepare yourselves and prepare your children for a new age, a golden age, to follow. Tomorrow we will all be citizens of a new and greater world." He nodded, and the flatscreens on the wall faded to a neutral gray.

Most of the audience burst out in wild applause. The foreign section did not. Some of its members were now at the edges of the *perator*'s retinue and being restrained by liveried guards.

The *perator* addressed them. "You must decide what is best for your own nations, of course," he said. His voice was artificially amplified and carried over the shouts of objection and cheers of approval. "Return to your delegations. Call your homelands. Do what you feel you must. But trust me, simple acquiescence will be best. Tomorrow all nations will be one, and governed from this palace. You want to be governed as friends and allies—not enemies of the state." His pose dignified, he turned and headed toward one of the side exits, a portion of his retinue accompanying him.

Wedge glared at Tomer.

But the diplomat did not look at all abashed. "You can't blame this on me," he said. "He's taken our suggestions about a world government and simply sliced them into his own ambitions for rule."

Wedge's anger didn't waver. "But are you going to press him to abandon this plan if it leads to war?"

Tomer shook his head. "This is a strictly internal affair, General. The *perator* might be using our presence, our organizational needs, as a rationalization for this move. But we're not involved, and we can't become involved."

"Cartann and its satellite nations, if I read things right, are powerful enough to conquer the nations most likely to resist," Wedge said. "So they form a world government, and it's what you've seen. A state where human life is only valuable when it's harvested for personal honor. You think the New Republic will want it? You think it will have anything in common with the New Republic?"

Tomer nodded, his expression confident. "We'll be able to work it out. Speaking of which—"

"More diversion for the attendees," cried the announcer. "Cheriss ke Hanadi accepts a ground title challenge from Lord Pilot Thanaer ke Sekae."

Wedge growled out something inarticulate. To Tomer, he said, "Later." Then he turned and plunged into the crowd, heading toward the open area already forming.

He spotted and reached Cheriss before she entered the circle. If anything, she looked more tired, more lifeless than before. He glowered at the men and women surrounding her until they retreated a step or two. "What do you think you're doing?" he asked her.

She looked at him, a sidelong glance without emotion. "I told you already."

"You lied," he said. "I'll tell *you*. You're committing suicide."

"No. I can beat him." Yet there was no anger in her voice, no emotion of any kind.

"Probably. If you do, will you accept another challenge?"

"Yes."

"And another?"

"Yes."

"Until what?"

"Until there are no challenges left."

"Or you're defeated." He leaned in closer. "You spurned the *perator* earlier today. You offered him the fate of your foe and then you chose the other way. Now, to avenge the insult and please the *perator*, anyone who defeats you will kill you. No one will offer you mercy ever again. Correct?"

She looked past him to where her opponent waited. Wedge caught a glimpse of him, a man of medium height, his dark tunic and beard tricked out with fringes of flowing red ribbons. "My opponent is waiting," she said.

"He can wait." Wedge drew a deep breath and tried to settle his thoughts. "Cheriss, I'm going to say some things to you now. They're going to sound egotistical. You're probably going to deny them. I don't really care. I know I'm right.

"You care about me, and you know I care about someone else, and you've decided to die rather than live with that."

She just looked at him.

"I'm waiting." That was Cheriss's opponent, standing alone in the ring.

Wedge didn't even look at him. "You've waited this long," he called out. "Another few minutes won't make you any homelier."

Members of the audience tittered. Wedge recognized Janson's laugh among the others.

He returned his attention to Cheriss. "I just wish," he said, "that in addition to caring about me, you had some respect for me."

"How can you say that?" At last there was emotion in her voice, unrestrained anger. "If I did not respect—"

"You wouldn't be pointlessly throwing your life away, in direct contradiction to everything I believe?" People surrounding them looked at him, and he struggled to lower his tone. "Cheriss, this is an act of dishonor."

Her tone turned contemptuous. "You really believe that."

"I can prove it to you. At least, I can prove to you that everything you think about me is wrong. What is it about me that you, and the other Adumari, think is so honorable?"

"Your success in killing the enemy—"

"No. That's dishonorable." He waited until her eyes widened, then he continued, "Or it would be, without the right intent. Why do I kill the enemy, Cheriss?"

"For—for the honor—"

"Circular thinking. I'm honorable because I kill the enemy, and I kill the enemy for the honor. There's nothing there, Cheriss. Here's the truth: I kill the enemy so someone, somewhere—probably someone I've never met and never will meet—will be happy."

She looked confused. "That doesn't make sense."

"Yes, it does. I told you how I lost my parents. Nothing I ever do can make up for that loss. But if I put myself in the way of people just as bad as the ones who killed my family, if I burn them down, then someone else *they* would have hurt gets to stay happy. That's the only honorable thing about my profession. It's not the killing. It's making the galaxy a little better."

She shook her head, unbelieving.

"And now you're here, thinking like an immature girl instead of a woman, anxious to throw away your life because you're unhappy now. And because you've been told all your life that there's honor in doing something like this. Tell me, where's the honor? Are you making Adumar a better place? Are you giving anyone a better life? Are you weeding bad men out of the court of Cartann, or are you just cutting them down randomly?"

"I . . . I . . ."

"Just stop doing this, Cheriss. Figure out how you're going to live and be happy, not why you can't. We'll talk. You'll learn how."

Something settled in Cheriss's expression, some pain behind her eyes. "Very well," she said. "After this fight."

"Refuse this challenge. It's meaningless."

"It's meaningless . . . but I've already accepted it." She drew her blastsword and examined the blade from guard to point. "I can't withdraw my acceptance now. I'd be shamed forever."

"Cheriss—"

"I can't, General." She moved past him to stand at the edge of the circle.

Wedge's pilots and Tomer moved in beside him as the announcer went through the usual ritual commencing a duel.

"No good, huh?" Janson asked.

"Some good," Wedge said. "If she survives." He looked around, caught sight of Iella. She was standing once more beside her minister escort, her expression mimicking the appreciation of blood sports Wedge could see on countless faces around her . . . but she saw Wedge looking, and he glimpsed worry behind her act.

Then Cheriss and Thanaer moved against one another.

Their duel was much like the last one, for Thanaer's blows were strong and lightning-fast . . . and it seemed to Wedge that Cheriss had slowed further. Nor had she the physical strength to beat her way past Thanaer's defense; with dagger and blastsword he swept each of her thrusts aside. They drove against one another in a clinch, each blastsword locked at its hilt against the other's knife, and when they parted, she managed to blood his sword arm's wrist with a sudden slash of her knife, but the wound did not slow him.

Then they came together, another furious exchange of thrusts and parries, and one of Thanaer's blows, almost too fast to trace, flicked past her defense to strike her in the chest. There was a crack of released energy. Cheriss was thrown back and down to the floor by the blow.

She lay unmoving, her eyes closed, her breath coming fast and shallow. Moving with exaggerated slowness and care, Thanaer sheathed his dagger, reached down to switch off the power to Cheriss's blastsword, and nudged that weapon away with the toe of his boot. Then he looked out into the crowd.

A lady at the edge of the crowd—blond, appealing, dressed in alternating shades of blue and violet, her features innocent and carefree—smiled at him and held out her hand. Palm down.

"So it is," Thanaer said, and raised the point of his blastsword.

Wedge took a step forward, opened his mouth to speak—but he was a half second behind Janson, who shouted, a bellow that filled the chamber, "Challenge!"

Thanaer and the crowd turned to look. Janson stood, one hand in the air and feet apart in a mockery of a heroic pose, his expression merry. "That's right, Ribbon-Beard. I challenge you."

Thanaer blinked at him. "Title or non-title?"

"Oh, non-title, I think. I don't want your title. Just some of that thin stuff you use for blood."

The Cartann pilot smiled at him. "Very well. As soon as I dispose of this ground-bound rubbish, we can begin."

Janson's tone became mocking. "No, no, no. You kill her and I withdraw the challenge."

A murmur rose in the crowd, a sound of surprise. Thanaer's face darkened. "You insult me, Major."

Tomer, behind Wedge and Janson, whispered, "You can't do that. If you put conditions on the offering of challenge, it suggests that you have no interest in dueling him. Only in the conditions."

Janson whispered back, "Thank you, Tomer. Now I understand." He raised his voice. "Yes, Thanaer, I insult you." The murmurs in the crowd grew louder. "You see, you're just not good enough to face me in the air or on the ground. I have no interest in dueling you. I'll do it for the girl's sake. Spare her, I'll give you this once-in-a-life-time chance. Kill her and I'll treat you like the nobody you are, and you'll never get to face me. Is that simple enough for you to understand?" With his last few words, he took on the tone of a school lecturer who had neither affection nor respect for his students.

There were gasps from the crowd at his words. Thanaer straightened, stiffening, and looked down at Cheriss. His thinking was very clear to Wedge: Kill the girl, not just for the honor, but to offend Janson, or accept the challenge and gobble up all the honor he could.

He sheathed his sword. "I accept," he said. "I will put your words on the tip of my blastsword and reinsert them in you." He moved away from Cheriss to stand at the edge of the crowd.

Wedge and his pilots moved to kneel beside Cheriss. Her face was covered in a sheen of sweat, and there was a grayness, a pallor to it. Steam rose from her wound.

"Upper left pectoral," Tycho said. "Not too deep. Survivable. But she's in shock. That can kill her."

Wedge swore to himself. The dress uniforms they wore didn't allow them to carry their headsets; the com-links they carried were very small, short-range only. He said, "Tycho, get her to the plaza. Don't waste time. Don't let anybody stop you. Hobbie, relay a message via the X-wings to *Allegiance*. Have them scramble a medi-cal team down to our arrival plaza in the shuttle. Then catch up to Tycho. Act as his wingman to the plaza."

Tycho nodded and gathered Cheriss up in his arms. In seconds both pilots were gone.

Wedge and Janson straightened and turned to look at Thanaer. The Cartann pilot was executing the same lunge over and over again for the enjoyment of the crowd.

"You jumped out ahead of me," Wedge said. "This was my fight."

Janson smiled. "Notice that, did you?"

"You don't think I can take him?"

"I know you can." Janson's smile changed from simple merriment to the cold, reptilian satisfaction he sometimes demonstrated when he finally got a target lock on a difficult opponent who richly deserved to become one with deep-space vacuum. "But there are three important reasons why I should take this fight and you shouldn't."

"Such as."

"First, the professional reason. You're the diplomat, the focus of what's going on. Should something go wrong, you're not expendable. I am. Second, a personal reason. You'd do this out of duty. Me, I'm going to enjoy it." He took off his belt and shrugged his way out of the jacket, exposing bare arms and the vibroblade sheath strapped to his left forearm. He handed both garments to Wedge and picked up Cheriss's blastsword.

"Third reason?"

"Also personal." He glanced past Wedge into the crowd. "I'm not sure what all went on last night . . . but you can consider this an engagement present. Or whatever." He turned from Wedge and stepped out into the circle, raising the blastsword high.

The audience roared.

"Before you die," Thanaer said, "I'm going to teach you the consequences of insulting your betters."

Janson smiled back at him. He gestured toward the woman who had pronounced the palm-down death sentence on Cheriss. "Thanaer, I have to admit, your widow sure is pretty."

The announcer interrupted their exchange. "We have a non-title ground challenge. Our new ground champion, Lord Pilot Thanaer ke Sekae, accepts the challenge of Major Wes Janson of the New Republic diplomatic envoy."

There was little applause from the crowd this time. Wedge sensed a breathlessness to their expectation. He shared it.

He didn't realize Tomer had joined him until the diplomat spoke. "Something of a no-win situation," Tomer said.

"Explain that."

"If Janson loses, obviously, your diplomatic party is reduced. Fewer pilots, fewer objects of admiration for the Adumari. The Imperials aren't obliged to reduce the size of their party. If Janson wins, well, Thanaer is very well respected here. Very much beloved of the court of Cartann and the *perator*."

Wedge shook his head. "Recalculate that, Tomer. If Janson loses, a man who does good things dies. If Thanaer loses, a man willing to gain some points at the cost of the life of a young woman dies. Are you capable of seeing the difference?"

Tomer sighed. "I think you and I speak very different dialects of Basic."

"For once we agree."

"To the *perator*," the announcer said. Thanaer turned toward the exit by which the *perator* departed and saluted in the ritual circle-and-cross pattern. Janson followed suit, his salute a sloppy one.

"Honor or death," the announcer said, and retreated into the crowd.

Thanaer assumed an on-guard pose.

Janson switched Cheriss's blastsword to his left

hand. "Wait! Look at this." He waved it furiously in the air before him. "Look! A bantha!"

The glowing trail left in the air by the tip of his blastsword did, in fact, resemble a child's scrawled impression of a bantha.

Wedge frowned. Janson wasn't left-handed. It wasn't a good idea to leave himself exposed this way—his sole ready weapon in his off hand.

Thanaer just stared, his expression confused.

"Not familiar with banthas?" Janson shrugged. "Try this." He waved again, creating an unrecognizable snarl of glowing blue lines in another volume of air. "An Adumari *farumme*! Here's another one." He waved again, and the result, had it been processed through a computer and extensively repaired, could have resembled one of the local fighter-craft. "A Blade-Thirty-two!"

Thanaer just waited. "Are you ready to die yet?"

"One more." Where the bantha scribble had faded, Janson traced another design. It was a stick figure of a man with a ridiculously tiny circle for a head. "It's Thanaer ke Sekae!"

Thanaer's jaw tightened, the only change to his expression Wedge could see through the beard and ridiculous ribbons. Thanaer, all business, lunged.

Janson twisted toward the attack and brought Thanaer's blade out of line with his own. Thanaer's forward momentum brought them together, their hilt guards crashing into one another.

Janson brought his right forearm up in a blow that snapped Thanaer's head back and smashed the man's nose flat. With his right hand, Janson seized Thanaer's sword hand and slammed it down across his upraised knee. Thanaer's sword point hit the floor with a loud blaster *pop* and the hilt followed, dropping from Thanaer's nerveless fingers.

Janson gave Thanaer a shove and the Cartann pilot

staggered backward, suddenly disarmed and disoriented. Janson brought his boot heel down on the other man's sword blade, just above the guard. The blade parted with a metallic sound and its point ceased hissing, ceased drawing glowing lines in the air.

Janson smiled at the man. "Your orders are simple." He switched off the power to Cheriss's blastsword and tossed the weapon, with feigned negligence, back in the direction he had come from. Wedge caught it out of the air. "I punch. You suffer. Got it?"

Thanaer responded by reaching for his dagger. Janson let him get it into his hand, then spun into a kick that further punished Thanaer's sword hand and sent the dagger flying. It clattered to the ground near the edge of the crowd and skidded past the feet of the foremost observers.

"Forgot to mention," Janson said, "on some worlds people fight with their feet, too. Feet, hands, rocks, pure cussed willpower—they're warriors. You, you're just a dilettante." He brought his hands up in a standard unarmed combat pose, left arm and left side leading.

Confused and uncertain, blood streaming from his nose, Thanaer brought up his own hands in an imitation of Janson's posture.

Janson smiled and waded in.

Wedge struggled to keep a wince from his face. It was a massacre. Janson fired off blows into Thanaer's midsection. When the Adumari pilot tried to block those shots, Janson concentrated on his ribs, and Wedge could hear occasional cracks as bones gave way under his blows. When Thanaer tried to strike, Janson took the blows on his forearms or shoulders, or, in the case of especially clumsy shots, withdrew a handspan or two and let Thanaer unload his blows into empty air.

And always Janson returned to pounding, to beating, his blows sounding like someone using a hardwood club on a side of hanging bantha meat.

He didn't hit Thanaer in the face again. Wedge knew this wasn't mercy, but common sense—jawbones being more likely to break fingers than the other way around.

Thanaer's final few blows made it clear that he could barely see and wasn't thinking at all; he lashed out against empty air half a meter to the left of Janson's position, then stared around, looking randomly for a foe in clear view a meter before him.

"At least you could say you were knocked out by a well-struck blow of the fist," Janson said. "If I were going to be nice to you, that is." He held up his open hand, palm toward his opponent, until Thanaer's bleary gaze fixed on it. Then he stretched his hand full out to his side—and slapped Thanaer, a blow that sounded like the crack of an energy whip.

He drew his hand back again.

But Thanaer's eyes rolled up in his head as a red mark the approximate shape of Janson's hand appeared on his cheek, and his knees collapsed under him. He hit the floor with a grunt and his eyes fluttered shut.

Janson waved jauntily at the crowd and returned to Wedge's side, whistling something Wedge recognized as a Taanabian dancing melody.

Applause broke out in the crowd, but it was not universal—exclamations and murmurs competed with it in volume.

Wedge helped him put his jacket back on. "That was it?" he asked. "You staked the entire fight on the assumption that you could block his first shot at you?"

Janson nodded. "Pretty much. I just couldn't see him throwing his best attack on the very first attack of the match. That gave me one crack at him, maybe two." He tied his belt back around him.

"You shouldn't have humiliated him," Tomer said.

Janson peered at him. "This whole world is full of 'shouldn't haves,' Tomer. Without that humiliation, there was no chance he'd learn anything. With it, I figure he has about a five percent chance of realizing that he's a big bag of Hutt droppings. Which is five percent more than he had a few minutes ago." He shrugged. "Who's hungry?"

Wedge grinned. "Let's get out of here. I'm buying."

9

The rest of the day offered hopeful news, and more than once.

By the time Wedge and Janson, joined by Hobbie, found a dining establishment where a small private room would afford them a certain amount of peace, the verdict was in on Cheriss. "She'll make it," Tycho explained via comlink. "She's responding well to the bacta and should be released in a day, maybe less."

"Good," Wedge said. "Make sure the medical staff knows to notify me when they're to release her. I want to be there as a friendly face when they cut her loose."

"Will do."

"And get down here. We have plenty to do today."

"Have you ever thought about sleeping, boss?"

Wedge grinned. "Which is, exactly, what?"

"Sort of like being shot until you're unconscious, except there's no bacta, and you often end up feeling better than when you started."

"Sounds good. I'll give it a try someday. Call in when

you reach groundside. Out." Wedge folded up his headset and returned his attention to the menu, a flexible flatscreen that showed the evening's available dishes as a series of animations running around the screen engaged in blastsword duels with one another. "I don't think I want to eat anything that looks like it wants to cut its way back out of me."

Hobbie gave him a dubious look. "Did you say we had plenty to do still?"

Wedge nodded.

"What, exactly?"

"We're going to try to subvert an Imperial admiral."

"Oh," Hobbie said. "Something easy. While you're doing that, why don't Wes and I smuggle ourselves aboard *Agonizer* and destroy her with thrown rocks?"

Wedge gave him a grin. "With the right tools—say, a hundred thousand Ewoks and a month to prepare—you could probably do that. In the meantime, we *have* the right tools to subvert our Imperial admiral."

"What tools?"

"Oh, Wes's maturity, your optimism, and my diplomatic skills."

Hobbie buried his face in his hands. "We're doomed."

Though he picked up a more powerful comlink from his quarters, Wedge kept its power output turned low, so that his signal could not possibly carry as far as *Agonizer* or even the nearest Cartann city. And every half hour, he or one of his pilots put in a call for Admiral Rogriss.

Shortly after Adumar's sun sank and the first of her two moons rose, he got an answer and arranged an appointment.

An hour later, he stood alone at the periphery of a Cartann plaza—not the one where he and his pilots had landed, days ago, but another of the same size some distance away. Its central feature was a large fountain; at its center was a round island of something like duracrete supporting a sculpture made of some brassy metal. The sculpture showed the *perator* in his younger days, wearing a Blade fighter-craft pilot's suit, waving to a crowd that was not present at this hour; behind him was a semicircle of seven fungus-shaped explosion clouds, representing, Wedge assumed, seven military campaigns or bombing runs.

Admiral Rogriss was not too long in coming. Wedge saw two silhouettes approaching from the opposite side of the plaza; one, larger, stayed back in the vicinity of the fountains, while the other moved unsteadily forward toward Wedge. Soon enough, moonlight illuminated his features, revealing him to be the admiral.

Wedge bit back a comment. Rogriss had deteriorated in the short time since Wedge had seen him last. Though the man's expression was cheerful and carefree, his posture and movements made it clear that he was as drunk as a new soldier on his first leave. In addition, something had changed in the man's face. Wedge had seen the expression before, the change that takes place when a cocky young pilot loses a battle but survives to realize that he isn't immortal, that he can be beaten.

Wedge nodded toward the figure who had hung back. "Your bodyguard? A local or an Imperial?"

"A faithful son of the Empire," Rogriss said, his tone jovial. "Come to protect me and to witness from afar your bribe attempt."

Wedge smiled and shook his head. "Bribe attempt? I'm afraid I'm here empty-handed."

"Ah. As skillful a spy as you are a diplomat, I see. You're not here to offer me a command, a salary, the gratitude of the Rebel Alliance if I'd only just betray those I've served faithfully for longer than you've been alive? I must say, my boy, I'm disappointed."

"No, that sort of thing is for the real spies. I'm just a pilot." Wedge lost his smile. "But I do have something to offer you. A way out."

Rogriss laughed. "A way out of what? My pension?"

"Out of your dilemma. Just listen for a minute, Admiral. I don't expect you to admit to anything I'm saying; you won't offer up any information, and that's fine. But I want you to hear what I have to say."

Rogriss considered, then nodded.

"It's obviously in your best interest if the Adumari choose to side with the Empire," Wedge said.

Rogriss laughed again. "Thank you for pointing that out. You really are adapting to life as a diplomat."

"Not because it's your mission, but because the alternative will mean your ruin. Probably your death. A suicide, I expect."

Rogriss didn't answer. He just cocked an eyebrow, his expression dubious, and waited.

"Because if Adumar sides with the New Republic, you're obliged to contact your superiors, in spite of the oath you swore on their behalf, and they send in an invasion force. The invasion force hammers Adumar so badly that it's shattered, probably not worth sweeping up the pieces. A metaphor, I suppose, for your word of honor, which will be just as ruined. Just as irreparable."

"See here, Antilles—"

"No, just listen, Rogriss. We're in kind of the same position here. Play by the rules, do as we're told, keep our careers—and lose everything. Or risk, and probably lose, everything—except our word. The thing is, our word is the one thing no one can take from us unless we leave it vulnerable. All I'm saying to you—if I'm right about what you're being called on to do—is that you shouldn't offer up your honor like that. You should refuse to break your word. And if your world suddenly becomes hostile to you because you choose to preserve your honor, you can come to us instead of going home and facing execution."

"You're absurd."

"I've been told that before."

Rogriss turned away . . . but did not move. After a moment he turned back. "Speaking hypothetically, if what you said were true, and I did what you recommended, my children could never be made to understand what I'd done."

"Have you raised them to be like you? Analytical, intelligent, suspicious, mean?"

Rogriss smiled again, this time showing teeth. "I'd express it a different way. But yes."

"Then they won't believe what they're told just because someone in authority told them. And you've got it backward. If my suspicions about your orders are correct, and you disobeyed them and went home, you'd be executed and might never even have last words to say to your children. If you come over, our Intelligence division can get messages to them, and I'll guarantee they'll do so . . . or I'll arrange to do it personally. You'll have your chance to make your reasons known to your daughter and son. Even a chance to offer them passage to the New Republic, if that's something they want."

"Ah." Rogriss shrugged. "You spin interesting fictions, Antilles."

Wedge held out a datacard to him. "On this is my emergency contact frequency. You should be able to reach me this way at any time. If you want to accept my offer. Even if you just want to gloat."

Rogriss took it. "I can't pass up an opportunity to gloat."

"What Imperial admiral could?"

"Good-bye, General."

"Good evening, Admiral."

Rogriss's walk, as he left, was slower than before, but more sure. Was he weighed down by Wedge's offer, or by being reminded of the dilemma before him? Or had he simply sobered up a bit? Wedge didn't know.

Before the pilots turned in for the evening, their datapads received a transmission from Tomer. The *perator* had called another gathering on the world government question for his palace the following evening.

Wedge and Red Flight spent the next morning and afternoon at their usual pursuit, what they were now calling "flight school"—accepting challenges from Adumari pilots and demonstrating to them the New Republic way of doing things. There were fewer challenges today, giving them some long, peaceful stretches when they could just fly for the joy of it.

Today, after the flying, there was no parade lining of well-wishers accompanying them on their way back to their quarters, just a few admirers crowded at the air base gates. There was no Cheriss to tell them how the Imperial flyers had done with their day's challenges. The ride back to their building was quiet and uneventful.

"No friends left," Janson said, leaning against the rail. "We've managed to make everyone hate us."

Tycho offered him a half smile. "I thought that's what you'd been trying to achieve your whole life."

"Good point." Janson straightened. "What am I complaining about? No, wait, I know—they haven't yet erected statues of us to throw rotten fruit at."

"Give us another day," Hobbie said.

They again wore their New Republic dress uniforms for the night's event. This time, entering the Royal Outer Court ballroom, they had no problem spotting the Imperial pilots—they, too, were in dress uniforms, the spotless grays that spoke of decades of the Empire's rule. Dull by the standards of Adumari dress, they still stood out in the crowd.

"They followed our lead," Janson said. His grin was infectious. "I bet they had to be ordered to. Stings a bit, doesn't it, General Phennir?" He was more than a dozen meters from the Imperial officer, who could not have heard his words, but Phennir still glowered at him.

Tomer joined them. "It's going to be war," he said, his tone regretful. "There's no stopping it now."

"Do me a favor and kill power to this performance," Wedge said. "Maybe you are a little sad that a war is resulting . . . but the rest of it is all according to your plan."

Tomer looked confused. "My plan? I think you're more than a little mixed up, General."

"No. It's pretty much cut and dried. Let's go back in time a little bit. You're assigned here as regional head of Intelligence with the task of bringing Adumar into the New Republic."

"I'm just a diplomat—"

"Shut up. But they need a world government to make the task a simpler one and you get to work persuading the rulers of Adumar's nations to consider such a change. All very well and good so far."

Tomer shook his head, a denial, but his attention was fully on Wedge.

"Now, it gets sticky. They want to talk to famous pilots, so you send for me, intending to keep me around as entertainment for the Cartann court, since I have no diplomatic skills to speak of. As soon as I arrive, you discover that the Empire is also here, which drastically moves up the time frame you're working in. The longer the Empire has to work on it, the more they can appeal to the Adumari love of blood sports and death in combat, so you have to act fast. That means creating a world government by the fastest means possible—by persuading the *perator* of Cartann to implement one through leverage and conquest, something that appeals to him anyway. We fly fighters for the public's amusement while you arrange to sacrifice hundreds, maybe thousands, of innocents in a war that will accomplish your mission."

"You're interpreting everything in the most negative possible way."

Wedge felt a surge of triumph; Tomer was no longer denying his role in the Intelligence side of these affairs. "And the thing is, you *have* to win. Bringing this off successfully is the only thing that will save you. You know that you can't explain your whole revised plan to General Cracken; he'd never go for it. Which is why you could never come up with an order from Cracken for me to play along with you. You had to implement a communications blackout to keep word of any kind, other than your own reports, from reaching him. It's success on Adumar or the end of your career, isn't it, Tomer? Your career might not even survive if you're successful. Chief of State Organa Solo, when she reviews these events, might just decide that you're a war criminal, not a successful diplomat."

Tomer glared for a long moment. "You could have helped. Things would have been better."

"I might have been able to help . . . if you'd been straight with me from the start. If you hadn't settled on Cartann running everything, through a war of conquest, as the only way to get your job done."

"You use the tools available to you—here's the *perator.*"

The ruler of Cartann emerged from his doorway, his retinue of guards and advisors around him like a set of living shields. Wedge saw Hallis, this time wearing subdued sea-green and her hair arrayed as it had been yesterday; she maneuvered to be as close as she could to the ruler, which was still outside the boundaries suggested by the placement of his outermost guards.

The *perator* offered up his charismatic smile for the assembly. This time, there were to be no flatscreens broadcasting his words, though once again they were amplified so all would hear. "It is with deep sorrow that I must announce that certain elements have chosen not to enter into our plans for the future. In specific, the seditious forces ruling the nation of Halbegardia and the Yedagon Confederacy have decided to issue statements of defiance. Their actions are clearly intended to endanger our future relations with other worlds and could leave Adumar a weak, disorganized planet, ripe for conquest from outside. So for the sake of the security of all Adumari everywhere, I declare Halbegardia and Yedagon to be outside our protection . . . and the targets of efforts of pacification to begin very soon."

He paused, and applause broke out among his courtiers. This day, Wedge saw smaller clusters of foreign dignitaries in the hall. He suspected that the ones present yesterday but not today were either under arrest or en route back to their native lands.

The *perator* raised hands against the applause and it died away. "Will the pilot-heroes of the Empire and the New Republic please approach?"

Wedge put on his business face and led Tycho, Janson, and Hobbie forward. To his right, the Imperial pilots had formed up in similar military precision. The crowd parted before them, and the two groups of pilots came to a halt at almost exactly the same moment, three meters from the *perator*.

The ruler beamed at them. "You eight pilots have brought considerable delight and knowledge to Adumar, but it has all been in circumstances somewhat different than those that brought you fame. I would now like to rectify that. Would you—and it would please us greatly if you would—lead units of the Cartann armed forces in action against our enemies, so that we might grasp the full measure of your skill and honor?"

Turr Phennir was first to speak, his voice nearly as rich and warm as the *perator*'s. "It would be my tremendous honor to demonstrate what we have to offer the people of Cartann and Adumar."

The *perator* smiled upon him, then turned to Wedge. "And our representatives of the New Republic?"

Wedge cleared his throat. This was not going to be good. "We must decline."

The ruler's expression became one of sorrow, regret. "But why? Can it be that you care for us less than your Imperial counterparts?"

Wedge considered his words for a split second. "No, I suspect we care more. But we must demonstrate it differently. In this case, with a refusal."

"I see." The *perator* nodded, his expression suggesting that he would remain reasonable in the face of hurtful treachery. "Please withdraw."

Wedge and his pilots about-faced and made their retreat.

They passed Tomer going the other way. "That was your last chance to do anything positive," Tomer said. "Now it's up to me to undo the damage you've done." The diplomat hurried on to join the *perator*'s retinue.

"So," Janson said. "What's it like to be an ex-diplomat?"

Wedge grinned. "I've been better."

"Think they'll escort us up to *Allegiance*, or just put us on the business end of a planetary defense laser cannon and blast us up there?"

Tomer had made it to the *perator*'s side. His eyes, his hand gestures, all said that he was pleading with the ruler. The *perator* shook his head again and again, then stopped to listen. But when Tomer finally turned away and left the ruler's retinue, his expression was downcast.

"General Antilles!" the *perator* called. "No, do not step forward. I do not wish you to be any closer to me than you already are."

Wedge stood, waiting, ignoring the rebuke implicit in the ruler's tone.

"I declare you to be an enemy of the state of Cartann," the *perator* said. "But I am told by Lord Tomer Darpen that it might cost Cartann friendships to have you executed as you deserve."

Hobbie murmured, "This has just gotten a lot worse."

"So I declare you and your pilots exiles. Remove yourself from Cartann, by gauntlet to Giltella Air Base, and never show yourselves before me again."

Wordlessly, Wedge turned away from the *perator*

and headed toward the chamber's exit. He felt blood draining from his head. The weight of his failure as a diplomat, anticipated for so long, was finally on him. The moment of failure did not feel good. In fact, he couldn't remember feeling worse in recent times.

Yes he could. It was worse when he became certain, for those brief moments, that he had lost Iella forever. He'd survived that and overcome it. He'd get through this.

Tomer, walking quickly, reached his side. "You're in trouble."

"I thought my troubles were over."

"No. You'll probably be dead before you get to your Blades."

Wedge stopped. "Blades? We're returning to our X-wings."

Tomer shook his head. "They're being impounded."

"Impound—"

"Even as we speak. They'll be gone from your balcony before you can get back, hauled off like cargo. You need to be thinking about the gauntlet if you're to survive."

Wedge took a look around. No members of the crowd stood nearer than half a dozen meters. Most regarded him with expressions of sympathy—or sudden revulsion. It matched what he was feeling at the thought of the Adumari touching his X-wings, at the realization that he needed answers from this man he wanted so desperately to punch. "All right. What does 'gauntlet to the air base' mean?"

"It means you have to get to Giltella Air Base by whatever means you can manage. They'll have four spaceworthy Blades ready for you. If you can get up to the *Allegiance* in them, past the Blades that are sure to be gunning for you up in the air, you get to live. But—" Tomer shrugged, helpless—"anyone can kill you, Wedge. It's legal. From the door out of the *perator*'s palace to the *Allegiance*, you're all fair game."

"Which means," Hobbie said, "the longer we wait, the more forces they can organize to bring to bear against us."

Tomer nodded. "Yes. In theory, you could also use the time to communicate with your friends and array them against your enemies. But you have no friends on-planet to aid you." He looked apologetic. "I'm sorry. The *perator* was in such a towering rage. He would have had you killed outright if I hadn't—"

"We'll discuss your contribution to this whole mess later," Wedge said. He felt very cold inside, cold with anger at Tomer and the *perator* and Adumar in general, cold with the realization that the gauntlet he was about to face was likely to kill him long before he was able to employ his most useful skills.

He turned back to the crowd and raised his voice. "Who'll offer blastswords to four doomed men?"

For long moments, no one moved.

Then a dignitary from a nation that had fallen in line with Cartann came forward, a slender man in a gold tunic, and wordlessly offered his sword belt and sheathed blastsword to Wedge. A pilot Red Flight had flown against came to put another in Tycho's hands. A woman, a minister by her age and dress, demanded the swords of her two guards and brought them forward to offer them to Hobbie and Janson. Wedge thanked each of them.

He saw Iella approaching, a surreptitious route that kept her toward the back of the crowd; he caught her eye and gave her a little shake of the head. She understood and stopped where she was. Nothing she could give him here would do him much good . . . and she could blow her cover, doing herself considerable harm. Wedge merely hoped Tomer hadn't caught their little exchange.

At the doorway, they reclaimed their blaster pistols. Moments later, they stood arrayed at the exit from the *perator*'s palace, steps down to the courtyard and main gates beyond, while an expectant crowd gathered behind them . . . and another crowd, expectant for another reason, gathered out in the courtyard. Seeing the distinctive New Republic uniforms waiting within the doorway, the courtyard crowd shouted for the pilots to come out.

"We have to get clear of pursuit and out of sight for a few minutes," Wedge said. "But we're not going to play their game." He pulled out his comlink and activated it. "Gate, relay this message up to *Allegiance*." He heard his astromech's answering whistle, and continued, "General Antilles to *Allegiance*. Requesting emergency evacuation from planetary surface."

There was no answer.

"Antilles to *Allegiance*, come in."

Nothing.

Wedge turned worried eyes to the other pilots. "All right. So I was wrong. We've somehow been countered. We're going to do it their way." He checked the charge on his blaster and the others followed suit with theirs. "Your orders," he said.

"Ready," Tycho said.

"Whatever they expect us to do, we don't do. Four, what do they expect us to do?"

Hobbie said, "Run out toward the gate and get shot."

"Correct. So we don't." Wedge scanned the courtyard. He saw gathered men and women, three dozen or more of them, waiting for them to emerge. He saw parked wheeled transports—and one repulsorlift transport against the wall, scores of meters to the left of the gate. He nodded in its direction. "That one's our target," he said. "Go."

They moved out and onto the stairs at a trot. As soon as men and women in the crowd raised blasters, Wedge and company opened fire and broke left, circling around the edge of the waiting crowd.

Incoming fire looked like stormtrooper new-recruit target practice, filling the air, inaccurate, but promising eventual deadly hits through sheer volume.

That wasn't to be. Janson lagged behind and shot precisely, using his sights and the native skill with blasters that had been his since childhood.

When the leading edge of shooters began collapsing, firer after firer taking Janson's blaster shots in face and chest and gut, the line wavered. Some of the shooters dove for cover—the only cover being provided by the bodies of their fellows. Others redoubled their efforts, firing faster and with even less accuracy.

Wedge, halfway across the courtyard, felt heat against the back of his neck and tensed himself against pain to follow—but there was no pain, just the sensation of superheated air from a near miss by a blaster bolt. He fired as he ran, his shots nowhere near as accurate as Janson's, but just as intimidating; the line of shooters did not surge toward him.

And then the repulsorlift transport was before him, hanging in the air. He hurtled over the rear, skidding forward toward the control mechanism, and leaned over the front to shoot the line tethering the craft to the wall. He felt the impact of Tycho landing in the bed behind him, more impacts of blaster shots hitting the vehicle's side.

Kneeling behind the control board to get as much cover as possible from the low lip at the edges of the vehicle, Wedge powered up its steering mechanism. "Call 'em as they come aboard," he said.

Tycho lay on his stomach at the transport's starboard side, his pistol braced against the lip. He fired once, twice, three times, and Wedge heard a shriek from the crowd of shooters. There was another thump, and Tycho said, "Four's aboard."

"Where's Three?"

"Thirty meters back."

"We'll pick him up." Wedge put the ungainly vehicle in reverse. It glided backward with frustrating slowness. Wedge reduced the repulsorlift power on the port side, increased it on starboard, so it tilted to port; this made it harder to control, but the vehicle's underside offered him and his pilots a little additional cover.

The vehicle shook again, harder than before, and Tycho announced, "Three's aboard."

Wedge glanced at his men. "Anyone hit?"

They shook their heads, not looking at him, concentrating on pouring blaster fire off the starboard side.

Wedge increased all repulsorlifts to full power. The transport soared upward—

To an altitude of four meters. Half the height of the walls of the *perator*'s complex. There was no way he could fly over the walls.

"We're going out by the gate," he announced. "Brace yourselves, pilots." He put the transport into forward motion, steering straight toward the crowd of shooters and the gate beyond.

The air was thick with the smell of blaster bolts, and thick with the bolts themselves. Only the shooters at the farthest edges of the crowd could get a good look at any of the men on the transport, and therefore get a decent shot at them; the others could see only the transport's underside.

Tycho uttered a yelp and stood as the metal under his stomach superheated. All over the transport, the flooring began to glow. In two spots, it gave way entirely and blaster bolts shot through, toward the sky. Wedge shifted his body as the flooring beneath him began to glow.

But meter by meter they approached the gates and began outrunning the shooters in the courtyard. A thin screen of attackers with blasters was lined up at the gate, and they poured fire up at the bottom of the transport as Wedge crossed overhead; he saw one blaster shot, reduced in strength, emerge to slice across Hobbie's hip. He hissed, leaned over the rail, took three quick shots in the direction of the screen of attackers.

Then they were past, floating at a good clip above a street heavy with pedestrian and transport traffic, pursuers trailing out behind them and losing ground—

The repulsorlift transport's engine coughed and the vehicle immediately lost speed. The pursuers began to gain ground on them, even while rushing across lanes of heavy traffic.

Hobbie, stanching his hip wound with a pocket torn from his jacket, offered up a bitter smile. "It just doesn't get better, does it?"

Tycho popped the metal plate over the transport's engine. "Shot," he announced. "Both ways. Blaster fire has ruined it."

"Right," Wedge said. "Janson, what do they expect us to do?"

"Set down and run on foot, or hop another transport. A wheeled one, since there are no floaters in sight." Janson, keeping low, leaned over the rear of the transport and fired off several shots at their pursuers. Wedge saw two men fall. One of them was immediately run over by a wheeled transport, its driver unable to swerve far enough aside in time.

"So we do something else," Wedge said. He aimed the dying transport toward the building opposite the palace gates—a tall residential building, its balconies deep, many furnished with elaborate tables or reclining furniture.

As they neared the building, Wedge could see the flatscreens on its exterior at ground level. All showed an identical image—the rear of Wedge's transport, from a distance of forty or fifty meters, on its approach toward the building. He offered up a growl. A flatcam was broadcasting their escape and it was probably up on walls and personal flatscreens all over Cartann. People at the base of the building he approached recognized the scene, turned, pointed up at their transport—and some unsheathed blaster pistols and began firing.

"Hobbie, suppression fire to starboard. Tycho, to port. Janson, keep it up off the stern." Then Wedge saw that their transport, even at maximum altitude, would not be high enough to climb over the rail of even the lowest balcony before them. It would probably slide in just beneath the balcony. "On my mark, prepare to abandon your posts, come forward, and *jump*."

"Got it, boss," Tycho said. He traversed to the port side of the transport and began unloading fire on the new enemies there.

In moments the balcony was mere meters ahead. On it were numerous ornate recliners—and several startled-looking Adumari nobles, brewglasses in hand. Wedge saw no flatscreens in their vicinity and supposed they were unaware of what was going on.

"Come forward!" Wedge shouted. And as his pilots abandoned their positions and moved to join him, he locked the controls down and moved up to the transport's forward rail. As it came within two meters of the balcony, he stepped up on it and launched himself upward, grabbing the balcony rail, swinging himself over onto the balcony floor. His pilots landed beside him, one, two, three.

He had his blaster pistol out before the balcony residents quite reached their feet. He waited a moment as the slow-moving transport crashed into the side of the building below, and said, "Don't move, we're just passing through."

He led his pilots through the sliding transparent door and into the nobles' main room. More people were here, adults, children, liveried servants. Wedge gestured with his pistol and they raised their hands.

"Jackets and belts off," he said. "Too distinctive. You people get to keep them as souvenirs. You." He gestured at one of the servants. "Where's your cloakroom?"

The man, his expression wavering somewhere between delight and alarm, pointed.

Janson kept the occupants under guard while Wedge slid the cloakroom door opened. He grabbed four dark cloaks, handed them out as Hobbie and Tycho took up positions on either side of the double doors out into what should have been the building's main hall.

Behind him, he could hear snatches of conversation from the nobles: "That one's the *diligent* one." "Why, they're no taller than our pilots. I thought they would be giants." "Is this a custom from their world? I rather like it. I think we'll visit the ke Oleans this way."

Wedge draped a cloak around Janson's shoulders and the last around his own, then the two of them also set up beside the doors. "Ready," he said, "go."

Janson pulled the door open, peered both ways. "Clear. Where to?"

"Straight across," Wedge said. "Now."

"Thank you for honoring our home," called one of the nobles.

"Happy to oblige," Wedge said, and followed his pilots across the hall.

He could hear shouting from the nearest stairwell, could even make out the words: "We must be allowed entry with our weapons. You have intruders on the first floor up—"

Wedge grinned. For once he was benefiting from, rather than being inconvenienced by, the local security measures.

Opposite was a big set of double doors, the main entrance into some other noble family's quarters. "The lock," Wedge said. "Fire."

"Wait," Hobbie said. He reached for the door handle, twisted it, gave it a pull. The door swung open toward him.

He shrugged, gave Wedge an apologetic look. "Worth trying," he said.

They charged into that set of quarters, surprising a trio of servants setting places at a long dinner table, and raced past them to the doors onto the balcony. It was unoccupied, though brewglasses were arrayed on the long bar to one side.

Wedge peered over the rail. Below was ordinary street traffic, mostly pedestrian, with two wheeled transports in view. In the distance to his left he saw a rarity for a downtown Cartann avenue—a pair of Adumari riding lizards and riders marching in stately fashion toward them. There were no maniacs waving blaster pistols to be seen.

Moments later, all four pilots dropped to the street and merged into the pedestrian traffic. At the intersection, they ducked faces and pulled up cloak hoods as survivors of the shooters' crowd turned the corner and raced toward the part of the building from which they had dropped, their attention high, blasters at the ready.

Wedge and his pilots passed through that crowd of amateur assassins and continued onward, forcing themselves to walk at a measured pace. "So far, so good," Wedge said, his voice low. "Keep your eyes on the flatscreens on the buildings. If we see ourselves on them in real-time, we know we're in trouble."

"What's the plan?" Tycho asked.

"They know where we're going. And we do have to go there if we're going to get off-planet. I suppose we could try to find enough privately owned Blades on balconies . . . but then we'd be stuck there, trying to get through security measures we're not used to, while they have time to recognize us and come after us again." Wedge shook his head. "No, we've got to get to the air base.

"They'll have people on the most obvious routes to the base, and probably a whole congregation at the base's main gates. So we go by side streets and back routes until we're near the base . . ." Wedge stopped, considering.

"Getting *into* the base is the hard part," Janson said. "It has transparisteel walls eight meters high, higher than those blasted reduced-power repulsorlift transports can go. Easily guarded gates are our only entry points. Wish we had Page's commandos or the Wraiths and a couple of days to prepare."

"We improvise," Wedge said. "We need a wheeled transport, one of the flatcam units our pursuers are carrying, and four sets of women's clothing."

Hobbie looked crestfallen. "Boss, please tell me you're not putting us in women's clothing."

"Very well," Wedge said. "I'm not putting us in women's clothing."

10

Half an hour later, the four of them sat, wearing Adumari women's clothing taken from a middle-class family's apartment, in a wheeled transport two blocks from the gates into Giltella Air Base. Hobbie stared with a hurt expression at Wedge, who ignored him.

On this ill-lit section of street, running between warehouses serving the air base, the pilots were well concealed by darkness. This was not to be the case when they neared the air base's front gates, which were brilliantly illuminated by glow lamps atop tall poles. Even at this distance, the pilots could clearly see the crowd that awaited them at the gates.

"You lied to me," Hobbie said.

"I did," Wedge said. "With my brilliant achievements in the diplomatic profession has come the realization that lies can be powerful motivators."

"My faith is shattered."

"You knew, when I said we needed four sets of women's clothing, that we were going to end up in them.

You *knew*. So any hopes you had to the contrary were just self-delusion."

"I understand that. But I'd rather blame you than me." Wedge grinned. "Tycho, what are we facing?"

"A hundred fifty, more like two hundred, easy," Tycho said. "So, fifty to one odds."

"Not too bad," Janson said, and cracked his knuckles. "So. Who's best-looking in women's dress? I vote for myself."

"Quiet," Wedge said. "Tycho, do you have the broadcast figured out?"

Tycho nodded. "I think so. But we're going to have to rely some on luck."

"We *are* doomed," Hobbie said.

Tycho gestured at the flatcam unit they'd taken from a man who now slept, with a bump the size of a comlink on his forehead, behind a stairwell in a residential building a few blocks from here. "I can't override the local flatcams," he said. "There's no equipment for that, no procedure. Just a specific broadcast protocol. My guess is that when we broadcast the recording, some manager at the local information distributor will decide whether or not to put it up on the flatscreens citywide."

"Which they will," Wedge said. "Considering the subject matter. All right, start broadcasting." He set the wheeled transport into motion, heading straight toward the two hundred eager killers awaiting them at the airfield's gates. Tycho hit a set of buttons on the flatcam's side and then carefully placed the device out on the street. Within moments it was lost to sight behind them.

The flatscreens on the buildings they passed—screens not so numerous as on the buildings in the richer quadrants of the city—showed edited scenes from their escape from the *perator*'s palace, and occasional glimpses of them in their stolen cloaks during their flight toward Giltella Air Base. They'd managed to avoid direct confrontations with the extraordinary numbers of shooters and flatcam wielders between there and here, even when breaking into a home to steal the women's clothing, though they'd had to lay down some long-distance suppression fire when eluding pursuit a time or two.

And now they were headed straight toward an enemy that was numerically superior and anxiously awaiting their arrival.

Each time they passed a flatscreen, Hobbie said, "Still the old stuff." Then they were a block closer, just coming into visual range of the crowd at the gate, and men and women there began to notice their approach, to point.

Wedge felt his stomach tighten. "Come on, come on . . ."

"Maybe we did something wrong," Hobbie said. "We might not have encoded the right security protocols or something. We probably failed to—oh, there it is."

On the flatscreen of the next building before them appeared new images. Four human silhouettes were suddenly illuminated against the side of a building. Two threw back cloak hoods, revealing their faces—Wedge Antilles and Wes Janson, their expressions at first startled, then vengeful.

On the flatscreen view, Wes Janson threw back his cloak and then drew his blastsword. The view wavered as if the flatcam holder was trembling, and then the distance to the pilots increased as though the holder was backing quickly away.

But Janson ran forward, lunging with his blastsword, its tip leaving a light blue trace in the air. There was a blue flash offscreen to the left, then the world spun as the flatcam holder flailed around and crashed to the ground.

In a moment, the view settled on the front of the building—with its distinctive red riding-*farumme* above the main entryway—and became still. The pilots, still barely visible at the left edge of the flatscreen, rushed out of view.

Wedge nodded. It was a crude attempt, but if the people of Cartann didn't take too much time to analyze it, it would withstand inspection—long enough to serve Wedge's purposes.

The pilots had made the recording minutes go, standing before a very distinctive building a short distance from the air base. Hobbie had held the flatcam in one hand, a piece of brick-colored street cover in his other. The fourth silhouette in the flatcam view was actually Hobbie's cloak, held up on the point of Tycho's blastsword. When Janson had lunged, his blastsword had hit the street cover, resulting in the flash of light suggesting the flatcam holder had taken the blow instead.

Ahead, the crowd must be seeing the recording. A roar of anger and expectation rose from the men and women there. Within moments, most were in motion, heading straight toward the pilots' transport—and beyond, Wedge hoped, to the building that had been their backdrop. "Get ready," he said, and drew the shawllike garment closer about his face.

In seconds, the leading edges of the crowd reached them. Most ran past. One man, chest heaving from his exertions, pointed with his blastsword toward the building of the red *farumme*. "Did you see them?"

Wedge nodded and pointed the same direction.

Behind him arose a terrified, high-pitched wail. Wedge jerked around to look, but it was Hobbie, uttering a noise of panic and suffering toward the sky, tearing at the clothes over his chest as though he were in mortal dread. Wedge blinked at the display and turned around again to steer.

"Never fear," panted the man who'd addressed them. "We will capture them, and rend them, and make them suffer for every—" Then the still-rolling transport was too far beyond him for his words to carry.

Moments later, the pilots were beyond the main

body of vengeful Adumari. "Good screaming, Hobbie," Wedge said.

"I practice a lot," Hobbie said, his voice hoarse. "Anytime Wes makes plans for the squadron, for example. Anytime a Corellian cooks for us."

Janson and Wedge both turned to glare at him.

Ahead, perhaps thirty men and women remained before the gates. Many appeared to be watching the flatcams posted on the transparisteel walls to either side of the gates themselves, but quite a few still had their attention on the approaching transport. Beyond the gates, themselves transparisteel, were two guards in the black-and-gold livery of the air base.

"On the command 'One,' " Wedge said, "fire on the gate locks. When I see them give, I'll issue the command 'Two.' That means spray suppression fire toward the crowd. Over their heads unless return fire starts coming in. Understood?"

He heard three affirmatives.

As they neared, the closest members of the crowd began shouting: "Did you see them?" "Did they kill the camwielder?"

As if in answer, Wedge shouted, "One." Then he drew and poured blaster fire into the locks on the gates.

Fire from the other three pilots joined his. One succession of blasts, probably Janson's, chewed away with extraordinary accuracy at the mechanisms. The guards behind the gates threw themselves away and down.

In his peripheral vision, Wedge saw members of the crowd flinch away, then realize they weren't being fired on. They began bringing blasters already in their hands to bear—

The locks weren't yet clearly destroyed, but Wedge shouted, "Two!" He leaned to port and fired repeatedly, blowing holes in street cover, firing once, with reluctance, at a young man too daring or stupid to demonstrate any self-preservative instincts; that man drew a careful bead on the transport and Wedge's shot took him clean in the gut, folding him over, depositing him with a fatal wound on the street cover.

The transport crashed into the gates, shuddering from the impact—and the gates flew open. The transport rolled through. Janson, Hobbie, and Tycho continued pouring suppression fire out the back.

One of the guards stood, hands up, and ran after the transport. "Wait, wait!"

"Another madman," Janson said. "Think I should shoot him?"

"If we shot every Adumari who was crazy, there'd be no one left," Wedge said. "Let's hear what he has to say." He slowed the transport's speed fractionally, allowing the guard to catch up.

"Cease fire, lord pilots," said the man, "please. You're upon air base grounds. You're safe until you take off again."

In fact, the crowd at the gate was no longer firing at the pilots. Nor were they entering the air base. Some were kicking the walls in frustration, shouting after the pilots.

An eerie wail bit into the air, rising and falling, its pitch and volume cutting at Wedge's ears. He resisted the urge to clap his hands over his ears. "What's that?"

The guard said, "Notification that you're on base. Now the street hunters will go home and the air hunters will know it's time to meet you. Your Blades are in the Lovely Carrion Flightknife hangar."

"That's somehow fitting." Wedge patted the rail. "Come aboard and guide us to our starfighters."

Liveried base personnel stood by at the hangar, ready with pilot's suits, helmets, personal gear. The four Blade-32s standing ready were colored a glossy red rather than black. "Seized from the pilots of the nation of Yedagon," one of the hangar mechanics said, a touch of apology to his voice. "The palace wanted declared enemies to look like enemies."

"Live weapons," Wedge said, "instead of paint, this time, I trust."

The mechanic nodded. Though he was a small man, his spadelike black beard made his face appear larger. "To sabotage your craft would be to sabotage your killers' honor—and our own. Your vehicles are in exquisite condition."

While Wedge and pilots ran through an abbreviated checklist, flight after flight of Blade-32s flew by the open hangar doors, close enough in to be seen easily. *Declaring their presence, announcing challenges we can't refuse this time,* Wedge decided. "Keep personal comlinks on Red Flight frequencies," Wedge said. "Tune Blade comm system defaults to the following frequencies: *Allegiance,* Rogue Squadron, Red Flight."

He got four acknowledgments. He switched to *Allegiance*'s frequency. "Red Flight to *Allegiance,* come in. This is General Antilles, and this is a direct order. *Allegiance,* come in. Acknowledge our transmission."

There was no answer. He hadn't expected any. The pilots of Red Flight were on their own. He switched back to Red Flight frequency. "Announce readiness. Leader had two lit and in the green."

"Two standing by, one hundred percent."

"Three, ready for a furball."

"Four is green-lighted."

"Up on repulsors." Wedge suited action to words by bringing his Blade-32 straight up two meters. Ahead of him, at the hangar exits, mechanics' crews cheered, but whether it was for Red Flight's success or merely for the fight to come, Wedge didn't know.

"What's our first order?" Wedge asked.

Tycho's voice came back immediately: " 'Whatever they expect us to do, we don't do.' "

"Correct, Two. Red Flight, come around one-eighty degrees." He swung the nose of his Blade around until it was pointed directly toward the thin sheet-metal rear of the hangar. "Arm missile systems. On my command, fire your missiles and all speed forward. Ready—fire."

Four missiles flashed instantaneously to the rear of the hangar and blew the sheet-metal panel into oblivion.

Wedge kicked his Blade-32 forward and began climbing as soon as he emerged through the hole.

His lightboard sensor data was confused, made erratic by the tremendous smoke cloud he was climbing through, but it clearly showed a half-dozen Blades hovering over the hangar, noses depressed, pointed toward the exit. Had Red Flight emerged the way they were supposed to, they would have done so right under the guns of this ambush party.

Wedge switched his weapons control to rear lasers— then switched them back again. "Red Flight, hold your fire until we're clear." He put his attention into climbing as fast as he could.

Had he fired and missed, had an ambusher Blade been hit and exploded, collateral damage would have punched through into the hangar, toward the front, just where the Lovely Carrion Flightknife mechanics waited.

His lightboard showed his pilots tucked in so close that he couldn't detect them as individual signals. Below, the ambushers above the Lovely Carrion Flightknife hangar were breaking up, beginning their climb in Red Flight's wake.

Other groups of flyers, circling at some distance, were turning in toward Red Flight. Two high-altitude formations began descents. Altogether, Wedge counted at least thirty enemy aircraft arrayed against Red Flight.

Thirty against four. In the past, he'd bullied his way

through such impossible odds, usually through use of stratagems set up well in advance. Here he had nothing like that working in his favor.

Red Flight was barely a thousand meters up when the first enemies, two separate half flightknives, neared attack range from overhead. "Loosen up the formation," Wedge said. "Remember it's me they're likely to concentrate on. Tycho, stand off, we're not in a normal wingman situation here. Fire at will."

The dozen enemies screamed down at them with lasers blazing—eight or nine of them concentrating fire on Wedge. Wedge returned fire with his lasers but mostly concentrated on evasive maneuvering. He juked and jinked from side to side, set his Blade into an axial rotation to constantly change the image he offered to enemy lightboards, and fired by reflex as targets presented themselves.

He saw his lasers shear through one incoming Blade and stitch scoring marks on the fuselage of a second. He felt his own craft shudder as lasers hammered at his fuselage. Then he was past the diving wave of enemies, seeing them—seven, not twelve—turn in his wake and follow. Behind him, Reds Two, Three, and Four followed in very loose formation.

Ahead of his flight path at several thousand meters was another blip, diffusing into a new squad of foes. Below, the fighters who had intended to ambush Red Flight at the hangar were now joining the Blades who had just exchanged shots with them.

"I have an idea," Wedge said. "Two, Three, Four, pull back and climb. Stay within a half kilometer of me. Set one missile each to detonate at a proximity of two hundred fifty meters. On my command, fire *at me*, then be prepared to prey on targets of opportunity."

"Leader, this is Three. Are you crazy? Acknowledge."

"Three, Leader. That's affirmative." Wedge put most of his attention on heading toward the new incoming enemies, but kept track of two sets of range-to-target numbers: those for the Blades ahead and the ones for those behind.

When the two sets of numbers were approximately equal, and just out of standard weapons-lock range, Wedge fired one missile at the targets ahead and then pulled a tight vector to port. In doing so, he rotated axially to expose his belly to the enemies ahead, his top hull to the enemies coming on from behind.

He saw puffs of smoke, the beginnings of missile trails, from the enemies ahead. "Fire," he said. He rotated again to narrow his cross section and climbed.

And his own pilots fired on him, as he'd instructed.

He felt a momentary chill of fear. What if the missiles malfunctioned? What if their proximity fuses ignited at a much closer distance than the quarter kilometer he'd dictated? He'd be dead before he felt the impact.

But three missiles detonated into huge clouds of opaque fire directly above and ahead of him. His Blade-32 rocked and shuddered as it met the overlapping shock waves from the explosions, and he heard countless metallic pings and clanks as shrapnel hit his hull.

A moment later, he was enveloped in fire and smoke. In his mind was a picture of the three explosions, placing him toward the westmost edge of one of the blasts; he snap-rolled, emerging belly-up from the cloud, then dove into it again. There was a moment of clear air as he crossed the open space between explosion clouds, then he was in fire and darkness again.

There was another detonation nearby, close enough to rattle his fighter and hurt his teeth. He heard equipment shattering within his Blade. Then he was in open air again. He glanced left and right, then at his lightboard, which now featured a crack across its crystal surface.

A moment ago, twenty-three Blades had been aimed at him. Now, only thirteen remained, their formations scattering, and the other members of Red Flight were now diving upon them, loosing lasers and missiles as fast as fingers could pull triggers.

Wedge could see it in his mind's eye, the way the opportunistic fighters had seen his lightbounce image improve to offer a target lock, the way they'd armed missiles and lasers and opened fire. He'd risen into friendly smoke clouds and the incoming missiles, deprived for a crucial second of their original target, sought out new ones . . . and found them in the oncoming friendly Blades. He looped after Tycho, dropping two missiles into the enemy formation before switching to lasers as he closed.

"One, Two. You all right?"

"I'm unhurt, Two." He glanced at the board that was supposed to display damage diagnostics. Text scrolled across it at a rate too fast for him to read, and he wished fervently that the Blades offered a diagrammatic display of damage the way New Republic fighters did. "Some damage to my Blade." He cocked his head as he realized he was hearing a new, persistent noise.

His stomach sank as he recognized it. Whistling. Air was passing through his cockpit making a constant, unmusical sound as it did so. "I've experienced a hull breach," he said, keeping his voice unemotional.

If he couldn't patch the breach, he couldn't reach space. Couldn't make the *Allegiance.*

Now was not the time to worry about it. Ten enemies still remained, and his Blade shuddered as he suffered a hit from the rear lasers of the fighter he was pursuing. He put more of his personal attention to evasive maneuvering and continued stitching his target with linked laser blasts.

Fire and smoke erupted from its cockpit and it began a slow descent toward distant grain fields. Nine enemies to go. No, eight. The fighter in Hobbie's sights exploded spectacularly, turning into a ball of black and red and gold that would have been beautiful if it had not been fueled by a human life.

Hobbie's Blade was now trailing smoke, a thin stream of it emerging from beneath his cockpit. "Four—"

"I see it, boss. Still functional."

Tycho pulled into wingman position behind and to the starboard of Wedge's Blade. Through his viewport, Wedge could see that Tycho's canopy was cracked and starred, with char marks indicating laser hits.

Wedge swore to himself. Tycho couldn't make space either; a canopy damaged that way would blow out under the pressure of its internal atmosphere. And these pilot suits weren't self-contained environment suits the way TIE fighter rigs were.

That left Janson the only one of them with a spaceworthy Blade, the only one who could reach *Allegiance* and tell the story of what had happened to them on Adumar.

Then Janson's Blade was enveloped in an explosion cloud.

He emerged from the far side of the cloud intact, or so Wedge thought at first; then his Blade began rolling to port and Wedge could see that the starboard wing was completely gone. "Punch out, Three," he said. "Janson, come in."

An enemy Blade diving in from directly above tore his attention away from Janson. He looped to starboard, causing the incoming Blade to alter his dive angle to follow. Tycho decelerated, slowing to the Blade's rated stall speed, and stitched the enemy with lasers from below. Wedge felt a tremendous bang to his rear quarters but watched, through his rear viewport and on the lightboard, as his attacker exploded. "Good shot, Tycho."

He heeled over until he could see Janson again. Janson's Blade was now sideways, its lone wing pointed toward the ground, and was beginning a looping descent to the ground.

But Janson was free of it. The pilot was in open air, a meter-square flat device above him; he hung by straps from it. Wedge nodded; this had to be the Blade's pilot-descent mechanism, a primitive repulsorlift device that lowered the pilot at a safe speed.

Safe, that is, unless someone was still shooting at the pilot. Wedge saw a Blade diving toward the defenseless pilot. He saw Janson pulling out his blaster pistol, as though a weapon that small could do any significant damage to a fighter, and open fire.

The incoming fighter exploded. Wedge resolved to find out just what sort of pistol Janson was carrying—and then saw Hobbie's Blade whip through the new debris cloud, lasers still flashing.

That left six enemies against three damaged Red Flight Blades.

"Stay with Three, Four," Wedge said. "When he reaches ground, land, join him, and tell him to take you to that club where he ate pastries the other night."

"Acknowledged, Lead."

"Two, you and I are going to finish this."

"I'm your wing."

"No, drift out in case they keep up the same tactics."

The six enemy Blades had gathered into formation, two triangles, and were on an approach vector. Wedge saw the two formations drift apart, each triangle heading toward one of the Red Flight fliers. He nodded; they'd finally learned something about not just mindlessly prosecuting the most prestigious enemy. That was too bad; now was not the time for them to get smart.

In these slow-maneuvering Blades, missiles gave his opponents a serious edge. He had to take that edge away.

He slammed his control yoke forward, diving straight toward the Cartann streets beneath him. He thought he detected a moment of hesitation in his enemies before they dove to follow.

It was a gambit he was reluctant to take. Back at the air base, he'd taken steps not to endanger civilians. He could afford to do so then; that choice did not have a direct bearing on his continued survival. But now it did, and he had to make use of available cover . . . or die.

Below, he could see only traces of lights indicating the outlines of streets.

But those streets were often blanketed by wires and cables at all altitudes, impediments that, even if they didn't tear his fighter's wings off, would throw him into a building side . . .

He nodded, remembering. They didn't have all those cross wires at street intersections. He made for the square light pattern of an intersection.

Columns of light poured past him toward the ground, his pursuers' lasers. He felt his stern rock from a graze impact. He returned fire with his rear lasers, was satisfied to see one shot punch through a canopy. It didn't kill the pilot, at least not immediately; that Blade turned clumsily away, heading off toward the air base or the forests beyond.

Wedge put his repulsorlifts on at full power and pulled back on his yoke, a full-strength effort to pull out of his dive. He angled to slide in under the unseen canopy of wires and cables, hoping he'd correctly calculated their height aboveground, and a moment later found himself roaring down a mere three meters above street level. Ahead, a repulsorlift transport clumsily turned out of his path.

Behind him, his two pursuers imitated his maneuver. The first one came in too high; Wedge saw it shudder, then saw its port wing disintegrate from an impact with one or more of the cables. The Blade spun, its other wing crumpling under multiple successive impacts, then crashed down onto the street, skidding forward almost as fast as Wedge was flying. In his rear viewport Wedge saw pedestrians dive out of the way of the flaming thing, saw it brush aside an abandoned wheeled transport as though the thing were a millimeter-thin flatscreen.

The other Blade continued relentlessly onward.

As he reached the next intersection, Wedge yanked the controls hard to port, turning into the new lane . . . and reduced strength to his repulsorlifts. His Blade dropped nearly to the street's surface and continued its spin until it was pointed back the way it had come. He brought strength up to the forward repulsorlifts, canting his bow upward, and slammed his thrusters forward as hard as he could.

His pursuer whipped around the corner, making better time than Wedge, coming so close to the building face on the outside of his turn that only his repulsors kept him from grazing the building. His nose was elevated far above Wedge's position, the pilot obviously expecting to catch Wedge in his sights farther down the street.

Wedge fired, his lasers raking the Blade from bow to stern at close range. He saw the underside of the Blade open up like a seam bursting under pressure. The Blade wobbled, roared past over Wedge's head, and slammed down into the street, skidding for a block in the direction it had been going, knocking wheeled transports aside like toys.

Wedge's lightboard showed only buildings all around him. "Red Two, report status."

"All clear," Tycho said.

"Let's see how clear we can get. Coming up to join you." Wedge sent his Blade forward to the intersection, then rose on repulsorlifts until he was well clear of the ubiquitous cabling. He pointed his nose up and climbed.

In seconds, Tycho joined him from points east. If anything, he looked worse than before, with laser scoring all along the starboard side of his fuselage. His cockpit was now shattered; his Blade couldn't hit very high speeds without wind hammering Tycho. "We're not going to make space, boss," he said.

"If I recall the maps right, Cartann's border to Halbegardia isn't outside our flight range," Wedge said.

"We'll use terrain-following flying to stay below their lightbounce sensors, and—"

His lightboard suddenly showed two fuzzy blips moving toward them, one from Giltella Air Base, one from Cartann Bladedrome. Within moments they resolved themselves into clouds of smaller blips, two entire flightknives. In the distance, Wedge could see the running lights of the incoming Blades; they were closer to one another than they were to Wedge and Tycho, but they would be on the New Republic pilots within seconds.

The tactical part of Wedge's mind, the one that was often at odds with the Corellian part, calculated odds and strategy. The answer wasn't good. Even if they could have ordinarily managed twelve-to-one odds, their equipment was too badly damaged to let them compete at full strength. Nor did they have time to land and get into hiding. Even if they punched out, experience had shown that the enemy pilots could spot them and were willing to shoot them out of the air as they descended.

Wedge suppressed a pang of regret. Not fair of him to offer a future to Iella and then rush off and get killed this way. He turned toward the incoming flightknives. He said, "Guess we're just going to have to rack up some numbers, Tycho." Despite his best effort, his voice was heavy.

"Understood, boss." Tycho stayed tight to him.

Then, on his lightboard, one of the two clouds of Blades looped toward the other, and the comm board was suddenly active with traffic: "Strike the Moons Flightknife issues a challenge to Lords of Dismay Flightknife!" "Ke Mattino, you madman, now is not the time—" "There is always time to crush incompetence and cowardice. Fire!"

The sky between the two flightknives, not so distant now, was suddenly lit up by lasers and ball-shaped explosions. A moment later there was no way to distinguish between the flightknives on the lightboard; they had merged into a single firefight.

"Red Two, we're going to ground," Wedge said. He switched to the standard Cartann military frequency. "Red Flight to Strike the Moons. Is that you, Captain ke Mattino?"

"It is I."

"Thanks, Captain."

"You have won your departure. I will not let some honor-grubber deprive you of it in this fashion. Confusion to your enemies."

"And frothing disease to yours. Antilles out." He pointed his nose toward the ground, toward the section of Cartann not so brightly lit by street illuminators.

It was hours later, the darkest and quietest hours of the night, when Wedge and Tycho arrived at the door of Iella's quarters. Wedge could not remember ever having been so tired. But when the door opened to his knock and he saw her there before him, his exhaustion evaporated in an instant. He took her in his arms and she dragged him inside. He heard Tycho follow and close the door behind them.

"You almost killed me," Iella said. Worry blunted the accusation in her tone. "Having to wait hour after hour to find out if you'd survived or not."

"I'm sorry." Wedge offered her a look of apology. "We needed to maintain comm silence as much as possible. To travel back streets and alleys and sometimes roofs and balconies to make sure we weren't spotted, weren't followed. Have you heard—"

The light in the apartment's main room clicked on and Wedge discovered he had an audience.

Janson and Hobbie were lounging on the sofa, Janson with his feet up on a small table, a brightly colored datapad, of the sort usually optimized for children's games, on his lap. His slicked-back hair suggested he'd recently had a bath, and his fresh clothes made Wedge long to be rid of the sweat-drenched garments he was wearing. Hobbie was similarly scrubbed, though his tunic was off to show a half-dozen places where his torso and arms were bandaged.

Cheriss stood at the wall, near the light control, and Hallis sat on another chair.

Wedge blinked at them. "I'm sorry," he said. "I seem to have interrupted a party."

Iella smiled at him. "More like a conspiracy." She led him and Tycho to additional chairs.

The room was crowded with more furniture than the last time Wedge had seen it; he supposed that she'd dragged it in off the balcony and out of other rooms. Wedge sat wearily and looked among the others. "You'll excuse me, I hope, if I look a little confused. Cheriss, how do you come to be here? And how are you?"

Cheriss, in dark blastsword-fighter's clothing, raised and lowered her left shoulder a couple of times, experimentally. "Better," she said. Her voice was low, her tone somber. "I need some more time before I can fight again. But I was out of danger, and they brought me down to Cartann, where I learned of the air duel you'd had. I went to your quarters, where I found Hallis but not you or your X-wings. I knew if you were to go anywhere, you would come here, so I did." When she finished, her expression suggested that she had more to say, but she bit back on it.

Wedge struggled with a way to suggest that bringing Hallis here was not a good idea, as it could compromise her identity, but Iella seemed to read his thoughts. She said, "After Cheriss came here and told me what she'd done and who she'd seen, I suggested she bring Hallis. It's all right, Wedge."

He nodded and sat back in his chair. "Hallis?"

She shrugged. "I robbed your quarters."

"Ah."

"Actually, when they said they'd taken your X-wings, I knew they'd ransack your quarters eventually. I went there intending to get Whitecap's remaining parts. But I overheard the two men who were packing up your belongings; they were stealing things like they were in a contest, laughing about the four of you like it was good entertainment that you'd been shot down, so I got mad. When they were apart, I hit them both with a hydrospanner and took all the stuff they'd gathered up."

Wedge couldn't help but laugh. "I was always under the impression that a documentarian shouldn't get so close to her subjects."

"Well . . . well . . . I was *angry*."

"What did you get?"

"Your civilian clothes, pilot's suits, Janson's fancy cloak, helmets, datapads, some datacards, four comlink headsets, your blastswords—one of them belonged to Cheriss so I gave it back to her—a whole pile of love notes Janson had been collecting . . ."

Janson looked up, his expression outraged. "Hey! You didn't look at any of them."

"No, certainly not."

He relaxed, a little mollified.

"Except for the ones that had been opened, that is. The one from Lady Marri was very poetic, I think."

Janson stood, his face flushing red. "I can't believe you—" Then his expression changed. "I don't recall any note from a Lady Marri."

Hallis grinned at him.

Janson sat again. "I've been had. General, I request permission to jump from an upper-story balcony, to ease my shame."

"Granted," Wedge said. "Now, Iella. You're the one in the most tricky situation here. I hate to be a demanding houseguest—but what *can* you give us without ruining your life?"

She gave him a wan smile. "Good question. I'm still bound by my orders and my duties, so the answer is 'not much.' But since my superior doesn't know of any direct connection between us, I have some latitude . . . for the time being. I can put you up, unless my superior asks a direct question whether I've seen you. And until the searches going on for you turn into door-to-door searches. You're going to have to get out of Cartann. I can get you Adumari money, some comm and computer equipment. Unfortunately, I don't have many contacts; the team that followed me here was responsible for setting up that sort of thing."

"How about a holocomm transmission back to the New Republic?"

She shook her head. "The holocomm unit was eventually moved to a site set up by my superior. I don't know where it is."

Wedge considered. "Still, the rest is very helpful. Is there any way you can find out what the status is of *Allegiance*? We need to know that before the next time we try to get up there."

Iella glanced over at one of her cabinets. "My comm gear picked up and recorded your open transmissions to *Allegiance*." Her expression grew bleak. "And their lack of a reply. But I know they're still up there. My comm unit has picked up coded transmissions from them continuously since before you went on your gauntlet run. There's been no irregularity to their comm traffic. No sort of activity to suggest they were captured, for instance."

Hallis said, "Iella, I need to talk to you. Privately."

Iella gave her a quizzical look.

"I'm going to persuade you to abandon your mission, to go with Wedge and the others. And to shoot your superior right in the guts if you ever happen to see him again."

"That'll take a lot of persuading." Iella gestured

toward one of the side doors. "But I'll give you the chance. After you."

They were gone only a couple of minutes, long enough for Wedge and Tycho to wearily drag their boots off and accept cups of water from Cheriss. Then Iella came slamming back through that side door, her face pale, her expression set and angry.

"Change of plans," Iella said. "I'm abandoning my post and my mission. I'll figure some way to get you out of Cartann. And if I see Tomer Darpen, I'm going to burn him down where he stands."

Wedge stared at her in shocked silence for a moment. Then he turned to Hallis. "How did you do that?"

Hallis shrugged.

"No, really, please. I have to know. It normally takes a vote of the Senate or a planetary collision to get Iella to change her mind. I need to learn how to do whatever you did."

Iella colored nicely. "Wedge."

"I'll show you." From beneath her sleeve, Hallis pulled out a standard datapad. With her other hand, she reached behind her and dragged a wire with a standard datapad coupler at the end of it. She jacked it into the pad and powered the unit up, then held the screen so Wedge could see. "You're not going to like this."

Tycho leaned in to see. Janson, Hobbie, and Cheriss also crowded in behind him to get a look. Iella turned away, perhaps unwilling to see this a second time.

The datapad view wavered across a sea of faces and the backs of heads. Wedge recognized the surroundings as the Outer Court chamber of the *perator*'s palace.

Finally the view stabilized. Wedge recognized the *perator* standing at the heart of his knot of advisors. The clothes worn by his advisors defined the scene—this was the last gathering Wedge had attended, the one where he and his pilots had been exiled and effectively sentenced to death.

The recording's sound kicked in, a meaningless babble of voices. Then the voices dropped out one by one; Wedge presumed that the recorder had to have been using a directional sound recorder to home in on a very few voices.

On the *perator*'s voice. He was saying, in hushed tones, "*. . . pity they couldn't have been persuaded to lend us their arts. That would have been spectacular, and Antilles's name alone would have been enough to cow some of the enemy forces . . .*"

Then Tomer Darpen was at his elbow. "*A moment of your time, my lord.*"

"*Only a moment. Time is pressing.*"

"*I wish to extend my personal apologies, and General Antilles's apologies, for what he has just been obliged to do.*"

Even in the somewhat blurry recording, the *perator* looked surprised. "*Obliged?*"

Tomer nodded. "*The general is pinned down between opposing forces. His natural desire is to aid you, of course; he knows it is the only honorable option. But ambiguous orders handed down by his diplomatic corps superiors, orders intended to keep him alive so that he remain valuable to them, prevent him from fighting. The situation has crushed him, has robbed him of all will to live.*"

The *perator* shook his head, his expression shocked. "*I cannot believe it.*"

Tomer lowered his eyes, his expression sad. "*It's true. He longs for death to burn away his shame. And so General Antilles begs a favor of you.*"

"*Speak.*"

"*He begs you to set your forces on him, assaults that he cannot decline . . . and cannot survive. So that he can die honorably and never again be used as a tool by the diplomatic corps. Do this, and not only will his memory be cherished, but you can be sure that the next pilot-representatives sent here will be unfettered by ridiculous orders restraining them from behaving as true pilots should."*

The *perator* nodded, his expression sympathetic. *"At last I understand. The poor man."*

"It must look like an act of justice on your part. But he will thank you with his dying breath."

"I understand."

"Thank you, perator."

Hallis's recording view followed Tomer as he left the ruler's side and moved toward Wedge and his pilots. Her audio lock remained with him, and though his next few words were muffled—doubtless by him holding a comlink up to his face and speaking quietly—Wedge could make out his words. *"En-Are-Eye-One to Allegiance, acknowledge. New orders, Allegiance. Do not accept, record, or acknowledge any transmissions from Adumar's surface or from vehicles not belonging to the New Republic until I rescind this order. Repeat it back to me to indicate you've understood . . . Correct, Allegiance. En-Are-Eye-One out."*

Hallis switched the datapad screen off.

They were all silent for a long moment. Finally Wedge looked at the documentarian. "Thanks, Hallis. But I have to ask—why didn't you tell me some of this before we left the *perator's* palace?"

"The first part, knowing that Tomer had set you up, couldn't help you. The second part, knowing that the *Allegiance* was off the comm waves—I was just getting up to you to tell you that when I heard you figuring it out for yourselves."

"Makes sense," Wedge said. He turned to Iella. "You know that you're next."

She nodded.

"I don't understand," Janson said.

"Tomer set things up to kill us," Wedge said. "Accomplishing a lot of things. It scored points with the *perator* by making him think that we pilots had been with him all along, just thwarted by bureaucratic orders, so the *perator* doesn't think we opposed him. And it scrapes us out of the way so I can't file my report, my conclusions on the way he set up this whole diplomatic mission—conclusions I now have to assume were largely correct. He wants everyone who can offer up a comprehensive report to the Chief of State to be dead. That means that Tomer's subordinates here, including Iella, will eventually end up facedown in an alley."

"It'll take me just minutes to pack," Iella said. "Which begs the question: Where do we go? I wasn't in charge of setting up safe houses."

"I know where," Cheriss said. "General Antilles—"

"It's about time you called me Wedge."

She didn't smile, but she did offer him a little nod of acknowledgment. "Wedge, there are some men and women who want to meet you. When I returned earlier tonight and made myself known at the *perator*'s palace, they tracked me down and told me so."

Wedge frowned. "What sort of men and women?"

"Political leaders. From nations not controlled by Cartann. From nations soon to be smashed by Cartann."

"Do you think they'd be willing to offer us use of a spaceworthy craft to get us to *Allegiance*?"

She nodded. "I think they would. But I don't think that is what is foremost on their minds. I think they want to ask a favor of you."

"I'd be happy to listen. All right, everybody. Tycho and I need to get cleaned up, and everybody is to get dressed up—nicely as we can. They're scouring the streets looking for four downed pilots hiding from their eyes, not seven upstanding citizens out for a late night of carousing."

"You're issuing orders to Intelligence," Iella said, her voice mild.

"Just to my pilots—and making some assumptions. Care to come along?"

"Anywhere," she said.

11

By dawn, Wedge and the other six refugees were in the passenger/cargo compartment of a *farumme*-class hauler, an aircraft Wedge suspected was constructed about the time he was being born. Air whistled through holes in the hull. Rings were imbedded in the compartment's framework, the better to allow for cargo to be lashed down securely, but the only thing being transported now was Wedge's party, seated on padded benches that ran the length of the compartment. The Yedagon Confederacy agent who had met them, a lean, very fair man of few words, rode with the pilots in their control compartment.

Wedge glanced around the compartment. Janson, Tycho, and Hobbie were all asleep. He was as tired as they were, in as great a need of sleep, but he had things to think about.

Cheriss sat alone on a bench on the other side of the craft. She had seldom looked at Wedge since their departure from Iella's quarters, and seemed lost in her thoughts.

Hallis was on the same side of the craft, alone, all the New Republic personnel's datapads piled up beside her.

She had, at Wedge's request, copied the recording of Tomer Darpen's treachery to each datapad. Now she was struggling with the most sophisticated of the datapads available to her, Iella's, to edit that and some other recordings into a portion of her documentary. Her occasional bouts of muttering and swearing suggested that it wasn't going well.

And Iella—Iella was tucked under Wedge's arm, her eyes closed, her expression serene.

Wedge smiled, knowing his was probably an idiot's grin but not caring. He was on the run, a death sentence on his head, on a world where his enemies and admirers alike would be happy to kill him, unable to get in touch with his superiors. But for this moment he was carefree, happy in a way he hadn't been in years.

Iella's eyes opened. She looked at him a little fuzzily, then smiled and burrowed her face into his neck. "Haven't you had any sleep?"

"I've been thinking. Putting things in order."

"Marshaling your troops, General?"

"Only when I could force myself to stop thinking about you."

Her shoulders shook a little and he realized she was laughing silently. "You know what's so wonderful about compliments from you?" she asked.

"What?"

"I know you always mean them. You have no skill at flattery."

Cheriss unstrapped herself and rose. She walked over to Wedge and Iella, her steps unsteady because of the craft's rocking motions and occasional battles with turbulence. Her expression was as serious as it had been back in Iella's quarters. "General . . . Wedge . . . may I speak to you for a moment? Privately?" She turned a look of apology toward Iella.

"Sure." Wedge looked down into Iella's eyes, tried to gauge her reaction. But her expression offered little but sleepy contentment. There was no concern, no jealousy to be seen in them.

Wedge joined Cheriss toward the front of the compartment. They held on to the rings in the framework to steady themselves against the craft's motion.

When Cheriss spoke, her voice was barely loud enough for him to hear over the engine's roar and the whistling of wind through rivet holes. "I just wanted to say . . . you were right and I was wrong."

"That's a hard admission," Wedge said. "It tries to stick in my throat whenever I'm obliged to offer it."

She managed a faint smile. "I didn't really understand it after I woke up on your big ship. My injury was almost healed and I knew I had nothing left to me—my title lost, the *perator*'s regard for me lost, your regard for me probably lost—"

"No."

"Let me talk. But I couldn't concentrate on all that because the medics kept asking me questions. How my wound felt. What I might be allergic to. Other conditions I had that were medical in nature. I told them of my dizziness with heights . . ."

Wedge was surprised to see tears form in her eyes. She wiped them away and continued, "They scanned my head and took my blood to look for chemicals in it, and decided that it was a chemical imbalance. They gave me a drug. Half an hour later I stood on the top walkway of your starfighter landing bay, over the great distance to the floor where the starfighters landed, even over the gap they flew out of—I could see all the way down to the clouds of Adumar's skies, and I felt not even a twinge. All I have to do is take a chemical once every few days. I can learn to fly."

"That's wonderful news."

"Yes . . . though I could not even make the medics understand that. To them, it was such a little thing. A diagnosis, a chemical, and their patient could be set aside and a new one brought in. For me, it was years of knowing I could never be anything in Cartann, suddenly swept away . . . and to those who helped me, it was nothing more than a minor task, successfully accomplished. I was almost angry with them for not understanding.

"And that's when I knew. If I had died the other day at the *perator*'s court, I could not even be resentful. I could never enjoy this thing, which is a few grains of chemicals to your medics and a miracle to me. So I understood that you were right. To throw away my life would have been dishonorable. It was the choice of a stupid girl. Someone I hope I no longer am."

"Having seen this, you have only one choice."

"Which is what?"

"To live your life well. To find a purpose and pursue it."

"I want to be a pilot," she said. "Not for Cartann. Not for Adumar. For your New Republic."

"If I'm still alive in a few days, I'll see what I can do to help you."

"I also wanted to say . . ." Her glance flicked to Iella and back to Wedge. "I wanted to wish you and your lady every happiness."

"Thank you."

"I—I don't know what else to say."

"Let me say something, then. One last piece of advice. Cheriss, you're always going to be too young for something important to you, too old for something else, and the timing is just not going to be right for a third set of things. That's life, and you can make yourself crazy by dwelling on that. Or you can figure out what you are the right age for, and what the timing is right for, and celebrate those things. Where do you suppose happiness lies?"

"I understand."

"Good."

He rejoined Iella and strapped himself back in, then wrapped his arm around her.

"All settled?" she asked.

He nodded.

"If I can ask, what was it all about?"

"She's just growing up. She's come along two, maybe three years since the other night."

"That's good."

"Maybe we can figure out how to build a weapon out of the process and shoot Wes a few times."

His eyes still closed, Janson said, "I heard that."

The briefing room where Wedge and company met the rulers of the Yedagon Confederacy was unlike anything they had seen in the city of Cartann. It was a circular chamber, half bounded by curving wall, half by a succession of ornate columns beyond which were close-cut grasses and artistically spaced trees. The portion of the room bounded by columns was open to the sky, though Wedge could see a panel at the edge of the ceiling of the room's other half that suggested some sort of light cover could be mechanically extended as a roof.

The floor and tables in the chamber were of a marblelike stone, the floor textured so that feet did not slip upon it; Wedge prodded at it with his toe to find that it was indeed solid, not the sort of cushiony cover that seemed to decorate every surface in Cartann.

Light winds stirred in the chamber. The place was airy and well lit, with no corners for skulking, no shadows to hide within. *A vast improvement over what we've been enjoying,* Wedge decided as he seated himself.

On the other side of the central table from him, Escalion, the *perator* of the Confederacy, settled into position. "I will be brief," he said. "You are a military man and doubtless have no taste for roundabout talk or circuitous approaches to the subject."

"Thank you," Wedge said, and studied the man. Yedagon's *perator* was also in contrast to Cartann's. Of average height, he was dark of hair and beard but pale of skin. The contrast gave his features the appearance of intensity even when he was at ease. He was a few years older than Wedge, and his physical condition seemed to be as good as Wedge's; the musculature of his upper body suggested regular exercise or workouts and his waist was flat. His uniform was a spotless white, reminiscent of an Imperial Grand Admiral's uniform except for the elaborate purple scrollery traced down the outside of his sleeves and trouser legs and the bank of medals and campaign markers on his chest—each a different size, shape, and color, decorations that the orderly Imperials would find offensive in the extreme.

"If it is your wish," Escalion said, "we would be happy to provide you transport to your orbital vessel. Your public refusal to fall in with Cartann's military aggression indebts us to you that far, and more. But we would like to present you with another alternative. A request."

"You want me to fly with your forces against Cartann."

"No," Escalion said. "To lead them. All of them."

Wedge leaned back. "I'm not sure it's a good idea to put an entire nation's military force in the hands of a man who has only the vaguest familiarity with it."

"You misunderstand me," Escalion said. "I'm not talking about one nation. I'm in constant communication with the ruler of Halbegardia, and she is in agreement. We wish you to lead the united forces of all nations arrayed against Cartann."

"Why?"

"Because you have done things on Adumar that are unprecedented. You have demonstrated piloting skills that surpass our best—your four-pilot unit shot down thirty opponents last night, lest we forget. You have sought to teach rather than accumulate honor at a cost of blood and lives. You have defied the most powerful man on Adumar and survived his wrath. All of which is only part of the answer." He leaned forward over the table, his expression genuinely intent. "It is my belief, and the belief of my advisors and Halbegardia's, that if it is known that you lead our combined forces against Cartann, many other nations will join us. Nations currently neutral, or siding with Cartann because they know they cannot withstand a direct attack by that nation, will join us, giving us a chance to win. Or at least be defeated in an honorable struggle rather than a massacre."

Wedge glanced among the others arrayed around his table. The members of his own party wore carefully neutral expressions. The six advisors Escalion had brought— men and women in uniforms similar to his—were more demonstrative, nodding as he made his points, turning eager and expectant eyes to Wedge.

"From what I've learned," Wedge said, "if I calculate things correctly, if every nation not under Cartann's direct control were to join us, we'd still have a united force about two-thirds the size of Cartann's."

Escalion nodded "Though even that number is optimistically misleading. Cartann's equipment is better than ours. For our fighter corps, we have fewer Blade-Thirty-twos than they do. Less than half our fighter fleet, in fact; we rely largely on older models."

"So, optimistically, we would, under the best of circumstances, have half their strength or less."

"Correct."

"I'll need a few minutes to think about this."

Escalion nodded and rose. "We will leave you this chamber and all the time you wish. Summon a servant when you have an answer for us. In the meantime, we will have food and drink sent."

"Thank you."

When the Yedagonians had withdrawn, Wedge said, "Pilots, Cheriss, Hallis, please give me a little space."

"Our proximity is interfering with his brain waves," Hobbie said as he stood. "We're jamming them."

"Something to be proud of," Janson said. "Anyone for a little sabacc?"

That left Wedge alone at the central table with Iella. She said, "Do you want to be alone to think?"

"What, send you away? I just got you."

She arched an eyebrow at him. "You make me sound like a marketplace purchase." But her voice sounded pleased.

"Never."

"I would have thought you'd have an answer ready for Escalion. Even before we reached here."

"I did. I was going to turn him down." Wedge sighed. "But then he threw a skifter into the deck. Flying with the Yedagon Confederacy is not the same thing as leading a union of nations against Cartann. One would be pointless. The other could actually accomplish some, or even all, of what I was sent here to do."

"How do you figure that? Wedge, you're no longer in the loop. Anything you do here constitutes rogue actions. Though I suppose that's appropriate for an ex-Rogue."

He smiled. "But that's where you're wrong. My duties and responsibilities and powers didn't remain in Cartann when we fled. I still have them here."

"I'm not sure I understand. Until Tomer Darpen is brought down—"

"He's not even relevant. It's obvious that the New Republic set this whole operation up under the control of the local Intelligence division, yes. And it hurts us that *Allegiance* is under his direct control. But, Iella, my orders don't even refer to Intelligence. I'm here to try to bring Adumar into the New Republic. I'm empowered to enter into negotiations and conduct treaties. I'm still the chief New Republic diplomat on this world—and I can choose to deal with this assembly of nations instead of Cartann."

"I hadn't considered it that way. So what's standing between you and making a decision?"

"One simple fact. Leading the non-Cartann forces is more than writing a treaty. It's deciding the fates of whole nations. Possibly of Adumar itself."

"Wedge, if you choose *not* to lead them, you're still deciding their fate."

"I—you're right."

"Get used to it. I usually am."

He grinned at her, a cocky grin that he knew other Corellians like Han Solo wore far more often than he. "We'll see about that." He stood. "Major Janson!"

Janson shot upright, military straight, then glared at Wedge. "I hope this is more important than my card game, young man."

"Inform Yedagon's *perator* that I have come to a decision."

"Yes, sir. Which is?"

"We're going to drop the heavy end of the hammer on Cartann."

Janson uttered a noise that was half cheer, half animal wail, and trotted to the door. He returned a moment later. "They're sending for Escalion."

"Good." Wedge looked among his pilots. "For me, this is technically a diplomatic matter and not a military one. I can't ask you to be part of it."

"You can't keep us out," Janson said. "We'll just overpower you. Two majors plus one colonel equals one general at least."

"I'm part of it, too," Iella said.

Wedge gave her a mock scowl. "You can overpower me?"

"I tickle."

"Maybe you can." Wedge stretched and yawned. "We'll begin strategic planning immediately. I'll need data on all available military resources—continuously updated if, as Escalion suggests, we'll be able to swing more nations over to our side. I need data and advisors on Cartann's forces and standard tactics. I want—"

"No," Tycho said.

Wedge stared at him. "What?"

"Go to bed, Wedge."

"Don't be ridiculous. We don't have a lot of time, and—"

"And you've had less sleep than any of us." Tycho approached to loom over Wedge where he sat. "Meaning that you'll do all your planning, then we'll hop into our fighters and roar off to meet the Cartann forces. And because you're exhausted, your reflexes are shot and your thinking processes crawl along like a dying Hutt, and some twenty-year-old twit will flame you down and be able to brag about it for the rest of his life. No, Wedge. Get some sleep."

"But who'll—"

"I will. I've plotted a few missions, you might remember. I also know how you think. No, you go get some sleep. You'll wake up fresh, you'll examine my plans, you'll fiddle with them to your satisfaction."

Janson and Hobbie flanked Tycho and stared down at Wedge with identical expressions of obstinacy.

"Mutiny," Wedge said.

Iella smiled at him. "I think it's time you learned how to do something."

"Which is what?"

"Delegate authority."

"You may be right." Wedge rose. It made him feel light-headed. His pilots were correct; if he did manage to force himself to endure several hours of planning and organizing, he'd be no good for anything else. "All right, mutineers, you win."

. . .

Eleven Coruscant hours later, freshly bathed and shaved, Wedge joined his party and the military leaders of the Yedagon Confederacy in their planning chamber. Like the meeting room where he'd met Escalion, this room was circular, but it was deep beneath the ground under Escalion's palace. The chamber was dominated by a table shaped as a broken ring; men and women could stand around its exterior and within the open space at its center. Its surface was dominated by flatscreen displays that glowed in the chamber's dim light.

Tycho waved him over to the portion of table surrounded by the New Republic representatives and several uniformed Yedagonians. "The nations of Thozzelling and Tetanne have come on board," Tycho said. "And a half-dozen smaller nations. Escalion was right—your name is like a bank full of credits here, especially after that four versus thirty fight."

Wedge smiled at Iella and got a smile in return. Then he turned his attention to the flatscreen on the table. It was a map showing an area reaching from the heart of Cartann to all of Yedagon. Military units of both sides were indicated with blinking colored dots. Wedge supposed that tapping on a dot would bring up information about it, as was the case with the lightboards on Blade-32s.

Tycho gestured at various units as he spoke. "Squadrons of Blades. *Scythe*-class bombers. *Meteor*-class Aerial Forts. *Cutting Lens*-class reconnaissance/intelligence craft. *Farumme*-class haulers configured as troop transports. The numbers are continuously updating on the main board as we get word of new units being added to our resources. Cartann's forces are similar to ours in composition—just superior in numbers and age.

"Here's Yedagon City." Tycho gestured at the grayish blob on the map indicating their current location. "If history is any judge, the forces of Cartann will be heading

here and to the capitals and other major cities of all 're-
bellious' nations. The *perator* of Cartann has demonstrated that he has a pretty limited agenda and consistent
deployment tactics. A screen of fighters to engage enemy
fighters, plus fighters acting as support for his bombers.
The fighter engagements are the ones that get all the attention, but it's the bomber usage that does the real damage. He starts by bombing military bases and any area
that has demonstrated high comm traffic within the most
recent observation period. Then he graduates to government buildings and the homes of higher-ranking nobles."

"What sort of bombs?"

"They're officially named Broadcaps, for the shape
of the cloud that results, but they're commonly called
Punch-and-Pops. They hit the ground and penetrate several meters—the idea being that they can get into underground chambers like this one—before detonating. A
single one can level several city blocks."

"Charming," Wedge said. "All right. What's your
plan?"

"The *perator* of Cartann likes noontime assaults.
They look very nice on the recordings, and a lot of his pilots enjoy diving down at their targets with the sun at
their backs. We can expect his attack on Yedagon City
perhaps as early as noon tomorrow . . . so we're not going to give him the opportunity. We'll be launching before dawn to be in Cartann airspace at sunrise."

Wedge nodded. Getting the hard-living, hard-drinking
Cartann pilots out of their bunks a mere handful of hours
after they reached them would provide the allied forces
with one more desperately needed advantage. "Go on."

"From there, our first tactic is to deny them their
strength by busting up their chain of command wherever
possible. The standard assault group of several fighter
squadrons and associated bombers and fortresses will
analyze the approach of Cartann forces. When they know
which portion of the formation is the Cartann target—

the 'center'—that portion will slow its approach and mill. The outer edges will swing out farther and increase speed, forming horns to either side of the Cartann formation and at a lower altitude, at distances that put our horns out of range of one another's weapons—but keep the Cartann forces within range of both sets of weapons. Since our firing plane is below the target plane, misses by missiles will not endanger our own forces—they'll just reach their programmed range limits and detonate themselves. Meanwhile, the Cartann forces will have to suffer an initial barrage in which we can concentrate fire and they have to diffuse theirs, and then will have to choose to maintain their original plan or break up to assault the diverse elements of our formation. Once they've committed themselves, we can choose whether to collapse our formation and pin them there, or send the horns—with their bombers—on to their primary objectives, the air bases and communications centers."

"Good," Wedge said. "Let me ask a few questions. On Adumari lightboards, a squadron tends to be a single signal until it's close enough to be perceived as individual fightercraft. How many Blades return the same-sized signal, at distance, as *Scythe*-class and *Meteor*-class vehicles?"

Tycho looked up at one of the uniformed officers standing by. "General ya Sethes?"

The officer, a gray-haired woman built like a champion wrestler, answered without hesitation. "Four for Scythes, six for Meteors. Unless the squadron is Blade-Twenty-eights or earlier, in which case five and eight."

"I want every bomber and aerial fortress transponder programmed to issue a false response," Wedge said. "When queried by a lightbounce signal, instead of responding with its true name and other information, it sends back that it's one Blade in a squadron. Three Scythes end up looking like one squadron, and two Meteors likewise, until they're close enough."

"So their projections on our composition are thrown

off just when it's time to mix it up," Tycho said. "I like that."

"That's not all. I want us to assemble a list of, oh, the thirty most prestigious pilots flying in our united force. I want the transponders of at least two Blades in each fighter squadron to be able to toggle between returning their correct data and the data for one of those pilots. Likewise, I want the real pilots on that list to be able to toggle to return the data for a novice pilot. Nobody's to switch to deceptive transponder data until the furball is under way, and only when they're not under weapons lock by an enemy."

General ya Sethes looked dubious. "If we wait until the fighters are all engaged, yes, then the deception will be harder to recognize. But what's the point?"

Wedge smiled at her. "The point is, within a single squadron's engagement, the pilots can tend to affect which of them is to be the focus of enemy assaults. Put someone who has good evasive skills up under the name of, say, Major Janson. The enemies will flock to him, possibly allowing the best shooters in his squadron an unanswered salvo or two. Then, if our ersatz Janson gets clear of weapons locks for a moment, he can take off his mask—switch his transponder back to his real identity—and confuse participants scanning for him. Any confusion we can sow in the enemy helps us, hurts them."

The general still looked unconvinced, but said, "If nothing else, this should be simple to program. I'll see to it."

"Thank you." Wedge turned back to the map. "Are Cartann's military responses predictable enough that we can map out where our forces will engage theirs?"

"Only if their squadron response drills are good indications." Tycho shrugged. "Hard to say, since those drills are non-weapon exercises and the Cartann flyers hate that. But my guess is, yes."

"So we send out one squadron an hour or two ahead

of each major formation. Pilots skilled at terrain-following flying. They fly beneath the altitude at which lightbounce sensors start to be active and set up in deep cover beneath the projected engagement zone. Because, until they break up to pursue enemies, Cartann squadrons tend to fly in pretty close formations—"

"So our advance units can fire their missiles up at their squadrons passing overhead," Janson said. "Perhaps taking out multiple fighters per missile in those first few seconds."

"Ooh," Hobbie said. "I volunteer. I want that. Let me do that. Please." Though his expression was, as usual, somber, he was practically hopping from foot to foot in his excitement.

Wedge and Tycho looked at one another. Wedge asked, "Have you ever seen behavior like this?"

Tycho shook his head. "Only when he really, really needs to run to the refresher. Hobbie, why?"

"Because I am *sick* of it," Hobbie said. "I'm sick to death of 'Hello, I'm so-and-so and I've killed this many enemies, and I challenge you, and we bow and go by the rules and say cute things to one another, and isn't it nice that we're all dead now?' Tycho, I want to *shoot* something. I want to blow something up. No apologies. No advance warning. Just lethal efficiency. Before frustration *kills* me."

"More words that he's strung together at once since I've known him," Tycho said. "All right, Hobbie. You'll be in charge of the advance squadron for lead group."

"I don't think he's entirely sane right now," Janson said. "I'd better stay with him."

"Good idea," Wedge said. "Anyway, Tycho, that's all the modifications I had to recommend for your plan. I do want to address the pilots, either directly or by recording, and lay down some rules. I want them flying New Republic-style. I see a pilot flying for glory instead of victory, I'll be happy to shoot him down myself."

"Done," said General ya Sethes.

Wedge caught Cheriss's eye. "Cheriss, will you be staying here?"

She shook her head. "I'm being flown in hours early, with a special ground unit. I could not bring myself to fire upon my city, or tell others where to drop the bombs . . . but I *can* help find your X-wings."

"I appreciate that. It might prove to be vital if Turr Phennir and his pilots are in their TIE Interceptors. Thanks." He turned to Hallis. "What about you? Staying here, I hope?"

"Are you crazy?" She frowned. "Let me rephrase that. Haven't you been paying attention? I'm a documentarian. They've granted me a place on one of the Meteors. I'll be recording all the way in, all the way out."

Wedge considered his responses, but knew he had no way to persuade her not to come. He could issue orders preventing her . . . but to do so would suggest, accurately, that he had no respect for her right to choose her own destiny. "Good luck," he said, and turned to Iella. "If you haven't already chosen something suicidal, I have a mission for you."

"Name it."

"I want you to go up to *Allegiance*, and beg, bribe, and bully your way aboard, and get a copy of our Tomer Darpen recording into their hands."

"Did that already."

"*What?*"

Heads raised all across the room at Wedge's shout. He waved people's attention away, then took Iella's arm and led her a few steps from the table. "How is that again?"

She smiled at him, her enjoyment at his discomposure very evident. "While you were sleeping. I asked Escalion for a spaceworthy Blade and a pilot. She flew me up to *Allegiance*."

"I wish you'd waited."

"For you to ask me to do exactly what I was going to do? What I was obliged by my duties as an Intelligence officer to do?"

"That's right." He grinned. "All right, so it's illogical. How did it go?"

"Strange," she said. "*Allegiance*'s officers, I found out later, were *not* happy with the no-communications order from Tomer. All we knew is that the ship wouldn't respond to our hails. So, very carefully and slowly, we flew up to her and into the main starfighter bay. There were a lot of soldiers there, a lot of blaster rifles there pointed at us . . . but things relaxed a lot when I identified myself, and I spoke with Captain Salaban. He's as frantic and resentful as a fighter pilot in a tractor beam with the orders he's under."

"What did you tell him?"

"Well, it was obvious that he intended to obey his orders no matter how hateful they were to him. Which is nothing more than what I expected. And even if I'd told him the whole story, it would have been my word—and a juicy bit of corroborating recorded evidence—against anything Tomer Darpen told him, just enough to cause Salaban distress but not enough to cause him to violate his orders, in my opinion. So I decided not to hang him on the hook of that dilemma. I told him about the war that was brewing, and how it came about—not including Tomer Darpen's role in it. I gave him a copy of the recording with a request that he forward it to General Cracken's office at the point the communications blackout was lifted. I also left a copy mislabeled as my will, and broadcast encrypted copies with a time-based decryption order to the R5 and R2 units of the X-wing squadron aboard."

"I would say you've done more than I could ask you to." He added, a growl to his voice, "Other than helpfully being out of harm's way when the shooting starts."

"I'm going to be in one of their reconnaissance craft,"

she said. "Doing unit coordination. Well away from the battlefront."

"Battlefronts tend not to have fixed lines, and missiles don't acknowledge what lines there are."

"That's the best you're going to get, Wedge. Don't push."

He sighed, exasperated. "Were you always this way?"

"No," she said. "I was pretty stubborn when I was younger."

"Just don't feel you have to stay close if things go bad," he said. "Our chances are still pretty low, even with all those new people and resources flooding in . . ." His voice trailed off as a new thought occurred to him.

"What is it?"

"I've commanded large forces before. The *Lusankya* has more combined firepower than the entire force I'll be leading today. But until now all the forces I've led have been assigned to me, routine unit assignments, with a healthy dose of volunteers. This is the first time that such a large group, so many recruits, have come in just on the strength of my name. It's disconcerting."

"Don't let it go to your head, Wedge. You won't be able to fit into your helmet."

"Thanks for the reassurance." He swung her back toward the planning table. "Back to work."

In the hours before dawn, Wedge stood on the ladder to his Blade's cockpit, a spotlight on him, a comlink on his collar to broadcast his words, and prepared to address the troops.

He'd never really understood the pre-mission pep talk—or, rather, had never shared the psychology of the pilots and soldiers who needed and expected one. He never flew a mission without becoming, at some point before the first laser was fired, completely committed to it; that was the only way to achieve the objective and maybe stay alive while doing it.

But since inheriting command of Rogue Squadron from Luke Skywalker a decade ago, he'd learned the hard fact that he often saved lives with the right words. He wondered if he had the right words with him now. He thumbed on the comlink and looked out over the vista before him—what seemed like an endless stretch of duracrete thick with fighter-craft, pilots, crewmen, mechanics. Most common were the dark red jumpsuits worn by Yedagon Confederacy pilots and workers; each person's was decorated by scarves, medals, piping, or other expressions of individuality. Jumpsuits of other colors, representing other nations, were in evidence. Wedge himself wore the garish orange of the New Republic starfighter pilot; Hallis had told the Yedagonians what to look for and they had obligingly equipped Red Flight with the familiar colors.

"People of Adumar," he said. "That's the phrase I have to use to address you, because it's not appropriate to refer to you by the nations of your birth. Today you're flying as pilots of your world, with the goal of keeping personal greed and ambition from ruining your world.

"Today, from this base and countless others, we're going to lift off and form the greatest air force your world has ever seen—except one. The forces of Cartann are greater. They're bigger. So to defeat them, we're going to have to be better. Here's how we're going to do that.

"Every pilot you line up in your weapon brackets is someone concerned with what he's going to get out of this conflict. How he's going to profit. Most plan to profit in the accumulation of honor. Honor bought with your blood.

"That pilot is thinking about himself. You're not going to do that. You're going to stay focused on your objective. Don't permit yourself to think about personal duels, about the accolades you're going to receive. Don't respond to challenges or personal remarks from the enemy; they don't deserve your answer. Don't worry about becoming heroes. The moment you committed yourself to defeating your enemy, at the possible cost of your own lives, you became heroes. That part is done. Now we move on to something more important.

"Focus on your enemy. How he moves. How he fires. What he must be thinking. Where his thoughts will take him. Shoot both at him and at where he's going. Fight now and a few moments in the future. That gives you the chance to kill him twice. That gives you twice as many guns as he has. And that's the only way you're going to win.

"If you let your thoughts stray from your enemy, focus them on what's waiting for you at home. Not the adulation. The wives, the husbands, the children, the parents. If we fail, they will be defenseless before the forces of Cartann. That should be enough to put your concentration back where it belongs . . . on the enemy.

"It's time to go. I salute you, Adumar." He paused, then said it again: "Adumar."

A moment later, the nearest fringe of people, including Tycho and Iella, took it up as a chant: "Adumar. Adumar. Adumar." It rolled across the assembled air armada, gaining in strength and volume.

Wedge let it go only for a few moments, only long enough for every one present to be caught up in it. Then he nodded to Tycho. Tycho thumbed his own comlink, and suddenly the air was split with the sound of a keening siren.

Like an insect mound suddenly disturbed by a giant intruder, the air base abruptly became a sea of running bodies as pilots returned to their fighters, mechanics scrambled to get last-second details in order, flight workers rushed to get late-arriving missiles loaded into aircraft.

Wedge stepped down to the duracrete. Iella came up

to him. "You understand," she said, "if you let yourself get hurt, it's going to go very badly for you. I'll make you regret it."

"I had that figured out," he said.

She waited as if hoping for him to say something more. The smile she gave him was an uncertain one. "That's Wedge. So honest he can't even reassure me."

He looked around to make sure no one was close enough to hear. "Here's some reassurance," he told her. "Two reasons why I'm not going to let anything happen to me. One: I'm the best there is. Two: I finally have someone to come back to."

She wrapped herself around him. "Don't forget that."

"I won't."

"I have to get to my station."

He kissed her, then watched her run—or perhaps flee—toward the large aircraft that was her assignment for the mission. It was built like a spoke-and-wheel space station whose every joining of spoke and wheel was a spherical sensor array.

He climbed back up to his cockpit. His mechanic, a middle-aged woman whose face was striped, tattoolike, with Blade-32 greases, was astride the fuselage, just behind the cockpit, dogging down the rear of the canopy with a hydrospanner. "How's it look, Grembae?" he asked.

"They gave you the best," she said. "And it's in as fine a shape as I can make it."

His helmet lay in the pilot's seat. He picked it up to put it on, then noticed the decorations upon it. Recently dried paint in gold on the dark red surface showed up as a succession of delta-shaped wedges, the decorative motif Wedge had added to most of the helmets he'd worn throughout his career. "Who did this?" he asked.

"My son," she said. "A mechanic on my team. Your lady said you'd like it."

"My lady." He put the helmet on, cinched it under his chin. "My lady." The words weren't new to him, but they were in a new combination, a configuration that had never meant anything to him before. He decided he liked them.

He levered himself into the pilot's chair. "She was right. Thanks, Grembae."

12

They rose from the Yedagon City air base, hundreds strong, fighters and bombers and fortresses and aircraft of all colors and description, and they were only one group of several involved in this all-out assault on Cartann and her satellite nations. One of the Blade units moving ahead of the group as a skirmish line was Running Crimson Flightknife, now being led by Wedge and Tycho.

This was a much faster flight than Wedge's departure from Cartann, and much more agreeable—it had just felt wrong to be in a vehicle he wasn't piloting. He watched moonlit forest tops and cultivated fields flash by beneath him. It was oddly peaceful, despite the fact that he was at the spearpoint position of hundreds of engines of war, for there was no comm chatter.

A few klicks from the Cartann border, the lightboard offered up a throbbing noise, indicating that he'd been hit by a lightbounce from ahead. Wedge nodded. That would be a border sensor installation. As the noise continued, Wedge got a fix on it with his lightboard. He looped away from the Running Crimson formation with Tycho tucked in beside him and headed straight for the source of the lightbounce signals.

The enemy sensor operators tried to save their installation: The lightbounce signals cut off. But the installation's coordinates were already locked into the Blade-32's computers. Wedge brought it up on his sensor board and designated those coordinates as the sole target. He armed his lasers, and as soon as the sensor board solidified the lasers' targeting brackets, he fired. He saw his lasers and Tycho's flash down into the forest below, and some hard target erupted into flaming explosion.

On the way back, they took a closer look. They'd hit a squarish bunker, perhaps fifteen meters on a side, and it was burning fiercely. Elaborate sensor gear on top was now char and slag. Satisfied, Wedge headed back to rejoin Running Crimson Flightknife.

All down the line, other members of the advance screen of Blades would be doing the same thing. They couldn't conceal their own approach to Cartann, but they could—if they hit enough sensor stations, and hit them early enough—conceal the size of the force approaching the enemy nation. The military forces of Cartann would have to go to an extra effort to get an idea of what was assaulting them.

Ahead, the sky was growing lighter. Wedge checked his chrono. The operation was still on schedule. And it was midday on the *Allegiance*; he supposed that the Star Destroyer's sensor crews would be having an interesting day of observation.

Minutes later, with the lightness in the east broadening and climbing, comm silence was finally broken. "Group One Leader, this is Eye Three." It was Iella's voice. "Electrocution Death Flightknife, at the extreme north edge of the group, reports an assault by a squad of Cartannese Blades. The furball's still continuing, but a unit of *Scythe*-class bombers tracked the enemy back to their base, a previously unknown one, and are pounding it flat. They say they caught another squadron on the ground."

Wedge looked northward. He could see distant, tiny flashes, and he wished luck to the members of Electrocution Death. "Thanks, Eye Three."

Minutes later, his lightboard lit up with signs of incoming squadrons—lots of them. They approached from north and south, from the major Cartannese cities in those directions.

Standard Cartannese tactics, had this just been a fighter raid, would have been to veer toward one or the other force, whichever seemed more prestigious, and engage it, with the hope of dispatching it before the other caught up . . . but Group One continued straight on its course, which led straight to the great city of Cartann. In minutes, those two Cartann units' lightboards would detect Groups Five and Twelve headed straight for their respective cities, and would be torn between the need to pursue Group One and to defend their cities. Wedge grinned. Cartannese society seemed to be tooled to keeping its people from having to address difficult questions. He planned to present them with quite a few more before this day was done.

"Eye Three to Red Leader. Main force detected from Cartann City air bases. Forming up and heading this way. Estimated strength twenty squadrons and growing."

"Thanks, Eye." That meant the enemy strength in fighters was already equal to Wedge's. "How's our pursuit?"

"Still pursuing. Groups Five and Twelve should just now be reaching their respective cities' lightbounce range."

"Acknowledged. Red Leader out."

The enemy would appear on the lightboard, Wedge knew, as a ragged line of tiny bright blips, each representing an enemy formation. As they neared, the blips would grow, gradually breaking down into clouds of dots representing individual fighters. And that's exactly how it happened, moments later. That's all Wedge would see until they were much closer; the enemy would be flying at them out of the rising sun, which was already peeking above the horizon.

Wedge lowered the goggles on his helmet. Yes, it was a disadvantage to fly into the sunlight. But it was a momentary disadvantage; as soon as the two forces broke up into individual dogfights, everybody would be at equal disadvantage. And the Cartann pilots' disadvantage, being too quickly roused after too short a night of sleep, would linger.

When the enemy force was about sixty seconds from distant firing range, when enemy squadrons were beginning to diffuse into individual enemy fighters, Wedge switched his comm board over to group frequency. "Red Leader to Group. Forward screen, slow to one-third to allow main body to catch up. North Horn, South Horn, begin your move into position. All other flightknives, slow to one-half standard cruise velocity and maintain formation."

He heard acknowledgments from the two horn formation leaders. On his lightboard, he saw the group's formation change shape. The leading edge, a thin line of fighters, dropped back until it was absorbed into the leading edge of the main body, an inverted triangle. The two leading corners of the triangle stretched forward, suggesting a pair of horns. Ahead, the roughly oval formation of Cartannese fliers continued toward them, not yet adjusting for the appearance of the horns, which would be to either side of them within seconds.

By squinting, and with polarization increased as high as it would go on his goggles, he could see traces of the oncoming force, little black dots at the heads of needle-thin white contrails.

Then specks of fire rose with blinding speed from the

forest. As they reached the heart of the Cartann force, they expanded out into ball-shaped clouds of fire.

Wedge jolted. That was Hobbie and Janson's force, Blastpike Flightknife, sent on ahead to do just this thing—and Wedge, nearly overwhelmed by other planning details, had all but forgotten about them. He saw the Cartann force begin to mill, with whole squadrons spiraling down toward the source of the missiles . . . missiles that kept rising into the group.

Wedge said, "North Horn, South Horn, that's your cue. Close and fire. Main group, advance. As you close, break by flightknives and fire at will." He accelerated back to cruise speed as, ahead, the first laser and missile crossfire by the two horn formations began.

He switched his targeting system back on and it immediately began howling at him, a wavering cry as distant targets flashed into and out of his brackets. He switched to missiles and fired every time the musical tone suggested a clean lock. Ahead, the Cartann force looked like the intersection of four sets of target practice, but lasers and missiles were now pouring back out of the cloud of enemy fighters. Wedge was rocked when a Blade to his port, Running Crimson-3, detonated; the blast buffeted Wedge and drove him meters to starboard before he recovered.

Then the two forces met, blurred into one wide-ranging engagement, clear distinctions no longer possible between them.

Wedge caught sight of an incoming Blade-32, on what looked like a collision course with him. He switched to lasers, fired, then looped to port, diving to get out of the madman's flight path. His sensor board howled that he was in an enemy's targeting brackets; he continued the dive, flashing between two enemy Blades, and the howl cut off. He began to pull up. Behind him, the sensors showed one of the two Blades he'd passed between now stitched with laser fire, its port side opened by a blast; the Blade was shaking violently as air hammered its way into the now-unaerodynamic vehicle.

His wingman was no longer beside him. "Tych?"

"Busy, boss."

Wedge said "Tycho" into the microphone of his targeting board. One blip on the lightboard began to blink. It was half a kilometer above him, directly between two enemy Blades. Wedge climbed.

He could pick out Tycho and the man's enemies, even against the dark sky, by the flashes of light between them. Tycho was in pursuit of a Blade, being pursued by another, and was sending laser fire in both directions, meanwhile slewing about in evasive action.

Wedge rose, caught the lead Blade in his targeting brackets, ignored it. He let his brackets flash back across Tycho and to the pursuit Blade. He opened fire, his first barrage of lasers missing the vehicle, his second chewing through its stern fuselage.

The tough Blade-32 did not explode, but its stern dropped away. The vehicle rolled, out of control. Wedge saw the canopy tear free and the pilot punch out a moment later. Wedge grinned; he must also have wiped out the repulsorlift system, else that pilot could have brought the Blade down to a safe landing.

No longer forced to divide his concentration, Tycho poured laser fire into the Blade ahead of him. Though the Blade returned fire, singeing the nose of Tycho's craft, Tycho's attacks relentlessly chewed away at its rear fuselage, riddling it with char and holes.

The Blade didn't look badly hurt, but abruptly it rose straight skyward, then heeled over in what looked like an uncontrolled dive. The pilot had to have been hit, a typically surgical Tycho kill.

Wedge continued his climb. At the upper altitude indicated for the engagement, he pulled back on the stick and rolled over to continue toward Cartann, though he was belly to sky, giving him a good look at the fight as it continued. Tycho pulled alongside.

It wasn't bad, Wedge decided. The united Adumari force was continuing to move toward Cartann, and Cartann's defenders were forced to keep with them. In minutes, if this continued, they'd be over the city itself. "Red Leader to Eye Three, report if you can."

"Eye Three to Red Leader. Red Three and Red Four report in unhurt, though their squadron took heavy losses. The pursuit forces have broken off and are returning to their cities to deal with Groups Five and Twelve. The Scythes from North Horn and South Horn have broken away from the horn formations and are now over Cartann, heading for the air bases. We have reports of ground-based defensive batteries firing."

Wedge looked toward the city. Yes, yellow-white streaks of laser light, four to a group, were flashing into the sky. Tiny as they seemed at this distance, each column of light would have to be half the diameter of a Blade or more.

"Sensors show another dozen or so squads rising from the air bases and Cartann proper," Iella continued.

"Any of Group One's units not yet engaged?"

"The six Meteors and their screens."

Wedge breathed a sigh of thanks that he'd assigned most squadrons and major aircraft numerical references in addition to their normal names—it was a choice that would allow him to address them even when he couldn't recall their normal designations. He switched to group frequency. "Meteors One and Two and screen flightknives, join the Scythes from North Horn. Meteors Three and Four and screen flightknives, join the Scythes from South Horn. Meteors Five and Six and screens, I want you to plow right into the middle of this furball. Give the enemy something new to think about." He switched back to command frequency. "Thanks, Eye Three." He pulled back on the stick and he and Tycho dove into the main engagement again.

He'd just taken a long-distance shot at a pair of Blades when a vehicle, unbelievably fast, cut across his flight path, leaving a blurry afterimage on his vision. It was a TIE Interceptor, flying an impossible-to-predict course full of sudden bends and course changes.

His lasers pointed at empty forest floor, he opened fire again. And as another three TIE Interceptors crossed his path, he had the pleasure of seeing his sustained laser fire clip the solar wing array of one of them. The shot didn't destroy the TIE, but he did see it roll out of formation and have to struggle to get back in position, and the spot where he'd grazed it was black with char. He turned in the TIE Interceptors' wake and was rapidly outdistanced.

"Good shot, Lead."

"Not good enough, Two. We've got no chance against Interceptors in these."

"Who are you now, Lead?"

Wedge tapped the centerpoint of his lightboard. The data sent by his transponder came up; it was his alternate identity, a Yedagon pilot with no kills to his name. "I'm not-Wedge."

"Good. Recommend you stay that way until and unless we get back to our snubfighters."

"I'll take it under consideration."

He could track the TIEs on the lightboard without consulting transponder data. They were the only craft in this engagement that moved at such high speed. He saw them streak to the edge of the engagement zone, reverse, then begin to shoot back through the thickest portion of the zone. All along the line of their passage, the blips representing Blades on the lightboard began blinking or vanished altogether. All along their flight paths, as Wedge checked visually, burning fighters began their final descents to the forest floor.

Two dark red Blades rose up to join Wedge and

Tycho. "Red Three and Four reporting in," Janson said, his voice cheery.

"Good timing," Wedge said. "Come about with me to one-eighty degrees." He began a hard loop around. "We're putting ourselves in the way of trouble."

On his lightboard, the four streaks representing the TIEs reached the edge of the engagement zone and looped around once more for another pass. Wedge calculated their likely path, just an estimate, and climbed higher to be in that path. "Here's the rules. This is not a one-on-one, not a duel. When the TIEs come in range, everyone hit the lead TIE. If you can, as soon as they flash past, switch to rear lasers and target the rear TIE. We'll see how much damage we can do them."

"Good." That was Hobbie's voice, more intent than usual. "Damage."

"Three, is Four all right?"

"He's fine, chief. Still deliriously happy from his missile barrage, I think."

The path of the oncoming TIEs changed slightly, continuing from what must have been an evasive move. Wedge sent his Blade into a hard vector to starboard. Now there was no way to get in the path of TIEs, but they could still fire upon them—

And there they were, two wing pairs streaking in from port. Wedge opened fire with his lasers, concentrating on the lead TIE, and was gratified to see three other pairs of lasers joining his.

The Interceptor exploded as if hit by a missile, leaving only an orange-and-yellow fireball and a spray of shrapnel behind. Wedge's Blade shook as he crossed in the wake of the TIEs and was hit by the explosion shock wave.

But because of their changed flight plan they hadn't concluded the exchange with their rear lasers pointed toward the TIEs. Wedge saw the three remaining enemy fighters split off, two one direction and one another, and begin to loop around at impossible speeds toward his Blades. "Whoops," Wedge said. "Red Flight, scatter." He rose and vectored to starboard, toward what looked like an incoming wing pair of friendly Blades.

A TIE Interceptor rose in his wake. He fired upon it, but the nimbler craft juked and jinked far too quickly for him to get a fix on it. It responded with lasers that hammered away at his rear fuselage; he felt his Blade shudder and text suddenly started scrawling across his diagnostics board.

"Red One, come to one-six-five." That was Iella's voice. He complied, as hard a turn as he could manage, the TIE adhering to his tail as if glued there.

As Wedge completed his maneuver, he found himself heading almost due west and into the path of something huge.

Shaped like a single curved wing, with a dozen laser cupolas atop the wing and a dozen below, the *Meteor*-class Aerial Fort was the largest flying vehicle the Adumari made, and among the most punishing. Each cupola held paired lasers the equal of the ones on the Blades and could turn 360 degrees around and depress to cover an entire hemisphere.

As Wedge turned into the craft's path, a half dozen of its gunners opened up on him—or so it looked, for their laser fire flashed all around him, above and below.

The TIE on his tail broke off with an almost ninety-degree turn and flashed out to the side faster than the *Meteor*'s gunners could turn their weapons. In a second he was out of sight.

"Thanks—" Wedge tapped the lightboard—"*Meteor* Six. Much appreciated."

"Our pleasure, Red Leader."

The Cartann Blades were not yet approaching the *Meteor*. Wedge saw some forming up into half squads, presumably for strafing runs at the enormous aircraft, but they weren't ready yet. He took the opportunity to catch up on his breathing. He also checked visually for the other members of his flight, couldn't spot them immediately. Into the lightboard microphone, he said, "Red Flight."

Three blips lit up.

Three.

He tapped each one in turn. Red Leader. Red Four. Red Three.

"Red Two, come in. Tycho, where are you?"

Janson's voice came back, strained. "I think he's gone, Lead. I saw him hammered by a TIE's laser fire, really bad. He banked away from me, not maneuvering well, and then a Blade's missile took him."

"Four to Red Flight, negative, negative. I was just queried by a Yedagon Blade-28, Sandstorm Six, who's following him down. Tycho punched out. No serious damage."

Wedge nearly slumped. Fear for Tycho had tightened every muscle in his body like they were an instrument's strings being tuned. "Red Leader to Eye Three."

"Eye Three."

"Please track Sandstorm Six. He's following Red Two down; Two is extravehicular. Send whatever you can to pick him up. We want him back in the air and with us, whatever it takes."

"Understood. And we have good news on another front. Cheriss with Holdout reports that her group has found your X-wings."

"That was fast."

"She said it was simple. They picked up your astromech's broadcasts."

"Tell her group to stand by. That just doesn't make any sense." The first thing an enemy would have done would be to disable the astromechs with restraining bolts and then go to work cracking the security measures limiting cockpit access only to authorized personnel. The astromechs would never be allowed to continue transmitting.

No, wait—that was the first thing an Imperial enemy would have done. It was the people of Cartann who'd seized the X-wings.

He tried to think like his enemy, and the answer was there almost immediately.

The *perator* ruled Cartann, not some diplomatic council. He could hand the X-wings over to the military, certainly, but as an ex-pilot himself—and an autocratic ruler—he might well have decided to keep them for himself.

But he didn't have time to investigate them. He was planning a war against those arrayed against Cartann. So he'd put them somewhere secure and worry about them when the war was done, or at least offered him some recreation time. He might not even be aware of the astromechs' capacity for self-motivation and action.

He switched to Red Flight frequency. "Red Leader to Gate, do you read?"

His communications board's text screen lit up with words. I READ YOU.

"Report your situation, please."

I AM IN A HANGAR SUITED FOR TWO OR MORE SQUADRONS OF STARFIGHTERS. RED FLIGHT'S X-WINGS AND FOUR BLADES, VARIOUS TYPES, ARE HERE. THE OTHER SNUBFIGHTERS' ASTROMECHS ARE HERE. WE ARE GUARDED BY SIX GUARDS WITH BLASTER RIFLES. THEY ARE TALKING, AND LISTENING TO DISTANT EXPLOSIONS AND THE SOUNDS OF LASER BATTERIES. WE HAVE NOT BEEN INTERFERED WITH AND THE X-WINGS HAVE NOT BEEN OPENED. WE AND THE X-WINGS HAVE SUFFERED ONLY COSMETIC DAMAGE.

"Cosmetic damage?"

THEY PUT STRAPS ON THE X-WINGS TO WINCH US OFF THE BALCONY AND TAKE US TO THE HANGAR. THE STRAPS RUBBED PAINT OFF ON BOTH THE SNUBFIGHTERS AND US.

"Stand by, Gate. We'll get someone to you soon."

The Cartann half squadrons preparing their runs on the Meteor banked and headed toward the gigantic aircraft. Wedge vectored to be away from the Meteor when it happened—not that the enemy odds worried him, but so that the Meteor's gunners would not have to worry about hitting him.

"Eye Three, when Red Two is picked up, assign the rescue craft to Red Flight. Red Flight, as soon as Tycho rejoins us, we're heading into Cartann to pick up our snubfighters."

He heard a wild, undisciplined cheer that had to be Janson's. Then Iella's voice came back: "Red Leader, if you head out in advance of the group, you'll be flying into antiaircraft laser barrages. They don't have to cut back on those until their own forces drift out over the city."

"Understood, Eye Three, but that's the plan. Red Leader out."

Wedge switched frequencies to that used by the insertion team in charge of finding the X-wings. "Red Leader to Holdout."

The response was immediate, but hard to hear; the voice was Cheriss's, and she was whispering. "Holdout to Red Leader."

"By any chance, did you end up with one of the New Republic datapads from our quarters?"

"No, Red Leader. All I have is standard Adumari gear."

"Including a flatscreen?"

"Yes."

Wedge pondered that. Gate could be told to transmit to a flatscreen, but anything he broadcast to Cheriss could be picked up by other flatscreens in the area. Unless . . .

"Can you adjust the frequency it receives on?"

"Yes, of course."

"Good. Set it to the most unusual or ill-used frequency you can think of and tell me what it is. Then, in a few minutes, your team is going to receive some very helpful visual images from within your target area."

"Understood." A moment later, she responded with a numeric sequence corresponding to one of the standard flatscreen reception frequencies.

"Acknowledged. Red Leader out." He sat back. He'd have to get Iella, who knew more than anyone else on all Adumar about translating between New Republic and Adumari systems, to get in communication with Gate to instruct the R5 unit in interfacing with the Adumar flatscreens. Then Gate and the other astromechs in the X-wings' hangar could broadcast 360-degree views of the hangar interior, with the holocam data reinterpreted to two dimensions and translated to the format understood by the flatcams.

It would be another desperately needed edge for his people. If only they would survive long enough to employ it.

In five minutes, the aerial situation had changed, though not in unexpected ways.

Cartann's fleet of Meteors and most of her Scythes had been caught on the ground and largely destroyed— the larger craft, requiring numerous crewmen, were not in a position to lift off by the time the united Adumari craft roared across the sky above them. Even at this distance, Wedge could see the columns of flame that marked where Cartann Bladedrome and Giltella Air Base had been. The united Adumari force's Meteors were doing substantial damage in the air, their lasers actually optimized to shoot down incoming missiles and used only when the opportunity arose to fire upon enemy fighters.

But that was almost the only good news. As the leading edge of the engagement zone began to drift over the western edges of Cartann, attrition was beginning to swing the tide of battle in Cartann's favor. Despite the fact that Wedge's tactics seemed to be keeping the united Adumari force focused, despite the fact that Adumari pilots and gunners were outfighting their enemies, the greatly superior numbers of Cartann defenders were taking their toll. Squadrons and partial squadrons were still lifting off from the city, doubtless composed of retired pilots and the aircraft they personally owned, and the Adumari force was growing low on fuel, owing to the hundreds of kilometers they'd had to cross before firing their first shots. Too, the three remaining TIE Interceptors were racking up a gruesome kill score, and had adjusted their strategy to head off the sort of mass-fire tactics Red Flight had employed against them. Any formation moving against them caused them to flash off at a new and unpredictable angle, making the TIEs impossible for the Blades to target and hit. It wouldn't be too much longer before the attrition from the TIEs made the Adumari force too weak to have any chance at victory.

A two-seater Blade-30, the canopy over its rear gunnery position shattered and its fuselage patched from numerous previous military engagements, rose to join Red Flight. The gunner wore New Republic orange and gestured at Wedge, a thumbs-up.

"Welcoming Blastpike Ten to Red Flight," Wedge said. "Pilot, be ready to fly low and evasive. We're entering Cartann."

"Understood, Red Flight."

The four Blades broke away from the engagement zone and headed east over Cartann City . . . and the sky lit up like a celebration for them, as countless ground laser batteries unloaded their energy into the sky. Wedge and his pilots dove almost to rooftop level to give the enemy gunners less time to spot and track them. "Red Leader to Holdout."

"Holdout here."

"We're inbound." A bank of lasers cut in just to starboard of Wedge's Blade. He felt heat from the flash of light, then his Blade rocked as the minor shock wave from expansion of superheated air hit him. The shock wave nearly slid him into Blastpike Ten, flying to his port; he corrected hastily.

"I'll transmit your destination." A moment later, a map of a portion of central Cartann City appeared on Wedge's main display. He gave it a quick look. Their destination, marked by a blinking X, was only a block from the *perator*'s palace. He whistled.

Before he could comment, Cheriss continued, "The area is *very* heavily defended. You can see why. And we need you to do something. To arrive at a particular time . . . and shoot something."

"Happy to oblige, Holdout." Red Flight flashed over a street; below, he could see a standard repulsorlift transport, this one with a small laser battery permanently mounted in the bed. The operator pointed up at him but had no time to fire before Red Flight was safely over the rooftop. Wedge glanced at his main board; the map graphic now included a countdown.

The permanent and mobile laser batteries were becoming more numerous, and were better-advised of Red Flight's course. Twice Wedge reacted to the body language of people on balconies, sending Red Flight into a sudden veer in a new direction, barely eluding a laser emplacement's sudden fire from street level. He sent Red Flight on a more unpredictable and dangerous course, dipping down to street level and flying just above the mostly empty avenues, risking the cables but making it that much harder for laser batteries to get word of their path.

Only once were they threatened by fighters. A pair of older Blade-28s, classic machines lovingly maintained by their owners, dropped down behind Red Flight and opened up with lasers. Hobbie and Janson destroyed them with sustained rear laser fire. The ruins of their

Blade-28s, burning, arced down to crash into the streets. They slid to smash into building fronts. "Old men," Janson reported, a catch in his voice. "Old men wearing big smiles."

As they reached the royal and governmental quadrant of Cartann City, the defenses become more capable and more numerous. Laser batteries arose from pods within building tops and could swivel to target enemies from the skies to the streets below. Reluctantly, Wedge rose to rooftop level again so as to see the pop-up batteries before they could target him. Red Flight fired upon and were fired upon by twenty of the installations before he lost count, and Wedge's Blade, though not even grazed, was so badly rocked by shock waves from laser blasts that he could hear mechanisms shattering within the craft.

Then it was before him, the gray, innocuous building beyond which was the *perator*'s palace. Laser batteries atop the palace tried to target him, but on this final portion of the run Wedge stayed down at street level, allowing the target building to shield him. Ahead, he saw hangar-style doors grinding open on the gray building, saw flashes of laser fire as men and women in dark, innocuous garments were fired upon by defenders within it.

A pair of laser batteries rose with breathtaking speed from within the gray building, turned to target Red Flight. All four Blades fired, three at the battery to port, Hobbie at the battery to starboard. The port battery exploded in a shower of sparks and fire. The starboard battery, though chewed and blackened by Hobbie's lasers, continued to sweep around and orient toward them; Hobbie launched a missile instead and the installation detonated, leaving behind only rubble and smoke.

Now they only had small-arms fire to contend with; shooters atop the gray building and clustered on balconies all around poured blaster fire into the four Blades.

The impacts rang like off-key musical notes; Wedge felt as though a brigade of mechanics were hammering on his hull with hydrospanners, but the armored fuselage held up against the barrage. Still, there was an ominous new signal on the lightboard, a swarm of fighters and a pair of larger vehicles following them.

He descended on repulsorlifts to the duracrete just outside the hangar doors, intending to whirl around and present his missiles to their pursuers, but his comm unit kicked in with Cheriss's voice. "Holdout to Red Flight, please come into the hangar."

"We have incoming—"

"They're ours. We need you in here."

Wedge glided forward. As he crossed into the comparative darkness of the hangar, his goggles depolarized and he could see the building's contents.

It was a spacious hangar, the duracrete floor meticulously clean, completely absent of the sort of lubricant spills he associated with a hangar that saw real use. He would have rated it as being spacious enough for two and a half to three squadrons of Blades, but there were only eight vehicles present: the four X-wings clustered against the back wall, toward the center, three Blade-32s lined up for quick departure to the left, and a brilliant gold Blade-28 all alone to the right.

The hangar's living occupants included at least a dozen men and women in unmemorable dark clothing. There were dead occupants, too, six guards in the livery of the *perator*'s palace, lying motionless on the duracrete. The members of the Holdout invasion force clustered near the hangar doors, returning blaster fire against the balcony snipers across the avenue.

Cheriss stood near the fabulous gold Blade-28. She held a comlink in one hand and a blaster pistol in the other. "We need you to hit that with missiles before you go." She pointed with the pistol to a bunkerlike cube of duracrete in the right rear of the hangar, then fired on it to illuminate it better. Her blaster shot did no perceptible harm to the hardened metal door at the front of the bunker.

"Will do," Wedge said. He gained a little altitude, putting his Blade halfway between floor and ceiling, and said, "Take cover." He waited until Cheriss ran to what he estimated to be a safe distance, then targeted the bunker and let fly with a missile.

The shock wave rocked his Blade-32, but when the smoke cleared, the bunker was merely singed.

"That's really reinforced, Cheriss." Wedge armed both missile ports and carefully targeted the front of the metal door. "What's behind it?"

"A tunnel . . . we think."

He glided backward on his repulsorlifts until he was nearly at the exit once more, and incoming sniper fire hammered away at his rear fuselage. Red Three, Red Four, and Blastpike Ten set down on the far side of the hangar, near Cheriss.

Wedge fired again. The shock wave actually pushed him halfway out into daylight. But when the smoke cleared, the metal door was gone and the bunker's ceiling was blown out. Wedge saw the roof lying atop one of the Cartann Blade-32s, which was now crushed.

Wedge's sensors showed that pursuit flight arriving. He turned around to see them: A half-dozen Blades in Yedagon red, most of them thickly decorated with burn marks, several of them trailing smoke, came across the near rooftops and set down on the duracrete outside, spinning on their repulsors to land with their missiles faced outward.

"Gate, begin power-on sequence and run through the portions of the start-up checklist you can handle. Instruct the other astromechs to do likewise." He waited for the astromech's confirmation, then shut down most power systems to his Blade-32. He raised his canopy manually and levered himself out to drop to the duracrete. The other members of Red Flight hurried to join him, but Cheriss reached him first. "What is all this?" he asked, and gestured at the destroyed bunker.

"When Gate broadcast the image of the inside of this hangar to us, we saw *that*." She pointed to the gold Blade-28. "There's only one Blade like it in existence. The Golden Yoke, *Perator* Pekaelic's own Blade, in which he won his greatest military victories. If it's here, this is the *perator*'s personal hangar . . . and you can be sure the *perator* is not going to be crossing the street and waving traffic to stop whenever he wishes to visit his favorite fighter."

"Meaning that tunnel has to be a direct access . . ."

"To the palace itself. If we act fast enough, perhaps they won't be able to array defenses against us like they have on the surface."

Outside, a *farumme*-class transport in Halbegardian blue settled down to the duracrete. Its front portions were afire. Side hatches opened and ground troops wearing the uniforms of Halbegardian elites poured out, streaming into the hangar in spite of the small-arms fire from the distant balconies. Ricochets flashed through the hangar sounding like bad musical notes when they hit metal, like meat sizzling when they hit duracrete.

"Good luck," Wedge said. There wasn't time for more. He hurried to his X-wing and its canopy rose for him.

It took moments to strap on the flak vest, systems controls, helmet and gloves, a ritual he could undertake in his sleep . . . and then he was behind the controls of his X-wing once more. "No time for full prep," he said. "Be prepared to go unless you spot a critical failure. Red Leader has four lit and looking optimal."

"Red Two. Four on-line, ready to fly."

"Red Three. Anxious to show 'em what we can do."

"Red Four. Four lit and in the green."

Wedge's sensor board howled, announcing an enemy target lock. He could see two black Blade-32s just coming over the horizon of buildings ahead of him. "Launch, S-foils to attack position, fire at will!" He rose on his repulsorlift, too fast and jerky, and saw incoming laser fire flash beneath him to strike the hangar wall. Flame erupted behind him. He couldn't tell whether Cheriss or any of the troops there had gotten clear, and there was no time to wait and find out.

He kicked the X-wing forward, firing as his strike foils locked in attack formation and his targeting brackets flickered from yellow to green. He saw the red pulses of his quad-linked weapons flash toward the incoming Blades, hammering through the bow of one of them, chewing mercilessly through its contents. That Blade banked to starboard and disappeared once more behind the line of buildings; even at this distance Wedge heard a tremendous impact, saw the fireball erupt from the crash site.

He was first out of the hangar, with none of the other members of his flight firing—they were too close in behind him. The lasers of the surviving incoming Blade hit his front shields. Reduced to negligible power, the laser strike played across the fuselage just in front of his canopy, doing nothing more than burning away at paint. He replied with another linked laser blast, a miss as the incoming pilot veered . . . then a laser shot from behind him caught the Blade-32, shredding the port wing. Wedge saw the pilot punch out. The Blade seemed to aim straight in toward the hangar, a ballistic course, and flashed by over Wedge's head, over the hangar roof, straight toward the *perator*'s palace. In his rear viewport, Wedge saw the bank of palace guns swing toward the out-of-control vehicle and burn it from the sky.

Wedge added power to acceleration. "Good shooting, Red Three. Now let's see what we can show General Phennir."

After so much work with the Blades, flying the X-wing again was more than mere improvement—it was a delight. He sent it up in an ascent that no Adumari vehicle could match, jinking and juking to give the laser battery gunners fits, and did a roll just for the sheer joy of it. This wasn't just flying; it was dancing in the air.

"Red Two, this is Three. Am I crazy, or is the general doing what he tells us never to do?"

"Three, Two. Yes you are, and yes he is. Pay no attention."

"Understood."

Wedge grinned and set his course due west.

In the time it had taken Red Flight to retrieve its X-wings, the engagement zone had drifted over the western portions of Cartann City. There, the laser batteries were silent, but they were the only thing that was. The sky was rocked from second to second by missile detonations, the ripping noise of Blades crossing the sky at full speed, the deadly scream of doomed fighters making their final, uncontrolled descents.

Red Flight came at the engagement zone from a higher altitude, the sun at their backs, and Wedge's sensors were quick to spot the three remaining TIE Interceptors, now making another lethal run through the thickest part of the zone. He plotted their likely return course and transmitted a simple intercept course to his pilots. "Between here and there," he said, "shoot anything in Cartann colors."

His X-wing flashed through the engagement zone. He fired when his brackets went live around an enemy, went evasive when his sensor board told him an enemy was seeking him with a target lock. Seconds later, he could visually spot the TIEs, approaching and heading across his path. He got the green of a laser lock on his targeting brackets and opened fire.

The three TIEs reacted almost instantly. The solo

pilot returned fire while going evasive in a corkscrew ma-neuver, a dazzling demonstration of evasive flying. The leader of the remaining wing turned straight toward Red Flight, a head-to-head that lasted fractions of a second; it fired, green lasers trying to find a target among the mem-bers of Red Flight, and then had flashed by and was be-hind them in an instant.

The third Interceptor, Wedge's target, detonated in a brilliant flash. He saw Tycho fly through the debris cloud. "Two, you all right?"

"Unhurt."

"I'm not." That was Hobbie's voice. "Took a couple of shots from the head-to-head. Power down to fifty-eight percent. Starboard lasers gone."

On the sensor board, the two Interceptors had joined up and were looping around to come in behind the X-wings.

"Four, full speed ahead, whatever you can manage," Wedge said. "Three, stay with him. Two, you and I play crippled." He reduced speed and began slewing back and forth in a manner that suggested damaged air surfaces and malfunctioning controls. "Gate, can you give me some smoke, sparks, anything to suggest I'm hit?"

I WILL APPLY A LASER TORCH TO THE SURFACE OF THE REAR HULL. THE PAINT WILL IGNITE AND CAUSE SMOKE. THE DAMAGE WILL BE COSMETIC ONLY.

"Do it." This was a gamble, drawing the Intercep-tors to him and Tycho, but if the enemy pursued Hobbie instead, they were more than likely to shoot down the damaged X-wing.

The enemy took the bait. The two Interceptors stayed together and arced to follow Wedge and Tycho.

Wedge switched to proton torpedoes and reduced forward speed, hard, a gambit normally used to force a novice or inattentive pursuer to overshoot. It didn't; the TIE pilot on his tail was too experienced, and fired off a laser salvo that hammered at the tail of Wedge's X-wing.

But Tycho shot on ahead, his pursuer staying tight behind him, and that pursuer crossed, in a smooth and predictable arc, into Wedge's brackets. The brackets flickered to red and he fired.

The Interceptor in his sights became a sky full of smoke and debris. Wedge headed straight into the destruction cloud. As soon as it surrounded him, he banked down and to port, hoping the Interceptor would lose him for a critical second or two.

It did; Wedge saw it shoot through the cloud, waver for a second, and then loop around in pursuit of him.

Then, as Tycho, at the end of his own loop, appeared in Wedge's forward viewport, the TIE pilot stood the Interceptor on its tail and rose skyward at a rate no vehicle on Adumari could match.

Wedge rose in its wake and fired after it, one laser barrage . . . but his targeting computer couldn't get a lock on the fast-moving, extraordinarily maneuverable Interceptor. "Phennir?" he asked.

There was no reply from the Interceptor, but Tycho said, "I think so. And I'll give you odds that he's about to tell his commanding officer that things aren't going so well down here, and it's time to bring in the rest of the Imperial fleet."

"If he is, you'd better pray that I've accomplished one thing with diplomacy while I've been here." He turned back toward the heart of the engagement zone. "Form up on me. We're going to give the pilots of Cartann what they've been asking for for so long."

The loss of the Interceptors did have an effect on the forces of Cartann. They flew against the united Adumari forces with increasing desperation and diminishing confidence. As their flying became more conservative, the Adumari forces' focus began to take a greater and greater toll on them.

And then there were the X-wings, roaring among the Blades at speeds none of them could match, dancing in and out of engagements almost effortlessly, sending enemy pilot after pilot down in flames, doing exactly what the Interceptors had been doing to Cartann's enemies moments before. Even Hobbie's crippled snubfighter could match a Blade's speed, and was superior to it in defenses, maneuverability, and firepower; Janson and Hobbie acted as a two-fighter screen for the surviving Meteor as the giant wing-shaped craft picked off Cartann's fliers with its long-distance lasers.

Wedge set his course for a half squadron of Blades now forming up at high altitude; doubtless they meant to dive into a strafing run on fighters at lower altitudes. But as soon as he had his nose pointed up toward them, one of his targets spoke up: "Hold your fire. Skull-Biters surrender."

Wedge rose toward them, his finger still on the trigger. "Say that again."

"Skull-Biters Flightknife surrenders to Red Flight. Our weapons are powered down."

Another voice cut in: "Lords of Dismay Flightknife, two reporting, surrenders to General Wedge Antilles."

Wedge switched hastily to command frequency. "Eye Three, what's going on?"

"Not sure, Red Leader. A lot of traffic from the *perator*'s palace. Now surrendering—wait." She was off the comm waves a few seconds. In that time, Wedge and Tycho surpassed the waiting Blades' altitude and looped over lazily for a return descent. Then Iella was back. "Surrenders confirmed. The palace is commanding air forces to surrender. And they're surrendering to *you*. Less honor lost than giving up to the 'lesser nations.' "

"Understood."

"Holdout requests your immediate presence at the *perator*'s palace."

Wedge growled to himself and switched back to the

general frequency. "This is Antilles. I accept the surrender of Skull-Biters and Lords of Dismay. Red Three and Red Four now authorized to accept surrenders in my name, during my absence." He switched back to squadron frequency. "Come on, Tycho. We have a royal appointment."

13

No laser installations fired on them as they crossed the city again. Small-arms fire from balconies all around struck the X-wings as they descended toward the *perator*'s palace outer yard, but that stopped as soon as the snubfighters were below the level of the walls.

In the outer courtyard, laser battery crews stood beside their pop-up emplacements with their hands up and behind their heads. Soldiers stood in similar positions. There were Blades, many of them damaged, on the grounds; their pilots stood by in attitudes of surrender. Wedge saw two men he thought were members of the elite Halbegardian invasion force keeping at least two hundred man and women under cover with nothing but their blaster rifles. And those two Halbegardians took the time to salute him as he slid out of his cockpit and dropped to the courtyard surface. A woman in the same uniform beckoned them from the steps up into the palace.

The Outer Court of the palace was not the place of festivities, or even gentility, it had been during previous visits. The air was thick with the smell of burned flesh, and the bodies of liveried guards still lay where they'd fallen. Courtiers were packed against one wall, held at bay by the blasters of invaders—members of the Holdout team and Halbegardian elites.

The *perator*, stripped of his retinue, stood with captors around him. Wedge saw, with relief, Cheriss among them. The flatscreens on the walls were bared and active; one showed Escalion, the *perator* of the Yedagon Confederacy, surrounded by advisors in the planning room at Yedagon City, while the other was broken into numerous smaller squares, some of which were blank and some of which showed scenes similar to the broadcast from Yedagon; the only difference was in the furnishings and the people staring out from the screen.

As he approached with Tycho, Wedge heard running feet approaching from behind. He turned to look, alert against some new attack, but it was Hallis who rounded the doorway and ran into the room; she skidded awkwardly to a halt, looked around, and then moved off to stand before a column from which she could record with the ordinary holocam she held in her hands.

"So you've brought the alien general," the *perator* said. There was mockery to his tone. "Why bother? It doesn't take a famous pilot to pull the trigger on me. Any of you could do it as well."

"That's not what we want to do." That was Tomer Darpen, standing among the captors present. "We'd really prefer—"

"I wasn't aware," Wedge said, "that you held a post with the united Adumari forces involved in this operation."

Tomer blinked. "Well, that's not relevant. We have to—"

"Be quiet, Tomer. Or I'll authorize Colonel Celchu to shoot you." Wedge approached Cheriss. "What's the situation?"

Her expression was an interesting study, a mix of exultation and guilt. "We hold the planning chambers and have compelled his senior officers to surrender—and to signal surrender to the flightknives."

"That's done."

"But the *perator* won't surrender."

The *perator*, clad in spotless white as if to suggest he had never taken an action to mar his reputation, moved forward, ignoring the blasters aimed at him, until he stood before Wedge. "Not honorable," he explained. His voice was weary but calm. "Surrender requires cooperation. I would rather die than cooperate."

"So we kill him," said one of the Halbegardian elites, but others turned to look at the flatscreens showing multiple images. It was evident to Wedge, from the way those shown in the flatscreens were intensely watching, that the images of the events taking place in this chamber were being broadcast to them.

One of the figures in one of the smaller flatscreen squares, a gray-haired woman with broad shoulders and an authoritarian bearing, spoke; her voice emerged from the flatscreen speakers. "No. Pekaelic can only be condemned by a council of his peers, and that is not the problem before us now."

Wedge leaned over to whisper in Cheriss's ear. "What happens if Pekaelic dies?"

"He has not named a successor. The council of nobles of Cartann would choose his successor. Some of the nations held in Cartann's grip would probably take the opportunity to break away. There would be much confusion . . ."

"I see." Wedge raised his voice. "*Perator*, let's speak simply. No diplomatic nonsense. If you persist in this posture and get yourself killed, your enemies will celebrate, but Cartann and its holdings become disorganized for a while. Long enough for the Empire to see that you're not going to be joining them willingly. Long enough for the Empire to send a fleet large enough to blow the *Allegiance* out of space and then pound your whole planet flat. In a week, you'll all be slaves, or worse. And where's the honor in that?"

"There is none," the *perator* said. "But I will still not surrender. I have never surrendered. It is not within me."

Wedge sighed, exasperated. Then a new thought occurred to him. "Could you retire?"

"What?"

"Retire. Without shame. Not surrender, not bow to your enemies. Just . . . quit."

"Abdicate." The *perator* considered. "I could honorably grant the throne to one of my sons. But my sons are pilots." His expression turned bleak. "After today, I don't even know if they are still alive."

"I suggest you find out." Wedge took a step back to give the *perator* space.

A minister was allowed to join the *perator*, then to go, with Halbegardian guards, to one of the palace's comm centers.

"Royal heirs are always in danger," Cheriss told Wedge. "At least in Cartann. They are usually raised away from their true parents, under assumed names, to keep them safe."

Wedge grimaced. "So they can't even be children to their living parents. Cheriss—"

"Don't say it. I can see that it is bad."

He pulled out his comlink and activated it. "Red Leader to Eye Three. Update, please." He turned the volume down and held it between his ear and his cupped hand.

"Except for a couple of minor skirmishes, the air battle is done," Iella said. "Cartann Blades are landing in fields all over the place under the lasers of the united force. But, more important, the *Cutting Lens*-class sensor ships showed one of the Star Destroyers, presumably *Agonizer*, leaving orbit. It left behind a small vehicle, which I'm tentatively identifying from a visual scan as a standard Imperial shuttle. It's descending toward Cartann City."

Wedge felt a surge of triumph. "Have a couple of Blades escort it in, all the way to the palace. I'm pretty sure it's a friendly."

"Will confirm and do so."

"Thanks. Red Leader out."

Minutes later, the minister returned and hurried to the *perator*'s side. The words he whispered to his ruler were good ones; the *perator* sagged for a moment, in what was obviously relief, then straightened. He beckoned Wedge to him, ignoring all others in the chamber.

"My sons survive," he said. "My oldest is being brought here now."

"Congratulations," Wedge said.

The *perator* gave him a close look. "Well done. I couldn't even detect the mockery."

"I didn't offer you any, *perator*. I think you should be punished for what you've done . . . but I'd never wish on anyone a punishment as severe as the loss of his children."

"Ah." Though he did not step back, the *perator* retreated, his thoughts and concerns suddenly light-years away.

Minutes later, a quartet of Halbegardian elites marched into the chamber, a pilot in Cartann black between them. The pilot was a young man with an earnest expression and thick black hair.

With a start, Wedge realized that he knew the young man. He was Balass ke Rassa, a pilot who'd flown against Wedge in simulated combat.

Balass did not acknowledge Wedge or any of the others near the *perator*; he marched up to his father and halted military style before him.

The *perator* looked upon him, searching his features. Wedge wondered how long it had been since he'd seen his son—months? Years?

"You know why I've had you brought here," the *perator* said.

Balass nodded.

"Will you accept?"

"If honor allows." Balass turned to one of his guards. "But I cannot in my present state. My pistol." He held out his hand and snapped his fingers, imperious.

The guard looked around, confused, then his gaze fell on Wedge.

Wedge nodded.

The guard pulled a small Adumari blaster pistol from beneath his coat and handed it to Balass. But the prince was not done; after he holstered the weapon, he said, "Blastsword."

Wedge nodded again. But when the guard reached for the weapon at his side, Balass said, "And not one of your Halbegardian toys. A proper Cartann blastsword."

Cheriss unbuckled the belt from her waist and put it around the prince. It barely fit, on the last notch, but he did not object. Cheriss stood back and away from him, her face solemn.

Balass turned again to his father. "Now I will accept."

The *perator* nodded. "I, Pekaelic ke Teldan, renounce my claim to the throne of Cartann and all titles pertaining thereto, in favor of my eldest son, Balass ke Teldan, known these last two-and-twenty years as Balass ke Rassa."

His son waited a beat, then said, "I, Balass ke Teldan, accept these rights and duties, and, though the circumstances be rushed and ceremony entirely absent, proclaim myself *perator* of Cartann."

There was no applause; there were no cheers to mark the sudden transfer of power from one set of shoulders to another.

Escalion, from the flatscreen, said, "I congratulate you on your poise, *Perator* Balass. Now, can you do what your father could not? Can you end this conflict by honorable surrender?"

Balass turned to the screen and shook his head. "No," he said. "We remain at war."

Wedge heard startled exclamations from the people in the hall and from both flatscreens. The Halbegardian guards in the chamber trained their weapons on the new ruler. Balass seemed unaffected by all this; he just stared into Escalion's flatscreen, or rather to the point at the top of the screen where its flatcam was installed, and kept a slight smile, possibly a mocking one, on his face.

"You understand," Escalion said, "you doom your nation to further punishment if you persist in this arrogance."

"I was about to say the same thing to you," Balass said. "Only substituting 'our world' for 'your nation.' Now be quiet a bit while I talk. I'll try to make you understand."

Balass paced, talking as he did so, turning from time to time so that he divided his attention between the dignitaries on the two flatscreens and those standing before him. "You lot seem to have concentrated so hard on the tactical situation before you that you have forgotten the strategic. Whether I surrender or not, the Empire knows Adumar will not be allying itself with them willingly. Indeed, I'm told that their giant ship has already left orbit . . . not a good sign for us.

"If I surrender, the New Republic cannot bring in ships to aid us in the conflict yet to come. Well, they can eventually. But they can bring in no more ships except under flags of truce with us or flags of war against us. And we cannot offer flags of truce as a united world until all ramifications of Cartann's surrender are explored. Which of Cartann's protectorates will splinter away and declare independence? Which will cling to Cartann and transfer loyalty to the united Adumari force you represent? These questions will take time to resolve."

Men and women, a few of them, were now nodding on the flatscreen that was broken into multiple images.

Balass continued, "But if I do not surrender—if you, the united Adumari coalition, accept at this moment my offer of truce without repercussion for our recent battles—then Cartann can join your union as an equal partner. Now, instantly, with terms to follow when we have time for negotiations. I can cast the votes of Cartann's protectorates, then free those nations when we have the luxury of time. Lords and ladies, if you abandon your grudge against Cartann, if you consider the old Cartann to have departed with my father's abdication and a new one to stand before you, we can forge a world union, in tentative form at least, *in minutes*. Or you can have your revenge and watch our world fall.

"Now, it is time for you to decide." He turned to face the many-faceted flatscreen, his hands on his hips, his expression imperious.

Wedge suppressed a whistle. If Balass pulled this off, he'd save his nation any number of troubles—years or decades of reparation payments, the perceived dishonor of wartime surrender, and much more. Wedge had seldom seen a leader take such a hurdle within seconds of accepting his position.

The figures on the flatscreens began talking with one another, their voices not broadcast over the speakers. One by one, the images of distant courtrooms and planning chambers winked down to neutral gray.

"We're going to do it," Tomer said. "He has them by the power cables. They have to accept. We're going to win."

"Yes, we are." Wedge smiled at him. It was easy to do so. All he had to do was imagine the man's fate.

"I was delighted when I heard that you and your pilots had survived the gauntlet, and then the rumors that you'd made it outside Cartann . . ."

"I imagine you were."

"And this raid!" Tomer gestured expansively. "More successful than you imagined, I'll bet."

"No, it's right on the money so far. But give it time. I predict that it will get even better."

Tomer's expression lost some of its glee, becoming more uncertain. "How so?"

The two flatscreens flashed back into activity. As before, Escalion of Yedagon dominated one of them, and it was he who spoke. "*Perator* Balass, much as we think Cartann should shoulder the major share of loss for the brief war we have suffered, you are correct. Everyone's circumstances have changed, and no one has time for even the most honorable prosecution. We offer Cartann a seat, a full vote, a full voice in what we now call the Adumari Union."

"I accept." Balass bowed to Escalion, then turned and bowed to the viewers on the other flatscreen. "Who will speak for us to the New Republic?"

Escalion said, "I think we would accept none other than General Antilles."

Wedge cleared his throat. "I'm sorry. I can't. Your elected speaker will be talking with *me*. I still have my duties as ambassador of the New Republic."

"Then we will choose from among ourselves," Escalion said.

As the *perators* and their advisors from around Adumar began a spirited—and, Wedge hoped, brief—discussion, Wedge turned to Tomer. "Tycho?"

Wedge drew his blaster, put its point up under Tomer's chin. Tycho drew in the same moment, putting his barrel to Tomer's left eye; the diplomat had to close his eye to keep it from being hurt.

"What is this?" Tomer asked. His tone was calm, even unconcerned. Wedge was impressed with his poise.

"It's time for you to call *Allegiance* and tell them to acknowledge and accept transmissions from all New Republic personnel and citizens on the ground," Wedge said.

"I don't know what you mean."

"And if you don't do it, we're going to hand you over to these Halbegardian guards. They'll conduct you back to Halbegardia or the Yedagon Confederacy. They'll put you on trial as a war criminal based on what I have to tell them about your interaction with Pekaelic. I doubt you can expect much mercy at their hands. On the other hand, comply and I'll turn you over to the New Republic for prosecution. Assuming neither Tycho nor I has a spasm and blows your head off."

Tomer heaved a sigh. "I admit nothing," he said. But he drew out a comlink. "Tomer Darpen to *Allegiance*, come in."

There was no answer. Tomer shrugged, an "I told you so" expression.

Wedge smiled at him. "Repeat after me. *'En-Are-Eye-One* to Allegiance. *Over.'* "

Tomer looked at him, expressionless, his one open eye flickering as if reading through a list of hints to find the one that would get him out of this situation. Finally he said, "En-Are-Eye-One to *Allegiance*. Over."

"*Allegiance* to En-Are-Eye-One, we read you."

Wedge just stared.

"I rescind the order concerning communications from the ground. You are authorized to respond to transmissions from Adumar."

"Rescind the comm blackout as well," Wedge said.

Tomer sighed. "Likewise, I rescind *Allegiance*'s hypercomm restrictions." He covered the microphone with his hand. "Is that all? Or should I have them send down a meal?"

"That's all."

Tomer removed his hand. "Acknowledge, please."

The distant comm officer said, "*Allegiance* acknowledges. Captain Salaban would like to talk to you."

Wedge took the comlink from Tomer's hand and gave it to Tycho. "Colonel Celchu, do me a favor and arrange for this prisoner to be transported to *Allegiance*. Inform the *Allegiance* of our situation and have Salaban stand by to communicate by hypercomm with the Fleet Command and General Cracken. Then give those two parties a quick report."

"Will do. What are you up to?"

"I'm going for a walk." Wedge gestured all around. "I'm sick of this place." He gave Tomer one last look. "You should have taken your chances with Adumari justice."

Tomer just stared, impassive.

On the palace steps, Wedge found Admiral Rogriss being escorted between two Halbegardian guards. Sniper fire from the near balconies was all but over.

Wedge dismissed the guards and gave the older man a salute. "Admiral. Good to see you. How are you?"

Rogriss gave him a slow shake of the head. "How can anyone be when his career has just been vaporized?"

"Meaning that *Agonizer* has left system without sending its holocomm message."

Rogriss nodded. "The holocomm is shut down and sealed tight. It can only be opened by my voice . . . or by the security codes of a superior officer. Which it won't reach for another three days or so."

"Will that matter? I mean, Imperial Intelligence could have a team on-planet, with its own holocomm unit . . ."

Rogriss shook his head. "Intelligence does have a team here. Good luck finding them; I won't tell you how. But they don't have a holocomm. You have the time you wanted . . . at the expense of my career."

Wedge offered his hand. "For what it's worth, you have my respect."

Rogriss took it. "You'll still get word to my children?"

"Yes."

"Even if General Phennir shoots you down when the Imperial forces return?"

"So he did survive . . . Yes, even then. First thing, I'll put together some orders concerning you that will be carried out in case of my death."

"And even if I don't come over to the New Republic?"

"Where would you go instead?"

Rogriss looked around. "I've spent considerable time lately planning how I was going to exploit the Adumari military weaknesses. Perhaps I can now show the Adumari where those weaknesses are, how to put armor over them. Perhaps they'd offer me a position here where I could do so."

"I imagine they would. Either way, I'll arrange to get word to your children."

"Thank you."

14

Wedge stood at the edge of the magcon field separating the atmosphere of *Allegiance*'s main starfighter bay from the vacuum of space beyond. Below, he could see *Mon Casima*, the Mon Calamari cruiser now assigned to the Adumar operation, less than two kilometers below. Other New Republic ships were out there, not visible to him but on-station—frigates, corvettes, aging cruisers that had once served the Empire or even the old Republic before it, as big a fleet as the New Republic could spare and assemble on such short notice. Not even *Lusankya*, the flagship—and sometimes only ship—of the task force Wedge normally commanded, would be present; in his absence, it had been dispatched on other duties.

The air was cold, as was common with starfighter bays in space; magcon fields were not good at retaining heat. The piercing noises of repulsorlifts being brought on-line cut through him, and the sound of engines being tested vibrated him to the bone.

To Wedge, it was almost like being at home.

Almost. From now on, he knew, home would be

where he and Iella chose to be together—quarters on Coruscant with its overwhelming press of population, a small house on some grassy patch on an insignificant colony world, even Corellia, someday, if things changed in the way that system was governed.

But that was a problem to solve tomorrow or the day after that. For now, there was Adumar.

Cartann City and a number of smaller metropolises had been seriously damaged during the Adumari Union raid. Hundreds of Blades and other vehicles on both sides had been lost, and many brave pilots. Wedge had been sorry to hear that Liak ke Mattino, captain of Strike the Moons Flightknife, who had risked his *perator*'s displeasure to give Red Flight a chance at escape, was among the dead, as were many of the pilots Wedge had trained against in the days before the outbreak of war.

The former *perator* was now hidden away on an estate somewhere within Cartann's borders, formally protected by his son from prosecution at the hands of the Adumari Union Council. Many of the world's other *perators* had protested, but Balass ke Teldan had stood fast by the terms he demanded for Cartann's peaceful and quick admission into the union, so it appeared that Pekaelic would avoid prosecution for his poor judgment and autocratic politics.

That would not be the case with Tomer Darpen. The onetime regional head of New Republic Intelligence was safely locked away in prison quarters, plotting his trial defense, blissfully unaware of the recording Hallis had made of the conversation that would doom him.

Tomer's temporary replacement would not be the detriment Tomer had been. Appointed by General Cracken, Iella Wessiri was now managing the New Republic's Intelligence matters on Adumar with her usual efficiency.

"Are you sure you don't want to direct your forces from *Allegiance*'s bridge?" Iella asked.

Wedge looked up, startled. Iella had appeared beside

him, in deceptive clothing, a naval lieutenant's uniform, and had joined Wedge in studying the skies beneath them.

Wedge looked around, saw that no one was near them, and affected surprise. "I'd swear you were talking to me. What an odd question to put to a pilot."

Iella managed a little smile. "Sorry. Lost my head for a moment. You can't blame me for trying."

"No, I can't."

She put an arm around his waist, rested her head on his shoulder. "I'm proud of you," she said.

"We haven't won, yet."

"Not for winning. For being willing to lose. For standing by your guns when the whole galaxy seemed to be arrayed against your decision."

"That wasn't fun. But when I was sure I was about to lose everything, and I discovered that I hadn't lost you after all . . . that made it all livable."

"But that leaves me with one big worry about the future."

"That I'm still flying?"

He felt her shake her head. She said, "No, that you're almost as stubborn as I am. I—"

Whatever her next words might have been, they were cut short by the single blare of an alarm, followed by words that echoed throughout the bay and, Wedge knew, throughout the ship: "Reconnaissance unit High Flight Three Beta reports arrival of Imperial vessels in Adumari space. Three repeat three *Imperial*-class Star Destroyers and numerous secondary vessels inbound. All personnel to battle stations. All pilots to muster stations."

Wedge sighed. "That's it." He pulled her to him for a quick kiss.

"I can't ask you to be safe," she said.

He shook his head.

"So shoot straight. And faster than they do."

"Count on it. I love you."

"I love *you*." She broke from him and hurried off to

her station, casting one last look over her shoulder at him before she joined the personnel streaming out the exit and was gone.

They formed up a kilometer off *Allegiance*'s bow, an impressive fighter group: Wedge's Red Flight, two shield-equipped TIE fighter squadrons, one slightly understrength A-wing squadron, a unit of B-wings, a Y-wing squadron, the High Flight X-wing unit off *Allegiance*, and three space-equipped Blade-32 flightknives from the planet's surface—two from Yedagon and one from Cartann. They were 106 fighters in strength.

"*Allegiance*'s sensors show the enemy TIE squadrons issuing from the Star Destroyers," Wedge said. "Fighters escorting bombers—a lot of bombers. They expect us to try to intercept with our fighters. Here's how we're going to play it instead.

"Our advance screen is Red Flight, High Flight Squadron, Lightflash Squad, and Contender and Skylight Squadrons." That put the X-wings, A-wings, and TIE fighters at the fore of Wedge's group. "The rest of you hang back in formation until we're fully engaged and you can calculate where the action is thickest—and where the enemy is less likely to be able to break away to engage you. Approach by those vectors and unload everything you have on *Agonizer*." That put the B-wings of Solar Wind Squadron, Y-wings of Remember Derra Squadron, and Blades of the Ice Edge, Frozen Death, and Sunwhip Flightknives behind on missiling duty. "You Blades remember to fire on the command of your flightknife commanders, in unison; your missiles lack the punch of proton torpedoes, so you're going to have to land precisely timed mass fire if you're going to do any harm to a Star Destroyer. Understood?"

He was answered by confirmations from each of the squadron commanders.

"All right. Let's go." He transmitted the intercept course to the group and vectored to lead the way to the enemy.

As his group formed up on him, he switched the comm board over to the main Adumari broadcast frequency. The two-dimensional image that was the continuous flatscreen broadcast filled his main screen. It showed an older man, a patch over one eye not quite concealing the scar that both rose and descended from his eye socket, addressing the flatcam.

". . . continues to hold out against Adumari Union forces," the man said. "Despite reports that Pekaelic's forces decline in number every day, assaults by units of his informal force continue to occupy Union attention and slow the Union efforts to bring peace to Adumar. At sunrise, Yedagon time, this morning, units of the Cartannese Lords of Dismay Flightknife, now allied with the former *perator*, escorted a bombing raid that destroyed six residential blocks in Yedagon's prestigious Accolux Township . . ."

Wedge switched it off. This was the third day of broadcasts that were, in essence, all lies. Scripted by Hallis Saper with the input of the Adumari Union's military advisors, the broadcasts told the tale of the former *perator*, Pekaelic ke Teldan, still mounting a mighty struggle against the conquering Adumari Union, keeping war raging across all the civilized nations of Adumar. The public followed the news accounts keenly. The guerrilla warfare always took place in communities that could be, and were, shut off from the outer world by military occupation . . . meaning that Imperial Intelligence agents on the ground would have a hard time disproving them.

Meanwhile, the true Pekaelic rested in the Cartannese township his son had chosen for his exile, barely aware of the events that were being attributed to him. All he knew was that he had a broadcast to make and a script to follow when instructed to do so.

If all went as it was supposed to, the Empire's Intelligence team or Adumar would have been recording all these transmissions for the last three days, analyzing them and interpreting them, but not discovering that they were all lies. Even now, they'd be transmitting their findings to the Imperial task force headed toward the planet. With luck, the task force would believe the accounts of a world still at war, its military might scattered.

Well before Wedge's group spotted the enemy Star Destroyers, *Allegiance* reported that elements of the 181st Imperial Fighter Group, escorting numerous squadrons of TIE bombers, was descending into Cartann airspace. Blips representing other Imperial fighter units were also detected in descent.

And then the Star Destroyer formation came into view, *Agonizer* at the point, *Retaliator* and *Master Stroke* well behind, other, smaller vessels throughout the convoy. Wedge set his course straight for the flagship. "Pilots, arm your weapons. X-wings, S-foils to attack position. Squadron commanders, you are free for individual deployment." He was not surprised to see the speed-happy A-wing pilots jump out ahead almost instantly. He switched to squadron frequency. "Red Flight, High Flight Squadron, call 'em as you see 'em."

"Red One, High Flight Twelve. I detect incoming TIE fighters and Interceptors . . . and two wing pairs of TIE Defenders. They've left behind a pretty ferocious screen."

Wedge grimaced. The TIE Defender was one of the best starfighters known. Equipped with three sets of solar wing arrays, equally spaced around the spherical fuselage, instead of two, and outfitted with shields equal to an X-wing's and weapons and speed superior to the X-wing, it was an extraordinary—and extraordinarily costly—starfighter. "Red Leader to Solar Wind Squadron. Solar Wind Seven through Twelve, move up to join the screen. We're going to need your help with the TIE Defenders."

"Acknowledged, Red Leader."

Space ahead lit up like interplanetary fireworks as *Agonizer*'s turbolasers and ion cannons went active. That meant the A-wings had come within range. Seconds later, he spotted the first of the incoming TIE fighters— mere blips on his sensor board that materialized into fast-moving blurs in his forward viewport.

He linked his lasers for quad fire, giving them a harder punch but a slower cycle rate. "Break by pairs and fire at will," he said.

The X-wings around him spread out, maintaining their course straight toward the incoming enemies. Head-to-head combat approaches were among the most dangerous tactics for starfighters, but they favored the shielded X-wings slightly over the unshielded TIEs.

On the heads-up display projected onto his forward viewport, Wedge's yellow targeting brackets tracked an incoming TIE Interceptor, the brackets trailing slightly behind the vehicle's lateral evasive movements. He sent his X-wing into the juking and jinking maneuvers that made it a more difficult target and manually swept his targeting brackets across the path he suspected the TIE would take next. His suspicion was right; the TIE dove straight through the path his brackets were tracing and the brackets went green. Wedge fired. He was rewarded only with a graze as one of his lasers charred the Interceptor's starboard solar wing black. The TIE veered off its intended course, away from Wedge and the X-wings.

Incoming green lasers matched outgoing red ones in number and intensity, and Wedge saw, in his peripheral vision, one of the High Flight X-wings explode, leaving only burning gas and rapidly cooking shrapnel behind.

Then the lines of TIEs and New Republic fighters met, merged, and separated again, the TIE squadrons flashing past. In a second the TIEs were behind him but coming around in their impossibly tight loops to come up behind the slower New Republic craft.

"Red Leader, got an eyeball," Tycho said.

Wedge checked by sensors and visually. A TIE fighter, or eyeball in pilot's parlance, had come up behind Tycho and was unloading a continuous stream of laser fire at him, though Tycho's erratic side-to-side motions had kept him from sustaining any but the most grazing of laser impacts.

"Read you, Two. I'm your wing." Wedge turned in Tycho's wake.

Tycho dove—"downward" being the direction of Adumar's orbital plane—in a shallow arc the most inexperienced of pilots could have followed. Less easy to follow would have been his extraordinary evasive maneuvering within the simple arc. The TIE fighter followed, keeping up his laser fire, and Wedge came up behind.

He fired once, his four lasers flashing through empty space where, a quarter second before, the TIE had been. The nimble eyeball flashed off to port, breaking away from its pursuit of Tycho.

"You'd think he wanted to stay alive or something, Lead."

"Let's disabuse him of the notion. Back to the furball." Wedge turned toward the most active portion of the engagement zone.

He could see on his sensor board the second wave of fighters, the missile-bearing craft, heading in two columns around the engagement zone toward Agonizer. And what he could see, the enemy could see. It would be best not to give the TIE Defenders a crack at those columns; Defenders would tear the slow-moving Y-wings and Blades to pieces. He identified the nearest Defender on his sensor board and headed straight for it.

It was engaged with two Allegiance TIE fighters and a B-wing operating in concert. As Wedge approached, the Defender's lasers chewed through one of the TIE fighters; the eyeball vented the gases in its cockpit and went dark. A linked ion-cannon blast from the B-wing missed the Defender by thirty meters or more, and the Defender's return ion blast eliminated the other TIE fighter, filling its cockpit with sparks before the vehicle went dark.

"Red Two, go wide. Let's give him nothing but guns to run toward." Wedge looped to starboard, away from his wingman, and Tycho looped to port; they arced toward the B-wing and Defender from opposite directions.

The Defender, itself looping around for a run at the B-wing, instead swung wide to keep clear of its original target and accelerated toward Tycho.

Wedge's targeting brackets flickered green across the Defender. He fired, but his lasers were meters off the mark.

Tycho and the Defender, skittering around like drops of ale on a cooking surface, came toward one another, Tycho unloading lasers, the Defender firing ion cannons. They passed one another seemingly undamaged . . . until Wedge noticed that Tycho was no longer maneuvering. Red Two's X-wing was dark, headed out to space like a missile with no guidance control.

Wedge bit back a curse. He didn't bother trying to raise Tycho on the comlink. Ion cannons tended to wipe out all a vehicle's electronics. Tycho was out of the game unless he could manage a cold start on his engines, an unlikely eventuality.

Instead, Wedge turned in the Defender's wake. He'd have only a shot or two before the other vehicle's superior speed and maneuverability would take it out of Wedge's range.

As his targeting brackets edged toward the Defender, its pilot detected the attempted targeting lock and went evasive, executing the kind of side-to-side maneuvers that only a TIE-style vehicle could manage. He also put on a burst of acceleration, drawing away from the

X-wing at a prodigious rate, and began a tight loop upward that would inevitably put him at Wedge's stern.

Wedge shook his head and held his fire. Instead, he maneuvered his brackets around and across his target, seeing which way the Defender jumped whenever threatened with an imminent hit. The Defender's response was always a spiraling loop down and to starboard, a fatal predictability . . . Wedge ran his brackets toward the Defender one last time, then, not waiting for the Defender's response, sent his X-wing into a loop down and to starboard.

The Defender rolled right into his targeting brackets. The pilot saw his mistake, began a reverse, but Wedge fired, quad-linked lasers punching through the vehicle's engines and into the cockpit. Fire flared through the hole he'd made, then the vehicle detonated.

Wedge found the B-wing on his sensors. "Red Leader to Solar Wind Eight. Tag Red Two, calculate his course and velocity, and transmit that data to *Allegiance* with a request for rescue."

"Will do, Red Leader."

Wedge turned back toward the heart of the engagement.

He could see, in the distance—not so great a distance as before—the B-wings, Y-wings, and Blades beginning their attack run on *Agonizer*. A little flare of light within the Y-wing formation had to be one of the wishbones intercepting a turbolaser blast, with fatal results.

Then bright lights began erupting on *Agonizer*'s hull, proton torpedo and Adumari missile impacts. A moment later the first barrage was done and Wedge could see char marks and buckled hull plates where the attack had hit.

No substantial penetration. "Red Leader to all Blade-Thirty-twos. Concentrate your fire or you'll never get penetration. Flightknife leaders, pick a target and transmit its location to your pilots for your next barrage or you might as well be throwing spitwads."

He heard the trio of acknowledgments, barely registering them, the Blades' problem already washed from his mental processes. Ahead, another TIE Defender, this one with red paint on its solar wing arrays, was turning into his path and accelerating toward him.

Red paint—that probably meant red horizontal stripes on the solar wings, and *that* meant it was piloted by a member of the 181st. Not many pilots of any unit, no matter how prestigious, rated a Defender. Turr Phennir was the logical candidate.

Wedge set logic aside. He needed his experience and his instincts now.

The Defender came straight at him, accelerating at full. Wedge bared a carnivore's grin. If he survived the head-to-head run, he'd have more time to turn about and confront the Defender again—the Defender's high rate of speed would make him overshoot Wedge and take his time turning around.

As he tried to target the madly maneuvering Defender, his brackets flickered from yellow to green and back again at a rate too quick for him to respond to—by the time he saw green and pulled his trigger, the brackets would have cycled through colors two or three more times. As the Defender came into optimal range, he fired anyway, saw his lasers flash through the gap between his target's solar wing arrays, felt an impact, and then he was past and looping around toward the Defender once more.

Diagnostics said his forward landing strut actuator was gone and indicated progressive problems with the launch mechanism for his proton torpedoes. He didn't need the diagnostics to see the black hole that had appeared in his X-wing's nose. For the laser shot to have pierced the top side of his fuselage and hit both proton torpedo launchers and landing strut, it would have had to have been a hard and accurate hit.

Not his problem now. He got turned around and headed toward the Defender again. He was aware of familiar voices over the comlink, but his call sign was not being used and he ignored them.

This time, he ignored the color changes on his brackets. He settled into his pilot's couch, felt its familiar contours around him, allowed his senses to spread out through his X-wing and ahead to—and into—the Defender rushing at him.

This wasn't use of the Force; to Wedge, the Force was as incomprehensible as astronavigation was to a bantha. But his long experience allowed him focus and responses that others sometimes considered mystical. He knew the change in engine pitch that said one of his generators was malfunctioning, the flash of light from his lasers that said one had drifted out of alignment, the subtle variations in acceleration that said his power was surging erratically.

He thought past the armor of the Defender, past the TIE pilot's suit, to the human beyond. He felt the pilot's twitch of response when he sent his X-wing swerving out of the pilot's own targeting brackets.

He felt his laser's aim rest on the pilot and he fired.

Then he was past, and looping around for another run.

The Defender, in the distance, wasn't looping back toward him. In fact, it wasn't quite a TIE Defender, anymore. The top solar wing array was gone, its pylon destroyed where it met the hull, and the Defender was venting atmosphere into space.

But it was still under control. The Defender picked up speed, heading out of the engagement zone at full acceleration. The pilot was supplied breathing air by his flight suit, but the loss of his cockpit atmosphere to space meant he was getting cold, and fast; he had only a few minutes before he'd freeze to death. He was out of the combat.

"Good shot, boss."

Wedge checked his sensor board, then looked to either side. "When did you get here?"

Red Three flew to his port side, Red Four to his starboard.

"Just now," Janson said. "You had a couple of opportunistic squints headed toward you. We scraped 'em off."

"Thanks." Wedge shook his head, trying to force himself out of the flow state he'd entered. "Was that Phennir?"

"According to our sensors, probably so."

"Tycho?"

"There's a damaged A-wing pacing him. The rescue shuttle has him on its list."

They were out of the main fight area and not engaged with enemies. Wedge turned back toward *Agonizer* just in time to see a brilliant fire flare up from its surface—the result of multiple missile hits breaching the shields and then the hull. The impact area, far starboard of the ship's center line, suggested that the damage would not be fatal to the Star Destroyer . . . but loss of atmosphere, structural integrity, and human life would be considerable. If the commander had any sense, the vessel would pull out of the engagement.

If.

"Red Leader to *Allegiance*. Give me a conflict status update, please."

"*Allegiance* here." It was, as he'd hoped, Iella's voice. "Imperial forces assaulting Aduma's surface are suffering heavy losses. They appear to have been anticipating a disorganized response and have been taken off-guard by the Adumari Union counterattacks. The TIE bombers have been especially hard-hit. The Imps also appear to have mounted a rescue operation to retrieve the *perator* of Cartann and, presumably, install him as a puppet ruler . . . but two transports full of stormtrooper elites are in Union hands now."

"Good to hear."

"In your group, the Blade squadrons were particularly hard-hit, with over thirty percent casualties and fatalities, but your group has inflicted heavy damage to *Agonizer*."

Indeed, as Wedge watched, the prow of the Star Destroyer slowly began to come about, away from Adumar's sun and the system's inner planets. In the distance, a point on the bow of the Star Destroyer *Master Stroke* flared into incandescence, sign of a serious detonation.

Wedge breathed a sigh of relief. This battle wasn't done, but the Imperials, calculating that the New Republic would be the only organized forces defending Adumar, had had the heavy end of the hammer dropped on them by united Adumari forces. When the spasms of pain from devastated TIE squadrons and damaged Star Destroyers finally hit the mission commanders—which appeared to be happening now—the Imperial forces would withdraw.

They'd be back someday. But before then, Wedge hoped, the New Republic would have taught Adumar more about defending itself.

"Thanks, *Allegiance*. Out." He switched back to squadron frequency. "Red Flight, let's do some hitting while we still have the chance."

15

He'd already made his good-byes to Adumar, another speech from the plaza receiving stand in Cartann City before a crowd.

The crowd wasn't quite so mindlessly enthusiastic this time. Some of its members chose to recall that Wedge had flown against them just days before. But others, still caught up in the worship of pilot excellence, or appreciative of the new configuration of Adumar's government, still cheered.

And now he stood as the centerpiece of the farewell party for Wedge Antilles, Ambassador. He was back in his Cartann quarters, once again in New Republic dress uniform, among a crowd made up of New Republic pilots and Adumari nobles—including pilots, ministers, and the *perators* of Cartann and the Yedagon Confederacy. And he had signs of progress to cheer him—such as Cartann's recent request for a set of flight simulators.

Iella took his arm. She was dressed once more in the moving-fire dress; he'd told her he liked it. "I know Intelligence has tried to recruit you once or twice," she said.

"But I have a feeling that the diplomatic corps just isn't going to."

Wedge smiled. "Good. I'd be obliged to shoot who-ever came to me with the offer. Saves me a murder trial."

Balass ke Teldan, Cartann's new *perator*, approached. "I am so sorry," he said.

"For what?"

"Your last flight in Adumar space and it gives you only a single kill."

Wedge shrugged away that concern. "That kill was a TIE Defender. Very prestigious. If prestige is your aim."

"Which, I know, is not one of your worries." The *perator* lost his slight smile. "My father's ways are old-fashioned. Not suited even to the world he wanted to build. But he is an honorable man, within the code he em-braces, and wishes to offer you an apology. He is furious that Tomer Darpen was able to convince him that you sought death when you did not, and deeply saddened that he offered it. I think he does not care for your forms of honor . . . but he recognizes them."

Wedge lowered his gaze for a moment. He had no doubt that the *perator* best served now by remaining in exile, with little or no influence on Cartann. Wedge had imagined that the former ruler would while away his re-maining years, doing little but polishing his memories of the successes of his youth, offering others little but bad advice and a growing dissatisfaction with what his world would become. But that was, perhaps, doing Pekaelic a disservice. The old man might change, might adapt. He might even lead again, by example, someday.

Wedge returned his gaze to Balass's. "Please tell him I accept."

"I shall. For now, though, I offer my last farewell. Duty calls." He offered a minimal bow, shook Wedge's hand, and was gone.

Iella said, "Poor boy."

"How do you mean?"

"He's a *perator* now. He can't lavish praise upon you and beg you to teach him all you know."

"As if he would."

"He would. Our profile on him says he's one of your biggest admirers. But now he's locked behind the ruler's mask and can never admit it."

"That's politics for you." Wedge looked around the chamber.

Janson and a crowd of admirers occupied a corner. Janson was in his dress uniform, but, in violation of regulations, had his favorite cloak on over it. The flatscreen panels on the cloak showed a line of Jansons, arms linked, doing high kicks like a dancing chorus. Wedge wondered where he'd gotten the image. He also wondered if there was any way to space that cloak, once they were headed back to Coruscant, without Janson knowing.

Tycho and Hobbie stood in a cluster of pilots, their hands moving, showing the respective positions of starfighters from some past dogfight.

Hallis was at the counter that served as the party's bar, her expression perplexed, as it had been for the last few days. The recordings she had made ever since Red Flight had been condemned to run its gauntlet had been increasingly inappropriate for the documentary she'd hoped to assemble. Some were now even classified. Yet the Adumari Union had settled a small fortune on her for her hard work in scripting the broadcasts that had successfully misled the Imperial invaders, and Wedge suspected, though Iella would not confirm it, that New Republic Intelligence had made an offer for her future services in the field of propaganda and deception. She looked like a woman with too many choices to make and not enough time to make them.

He turned, looking for Cheriss, and there she was beside him. "Ah. Cheriss. I wanted you to know that I've transmitted your application to the academy, along with my recommendation."

"Thank you. May I ask another favor?"

"Certainly."

"May I leave Adumar with your ship?"

Wedge hesitated. The last thing he needed was for her crush on him to interfere with his time with Iella . . .

"You see," she continued, "the new *perator* is obliged to dislike me. I was a member, the chief guide actually, of the party that captured his father. My—what did Hobbie call it?—endorsement arrangement has already been canceled, and the owner of the building where I keep my quarters has issued a decree of eviction. If I'm to move, I might as well move all at once. Even if your academy does not accept me—"

"You'll find work teaching the art of the sword, believe me. Of course, Cheriss. I'll arrange it with Captain Salaban."

"Thank you." With a smile, she returned to the group Hobbie and Tycho were entertaining.

Wedge couldn't quite suppress a rueful grin, and Iella saw it. "What?"

"I was in the process of flattering myself," Wedge said, "and I got caught doing it."

"You just flatter yourself anytime you want. I'll always be here to bring you back to ground."

He drew her hands up around his neck, took her about the waist, and began a slow dance of Corellia.

"Wedge, there's no music."

"Well, for the next few hours anyway, until we pack up and jump out of system, I can snap my fingers and have anything I want. One of the rewards of fame. You want music?"

"No." She rested her head on his shoulder. "This is perfect."

He nodded, feeling her hair soft beneath his chin.

Perfect it was.

About the Author

Aaron Allston is a novelist from the Austin, Texas, area. His interests include science fiction and fantasy, mysteries, ancient history, archaeology, anthropology, role-playing games, table tennis, cats, gruesome puns, and (whenever possible) ruining people's brains.

Starfighters of Adumar is his tenth completed novel and his fourth in the X-wing series.

His Web page is on-line at *www.io.com/~allston/*.

The World of
STAR WARS Novels

In May 1991, *Star Wars* caused a sensation in the publishing industry with the Bantam Spectra release of Timothy Zahn's novel *Heir to the Empire*. For the first time, Lucasfilm Ltd. had authorized new novels that *continued* the famous story told in George Lucas's three blockbuster motion pictures: *Star Wars, The Empire Strikes Back,* and *Return of the Jedi.* Reader reaction was immediate and tumultuous: *Heir* reached #1 on the *New York Times* bestseller list and demonstrated that *Star Wars* lovers were eager for exciting new stories set in this universe, written by leading science fiction authors who shared their passion. Since then, each Bantam *Star Wars* novel has been an instant national bestseller.

Lucasfilm and Bantam decided that future novels in the series would be interconnected: that is, events in one novel would have consequences in the others. You might say that each Bantam *Star Wars* novel, enjoyable on its own, is also part of a much larger tale.

Here is a special look at Bantam's *Star Wars* books, along with excerpts from the more recent novels. Each one is available now wherever Bantam Books are sold.

The Han Solo Trilogy:
THE PARADISE SNARE √
THE HUTT GAMBIT √
REBEL DAWN √
by A. C. Crispin
Setting: Before *Star Wars: A New Hope*

What was Han Solo like before we met him in the first STAR WARS movie? This trilogy answers that tantalizing question, filling in lots of historical lore about our favorite swashbuckling hero and thrilling us with adventures of the brash young pilot that we never knew he'd experienced. As the trilogy begins, the young Han Makes a life-changing decision: to escape from the clutches of Garris Shrike, head of the trading "clan" who has brutalized Han while taking advantage of his piloting abilities. Here's a tense early scene from The Paradise Snare *featuring Han, Shrike, and Dewlanna, a Wookiee who is Han's only friend in this horrible situation:*

"I've had it with you, Solo. I've been lenient with you so far, because you're a blasted good swoop pilot and all that prize money came in handy, but my patience is ended." Shrike ceremoniously pushed up the sleeves of his bedizened uniform, then balled his hands into fists. The galley's artificial lighting made the blood-jewel ring glitter dull silver. "Let's see what a few days of fighting off Devaronian blood-poisoning does for your attitude—along with maybe a few broken bones. I'm doing this for your own good, boy. Someday you'll thank me."

Han gulped with terror as Shrike started toward him. He'd lashed out at the trader captain once before, two years ago, when he'd been feeling cocky after winning the gladiatorial Free-For-All on Jubilar—and had been instantly sorry. The speed and strength of Garris's returning blow had snapped his head back and split both lips so thoroughly that Dewlanna had had to feed him mush for a week until they healed.

With a snarl, Dewlanna stepped forward. Shrike's hand dropped to his blaster. "You stay out of this, old Wookiee," he snapped in a voice nearly as harsh as Dewlanna's. "Your cooking isn't *that* good."

Han had already grabbed his friend's furry arm and was forcibly holding her back. "Dewlanna, no!"

She shook off his hold as easily as she would have waved off an annoying insect and roared at Shrike. The captain drew his blaster, and chaos erupted.

"Noooo!" Han screamed, and leaped forward, his foot lashing out in an old street-fighting technique. His instep impacted solidly with Shrike's breastbone. The captain's breath went out in a great *houf!* and he went over backward. Han hit the deck and rolled. A tingler bolt sizzled past his ear.

"Larrad!" wheezed the captain as Dewlanna started toward him.

Shrike's brother drew his blaster and pointed it at the Wookiee. "Stop, Dewlanna!"

His words had no more effect than Han's. Dewlanna's blood was up—she was in full Wookiee battle rage. With a roar that deafened the combatants, she grabbed Larrad's wrist and yanked, spinning him around and snapping him in a terrible parody of a child's "snap the whip" game. Han heard a *crunch,* mixed with several *pops* as tendons and ligaments gave way. Larrad Shrike shrieked, a high, shrill noise that carried such pain that the Corellian youth's arm ached in sympathy.

Grabbing the blaster from his belt, Han snapped off a shot at the Elomin who was leaping forward, tingler ready and aimed at Dewlanna's midsection. Brafid howled, dropping his weapon. Han was amazed that he'd managed to hit him, but he didn't have long to wonder about the accuracy of his aim.

Shrike was staggering to his feet, blaster in hand, aimed squarely at Han's head. "Larrad?" he yelled at the writhing heap of agony that was his brother. Larrad did not reply.

Shrike cocked the blaster and stepped even closer to Han. "Stop it, Dewlanna!" the captain snarled at the Wookiee. "Or your buddy Solo dies!"

Han dropped his blaster and put his hands up in a gesture of surrender.

Dewlanna stopped in her tracks, growling softly.

Shrike leveled the blaster, and his finger tightened on the trigger. Pure malevolent hatred was etched upon his features, and then he smiled, pale blue eyes glittering with ruthless joy. "For insubordination and striking your captain," he announced, "I sentence you to death, Solo. May you rot in all the hells there ever were."

SHADOWS OF THE EMPIRE √
by Steve Perry
Setting: Between *The Empire Strikes Back* and *Return of the Jedi*

Here is a very special STAR WARS story dealing with Black Sun, a galaxy-spinning criminal organization that is masterminded by one of the most interesting villains in the STAR WARS universe: Xizor, dark prince of the Falleen. Xizor's chief rival for the favor of Emperor Palpatine is none other than Darth Vader himself— alive and well, and a major character in this story, since it is set during the events of the STAR WARS film trilogy.

In the opening prologue, we revisit a familiar scene from The Empire Strikes Back, *and are introduced to our marvelous new bad guy:*

He looks like a walking corpse, Xizor thought. *Like a mummified body dead a thousand years. Amazing he is still alive, much less the most powerful man in the galaxy. He isn't even that old; it is more as if something is slowly eating him.*

Xizor stood four meters away from the Emperor, watching as the man who had long ago been Senator Palpatine moved to stand in the holocam field. He imagined he could smell the decay in the Emperor's worn body. Likely that was just some trick of the recycled air, run through dozens of filters to ensure that there was no chance of any poison gas being introduced into it. Filtered the life out of it, perhaps, giving it that dead smell.

The viewer on the other end of the holo-link would see a close-up of the Emperor's head and shoulders, of an age-ravaged face shrouded in the cowl of his dark zeyd-cloth robe. The man on the other end of the transmission, light-years away, would not see Xizor, though Xizor would be able to see him. It was a measure of the Emperor's trust that Xizor was allowed to be here while the conversation took place.

The man on the other end of the transmission—if he could still be called that—

The air swirled inside the Imperial chamber in front of the Emperor, coalesced, and blossomed into the image of a figure down on one knee. A caped humanoid biped dressed in jet black, face hidden under a full helmet and breathing mask:

Darth Vader.

Vader spoke: "What is thy bidding, my master?"

If Xizor could have hurled a power bolt through time and space to strike Vader dead, he would have done it without blinking. Wishful thinking: Vader was too powerful to attack directly.

"There is a great disturbance in the Force," the Emperor said.

"I have felt it," Vader said.

"We have a new enemy. Luke Skywalker."

Skywalker? That had been Vader's name, a long time ago. What was this person with the same name, someone so powerful as to be worth a conversation between the Emperor and his most loathsome creation? More importantly, why had Xizor's agents not uncovered this before now? Xizor's ire was instant—but cold. No sign of his surprise or anger would show on his imperturbable features. The Falleen did not allow their emotions to burst forth as did many of the inferior species; no, the Falleen ancestry was not fur but scales, not mammalian but reptilian. Not wild but coolly calculating. Such was much better. Much safer.

"Yes, my master," Vader continued.

"He could destroy us," the Emperor said.

Xizor's attention was riveted upon the Emperor and the holographic image of Vader kneeling on the deck of a ship far away.

Here was interesting news indeed. Something the Emperor perceived as a danger to himself? Something the Emperor feared?

"He's just a boy," Vader said. "Obi-Wan can no longer help him."

Obi-Wan. That name Xizor knew. He was among the last of the Jedi Knights, a general. But he'd been dead for decades, hadn't he?

Apparently Xizor's information was wrong if Obi-Wan had been helping someone who was still a boy. His agents were going to be sorry.

The Bounty Hunter Wars
Book 1: THE MANDALORIAN ARMOR√
Book 2: SLAVE SHIP √
by K. W. Jeter
Setting: During *Return of the Jedi*

Boba Fett continues the fight against the legions of circling enemies as the somewhat hot-tempered Trandoshan Bossk attempts to re-establish the old Bounty Hunter Guild with himself as its head. Bossk has sworn undying vengeance on Boba Fett when his ship, Hound's Tooth, *crashes.*

In the excerpt that follows, Bossk attempts to kill Boba Fett in a violent confrontation:

Fear is a useful thing.

That was one of the best lessons that a bounty hunter could learn. And Bossk was learning it now.

Through the cockpit viewport of the *Hound's Tooth,* he saw the explosion that ripped the other ship, Boba Fett's *Slave I,* into flame and shards of blackened durasteel. A burst of wide-band comlink static, like an electromagnetic death cry, had simultaneously deafened Bossk. The searing, multi-octave noise had poured through the speakers in the *Hound*'s cockpit for several minutes, until the last of the circuitry aboard Fett's ship had finally been consumed and silenced in the fiery apocalypse.

When he could finally hear himself think again, Bossk looked out at the empty space where *Slave I* had been. Now, against the cold backdrop of stars, a few scraps of heated metal slowly dwindled from white-hot to dull red as their molten heat ebbed away in vacuum. *He's dead,* thought Bossk with immense satisfaction. *At last.* Whatever atoms had constituted the late Boba Fett, they were also drifting disconnected and harmless in space. Before transferring back here to his own ship, Bossk had wired up enough thermal explosives in *Slave I* to reduce any living thing aboard it to mere ash and bad memories.

So if he still felt afraid, if his gut still knotted when Boba Fett's dark-visored image rose in his thoughts, Bossk knew that was an irrational response. *He's dead, he's gone . . .*

The silence of the *Hound*'s cockpit was broken by a barely audible pinging signal from the control panel. Bossk glanced down and saw that the *Hound*'s telesponder had picked up the presence of another ship in the immediate vicinity; according to the coordinates that appeared in the readout screen, it was almost on top of the *Hound's Tooth.*

And—it was the ship known as *Slave I.* The ID profile was an exact match.

That's impossible, thought Bossk, bewildered. His heart shuddered to a halt inside his chest, then staggered on. Before the explosion, he had picked up the same ID profile from the other side of his own ship; he had turned the *Hound's Tooth* around just in time to see the huge, churning ball of flame fill his viewscreen.

But, he realized now, he hadn't seen *Slave I* itself. Which meant . . .

Bossk heard another sound, even softer, coming from somewhere else in his own ship. There was someone else aboard it; his keen Trandoshan senses registered the molecules of another creature's spoor in the ship's recycled atmosphere. And Bossk knew who it was.

He's here. The cold blood in Bossk's veins chilled to ice. *Boba Fett . . .*

Somehow, Bossk knew, he had been tricked. The explosion hadn't consumed *Slave I* and its occupants at all. He didn't know how Boba Fett had managed it, but it had been done nevertheless. And the deafening electronic noise that had filled the cockpit had also been enough to cover Boba Fett's unauthorized entry of the *Hound's Tooth;* the shrieking din had gone on long enough for Fett to have penetrated an access hatch and resealed it behind himself.

A voice came from the cockpit's overhead speaker, a voice that was neither his own nor Boba Fett's.

"Twenty seconds to detonation." It was the calm, unexcited voice of an autonomic bomb. Only the most powerful ones contained warning circuits like that.

Fear thawed the ice in Bossk's veins. He jumped up from the pilot's chair and dived for the hatchway behind himself.

In the emergency equipment bay of the *Hound's Tooth,* his clawed hands tore through the contents of one of the storage lockers. The *Hound* wasn't going to be a ship much longer; in a few seconds—and counting down—it was going to be glowing bits of shrapnel and rubbish surrounded by a haze of rapidly dissipating atmospheric gases, just like whatever it had been that he had mistakenly identified as Boba Fett's ship *Slave I.* That the *Hound* would no longer be capable of maintaining its life-support systems wasn't Bossk's main concern at this moment, as the reptilian Trandoshan hastily shoved a few more essential items through the self-sealing gasket of a battered, much-used pressure duffel. There wouldn't even *be* any life for the systems to support: a small portion of the debris floating in the cold vacuum would be blood and bone and scorched scraps of body tissue, the rapidly chilling remains of the ship's captain. *I'm outta here,* thought Bossk; he slung the duffel's strap across his broad shoulder and dived for the equipment bay's hatch.

"Fifteen seconds to detonation." A calm and friendly voice spoke in the *Hound's* central corridor as Bossk ran for the escape pod. He knew that Boba Fett had toggled the bomb's autonomic vocal circuits just to rattle him. "Fourteen . . ." There was nothing like a disembodied announcement of impending doom, to get a sentient creature motivated. "Thirteen; have you considered evacuation?"

"Shut up," growled Bossk. There was no point in talking to a pile of thermal explosives and flash circuits, but he couldn't stop himself. Under the death-fear that accelerated his pulse was sheer murderous rage and annoyance, the inevitable-seeming result of every encounter he'd ever had with Boba Fett. *That stinking, underhanded scum . . .*

The scraps and shards left by the other explosion clattered against the *Hound's* shielded exterior like a swarm of tiny, molten-edged meteorites. If there was any justice in the universe, Boba Fett should have been dead by now. Not just dead; atomized. The fury and panic in Bossk's pounding heart shifted again to bewilderment as he ran with the pressure duffel jostling against his scale-covered spine. Why did Boba Fett keep coming back? Was there no way to kill him so that he would just *stay* dead?

THE TRUCE AT BAKURA ✓
by Kathy Tyers
Setting: Immediately after *Return of the Jedi*

The day after his climactic battle with Emperor Palpatine and the sacrifice of his father, Darth Vader, who died saving his life, Luke Skywalker helps recover an Imperial drone ship bearing a startling message intended for the Emperor. It is a distress signal from the far-off Imperial outpost of Bakura, which is under attack by an alien invasion force, the Ssi-ruuk. Leia sees a rescue mission as an opportunity to achieve a diplomatic victory for the Rebel Alliance, even if it means fighting alongside former Imperials. But Luke receives a vision from Obi-Wan Kenobi revealing that the stakes are even higher: the invasion at Bakura threatens everything the Rebels have won at such great cost.

STAR WARS: X-WING
By Michael A. Stackpole
ROGUE SQUADRON ∨
WEDGE'S GAMBLE
THE KRYTOS TRAP
THE BACTA WAR

By Aaron Allston
WRAITH SQUADRON
IRON FIST
SOLO COMMAND

By Michael A. Stackpole
ISARD'S REVENGE ○
Setting: Three years after *Return of the Jedi*

The Rogues have been instrumental in defeating Thrawn and return to Coruscant to celebrate their great victory. It is then they make a terrible discovery—Ysanne Isard did not die at Thyferra and it is she who is assassinating those who were with Corran Horn on the Lusankya. *It is up to the Rogues to rescue their compatriots and foil the remnants of the Empire.*

The following scene from the opening of Isard's Revenge *takes you to one of the most daring battles the Rogues ever waged:*

Sithspawn! When his X-wing reverted to realspace before the countdown timer had reached zero, Corran Horn knew Thrawn had somehow managed to outguess the New Republic yet one more time. The Rogues had helped create the deception that the New Republic would be going after the Tangrene Ubiqtorate Base, but Thrawn clearly hadn't taken the bait.

The man's incredible. I'd like to meet him, shake his hand. Corran smiled. *And then kill him, of course.*

Two seconds into realspace and the depth of Thrawn's brilliance became undeniable. The New Republic's forces had been brought out of hyperspace by two Interdictor cruisers, which even now started to fade back toward the Imperial lines. This left the New Republic's ships well shy of the Bilbringi shipyards and facing an Imperial fleet arrayed for battle. The two Interdictors that had dragged them from hyperspace were a small part of a larger force scattered around to make sure the New Republic's ships were not going to be able to retreat.

"Battle alert!" Captain Tycho Celchu's voice crackled over the comm unit. "TIE Interceptors coming in—bearing two-nine-three, mark twenty."

Corran keyed his comm unit. "Three Flight, on me. Hold it together and nail some squints."

The cant-winged Interceptors rolled in and down on the Rogues. Corran kicked his X-wing up on its port S-foil and flicked his lasers over to quad-fire mode. While that would slow his rate of fire, each burst had a better chance of killing a squint outright. *And there are plenty that need killing here.*

Corran nudged his stick right and dropped the cross-hairs onto an Interceptor making a run at Admiral Ackbar's flagship. He hit the firing switch, sending four red laser bolts burning out at the target. They hit on the starboard side, with two of them piercing the cockpit and the other two vaporizing the strut supporting the right wing. The bent hexagonal wing sheered off in a shower of sparks, while the rest of the craft started a long, lazy spiral toward the outer edges of the system.

"Break port, Nine."

As the Gand's high-pitched voice poured through the comm unit, Corran snaprolled his X-wing to the left, then chopped his throttle back and hauled hard on the stick to take him into a loop. An Interceptor flashed through where he had been, and Ooryl Qyrgg's X-wing came fast on its tail. Ooryl's lasers blazed in sequence, stippling the Interceptor with red energy darts. One hit each wing, melting great furrows through them, while the other two lanced through the cockpit right above the twin ion engines. The engines themselves tore free of their support structure and blew out through the front of the squint, then exploded in a silver fireball that consumed the rest of the Imperial fighter.

"Thanks, Ten."

"My pleasure, Nine."

Whistler, the green and white R2 unit slotted in behind Corran, hooted, and data started pouring up over the fighter's main monitor. It told him in exact detail what he was seeing unfold in space around him. The New Republic's forces had come into the system in the standard conical formation that allowed them to maximize firepower.

THE COURTSHIP OF ✓
PRINCESS LEIA
by Dave Wolverton
Setting: Four years after *Return of the Jedi*

One of the most interesting developments in Bantam's STAR WARS novels is that in their storyline, Han Solo and Princess Leia start a family. This tale reveals how the couple originally got together. Wishing to strengthen the fledgling New Republic by bringing in powerful allies, Leia opens talks with the Hapes consortium of more than sixty worlds. But the consortium is ruled by the Queen Mother, who, to Han's dismay, wants Leia to marry her son, Prince Isolder. Before this action-packed story is over, Luke will join forces with Isolder against a group of Force-trained "witches" and face a deadly foe.

HEIR TO THE EMPIRE ✓
DARK FORCE RISING ✓
THE LAST COMMAND ✓
by Timothy Zahn
Setting: Five years after *Return of the Jedi*

This #1 bestselling trilogy introduces two legendary forces of evil into the STAR WARS literary pantheon. Grand Admiral Thrawn has taken control of the Imperial fleet in the years since the destruction of the Death Star, and the mysterious Joruus C'baoth is a fearsome Jedi Master who has been seduced by the dark side. Han and Leia have now been married for about a year, and as the story begins, she is pregnant with twins. Thrawn's plan is to crush the Rebellion and resurrect the Empire's New Order with C'baoth's help—and in return, the Dark Master will get Han and Leia's Jedi children to mold as he wishes. For as readers of this magnificent trilogy will see, Luke Skywalker is not the last of the old Jedi. He is the first of the new.

The Jedi Academy Trilogy:
JEDI SEARCH 𝒟
DARK APPRENTICE ℂ
CHAMPIONS OF THE FORCE 𝒪
by Kevin J. Anderson
Setting: Seven years after *Return of the Jedi*

In order to assure the continuation of the Jedi Knights, Luke Skywalker has decided to start a training facility: a Jedi Academy. He will gather Force-sensitive students who show potential as prospective Jedi and serve as their mentor, as Jedi Masters Obi-Wan Kenobi and Yoda did for him. Han and Leia's twins are now toddlers, and there is a third Jedi child: the infant Anakin, named after Luke and Leia's father. In this trilogy, we discover the existence of a powerful Imperial doomsday weapon, the horrifying Sun Crusher—which will soon become the centerpiece of a titanic struggle between Luke Skywalker and his most brilliant Jedi Academy student, who is delving dangerously into the dark side.

I, JEDI ✓
by Michael A. Stackpole
Setting: *During that time*

Another grand tale of the exploits of the most feared and fearless fighting force in the galaxy, as Corran Horn faces a dark unnatural power that only his mastery of the Jedi powers could destroy. This great novel gives us an in-depth look at Jedi powers and brings us inside the minds of the special warriors learning to use the Force:

I switched to proton torpedoes, got a quick tone-lock from Whistler and pulled the trigger. The missile shot from my X-wing and sprinted straight for her ship. As good as she was, the clutch pilot knew there was no dodging it. She fired with both lasers, but they missed. Then, at the last moment, she shot an ion blast that hit the missile. Blue lightning played over it, burning out every circuit that allowed the torpedo to track and close on her ship.

I'm fairly certain, just for a second, she thought she had won.

The problem with a projectile is that even if its sophisticated circuitry fails, it still has a lot of kinetic energy built up. Even if it never senses the proximity of its target and detonates, that much mass moving that fast treats a clutch cockpit much the way a needle treats a bubble. The torpedo drove the ion engines out the back of the clutch, where they exploded. The fighter's hollow remains slowly spun off through space and would eventually burn through the atmosphere and give resort guests a thrill.

CHILDREN OF THE JEDI √
by Barbara Hambly
Setting: Eight years after *Return of the Jedi*

The STAR WARS characters face a menace from the glory days of the Empire when a thirty-year-old automated Imperial Dreadnaught comes to life and begins its grim mission: to gather forces and annihilate a long-forgotten stronghold of Jedi children. When Luke is whisked aboard, he begins to communicate with the brave Jedi Knight who paralyzed the ship decades ago, and gave her life in the process. Now she is part of the vessel, existing in its artificial intelligence core, and guiding Luke through one of the most unusual adventures he has ever had.

DARKSABER by Kevin J. Anderson √
Setting: Immediately thereafter

Not long after Children of the Jedi, *Luke and Han learn that evil Hutts are building a reconstruction of the original Death Star— and that the Empire is still alive, in the form of Daala, who has joined forces with Pellaeon, former second-in-command to the feared Grand Admiral Thrawn.*

PLANET OF TWILIGHT ○
by Barbara Hambly
Setting: Nine years after *Return of the Jedi*

Concluding the epic tale begun in her own novel Children of the Jedi *and continued by Kevin Anderson in* Darksaber, *Barbara Hambly tells the story of a ruthless enemy of the New Republic operating out of a backwater world with vast mineral deposits. The first step in his campaign is to kidnap Princess Leia. Meanwhile, as Luke Skywalker searches the planet for his long-lost love Callista, the planet begins to reveal its unspeakable secret—a secret that threatens the New Republic, the Empire, and the entire galaxy:*

The first to die was a midshipman named Koth Barak. One of his fellow crewmembers on the New Republic escort cruiser *Adamantine* found him slumped across the table in the deck-nine break room where he'd repaired half an hour previously for a cup of coffeine. Twenty minutes after Barak should have been back to post, Gunnery Sergeant Gallie Wover went looking for him.

When she entered the deck-nine break room, Sergeant Wover's first sight was of the palely flickering blue on blue of the infolog screen. "Blast it, Koth, I told you . . ."

Then she saw the young man stretched unmoving on the far side of the screen, head on the break table, eyes shut. Even at a distance of three meters Wover didn't like the way he was breathing.

"Koth!" She rounded the table in two strides, sending the other chairs clattering into a corner. She thought his eyelids moved a little when she yelled his name. "Koth!"

Wover hit the emergency call almost without conscious decision. In the few minutes before the med droids arrived she sniffed the coffeine in the gray plastene cup a few centimeters from his limp fingers. It wasn't even cold.

THE CRYSTAL STAR
by Vonda N. McIntyre
Setting: Ten years after *Return of the Jedi*

Leia's three children have been kidnapped. That horrible fact is made worse by Leia's realization that she can no longer sense her children through the Force! While she, Artoo-Detoo, and Chewbacca trail the kidnappers, Luke and Han discover a planet that is suffering strange quantum effects from a nearby star. Slowly freezing into a perfect crystal and disrupting the Force, the star is blunting Luke's power and crippling the Millennium Falcon. These strands converge in an apocalyptic threat not only to the fate of the New Republic, but to the universe itself.

The Black Fleet Crisis
BEFORE THE STORM ✓
SHIELD OF LIES ✓
TYRANT'S TEST
by Michael P. Kube-McDowell ✓
Setting: Twelve years after *Return of the Jedi*

Long after setting up the hard-won New Republic, yesterday's Rebels have become today's administrators and diplomats. But the peace is not to last for long. A restless Luke must journey to his mother's homeworld in a desperate quest to find her people; Lando seizes a mysterious spacecraft with unimaginable weapons of destruction; and waiting in the wings is a horrific battle fleet under the control of a ruthless leader bent on a genocidal war.

THE NEW REBELLION
by Kristine Kathryn Rusch ○
Setting: Thirteen years after *Return of the Jedi*

Victorious though the New Republic may be, there is still no end to the threats to its continuing existence—this novel explores the price of keeping the peace. First, somewhere in the galaxy, millions suddenly perish in a blinding instant of pain. Then, as Leia prepares to address the Senate on Coruscant, a horrifying event changes the governmental equation in a flash.

The Corellian Trilogy:
AMBUSH AT CORELLIA ○
ASSAULT AT SELONIA ○
SHOWDOWN AT CENTERPOINT ○
by Roger MacBride Allen
Setting: Fourteen years after *Return of the Jedi*

This trilogy takes us to Corellia, Han Solo's homeworld, which Han has not visited in quite some time. A trade summit brings Han, Leia, and the children—now developing their own clear personalities and instinctively learning more about their innate skills in the Force—into the middle of a situation that most closely resembles a burning fuse. The Corellian system is on the brink of civil war, there are New Republic intelligence agents on a mysterious mission which even Han does not understand, and worst of all, a fanatical rebel leader has his hands on a superweapon of

*unimaginable power—and just wait until you find out who that
leader is!*

The Hand of Thrawn
SPECTER OF THE PAST
VISION OF THE FUTURE
by Timothy Zahn
Setting: Nineteen years after
Star Wars: A New Hope

*The two-book series by the undisputed master of the STAR WARS
novel. Once the supreme master of countless star systems, the
Empire is tottering on the brink of total collapse. Day by day,
neutral systems are rushing to join the New Republic coalition.
But with the end of the war in sight, the New Republic has fallen
victim to its own success. An unwieldy alliance of races and tradi-
tions, the confederation now finds itself riven by age-old animosi-
ties. Princess Leia struggles against all odds to hold the New
Republic together. But she has powerful enemies. An ambitious
Moff Disra leads a conspiracy to divide the uneasy coalition with
an ingenious plot to blame the Bothans for a heinous crime that
could lead to genocide and civil war. At the same time, Luke
Skywalker, along with Lando Calrissian and Talon Karrde, pur-
sues a mysterious group of pirate ships whose crew consists of
clones. And then comes the worst news of all: the most cunning
and ruthless warlord in Imperial history has returned to lead the
Empire to triumph. Here's an exciting scene from Timothy Zahn's
spectacular STAR WARS novel:*

"I don't think you fully understand the political situation the
New Republic finds itself in these days. A flash point like
Caamas—especially with Bothan involvement—will bring the
whole thing to a boil. Particularly if we can give it the proper
nudge."

"The situation among the Rebels is not the issue," Tierce
countered coldly. "It's the state of the Empire *you* don't seem to
understand. Simply tearing the Rebellion apart isn't going to re-
build the Emperor's New Order. We need a focal point, a leader
around whom the Imperial forces can rally."

Disra said, "Suppose I could provide such a leader. Would you
be willing to join us?"

Tierce eyed him. "Who is this 'us' you refer to?"

"If you join, there would be three of us," Disra said. "Three who would share the secret I'm prepared to offer you. A secret that will bring the entire Fleet onto our side."

Tierce smiled cynically. "You'll forgive me, Your Excellency, if I suggest you couldn't inspire blind loyalty in a drugged bantha."

Disra felt a flash of anger. How dare this common soldier—?

"No," he agreed, practically choking out the word from between clenched teeth. Tierce was hardly a common soldier, after all. More importantly, Disra desperately needed a man of his skills and training. "I would merely be the political power behind the throne. Plus the supplier of military men and matériel, of course."

"From the Braxant Sector Fleet?"

"And other sources," Disra said. "You, should you choose to join us, would serve as the architect of our overall strategy."

"I see." If Tierce was bothered by the word "serve," he didn't show it. "And the third person?"

"Are you with us?"

Tierce studied him. "First tell me more."

"I'll do better than tell you." Disra pushed his chair back and stood up. "I'll show you."

Disra led the way down the rightmost corridor. It ended in a dusty metal door with a wheel set into its center. Gripping the edges of the wheel, Disra turned it; and with a creak that echoed eerily in the confined space the door swung open.

The previous owner would hardly have recognized his one-time torture chamber. The instruments of pain and terror had been taken out, the walls and floor cleaned and carpet-insulated, and the furnishings of a fully functional modern apartment installed.

But for the moment Disra had no interest in the chamber itself. All his attention was on Tierce as the former Guardsman stepped into the room.

Stepped into the room . . . and caught sight of the room's single occupant, seated in the center in a duplicate of a Star Destroyer's captain's chair.

Tierce froze, his eyes widening with shock, his entire body stiffening as if a power current had jolted through him. His eyes darted to Disra, back to the captain's chair, flicked around the room as if seeking evidence of a trap or hallucination or perhaps his own insanity, back again to the chair. Disra held his breath. . . .

STAR WARS ®

THE FORCE IS WITH YOU
whenever you open a *Star Wars* novel
from Bantam Spectra Books!

The novels of the incomparable
Timothy Zahn

___29612-4	HEIR TO THE EMPIRE	$5.99/$6.99 Canada
___56071-9	DARK FORCE RISING	$5.99/$6.99
___56492-7	THE LAST COMMAND	$5.99/$6.99
___29804-6	SPECTER OF THE PAST	$5.99/$7.99
___10035-1	VISION OF THE FUTURE	$24.95/$34.95

The original Star Wars *anthologies*
edited by Kevin J. Anderson...

___56468-4	TALES FROM THE MOS EISLEY CANTINA	$5.99/$7.99
___56815-9	TALES FROM JABBA'S PALACE	$5.99/$7.99
___56816-7	TALES OF THE BOUNTY HUNTERS	$5.99/$7.99

...and by Peter Schweighofer...

___57876-6	TALES FROM THE EMPIRE	$5.99/$7.99

Please send me the books I have checked above. I am enclosing $_____ (add $2.50 to cover postage and handling). Send check or money order, no cash or C.O.D.'s, please.

Name _____

Address _____

City/State/Zip _____

Send order to: Bantam Books, Dept. SF 11, 2451 S. Wolf Rd., Des Plaines, IL 60018.
Allow four to six weeks for delivery.

Prices and availability subject to change without notice. SF 11 1/99

®, ™, and © 1997 Lucasfilm Ltd. All rights reserved. Used under authorization.

JOIN

STAR WARS®

on the INTERNET

Bantam Spectra invites you to visit their
Official STAR WARS® Web Site.

You'll find:

< Sneak previews of upcoming STAR WARS®
novels.
< Samples from audio editions of the novels.
< Bulletin boards that put you in touch with
other fans, with the authors, and with the
Spectra editors who bring them to you.
< The latest word from behind the scenes of
the STAR WARS® universe.
< Quizzes, games, and contests available only
on-line.
< Links to other STAR WARS® licensees'
sites on the Internet.
< Look for STAR WARS® on the World Wide
Web at:

http://www.bantam.com/spectra

SF 28 1/99

®, ™, ©